THE COLOR OF HER PANTIES

BY PIERS ANTHONY

Xanth
(Books One Through Fourteen)
Adapt
(Books One Through Seven)
Incarnations of Immortality
(Books One Through Seven)
Bio of a Space Tyrant
(Books One Through Five)
Cluster
(Books One Through Five)
Orn
(Books One Through Three)
Tarot
Macroscope
Mute
Battle Circle
Rings of Ice
Prostho Plus
Shade of the Tree
Ghost
Anthonology
But What of Earth?
Hasan
Race Against Time
Steppe
Triple Detente
Bio of an Ogre
Balook
Chthon Phthor
Total Recall
Parnucopia
Firefly
Tatham Mound

PIERS ANTHONY

THE COLOR OF HER PANTIES

William Morrow and Company, Inc.
New York

The Color Of Her Panties is an original publication of William Morrow and Company, Inc., published simultaneously in paperback by Avon Books. This work is a novel. Any similarity to actual persons or events is purely coincidental.

Jacket illustration by Darrell K. Sweet
Published by arrangement with the author

It is the policy of William Morrow and Company, Inc., and its imprints and affiliates, recognizing the importance of preserving what has been written, to print the books we publish on acid-free paper, and we exert our best efforts to that end.

ISBN: 0-688-10916-0
Library of Congress Catalog Card Number: 92-90168

Printed in the United States of America

2 3 4 5 6 7 8 9 10

CONTENTS

Chapter 1. Mela

Mela Merwoman swam restlessly around her sea cave garden, brushing the treelike seaweeds that formed the walls and canopy. Her hair swirled greenly behind her, and her flukes caused little eddies that toyed with whatever strands of hair they could catch.

She swooped down near the glowing colored stones of her floor, so that her breasts almost brushed them. Then she halted at her central fireplace and stoked up the waterlogs so that her fire blazed more brightly. "Oh, brimstone!" she swore, severely out of sorts. "I need a husband!"

She brought out her mirror and stretched the glass out to full length so she could see all of herself. It merely reflected what she already knew: she was a splendiferous creature, with fuller breasts than any mere mermaid and a flashier tail than any fish could boast. About her neck she wore a necklace supporting two precious glowing firewater opals, surely sufficient to attract the best quality husband.

So why wasn't she married? It wasn't as if she were choosy. All she wanted was the nicest, handsomest, most manly and intelligent unmarried prince in Xanth, who would be pleased to let her do anything she wanted. Such as swimming in the salt sea for hours and eating raw fish, and who would love to brush out her hair for her. Once she had captured Prince Dolph, but he had been a trifle young at the time, nine years old. She had traded him off for her opals, and later he had grown up and married a girl of his own species whose endowments weren't nearly as impressive as Mela's own. Human men just didn't have much sense.

The problem was that there weren't many males who met her modest standards, and most of those were already married. She had scoured the seas and found nothing worth her while. So what was she to do?

She sighed, and the effort sent ripples down through her fabulous flesh. There was no help for it: she would have to go ask the Good Magician. That meant doing him a year's service, which would surely be a colossal bore, but if he landed her a suitable husband it just might be worth it.

No time like the present. Mela gathered together the few useful spells she had collected during her explorations of the bypaths of the sea and tucked them into her invisible purse. Then she swam out of her cave and up toward the surface of the sea. She didn't worry about the fire spreading during her absence, because fire could not burn under water without the magic presence of the merfolk. Only if another merwoman or merman came would it flare up, and no one would intrude on her private premises.

Mela's undersea cave was near the Isle of Illusion, by sheerest coincidence, so she came up in sight of the isle which had once appeared to be the most illustrious of regions. Her hair yellowed as it broke the surface. She remembered again how she had captured Prince Dolph here, despite the objection of his skeletal companions Marrow Bones and Grace'l Ossein. They had in the end turned out to be decent folk despite their gauntness; indeed, they had helped her get her opals. She wondered how they were doing; they had made a nice if somewhat emaciated couple.

The Isle of Illusion no longer had much illusion, because the Sorceress of Illusion, Queen Emeritus Iris, had long since departed it. But a faint tinge of great fancies still surrounded it, suggesting the greatness of past imaginings. Perhaps some day another great illusionist would inhabit it, and once again no one would know its rather pedestrian reality.

She swam directly to the shore where the Gap Chasm debouched into the eastern sea. She came as close to the small beach as she could without getting out of the water. Then, when the sand threatened to abrade her satiny skin, she sat up, her tail folded before her. She concentrated, and her beautiful flukes became misshapen lumps, while the main portion of her tail turned a sickly pink. A lengthwise crease appeared, which deepened, until the entire tail split into two ungainly limbs.

Mela bent these limbs at their knobby knees and set the bony feet firmly against the sand. Then she heaved herself up, until she balanced precariously on those awkward legs, knee-deep in the surf. It had been a long time since she had gone on land, and it was hardly her notion of fun, but it was the only way. The Good Magician lived on land, and would not come to the sea.

Once she was sure of her equilibrium, she waded on out to the dry sand. Her new legs were getting stronger as she got the hang of them, and her balance was improving. She did know how to do this; she was merely out of practice.

But when she walked away from the water, the sand grew hot, burning her feet, and little sharp stones tried to cut her soles. Her extremities might be ugly, but they were also tender. Fortunately she knew where there was a lady's slipper patch; she had seen it from the water. She limped to it and picked two slippers. Naturally they fit perfectly, and they protected her feet so that she could walk in comfort.

She came to the edge of the Gap, where the way turned steep. Now she had to climb, but she could do that too, and clambered up across the rocks and slopes without much trouble. She knew that she had to get out of the chasm immediately, for two reasons. First, the sides became considerably steeper farther in—everyone knew that!—and second, there was the Gap Dragon. Only a few folk knew that, because most of those who had encountered the dragon had been eaten. There had been a Forget Spell on the chasm for a long time, but now it was gone and so it was possible to know things about the Gap. That was just as well, because she would not have wanted to try to run from the dragon on her wobbly legs. She wondered how the land folk ever endured such an ungainly mode of travel.

She came to the brink and climbed over. Now the land was reasonably level, and she could walk upright. She understood that the Good Magician's castle was slightly south of the Gap, so she walked generally westward. There were supposed to be enchanted paths, and once she found one of those she would be able to proceed to the castle without having to worry about stray monsters.

Unfortunately she was still in the wilderness. "Ho!" someone shouted to the side. "A nymph! Hit her!"

Mela looked, alarmed. She was no nymph, for they were mostly brainless creatures who kept company with similarly brainless fauns. For some reason human men seemed to like nymphs, while lacking interest in the fauns. She saw that the shouter was a man the size of an elf, standing hardly taller than her knees. His hands were relatively huge. She didn't have to worry about him.

Then about six more like him appeared. "Hit her! Hit her!" they cried, charging toward her in a messy mass.

Now she recognized their nature: these were hit men! Their hands were huge because they used them to make tremendous fists, the better to hit innocent folk. They were erupting from a blackjack bush, which was a plant that liked to be hit. It was always exclaiming "Hit me!" and "Hit me again!" though its leaves were so thin and flat that they could hardly stand up long to such abuse. Maybe that was why they had all those little red and black marks on them in the shapes of things like spades and hearts and clubs. But hitmen were notorious for making hits on anything that came within reach, and a luscious bare female like herself was a prime target. They certainly wanted to hit on her.

Mela quickly took stock. She was too far from the sea to reach it before the obnoxious little men caught up with her. Maybe in time her clumsy legs would be able to carry her swiftly, but she was still concentrating on things like balance and locomotion. If she tried to run fast, she would fall on her face, and they would swarm all over her.

Could her magic stop them? She had a spell to splash water into the eyes of a person, but that only worked on one person at a time, and she doubted it would discourage even a single one of these hit men for long. She had a small waterlog, but that would burn only in water. There was her mirror, but that had very limited power. Not much hope there.

However she also had a little magic manual that was supposed to list many of the useful things of Xanth, as well as the things best avoided. She snatched it out of her purse and checked quickly through it. She saw pictures of various creatures and plants, including the hit men and blackjack bush. "Well, I already knew about those!" she snapped. "How about something that will help me that's close by?"

The manual showed a picture of a mitten bush, with neat little white mittens. A mitten bush? Mela rolled her eyes. She was no kitten, and she needed no mitten.

Then she spied a mitten bush close by. Well, that might not be what she wanted, but she would have to make do with it. She hurried to it, not quite managing to lose her balance in her haste. The hit men were now almost upon her, their big ugly hands forming into bigger uglier fists.

She dodged around the bush. The hit men piled into it—and its mittens expanded to swallow their fists. In a moment the hit men were all caught by their hands, unable to get them from the tight mittens. They cursed, swore, and obscened, turning the air bilious blue, which was an unusual effect. Bilious green or yellow were the normal hues. But even with the blue they couldn't get free, because the mittens were firmly tied to the bush.

Mela went blithely onward. Sometimes all it took was a little luck and the common sense to use it. Plus a little help from a manual. This was, after all, the Land of Xanth, where almost everything was magic, and the rest was probably lying about it. The land was more dangerous than the sea, because she was used to the sea, but she could manage.

In due course she came to a river. This was wonderful; it gave her a chance to wet her tail. She waded in—and right out again. It was fresh water! What a horrible sensation. She would have to make do on dry legs until she could return to the sea.

Rather than touch the bad water again, she walked upstream. It stood to reason that if she went far enough, the river would give up and fade out, and then she could proceed without touching it.

Soon she encountered an odd little creature. It had pinkish hairy skin and a squared-off snout, which it used to nose around in the ground. She brought out her manual again and sifted through the pages until she found a picture and managed to recognize the thing: it was a pig. The description was reassuring: they were harmless if not bothered. So she ignored it and walked on.

She came across another pig, and a third. In fact there was half a slew of pigs along the bank. It was a piggy bank!

She moved away from the bank and found a path. This expanded as if glad of her attention to it, and became a paved road. She knew that some paths were treacherous, because they led to dragon lairs or tangle trees, but this was not that type. It was a straight road that liked to be used, and she was happy to oblige it. It would enable her to get farther faster, with less wear on her tender extremities.

Suddenly there was a huge honking, and a tremendous

pig came charging down the road. Mela had to leap into the brush to avoid it. She got no thanks. "Outta my way, nymph!" the huge pig grunted as it passed.

Mela did not like being called a nymph, when anyone could see she was a merwoman on legs. "Hey, do you think you own this road?" she demanded angrily.

The pig halted, and turned its porcine snout to look at her. "As a matter of fact, I do," it said.

"What kind of creature are you?"

"I'm a road hog, of course. Now stay out of my way." It resumed motion, and in a moment was out of sight.

A road hog. That figured. When the piggies of the bank grew large and arrogant, naturally they became hogs. She should have checked another page in the manual and found it before it found her.

Mela shrugged and tried to get back on the road. She discovered that she was stuck in the foliage of the most ugly and useless tree she had encountered. Its leaves were misshapen, its bark was falling off, and its fruit was rotten. It just seemed to have grown all wrong. It was a good thing she wore no clothing, because the erratic thorns would have caught in it. As it was, she was smarting from two mentionable places and one unmentionable place.

She extricated herself, and brought out the manual. There it was: a lemon tree. Anyone who got one of these was supposed to get rid of it in a hurry, because it was no good. She had already caught on to that fact.

This was wearing. Did she really need a husband? But Mela decided that there was almost as little point in turning back now as there was in moving on forward. She might as well plow on and see what the Good Magician had to say.

The road wound on through the forest, passing some nice pie trees. Mela paused to have some watermelon pie. Farther along she found water chestnuts and watercress. That was the best that offered, as the land did not seem to have seaweed soup or sea cucumbers. She could tell by the taste that fresh water had been used, but that was all right for food. It was swimming and bathing that required salt water.

However, time was sneaking by, and the shadows were taking advantage of it to grow longer. Mela was intrigued by this phenomenon, because there were not many shadows on the sea floor, but she realized that this was a magic signal that night was approaching. She did not feel at ease traveling in the dark, and anyway, her new legs were tired. She needed a safe, comfortable place to sleep. Now where would that be?

She checked the manual. It showed a picture of a beerbarrel tree. Mela wasn't sure about that; she didn't like the notion of swimming in beer much better than that of swimming in water. Then she realized that it was a dead, hollow beerbarrel tree it meant. So she looked around as she walked, and sure enough, in due course she found one.

She went to the tree and examined it. She found a crevice that led to a crack that led to a fissure that became the square outline of a door. This was the place!

She felt along the edge until she found a latch. She worked it, and the door opened. There inside was a dark abode girt about by fluffy pillows. Not as appealing as salt water, but ideal in terms of roughing it on the land.

Mela entered and closed the door behind her. Immediately a soft light glowed from colored fungus. It didn't compare to that of deep-sea plants and creatures, but it did give her a feeling of the depths, and that was very nice. Whatever male she married would have to love the sea, because she was a creature of the sea, inside as well as outside. She lay blissfully on the bed of pillows.

"Mmmmph, mmmph mph mmmmmmmmph!"

Mela jumped. What was that?

"MmmmmMmmmmmph!" The muffled sound came as she landed from her jump, squishing the pillows flat.

She scrambled to her tired feet. "What is going on here?" she demanded of the situation in general.

The center pillow formed a mouth and opened it. "A

better question is what is coming off here! How dare you plop your fishy backside in my Eskimo!''

"In your what?'' Mela asked, bemused.

"My Inuit, Aleut, Finn, Sami—''

"Lapp?'' Mela inquired.

"Whatever. Can't a creature get a decent nap without getting squished by an ugly sea monster?''

Mela began to take umbrage. "Um—I am considered by some to be a rather attractive sea monster.''

The mouth grimaced. "By whom, fish-head? A hungry kraken weed?''

Mela finished her taking umbrage. "Brage!'' she swore. "You don't exactly have much sex appeal yourself, cushion-face!''

The pillow exploded. The mouth flew up and hovered before Mela's nose, while feathers swirled around it. "I have all the sex appeal I want, seaweed-hair!'' it exclaimed.

Mela realized belatedly that magic was operating here. "You are not what you seem,'' she charged with a certain justice.

The feathers closed in around the mouth, forming the shape of a head. "I am whatever I choose to be, manrear!''

That was a low blow. No one had ever before mistaken Mela's posterior for male. "And what kind of rear do you have, pillow-cheeks?'' she demanded.

The feathers shaped themselves into a human outline and faded into flesh tone. Now a voluptuous woman stood there. "*This* kind of rear, gills-for-brains!'' she said, turning to show a set of buttocks almost as generous as Mela's own.

"You're a demoness!'' Mela said, catching on. However, the creature moved away so that Mela could not keep her catch.

"The Demoness Metria, of course. And who in conniption are you?''

"I am Melantha Merwoman.''

"What are you doing out of your ingredient?"

"My what?"

"Your component, aspect, fragment, division, portion, segment—"

"Oh, you mean my element! The sea."

"Whatever. Why are you here on land?"

"I am in quest of a husband. I can't find what I want in the sea."

Metria gazed at her appraisingly. "Considering what men are interested in, it seems that you should be able to nab one. What kind are you looking for?"

"A prince would do, if he's handsome and manageable. I caught one once, but he was too young and I had to throw him back."

"Oh? Which one was that?"

"Prince Dolph of the human folk. He was nine years old, but would have grown in time."

"Prince Dolph! I know him. He's seventeen now, and married."

"I know," Mela said sadly. "I heard she wasn't even a princess."

"She is now. And a mother, too. The stork brought them twin girls, Dawn and Eve."

"Oh, those should have been my girls!" Mela cried. "I should never have let him get away."

"Well, you're mortal. You make mistakes."

"So now I am going to see the Good Magician to find out how to nab some other prince," Mela concluded. "I'm sorry if I intruded on your domain. I thought it was available."

"Oh, go ahead and use it," Metria said. "I took it from Esk Ogre some years back, and the truth is, things were more interesting when he was around."

"Things always are, when a male's around."

"How true! But now he's gone and married a brassie girl from the gourd named Bria, and they have a son named Brusque."

"Everybody's getting married!" Mela said petulantly.

"But the son of an ogre and a brassie—does he have a talent?"

"Yes. He can make himself or other things hard and heavy, or light and soft. That should be handy, when he is grown."

Mela nodded knowingly. "Surely so. But it doesn't solve my problem. I need a prince."

"Why not a regular man?" the demoness asked. "There are more of them."

"Well, after almost nabbing a prince, I fear it would feel like backsliding to settle for an ordinary man."

"I suppose so. My friend Dana Demoness married a king. Now she won't settle for anything less."

"Oh? What king?"

"King Humfrey."

"I didn't know there was a King Humfrey! Is he any relation to the Good Magician Humfrey?"

"The same."

"But Humfrey's no king! He's the Magician of Information."

"He's no king *now*. But he was then. She got bored and left him, but after a century or so she got bored being single, so she returned to him, and is married to him today."

"But I thought he was married to the Gorgon."

"He is. It gets complicated to explain."

"It must!" But Mela was too tired at the moment for complexity. "Is it all right if I sleep on the other pillows?"

"Be my guest," Metria said grandly, fading away.

In the morning Mela left the cozy den and searched out some fruits and nuts. She needed to do something else, but wasn't sure how to manage it cleanly while wearing the clumsy legs; she wished she could return to the sea for a while or even an (ugh!) freshwater pond, and not just for that. The land was just such an awkward place!

The Demoness Metria appeared, in her human form, standing in the air. "Must you go so soon?" she inquired.

"I thought you wanted to be rid of me."

"I do. I was being facetious."

"That's more like it." Mela had relatively few illusions about demons, having encountered them on occasion.

"You look squirmy."

"I would ask you whether there is water near, but you would only misdirect me."

"No, I would answer truly, because then you wouldn't believe me and would go the wrong way." The demoness evidently understood why Mela wanted water, so was teasing her, demon fashion.

"Never mind. I'll do it in the den." Mela headed for the beerbarrel tree.

"Oh no you don't! Go to that purpose bush over there." Mela's left arm stretched out and her hand assumed the form of an arrow.

"What kind of bush?"

"Aim, design, province, sphere, object, what it's made for—"

"Function?"

"Whatever," Metria agreed crossly.

"What's a function bush?"

"Just go there and see. It's really quite natural."

Mela knew that this was mischief, but it was better to humor the demoness, whose mischief was surely not as bad as her anger. She walked to the bush, which had the smell of manure. Then suddenly she folded over and accomplished her business despite her clumsy form.

A function bush: now she understood its name. It had its own way of collecting fertilizer.

Mela straightened up and walked away from it. "Thank you, Metria," she said. For the demoness had after all facilitated the necessary chore.

"You're not mad?" Metria inquired, disappointed.

"Furious." There was an art to managing demons.

"You're not going to throw any of it at me?"

"That wouldn't be ladylike."

"It would just loop around and splat on you."

"That, too."

"You're just trying to be dull, so I'll lose interest and stop pestering you."

"Demons are getting smarter all the time."

"Well, it won't work! I'll just tag along and see you mess up some other way."

"Suit yourself."

"Confound it! I can't tell whether you even want to get rid of me! Maybe you prefer to have my company."

"I would prefer it even more if you were a male prince demon. Perhaps you can get one to come and pester me in lieu of you. Males can be such brutes."

"That does it! I am going to stay and be perfectly nice to you! What do you think of that?"

Mela sighed. "You are very sophisticated in your pestering." The truth was that she didn't really care whether the demoness remained or departed; she just wanted to keep her on good behavior.

They walked generally west, but the freshwater river threatened to return, with its pigs and things, so they veered south. The land became hilly, so they veered some more to move along a contour. The demoness was now walking on the ground, so that she seemed just like another mortal creature. She was even solid, now; Mela could tell, because she left footprints.

Then she heard a faint booming sound. "What's that?"

"A pronoun used to indicate a person, place, thing, idea, or state of being. I keep confusing it with which."

"I don't mean the word! I mean that sound."

"What sound?"

Mela saw that the demoness was still teasing her. She surely heard the booming and know all about it, but wouldn't tell. So Mela shut up and walked on.

The booms became louder. Finally she came to a series of small hills shaped like little mountains. At the top of each hill was a human baby. Every so often each baby opened its mouth and let out a surprisingly loud boom. "Why, they're baby boomers," Mela said, surprised. "There certainly are a lot of them!"

"They will be something when they grow up," Metria remarked. "They'll be big boom-booms."

"But what's the point?"

"There is no point. They're just there. They strayed from Mundania, where there are even more of them."

Mela shook her head. "Mundania is a strange place!"

"That is true. Even the Mundanes don't understand it. That is why they come to Xanth whenever they can. Fortunately most of them don't know the way, any more than you know the way to the Good Magician's castle."

"But if I asked you, you would merely direct me wrong. Or right, if I didn't believe you."

"Of course. Isn't it beautiful?"

"Lovely." Despite her best effort, Mela was getting annoyed by the demoness.

They passed beyond the baby boomers and came to a big lake. It looked very pleasant. Mela stood and gazed at it.

"Aren't you going for a swim?" Metria inquired innocently.

"No."

"Oh, you already know its nature."

This made Mela pause. Suddenly she suspected that the demoness wasn't thinking of fresh water. But the demoness wouldn't tell, if she asked. So she shrugged. "I'll go around it."

"Actually, it's not as if the Kiss-Mee Lake hurts anyone. It's not nearly as bad as a love spring."

So this was the Kiss-Mee Lake! She had heard of it. "Wasn't there some trouble with the associated river? I heard that your friends pulled it straight, and then it was known as the Kill-Mee River."

"Yes, the hummers got really bad. That's when I had to leave, and I found the ogre's den. But I helped him restore the river. That was interesting."

"So I will just walk around it to the south," Mela said.

"By all means. I will walk with you."

That meant that there promised to be something interesting for the demoness to the south, which in turn meant that Mela wouldn't like it. "Oh—the Kiss-Mee River flows from the south shore!" Mela said, realizing. "So I can't go that way, unless I want to mess with fresh water anyway."

"Sure enough," Mela agreed, disappointed.

"So I'll have to walk around it to the north instead."

"By all means."

That did not sound promising either. But what other choices were there? Mela certainly didn't want to swim across it, and she couldn't fly across it.

She opened her invisible purse and took out her manual. What she wanted was surely in there, but she didn't know what to look for. That was why she couldn't use it to locate a husband; it showed all the creatures of Xanth, but couldn't point out individuals or give their marriage status. Now she needed a way to cross the lake without soiling her body with fresh water, and the manual couldn't tell her how.

The sky darkened, dimming the page. She looked up. There over the water a nasty little cloud was forming. So she flipped the pages until she came to clouds, and there it was: King Cumulo Fracto Nimbus, the meanest of clouds. But since she had nothing either to gain or fear from a cloud, she ignored Fracto, and he ignored her.

Then she saw something strange. It was a little red boat, zooming along backwards, rowed by a very big man. No, by a very small giant. No, something even odder. But what?

"Fascinating," Metria said, and faded out.

That surely meant trouble. But it just might be a ruse. If this was someone who could help her cross the lake, the demoness might be trying to scare her away, so that she would after all be stranded. So she couldn't be sure. The best thing to do was chance it. If she got into the boat with the man, and he tried to get fresh—how she hated freshness!—she could always jump into the water, loathsome as it was, and escape. So she waited. But she took the precaution of hiding behind some redberry bushes.

The boat plowed right on toward the shore not far distant. The rower didn't seem to realize. He banged right into the bank, and grunted as the boat suddenly stopped. "Oh, everything's wrong!" he cried in a high voice. "I'll never find the Good Magician!"

Mela's ears perked up. He was looking for the Good Magician? This could be a wonderful break!

She stepped forward. "Hello," she said brightly.

The stranger jumped right into the air and screamed, bursting into tears. Startled, Mela fell back into the bushes, scratching her nevermind. "Well, I didn't mean any harm," she said, nettled. "I just happen to be looking for the Good Magician myself, and I wondered—" She broke off, staring at the huge creature. "Why, you're not a man at all! You're a—well, just what *are* you?"

"I'm an ogre girl," the other responded. "You frightened me."

"An ogre! But they're very strong, ugly and stupid, and justifiably proud of it. You're—"

"A very poor excuse for an ogress," the other said. "I can't even crunch bones very well."

Mela decided to let that pass. "Do you think you might row me across the lake? I think the Good Magician is somewhere on the other side."

"He is?" the ogress said, brightening. "Sure! Do you know the way?"

"Not exactly. Just in a very general sense. But if you want to go there too—"

"Yes!"

"Then let's introduce ourselves. I'm Mela Merwoman. I'm looking for a husband."

"I'm Okra Ogress. I'm looking for my fortune. I want to be a Main Character."

"A main character? Why?"

"Because nothing really bad ever happens to a main character, and a whole lot of bad things are going to happen to me if I don't get away from them."

"Now that's interesting! Do you mean I could get a good husband if I became a main character?"

"Sure. Main characters always live happily ever after, so if you need a husband to make you happy, then you'd get one."

"Well, Okra, I'm glad I met you! Let's get on across Lake Kiss-Mee, and we'll see if we can find the Good Magician together."

"Lake what?"

"Kiss-Mee. Didn't you know?"

"But I was rowing on Lake Ogre-Chobee!"

"You must have rowed right up the river to Lake Kiss-Mee without knowing it!" Only a very strong and stupid person could have done that, but that made sense in this case.

"Okay." Okra hauled the red boat around and plopped it back into the water. "I'll row. Maybe it will work better if you can tell me where we're going."

"It should," Mela agreed, realizing that this was part of the ogress's problem: she had not been able to look forward.

So they got into the boat, and Okra started to row. The boat fairly leaped through the water with each heave. Mela looked ahead—and saw the cloud, King Fracto, changing course to intercept them. "Um, maybe we should turn back and wait for Fracto to go away," she said.

But the ogress was working so hard that she didn't hear. Well, maybe they could make it across before the storm hit. Mela hoped so. She did not relish the thought of getting doused with fresh rainwater.

Chapter 2.   Gwenny

It was a perfect day for a picnic. They would smell flowers and eat red, yellow, and blueberries and sun in the sun. With luck they would encounter a winged dragon or a griffin. From the time of her association with Che Centaur, she had had no fear of winged monsters, for all of them were his friends.

Gwendolyn Goblin could not remember when she had been as happy as during these last two years as the guest of the winged centaur family. She had been well treated at home in Goblin Mountain, but confined to her apartment, because, well, because. Then little Che Centaur had come to be her companion, and his friend Jenny Elf who was the same age as Gwenny, and they had gone to be with Che's family. For the first time Gwenny had experienced the freedom of the great outside, and she reveled in it.

Of course there were bad things too. Che's parents, Cheiron and Chex, insisted that every creature in their household be properly educated. Thus the teenage goblin girl and elf girl shared seven-year-old Che's fate, and had to spend weary hours learning how to count and figure and read and write, and all about the geography and history of Xanth. They even had to learn the various types of magic, and the rules of human and nonhuman cultures. What a bore! Sometimes Gwenny and Jenny pretended to lose their spectacles so that they couldn't study, but the adults were hideously astute at finding them. It was the one awful thing about centaurs: they were intellectual. They represented the very most extreme case of the dreadful Adult Conspiracy, which dictated that anyone young enough to be a non-Conspirator must Know and Not Know a rigorous schedule of things. Naturally most of the interesting things were in the Not-Know category.

But overall, the positives outweighed the negatives. Gwenny was well fed and well cared for and safe, and she had close companions who didn't like studying any better than she did. The alternative was to be locked in her suite at home with only her mother, Godiva, for company—and the truth was, Godiva also had distressingly adult notions about education and behavior. The rest of Goblin Mountain was a total loss; it was dark and gloomy and full of goblins. Who wanted to be in a mountain full of goblins?

They skipped along the path, Che running beside Gwenny so that she would be guided by him and would not misstep. A visit to a healing spring had cured her lameness, but not her eyesight. Her eyes weren't ill; they merely were unable to focus quite right at ordinary distances. Jenny Elf had the same problem. Healing water restored a person's body to its natural state, and their natural state was a different way of seeing than that of most folk.

They had hardly reached the first field of flowers before there was a figure in the sky. Gwenny put on her spectacles so she could make out what it was. It was Chex, Che's dam, flying down to intercept them. She landed lightly on her four hooves and folded her wings. "Gwenny, I have what may be bad news. Your mother is here."

There was a pause. Then the three young folk burst out laughing. They knew Chex didn't mean it the way it sounded. All of them liked Godiva Goblin despite her adult tendencies.

But in a moment they sobered. Godiva would not have come here without good reason, and that was indeed likely to be bad news. "Did she say—?"

"No. But I think you had better talk with her immediately."

"I'll hurry back to the house!"

"I will take you."

"But Che and Jenny—"

"We shall get back on our own," Che said quickly.

So Gwenny climbed onto Chex's back, and Chex flicked her with her tail, making her feather light. Then Chex spread her wings and leaped into the air. They were airborne.

Gwenny still thrilled to this experience. She hung on to Chex's mane and peered down as the centaur circled to gain elevation. There were Che and Jenny, waving. Jenny was holding her little orange cat, Sammy. Then Chex straightened out and headed across the forest, not far above the treetops. It seemed almost like walking through waist-high bushes, looking down on them, only these were full trees.

Soon they landed in the yard before the house. Godiva was there, her flowing black hair forming a cape about her body.

Gwenny jumped off—and sailed high into the air, because she had forgotten how light she was. Chex reached up with a hand and caught her ankle, bringing her down. She set Gwenny gently on the ground. It took a while for the lightening effect to wear off.

Gwenny walked—carefully—to her mother and hugged her. "My dear, you have lost weight! Have you been eating enough?" Godiva exclaimed. Of course it was humor, because she understood the centaur magic and could see that Gwenny, far from being underfleshed, was now a rather pretty figure of a gobliness. She was, after all, fourteen years old, which was just about old enough for a goblin girl. Naturally no adult would tell her *what* she was old enough for. Adults could be real pains at times.

"Why are you here, Mother?" Gwenny asked.

Godiva became extremely serious. "Your father is dead. You know what that means." She did not pretend any grief; Gouty Goblin had been a typical male, which meant that he had few if any endearing traits, and had done his best to eradicate those.

Gwenny felt a sudden chill. Indeed she knew what this meant: that her idyllic time with the centaur family was over, and perhaps her life itself. For she was the next in line to be the chief of the goblins of Goblin Mountain—the first female ever to aspire to that role.

"Mother, I'm not ready!" she said.

"I know that, dear. I had hoped that your father would hang on a few years longer, to give you time. But he was unobliging even in this. It is now or never."

"But the spectacles—I can't wear them at home, and I can't see well enough without them to do anything. That would disqualify me immediately."

"I know that too, dear. But there are other ways. We must find you some magic contact lenses."

At this point Chex cut in. "We have been searching for a suitable lens bush for two years, but there seems to have been a blight on them."

Godiva sighed. "I was afraid of that. Then there is only one thing to do: we must take her to the Good Magician to find out how she can nullify this liability."

"Wait, Mother," Gwenny said. "You mustn't do this for me."

"But, dear, time is short. There is only one month before the ascension of the new chief. Only the Good Magician can possibly know where contact lenses may be obtained immediately."

"I agree, Mother. But I must go to him myself. If I am unable to do that much without adult help, how can I ever be chief?"

"She is correct, Godiva," Chex said. "She must rise to her own challenges, now. They will not allow you to assist her at Goblin Mountain, and the challenge of reaching the Good Magician is surely less arduous. She must have practice in the intervening time, little as it may be.''

The gobliness was silent in an appalled way. Centaur logic was impossible to refute.

''But I think it would be legitimate for her companion to accompany her,'' Chex continued.

''But Che is even younger,'' Godiva said. ''The danger—''

''The winged monsters will protect him as one of their own.''

Godiva nodded. ''We have seen the manner of that protection.''

Gwenny knew it was all right, then. Recently she had been coming to understand some of the nuances of adult dialogue, which were sometimes more subtle than children appreciated. The centaur had in effect said that the winged monsters would take care of Che and his companion, which was Gwenny herself. Chex herself was a winged monster, and she had been taking care of both of them all along. Godiva had acknowledged it: she was complimenting Chex on it.

So they would allow Gwenny and Che to travel by themselves to see the Good Magician. If anything really bad threatened, the winged monsters, all of whom had taken an oath to protect Che, would intervene. That intervention could be formidable; they had at one time almost destroyed Goblin Mountain itself when they had thought Che was captive there.

''We'll start tomorrow,'' Gwenny said. ''We can use the magic paths and Grandam Chem's map.'' Actually that would be a copy, for Chem Centaur's maps manifested in air. They were extremely accurate.

So it was decided. Godiva Goblin agreed to stay the night, and in the morning they would go their separate ways, for the nonce. Godiva had to keep an eye on things at Goblin Mountain, until the new chief took office. With luck and management, that chief would be Gwenny.

Che and Jenny Elf arrived back from the field. Gwenny

explained about her need to go to see the Good Magician, and how it was all right for Che to come along.

"But what about Jenny?" he asked.

Gwenny hadn't thought of that. Of course she didn't want to leave Jenny Elf behind! Jenny had been Che's friend before he came to Goblin Mountain, and she had been Gwenny's friend too. "Jenny, too, if she wants to come," she agreed.

"Of course I want to come!" Jenny said. "I'd like to see the Good Magician's castle when I'm not distracted."

"Maybe he can tell you how to get back to the World of Two Moons," Gwenny said.

"Yes, maybe he could," Jenny agreed. But she did not seem completely excited by the prospect.

In the morning they bid farewell to Che's sire and dam, and to Gwenny's mother. Then Godiva took one path, heading east toward Goblin Mountain, and the three of them took another, heading south toward the Gap Chasm and the Good Magician's castle. The copy of Chem's map showed that they could use the invisible bridge to cross the Gap and then go right on down to the castle. Then they would have three challenges to surmount before they could get into the castle, and after that—

"Oops," Gwenny said. "I will have to give a year's service to the Good Magician, for his Answer to my Question, but I have only a month before I must be chief."

"Then I will ask on your behalf," Che said.

"No, I will," Jenny Elf said. Her cat, Sammy, was riding in her backpack. "You two must stay together."

"But—" Gwenny started to protest. Then she realized that this was help she needed, and that perhaps Jenny had looked ahead and realized that their juvenile friendship could not endure beyond the settlement of the chiefship. Gwenny would then either be chief, with its pressing responsibilities, or dead. In either case, she could not truly be with Jenny. So their separation was coming, regardless. It was not as if service to the Good Magician was onerous; the word was that often it was as beneficial for the person as for the Magician. "Thank you, Jenny." There was more to be said, but she couldn't figure out how to phrase it.

They walked down the path, not hurrying. They had a fair way to go, and there was no point in wearing themselves out. Also, perhaps, they were not eager to separate, and that separation could occur at any time after they reached the castle. This was the last of their carefree association.

The abode of the winged centaurs was not far from the Gap Chasm. They reached it in the afternoon. The path led right up to it, and stopped. There was nothing but the great deep awesome expanse of the Gap ahead.

Che looked at the map. "The invisible bridge is supposed to be right here."

"I don't see it," Jenny said, smiling.

He flicked her hair with the tip of his tail, making it float about her head. "We must verify its location, and cross, making sure no creature is below it."

"What does it matter whether there is anyone below?" Jenny asked. "I mean, we aren't going to drop rocks on him."

"Gwenny is wearing a dress."

Jenny laughed. Gwenny felt her dark face doing its best to blush. She was indeed in a dress, because she had deemed it to be more ladylike than jeans. Now she wished she had followed Jenny's example and settled for the jeans, because it would be a horrible disaster if anyone below looked up and saw the color of her panties. No one was supposed to know that they were goblin black. No male, anyway. Jenny knew, but not Che. She hoped.

"Well, first we have to find it," Jenny said. "I'm not stepping out there until I'm sure there's something to step on." It seemed that there were not such things as invisible bridges on the World of Two Moons where Jenny came from, so she was slow to accept them. She found a length of wood that would do for a pole, and used it to poke along the edge of the cliff.

When she passed the section where the path ended, without result, she extended the pole farther and tried going back. But there still seemed to be nothing solid. "Are you sure it's here?" she asked.

Che took another stick and probed for the bridge himself, with no better success. "I must admit that it doesn't seem to be. Perhaps someone misdirected the path."

"Who would do that?" Jenny asked.

"Oh, anyone with mischief in mind. Perhaps Com-Pewter, the evil machine who can change reality. He's been in a snit, I understand, ever since his plot to make Grey Murphy his slave was foiled."

"But how will we find it, if we can't see it and don't know exactly where it is?" Then she turned her head to address her cat. "No, I'm not setting you loose to find it, Sammy! I'm afraid you'll forget what you're after, and bound into the Gap." Sammy pretended he was asleep.

Che shook his head. "I fear that finding it could take a long time. It will probably be better to walk on along the Gap until we come to the main bridge, which is both substantial and visible. I believe it is not unduly far out of our way. I can make us all lighter so that we will not get tired from the extra walk, and we can perhaps proceed more rapidly."

They did that. They walked along the cleared region near the brink—it seemed that trees did not want to grow too close, lest they fall off—toward the west. It was fast going, because Che had flicked them, making each girl weigh only a fraction what she usually did. This could have been dangerous when the winds were high, but this was a quiet day.

They came to the main bridge—and paused, dismayed. There was a horrendous demon standing on it, blocking their way. The thing stood ogre tall, had tremendous tusks, and a glare so intense that the air in its path flickered and smoked.

"I don't think that creature likes us," Jenny whispered.

"But how can a bad creature be on a charmed bridge?" Gwenny asked, adjusting her spectacles to see it better. "There aren't supposed to be any hostiles along the magic paths."

"The charm may not work well against demons," Che said. "Or the magic of the bridge may be weakening. We shall have to tell the Good Magician, so he can fix it."

"But first we have to get to his castle," Jenny said. "And I don't think we're going to do it by crossing this bridge."

"There is a third bridge," Che said, checking the map. "I suppose the sensible thing to do is go to it."

Gwenny sighed. "I suppose so. But it is getting late."

They walked on west, leaving the glowering demon behind. When they slowed, Che flicked them all, including himself, and they got lighter and faster.

They came to the third bridge. It was narrow but looked solid. Jenny stepped toward it.

"Wait," Che said. He took a stick and poked it at the planking. "I was afraid of that."

"Afraid of what?" Jenny asked.

"It isn't solid. See, the stick pokes right through it without resistance."

"But the map shows it!" Gwenny protested, upset. "It's not supposed to be illusion."

"It isn't. It's one-way—going the other way."

"But we have to go our way!"

"I am not certain of the mechanism of it," Che said. "I suspect that someone recently used it, and that it reverses after use, to allow the person to return, or just to be fair to the other side. We just happened to arrive at the wrong time."

Gwenny stamped her delicate little foot. "Oh, this is so frustrating! Were I not the daughter of a chief, I would say something disreputable."

"Perhaps Jenny could say it instead," Che suggested.

"She's not royal, as far as we know. What expression did you have in mind?"

"Big mice. Maybe even—"

"Rats!" Jenny cried.

The bridge trembled, smarting under the disreputable expression. Gwenny giggled, feeling better.

Nevertheless, they could not cross. What were they to do? All three bridges had been denied them, and the day was fading.

"Perhaps if I made us even lighter, we might walk down the face of the cliff," Che said. "We could not fall, or if we did, we would land so lightly we would not be hurt."

"In that case we could just jump," Jenny pointed out.

Gwenny considered. "I suppose, if it's the only way."

They stood at the brink, ready to be lightened. Then a gust of wind came, followed by another.

"I just thought," Jenny said, "if we are feather light, couldn't that wind blow us away?"

"Unfortunately it could," Che agreed. "I fear that our timing is wrong again."

"But there has to be *some* way!" Gwenny exclaimed. "We have to reach the Good Magician's castle."

"Perhaps we can go around the Gap Chasm," Che said. "The map indicates that it ends at the water."

"Then how will we cross the water?" Jenny asked.

"We shall have to fashion a raft or similar craft," Che said. "We should be able to do that in a day or so, if we can find suitable materials."

"Oh, this is getting so complicated!" Gwenny wailed.

"I could summon a winged monster," Che offered.

"No! I have to get through this myself, or it doesn't count. I mean, with your help and Jenny's, but not with adults or monsters. Otherwise I won't have what it takes to be chief and might as well give up, and I absolutely refuse to do that."

"We'll get through," Jenny said reassuringly.

So they proceeded on west, and as the day expired they reached the shore of the sea. They scrounged for food, and found a pie tree with an overripe cherry pie and a somewhat soggy chocolate pie. It would have to do.

Che found a deserted shed, and some old pillows. The shed seemed to have an old debug spell on it, because there were no bugs inside. They made themselves as comfortable as they could for the night, the two girls lying down on either side of the little centaur. "I don't mean to complain," Gwenny said, "but somehow I never thought about the awkward little details of adventuring. It's really more comfortable at home."

"It's better than being a prisoner of the goblins," Jenny said. "I mean, when the Goblinate—"

"I know what you mean," Gwenny said. "Male goblins are brutes. That's why I have to be chief, if I can. Then we'll try to be civilized."

"I think it is my destiny to help you do that," Che said. "I am supposed to change the history of Xanth, and I think that will happen if you become the first female goblin chief."

"I don't know about the history of Xanth, but I'll do my best to change the history of the goblins!" Gwenny said.

"The goblins are a significant part of Xanth."

They lapsed into silence, and then into sleep. But Gwenny was uneasy. She had no certainty that she could even manage to become chief, at her tender teen age, or that she could do the job thereafter.

In the morning, shivering, they ate more aging pie and set about making a raft. The map indicated a copse of deadwood trees nearby, and sure enough, there was enough deadwood lying around to make several rafts. But how were they to tie it together? There seemed to be no suitable vines, unless they wanted to try to hack some from a tangle tree. They knew better than that!

But Jenny had an answer. She addressed her cat. "Sammy, we are looking for some nice, strong, safe vines that are close by. Do you think you can find—"

Sammy bounded away. "I'll follow him," Jenny said, hurrying after.

There was a swirl of dust before Gwenny. She retreated, not trusting it, but it followed her. "There's something here," she said. "I think it's magic."

Immediately Che came to join her. "That's a dust devil," he said. "But there's no dust. So it's probably a demon."

A face appeared at head height on the swirl: two round eyes made from vortices of dust, and a mouth formed from a wriggling dust snake. "No, a demoness. What are you tankards up to?"

"What?"

"Cups, glasses, containers, bottles, mugs—"

"Goblets?"

"Whatever."

"Nothing interesting," Gwenny said, hoping the demoness would go away. There was no point in correcting her about the distinction between a goblet and a goblette, or in reminding her that there was only one goblin in this party. They had enough problems without having them complicated by a supernatural creature. Demonesses were supposed to be less worse than demons, being mischievous rather than mean, but their mischief could be formidable.

More of the form appeared. Smoky hair sprouted and curled downward. A larger swirl of dust became a voluminous skirt. There was nothing between the skirt and the head, but they were evidently connected. "I don't believe that. You seemed most eager to get across the Gap."

Gwenny caught on. "That horrible demon blocking the way! That was you!"

"Of course. That path is enchanted. A real monster couldn't be on it, but since I mean no harm and the menace was illusory, no problem. I just wanted to see what you'd do."

"Gee, thanks," Gwenny said sarcastically.

"You're welcome." Sarcasm was of course wasted on demons.

Jenny returned, realizing that something was happening here. "A demoness?" she asked.

The dust coalesced into a rather shapely figure of a woman. "Metria!" Che and Jenny exclaimed, almost together.

"You know her?" Gwenny asked, surprised.

"She pestered us when we were coming to Goblin Mountain," Jenny said. "She pretended to be Nada Naga, and talked to Prince Dolph."

"Well, a winged centaur foal traveling with goblins and an outsized elf girl on the back of a sphinx was interesting," Metria said defensively.

"Well, we're dull now," Gwenny said.

"I doubt it. Why are three young folk traveling alone, when they are under the protection of the winged monsters?"

"Because we're trying to learn to be independent."

"And what would a long-haired goblin woman have to do with any of this?"

"She's my mother," Gwenny said shortly.

"So your mother left Goblin Mountain to come to the centaur family, and next day you three depart alone, going in another direction. You say that's not interesting?"

Gwenny realized that Metria would not be denied. "If we tell you what we're up to, will you leave us alone?"

"That depends. Let's make a different deal: if what you tell me is interesting, I'll tell you something interesting."

Gwenny looked at Che. "Is that a good deal?"

"It probably is," the centaur said. "I understand that Metria always honors her deals, and always tells the truth. But that often the deal doesn't turn out the way the other party thinks it will, and often the truth is not what he wants to hear."

Metria shot him a glance. "Even little centaurs are entirely too intelligent."

"However," Che continued, "it will be necessary to

obtain her commitment to privacy, because our mission is of a private nature.''

Metria grimaced. ''That ruins half the fun of it. But secrets are more interesting than what everyone knows. I'll agree.''

''Very well,'' Gwenny decided. ''I'll make that deal.'' For she realized that if their story bored the demoness, she would go away, and that was what they really wanted. ''My father, Gouty Goblin, just died, and I have to try to be the first female goblin chief of Goblin Mountain. But I can't see very well without spectacles, and I'll never get to be chief if the other goblins know that, so I've got to get contact lenses instead. I'm going to ask the Good Magician where I can get them.''

''The first female chief,'' Metria said. ''Does that mean your tribe of goblins will start acting civilized?''

''Yes.''

''I can see that there will be no entertainment there. But of course you may not win the chiefship, in which case the goblins will continue to be interesting.''

''Yes.''

''That must be what Che Centaur is fated to accomplish: getting you to be chief. That certainly would change the history of Xanth.''

''Yes. Now what do you have interesting to tell?''

The demoness made an expansive gesture. Her arms seemed to jump from one position to another in a series of placements, instead of smoothly the way mortal arms did. ''Only that there is another group of three traveling to see the Good Magician. They are Mela Merwoman, Okra Ogress, and Ida Human. Only the other two don't know yet that Ida is to be part of their party.''

''Mela Merwoman,'' Che said thoughtfully. ''Isn't she the one who—?''

''Yes, the color of whose panties represents the Question the Good Magician couldn't answer. It seems the time is coming for her to don them. She doesn't know this, of course; she's entirely innocent, which is a paradoxical appellation to apply to such a brute.''

"Such a what?"

"Animal, beast, critter, freak, monster—"

"Creature?"

"Whatever," Metria agreed crossly. "How come you didn't stumble over 'paradoxical appellation'?"

"I am a centaur. Such vocabulary is natural to me."

"Well, *I* stumbled," Jenny said. "What does it mean?"

Metria was pleased. "It means that this is the only way in which Mela is innocent. When it comes to males, she—oops, just how old are you?"

"Fourteen," Jenny said, just as crossly as Metria had been before. "I haven't joined the Adult Conspiracy."

Metria looked her over. "But you're about to. It isn't just a matter of age. After all, mice grow up and join in a matter of weeks."

"But why should Mela Merwoman's excursion be of interest to us?" Che asked.

"Well, she isn't, of course. Your kind has no interest in panties, and the girls already know about them. But Okra Ogress is of interest to Jenny Elf."

Jenny was startled. "She is?"

"Yes. Aren't you aware of the rationale behind your arrival in Xanth?"

"It was an accident. I was trying to catch Sammy, and we wound up in Xanth."

"It was no accident. You were chosen to come here. Someone had to be Jenny in Xanth, and you were the one."

Jenny was flustered. "I don't understand."

"There were two finalists: a foreign elf and a local ogress. The elf was chosen, so you were guided through the hole in Xanth, and the ogre girl was dumped."

"Chosen?" Jenny asked, bewildered.

"Someone wanted a Jenny here, so she was brought. That's why the Muses were so interested; they hadn't done it."

"But then the ogress—"

"Had to take whatever name and role were left over. So Okra Ogress is a minor character, and not too pleased about it. It should be interesting when you two meet."

"When we meet!" Jenny exclaimed, appalled.

"Maybe it will happen at the Good Magician's castle. Ida, of course, is even more remarkable, in a weirder way. So the future of that trio is a good deal more intriguing than your future. With that interesting news I leave you." Metria faded out.

"You were right," Gwenny said. "We don't like her truth. Who wants to meet an ogress?"

"Nevertheless, we learned something unexpected," Che said. "When I started to ask about Mela Merwoman, I was thinking of the way she kidnapped Prince Dolph, intending to marry him when he came of age. But Metria told me something of which I had no inkling; it must be known only to the demons. Now at last we know the Question the Good Magician could not answer."

"But that's such a simple Question," Gwenny said. "Any magic mirror could answer it, just by looking ahead."

"There must be more to it than we know," Che said.

Then they both looked at Jenny, who was oddly silent. "You don't have to meet any ogress, Jenny," Che said reassuringly.

"It isn't that. It's that I didn't know I was chosen. That someone else got excluded. I didn't mean to do that. I thought it was just an accident, my coming here."

"You didn't exclude anyone," Che said. "You have no responsibility for that."

"Still, I feel guilty. That poor ogre girl."

Gwenny laughed. "Poor ogress! That's impossible. All ogres are brutes."

"How do we know?" Jenny asked.

Gwenny exchanged a glance with Che. It was evident that Jenny had not had much experience with ogres.

Che changed the subject. "We must build our raft."

"That's right!" Jenny agreed. "I forgot about Sammy. I hope I can find him." She hurried off again, in the direction the cat had gone.

This time the other two followed her. The three spread out, so as to be able to cover more territory. The little orange cat could be anywhere. He was able to find anything except his way back from wherever he went. That was why Jenny was so careful about letting him go in strange territory. The demoness had appeared at just the wrong time, perhaps by no accident.

But it was all right. Sammy was just a short distance away, playing in a pile of vines. There was a quiescent tangle tree nearby. They were able to recreate what had happened: an ogre had passed by, and the tangle tree had made a grab for it, and the ogre had twisted off a number of tentacles and thrown them away. Such incidents occurred all the time in Xanth, because neither ogres nor tangle trees were noted for their intelligence or caution.

They hauled the drying vines to their assembled wood. They bound the wood together until they had a ragged but serviceable raft. It took only half the day, because it was no fancy job.

They hauled the raft to the water, clambered onto it, and used deadwood poles to push off. When the water became deep, they used deadwood paddles to move the raft forward.

"I hope Fracto doesn't spy us," Jenny said.

There was a rumble of thunder. Horrified, they paddled madly, but the raft moved as slowly as it could. The inanimate tended to be perverse.

The thunder turned out to be a false alarm. It wasn't Fracto, but a routine action of offshore clouds that did not come closer. They nudged on toward the shore to the south of the Gap.

Then the current caught them. The raft was carried out to sea, and they were unable to stop it. They watched helplessly as they moved away from the land.

But there was an island. The current carried them tantalizingly close to it. Yet they were afraid to try to swim to it, because there could be lurking water monsters waiting to gobble them.

The raft passed the northern tip of the island and started out into the larger part of the sea. They watched despairingly. As adventures went, this was a bleak one.

There was a breeze here, blowing from the sea toward the land. But it wasn't enough to reverse the effect of the current. It merely slowed their outward travel, prolonging the agony.

Then Gwenny had an idea. "Che! You can make the raft light! Then we can use the wind to get to the island!"

Che did it. He flicked every log of the raft with his tail, and the raft rose in the water, floating very high. Then they braced themselves and stood with their backs broadside to the wind. Now the current had less raft to work on, and the wind had more to work on. The raft slowed, jogged a bit, twisted around, and finally nudged back toward the island. It was working!

Finally they reached the beach and jumped back onto firm land. They hauled the light raft after them, for they would need it to cross from the island to the mainland. But meanwhile it was getting dark, and they had to make camp for the night.

"Find us a good place to sleep, Sammy," Jenny said, putting her cat down on the sand. Because this was an island, she didn't need to worry as much about his getting lost.

Sammy bounded toward the center of the island. They followed. And there, suddenly, they spied a tent.

"That looks familiar," Che said.

"It certainly does," Gwenny agreed. "It's almost as if we have been here before."

"Playing in the sand," Jenny agreed.

Then it came to them. "This is the Isle of View!" Gwenny exclaimed. "Where Prince Dolph married Electra!"

"And that tent is where they summoned the stork," Che agreed.

"So well that the stork brought them two babies," Jenny added.

"Dawn and Eve," Che said.

They looked at each other. A naughty thought flitted between them. "Do you think—" Gwenny started.

"That if we spent the night here—" Jenny continued.

"That we might learn the secret of summoning the stork?" Che concluded.

"Let's find out!" Gwenny said.

So it was that they spent the night in comfort, using the same pillows that Dolph and Electra had left. They had a fine pillow fight, for there was no adult to tell them no.

But they didn't learn the secret of summoning the stork. It seemed that Dolph and Electra had taken it with them. They had joined the dread Adult Conspiracy. What a pity.

In the morning they lightened the raft again, hauled it to the east shore of the island, and paddled it across to the mainland. A sea monster poked its head out of the water and eyed them, but a huge roc bird just happened to fly by, and the sea monster ducked out of sight.

Gwenny realized that the winged monsters were indeed keeping an eye on them. That left her with mixed feelings. She wanted to make it on her own, but still it was comforting to know that they would not be gobbled by a monster. So maybe this was a reasonable compromise: the three of them were being allowed to proceed without interference from either hostile or friendly creatures. Maybe they would have less need for protection as they gained experience.

They found a magic path and followed it inland. It would lead to Castle Roogna, because all the paths of the region did. Gwenny had visited the castle once, with her companions after Dolph and Electra's wedding. It was an impressive edifice. Much nicer, if the truth be confessed, than Goblin Mountain.

Suppose she just came to Castle Roogna, and didn't leave it? Then she would lose her chance to be lady chief, but she would be safe.

She shoved away the temptation. It wasn't that she *wanted* to be chief, it was that she *had* to be, so as to change the course of goblin history, and therefore Xanth history. It was her duty and her destiny. She dreaded it, but she could not flee from it.

Then she realized something. She had been making decisions. She had thought of a good idea that got them to shore. She was learning how to be a leader. She might not be very good at it, yet, but she was getting better. Maybe, just maybe, by the end of this journey, she would have learned it well enough. So there was a scintilla, or perhaps even two iotas, of hope for her.

So, resolutely, she proceeded on toward Castle Roogna.

Chapter 3. Okra

Okra's mind tended to keep pace with her
body. Since that was now rowing hard, she was thinking
hard, but since there wasn't much to think about at the
moment, she thought about her past, seeming almost to
relive it.

She had been delivered by the stork fourteen years before, to a small community of ogres still living beside
Lake Ogre-Chobee. It seemed that they had gotten turned
around during the migration to the Ogre-Fen-Ogre Fen
and returned here without quite realizing. After a few decades they had caught on, but by then it was too late to
catch up to the main party, so they had remained.

Okra's ogress mother, disappointed by Okra's pipsqueak
size, had tried to compensate by giving her a name to
grow into: Okra Cordata Saxifraga Goatsbeard Ganas
Ogress. Unfortunately she hadn't grown enough and was
singularly small and plain for her kind. She didn't even
have any warts or fangs; her stare would never curdle milk.
She was also embarrassingly weak; she had to use both
hands to crush juice from a rock. But her worst failure
was in her mind: she was not nearly stupid enough. This
defect had a minor compensation: she was smart enough
to hide this fault and to pretend to be only a little less

stupid than the other ogre whelps. But she could not hide it from herself, and it was her constant shame.

Okra tended to stay close to home, so as not to be teased by her peers. Other ogres thought that peers were wooden structures that projected into the water of Lake Ogre-Chobee and had no concern about them, but Okra knew better. Peers were other ogres her age, and they were the very worst company for her. She was content to stir the pot and scrape the dirt off the floor, and to think her frustratingly smart thoughts. If she ever let slip how unstupid she was, they would throw her away.

But some events she had been unable to escape. Her stylishly brutish parents had taken her to the monster marriage mash of Conan the Librarian and Tasmania Devil. Conan was said to have been able to squeeze a big dictionary into a single word, and to be able to use two heavy tomes to pound the civilization right out of any creature in short order. Tasmania was hailed as the meanest she-canine of an ogress of her generation. So it was a perfect match. Alas, the marriage did not work out well. Conan was too literate for Tasmania's taste, and she had a restless spirit. When the blood was on the moon she would feed him wild poison mushrooms that she ground up and mixed into his sea oat cakes. He loved the taste of those cakes, but the poison only gave him romantic notions. She wished he would lie down and die so that she could marry her first cousin Tasmaniac and gain status, but instead he was fired up for twice the usual amount of stork summoning, and their family grew at an ogreish rate.

But that was irrelevant. It was at this wedding that Okra's mother, Fern Kudzu, had gotten Okra's horrorscope cast in iron. The ogre tribe's midwife, who helped point out the right families when the stork couldn't tell one from another, was also the diviner. She announced that the runes, ox entrails, and stars pointed to good news and bad news. The good news was that Okra would eventually become a significant figure in Xanth. The bad news was that she had been cursed by a stray random accidental curse that escaped from a curse fiend without finding its proper object, and so had a magic talent.

Kudzu had reacted to this outrage as any ogress would: she had smashed the diviner into the lake, where she had disappeared without significant trace; only a few fragments of bones showed at the water's edge, and the chobees soon gulped those down. She jammed the iron cast down into the ground so deeply that molten lava filled in the hole it left. Then she hauled Okra back into the midst of the festivities—the mashing and bashing, the slam dancing, and the floor show with the drunken harpies harping—and pretended that the horrorscope had never been cast.

But Okra knew better. Ashamed, she slipped away from the festivities and hid in the cold, slimy, rat-infested cellar. That was a pleasant place, but still someone might find her, so she went down the winding narrow stone steps, down, down to the main kitchen where the wedding feast had been prepared. Pieces of chopped monsters lay scattered around; they must have fallen off the platters. As Okra's reddened eyes grew accustomed to the smoky gloom she saw sea oat cakes, both plain and poison (tastes differed), strewn on the stone floor. Someone had spilled a keg of wine dregs all over the kitchen table, the floor, and a drunken rat who lay in a stupor under the table. It was a very pleasant retreat, and Okra was able to hide there until the commotion above ground down into a dull roar.

That was one of Okra's early memories, and not unpleasant as ogre experiences went. But the knowledge that she was cursed with a magic talent haunted her thereafter. All ogres had magic, of course, and plenty of it; it was magic that gave them their vaunted strength, ugliness, and stupidity. But a separate talent? That was awful! No wonder she was small and plain and unstupid; her natural magic had been siphoned away to make this other talent. But maybe with luck she would never discover what it was.

Her other big memory was when she was thirteen. It

rained, as it did every afternoon in this season. Thick steamy clouds wet on those below with torrents of sheets of deluge that drenched the hot rocks and cooled the hot pools. Steam puffed up, but the freezing rain sliced on through, making a turmoil of vapor that suffused the caves and made it almost impossible to breathe. It was wonderful.

The dining room smelled of spoiling cabbage and stewed carcasses. That, too, was wonderful. Okra mussed up her unogreishly blond hair so that it would better hide the IQ vine circlet she wore as a wreath, and went inside. IQ vines had little effect on most ogres, because twice nothing remained nothing, but it helped Okra be alert enough to conceal her other liabilities. One was asthma; a siege of it had somehow found her, and it refused to depart. So she had to pretend to be fashionably hoarse, though actually she was having trouble breathing.

She remained naive enough to fancy that a birthday was important to anyone other than the owner of it. This was the day that cured her of that notion. It was just a pretext for another bash, and a new horror. She would later wish she had never had that birthday, but at the time she hadn't known how it would turn out. She had retained a tatter of innocence.

In an effort to sweeten the air, Okra's grandmother, that great burgundy queen Opuntia, had arranged to intermix heaps of wilted flowers with the rushes strewn about the dining room. There was a riotous show of color: white magnolias, yellow, orange, and red hibiscus, deep purple jacaranda, bougainvillea, and the famous fragrant lavender blooms from which Grandmother Ogre's medicinal soap was made. All of this was quickly trampled under the humongous hairy feet of the ogre clan as they pounded in to eat. Soon the dining room looked like an elegant woman dressed in soiled and tattered rags, feeling somewhat the worse for wear.

The door from the kitchen opened, and the old servant Troika Troll tromped in, bearing the largest soup tureen.

Behind her other servants came, each bending under the oppressive weight of the food piled on their serving platters. The last person in was Magpie, Okra's tutor. She was in black leather and black feathers. Her outfit was dated by a century or two, but that was understandable, for Magpie was a demoness who had served similarly in many places and times. She had even been at the fabulous human Castle Roogna, with Princess Rose, serving at her wedding to Good Magician Humfrey. Later Rose had gone to Hell in a handbasket, but remained a good person; Hell needed more roses, and roses were her talent. Who knew what else Magpie had seen during her immortal existence! No wonder she liked being a servant.

But someone tripped and dropped a platter, and its contents spewed across the table and floor. "Incompetent!" screamed the cook. Enraged, she threw crockery, handfuls of ground pepper, and finally Okra's birthday cake across the room. That caused the ogres to think that there was a food fight in progress, and they gleefully pitched in, filling the air with flying food. The original purpose of the party was forgotten. Now the dining room smelled not only of spoiled cabbage and wilted flowers, but also of every other type of bad food.

Okra, appalled, wept. That was of course a giant yes-yes of a no-no, and gave her an ogre-sized headache. She fled the hall—only to collide with Great Auntie Fanny. "Why ogrette, whatever's the matter?" Fanny inquired. A male ogre child was an ogret, and a female an ogrette, of course, not that anyone cared. Well, maybe the goblins cared, but only because they had goblets and goblettes.

"They r-ruined my birthday party!" Okra cried.

"Oh, is *that* the occasion! I thought it was a routine food fight."

"It is now."

"Well, then, there will surely be other birthdays! How old are you?"

"Thirteen today, Auntie," Okra replied, beginning to feel less worse.

"Great gobs of gook!" Auntie exclaimed politely. "Petard and brimstone! You are overdue for marriage! You're so small it never occurred to me—but I will speak to my husband, Bareface Von Wryneck, at once. We will check the grapevine to see which first cousin ogres are available."

"But—" Okra tried to protest.

"Let's see. There's young Crawling Banks. He's so stupid that if he had dynamite for brains, he could not clear one hairy nostril. He's ideal! But I think another ogress has her eye and maybe a ham hand on him already. There's the twins Slow Comb and Fast Comb, but it's too hard to choose between them because each one's duller than the other. Well, you'll probably have to wed the widower Zoltan Dread Locks."

That name was unfamiliar. "Who?"

Auntie poked her head through the door, because it happened to be closed. The wood splintered. It was the door's own fault for being in the way. She pointed a ham finger. "See that dirty old ogre dressed in animal-skin slippers and the mask of the black death? That's him. Yes, I think he's the one. You know, my first, second, and third husbands were widowers when I wed them, so I can recommend the type. An ogre doesn't get to be a widower unless he treats his ogress pretty roughly, it stands to reason. So he'll be fine for you."

Okra backed away and stared around her, petrified with a little loathing and a lot of fear. Just before she fainted she had a vision of a great gray city crowded with gargoyles made of stone.

Fortunately Auntie Fanny thought she must have knocked Okra out with an accidental sweep of her ham hand and didn't realize how unogreishly sensitive and weak she really was. Fanny proceeded forthwith setting up the marriage. However, none of the top prospects was interested in Okra; they pointed out with some justice that she was too small and scrawny to stand up to much punishment, and her looks were so plain as to be disgusting, and there was even an ugly suspicion that she wasn't as stupid as she pretended to be. Her parents finally gave up and turned her over to her more understanding grandparents, and the search began anew.

So it was another year before a suitable prospect was lined up: Smithereen, an ogre from the far Ogre-Fen-Ogre Fen who had never seen Okra so didn't know her liabilities. He started down to meet her, but there were distractions along the way, such as trees that had not been twisted into pretzels and small dragons who had not learned fear. Thus his progress was slow, for of course he was doing what it was in an ogre's nature to do: setting the world along his route into ogreish order. When he arrived, he would do the same for Okra, everyone fondly hoped, for her need was obviously great.

When the blood was on the moon shortly after Okra's fourteenth birthday—there was no party, because she was getting entirely too long in the tooth for marriage, as if her faults weren't already bad enough—the third big ugly event in Okra's life occurred. Her kindly (for ogres) grandparents disappeared, leaving her in the charge of her uncle Marzipana Giganta la Cabezudos fen Ogre, and his toady henchmen Numb Nuts and Big Blue Nose. Marzipana was a fine specimen of an ogre; he liked to stick pins into living butterflies and wear them on his head. Every time he suffered a difficult thought his laboring brain heated up his head and the butter melted, but that was no problem. He seldom bothered with difficult thoughts, and it was easy to catch new butterflies.

Okra knew that creatures disappeared on occasion. Ogres did all manner of stupid things, such as barging through dragon conventions or walking off sheer cliffs, and were generally then heard from no more. No one thought anything of it except Okra, who discovered yet another peculiarity of her nature: grief. She missed her grandparents, and was sorry to think that anything bad could have happened to them. Naturally she kept this sentiment to herself, because of her primary flaw: her intelligence.

Unable to sleep, Okra roamed the dank chambers and dusky tunnels of their home caves by night. During one of these dismal jaunts she happened to overhear the voices of her Uncle Marzipana and his henchmen. It seemed that the Ogre-Fen-Ogre Fen ogre Smithereen had been spied bashing small dragons over their heads with fresh pretzel treetrunks, and would bash his way on to Lake Ogre-Chobee any day now. They were afraid he would balk when he actually saw Okra. So they planned to carve a petrified pumpkin into the shape of an ogre face—any random pounding and slashing would do for that—and jam it on Okra's head so that she would look uglier than she was, at least until after the wedding. Then it wouldn't matter, of course; the ogre would pull out her hair and bash her real head into any new ugliness he preferred.

For some reason Okra wanted neither the pumpkin treatment nor the marriage. She realized that she just didn't fit in ogre society. So with shame she did her final un-ogreish thing: she bugged out. She packed her dragon-leather knapsack and made her way out to the dark slurpy shore of the lake where her little homemade oxblood boat lurked. Ogres were no sailors, so none of the others had ever recognized the nature of this craft, let alone connected it to her. She had often rowed around the lake by night, finding it blissfully peaceful. That of course marked one more flaw in her nature: no good ogre desired peace.

But once she was in her boat and fleeing the ogre caves, she realized that she had nowhere to go. She was unlikely to get anywhere if she had no destination, so she pondered, and by and by it came to her. She would go to the Good Magician for an Answer! Since she didn't have a Question, she would have to come up with one. She cogitated and pondered and considered and thought about it until her skull began to overheat, and finally decided that she would simply ask for her fortune. Whatever the Good Magician had to offer was bound to be less worse than whatever else she faced.

But she didn't know where the Good Magician lived.

So she solved that problem ogre fashion: she just rowed and rowed until maybe she'd get where she was going. While she did, she continued to think—that was a lifelong fault of hers—and realized that she might have a better chance if she did not leave her fortune up to the Good Magician. She should frame her Question so that the Answer would give her the clue to improving her fortune. But how could she do that?

Questions flitted tantalizingly around her ears, never quite entering her head. She began to get annoyed. That gave her a notion. Maybe she should ask whether she should keep her temper, and if so, where should she keep it? But after a time she realized that the Good Magician might simply answer "No," and charge her a year's service. So she discarded that one and continued to ponder.

She rowed and rowed, because she couldn't see where she was going but obviously wasn't there yet. That gave her plenty of time to think. Finally she came up with what she thought was the perfect Question: how could she become a Main Character? For it was evident that every creature was a character in the realm of Xanth, but some were more important than others. All of them suffered sundry travails, but the main characters had a much better record of survival and success than did the throwaway characters. Most ogres were obviously throwaways, which was why their lives were so wretched. But if she could somehow manage to become important, then her fortune would take care of itself.

The night had brightened into day, and the day had darkened into night, several times during the course of these deliberations. Still she hadn't gotten there, and she was beginning to get somewhat tired and hungry. But she was afraid that if she stopped rowing, she would get distracted and never get there.

Then there was a horrendous bump. She had gotten there! But when she looked around she discovered that it was only a bare shore; there was no Magician's castle in sight. "Oh, everything's going wrong!" she exclaimed. "I'll never find the Good Magician!"

"Hello."

Startled, Okra screamed and leaped into the air. She came down on her feet outside the boat, halfway frazzled. She hadn't realized that anyone was close.

It turned out to be a merwoman in nymph form named Mela. They talked, and decided to cross the lake—it was now the Kiss-Mee—together, because Okra had the boat and Mela knew where to go. Okra tossed the boat back into the water and they started off. Okra rowed vigorously, having recovered some strength during the brief pause, and encouraged because now there was someone to show the way.

Mela was saying something, but Okra couldn't hear over the sound of her rowing. But when her thoughts had run their course, catching her up to the vicinity of the present, she became aware of something else: the sky was darkening. Was it night already? No, it was a big thick cloud getting ready to rain on them. Well, a little rain wouldn't hurt, unless it filled the boat. Maybe it would be better to go to land and wait out the storm, as they would not make much progress in a storm.

She paused in her rowing. "Do you think we should—?" she inquired.

"Too late!" Mela cried. A gust of wind chose that moment to blow her hair halfway across her face. "Fracto has cut off our retreat."

"Fracto?"

"King Cumulo Fracto Nimbus, the worst of clouds. He always makes trouble."

"But ogres like trouble!"

"Can you swim?"

"No."

"Then you won't like Fracto's kind of trouble."

She had a point. Okra tried to turn the boat around and row toward shore, but the wind gusted up hugely and blew them the opposite way. Now she saw that the cloud had

formed a big misty mouth and was blowing right at them.
The wind was whipping up the waves, which were becoming mountainous.

Rain started, first a few fierce drops, then a drenchpour.
"Eeeek!" Mela screamed, pulling her bare legs up.
"Fresh water!"

"What's wrong with that?"

"I'm a saltwater creature. Fresh water foozles my tail."

"But you're wearing legs."

"I don't know how to swim with legs. Anyway, it foozles
my skin, too." Indeed, her skin was getting all blotchy
where the rainwater was striking it.

Okra tried to scoop out the water in the boat with her
hands, but it was coming in too fast. So she grabbed her
oars again. "Maybe we can get somewhere," she said.

Mela looked doubtful, but whatever she was trying to
say was lost in the howl of the wind and roar of the waves.
Okra saw a huge wave looming, trying to swamp them,
but she managed to heave the boat forward enough to elude
it and ride its swell after it settled a little. Waves could be
handled; they were like dragons—not too bad if closely
watched and tackled from behind.

But it just got worse. Sheets of water swept across, making Mela scream piercingly enough to be heard even above
the storm, and filled the boat rapidly. Okra couldn't row;
she had to bail. So she shipped the oars and started scoop-
ing out water with both hands. It flew out in gouts, low-
ering the level, and that saved the boat from sinking. But
that meant that they were entirely at the merciless mercy
of the wind and waves. In addition, Okra could feel an
asthma attack coming on; the exertion, wind, and soaking
were making her breath clog. Asthma always waited for
the worst times.

Then the awfullest wave yet charged them. It picked
them up and carried them at a horrendous rate into obscurity. All they could do was hang on, soaked through by
the seething foam; they were doomed to go wherever the
wave took them, with no argument.

The boat crashed onto a sandy, hairy crumb of a rock. It overturned, dumping them out. The water receded, leaving them sitting high and wet. Mela was huddled and shivering, and even Okra was cool. That had been a nasty storm, but they had after all made it to land.

The storm moved on, leaving only a few satisfied rumbles behind. It was through with them.

"Oh, no!" Mela exclaimed as she straightened up and sat down, more or less in one motion.

Okra looked. There was a great moving mound of sand coming toward them, giggling. "Gotcha in my sand trap!" it said. "Hee hee hee!"

"No, she she," Okra gasped. "Two she's, not three he's." She hoped her breath would unclog soon.

"It's a sandman," Mela said. "And he's caught us in his sand trap. That's why Fracto dumped us here."

"Sand trap?" Okra stood—and sat again as the sand went out from under her.

"It catches you so you can't get out of it. I've heard about it, but never been in it before. The sandman will cover us over until we smother, and then we'll dissolve away until only our heads are left, and we'll be beachheads."

"Hee hee hee!" the sandman repeated, agreeing.

Okra focused her brain and thought heavily for a moment. She knew she couldn't fight the sandman, because she could hardly breathe and was getting horribly weak. So she had to use her brain, such as it was.

A dim bulb flashed, heating her head. She had a feeble notion! She reached into her soaking wet knapsack and pulled out her lunch: a bottle of door jam. She hated to waste it, but it seemed necessary. She twisted the cap, making it ajar, and dumped the jar of it into the sand around her.

The sand swarmed over the sticky stuff and got jammed. More sand came in, and it too got jammed. Soon there was nothing but jammed sand.

Okra got to her feet and stepped on it. The surface was

now firm because of the sand. The jam nullified the loose-
ness of the sand, and the sand nullified the stickiness of
the jam. She could walk on it.

But the effect did not reach to Mela. So Okra stood at
the edge of the jammed sand and reached out to catch the
merwoman's hand and draw her in. Then the two of them
stepped out of the sand trap.

The sandman was so annoyed that he sank back into a
blah mound. Good riddance.

But this turned out to be an island, not the far shore of
the lake. They would have to stay here overnight, for the
storm could turn around and get them again if they tried
to leave before it did. Okra dumped the remaining water
out of the boat and set it out to dry in the sun.

They found a pool of firewater. Mela decided that this
was better than fresh water, so they had a bath in it, using
a cake of carved soapstone they found nearby. Soon they
were free of the last of the horrible froth Fracto had
dumped on them. Okra's asthma gave it up as a bad job,
and let her breath unclog. They rubbed their hair dry with
a towel from a cottonwood tree. Then Mela sang a siren
song as she combed her long tresses, making them magically lustrous.

Okra watched, intrigued. She pulled out a lank strand
of her own hair. It had never occurred to her that hair
could be beautiful, and it was not the ogre way to—but
still . . .

Mela smiled. "Would you like me do your hair, too?"

Okra blushed, which was another unogreish thing to do,
and agreed. So Mela used her magic brush and song, and
soon Okra's hair had changed from dank strands to lustrous tresses. She looked at her reflection in the pool, and
was amazed.

The light was getting all lavender, purple and soft. It
was time to find something to eat, before the light moved
on to deep purple and black. They gathered beach nuts,
sand dabs, beached banana boats, and finally found a coconut tree with several nuts full of fresh cocoa. That gave

them plenty to eat and drink, despite the loss of Okra's door jam.

Then they collected driftwood and made a drifter's hut to sleep in. Okra's boat, turned upside down, made the roof. They gathered fresh pillows and sheets from pillow bushes, forming a comfortable bed. They slept.

In the morning they scrounged for more food, finding some crabapples they cooked in the hot spring until they stopped squirming, and set out again. Okra had new confidence, because she discovered she liked having a companion instead of being alone. Mela was not at all like an ogre; she was beautiful and nice and fun to be with.

"May I ask you something, Okra?" Mela asked.

"Sure. But I may not know the answer. Ogre's aren't very smart."

"You seem smart enough to me. What I want to know is, why is it that you don't talk like an ogre?"

"I do talk like an ogre, but not as loud."

"No, you don't. You don't rhyme."

"Ogres don't rhyme!"

"Yes, they do. They say things like 'Me think you stink.' Crude rhymes. You don't talk that way."

Okra considered. "Maybe we just sound that way to others. We don't to ourselves."

"Or maybe your ogre tribe is different from the other ogres."

"Maybe. I'll try to rhyme if you wish."

Mela laughed musically. "Don't bother! I like you as you are."

Okra rowed, and they made progress toward the far shore of the lake. But Okra, facing back, spied a cloud on the horizon which rapidly grew larger as it approached. "I think Fracto is coming after us again," she said.

Mela turned back to look. "You're right! That's the demon cloud. Can we get to land before he reaches us?"

"We can try." Okra bent to it with new vigor, and the light craft leaped ahead. Still, Fracto gained, and would have caught them except that his leading winds just blew them farther ahead. He couldn't suck them back into himself.

However, they didn't have much choice about where they landed, and didn't have much chance to check around before the storm hit. They snatched burlap from a tree, strung it over a branch, and weighted down the ends with heavy shells. This gave them some shelter from the wind and rain, and they huddled inside it while the storm raged outside. At least they had made it all the way across the lake.

It remained day, but there was nothing to do except wait out the storm. Okra was really getting to dislike Fracto! It rained every day at home, too, but that wasn't malignant; Fracto evidently stormed just to make trouble for travelers. So they lay down and slept.

Okra was a light sleeper, for an ogress; anything out of the ordinary made her alert. Thus she woke when the burlap and shell curtains shook and tinkled as if blown open by a wet breath of wind. The thing was, there was no wind at this point; the storm had wandered elsewhere.

A billowing dribble touched Okra's arm and then landed with a soft splat on the floor. It was a very faint sound, but it was unfamiliar, so it brought her fully awake. Once when she had slept in the garden at home, a snake had paused and thought about performing a snakely function, and the sound of that thought had awakened Okra.

As it happened, she was glad to wake, because she had been dreaming of riding a night mare, and that was not her favorite occupation. She had never ridden anything, preferring to use her legs on land or her rowing arms in her boat on the water. But she was aware that the dangers of the waking state could be almost as bad as those of dreams.

She opened her eyes and looked at what had fallen beside her. It was a fat luna-tick, ready to gorge itself on her blood. Even now it was using its stubby legs to crawl toward her, hoping to bite her in an unseen place and get her blood without waking her. It was about the size of her fist, and twice as ugly. A nest of such ticks could drain a person's whole body during sleep, so that the victim never did wake up. Of course that meant that there was no more for the ticks to eat, and most of them died. That was one reason they were called luna-ticks: they were crazy.

But how had the tick come here? Her eyes flicked to the sloping side of the impromptu tent, but there was no hole there. So it hadn't dropped in from outside. Since luna-ticks couldn't fly, it must have been thrown there.

It was not true that ogres always blundered noisily when they moved; they could act quickly and silently when they had to. They seldom had to, as it was normally easiest simply to bash something into oblivion. But Okra, being the least of ogres, had learned more of silence than was useful. Her hand went soundlessly to her knapsack beside her and her fingers closed about the handle of her skinning knife. But she didn't stab the tick; that was a minor pest. She wanted to be ready for the major one she knew had to be near.

Then, carefully, she turned her head. There was an awful figure standing over Mela's still form. There was the smell of fresh blood. She had thought it was from the tick, but now she knew better.

Okra recognized the figure. It was a geek. They were lesser humanoid monsters, smaller and weaker than ogres or trolls, but they made up for it by being nastier in personality. No geek was ever up to any good; that was in the big book of monster rules.

Okra's arm moved. She threw the knife at the geek. But the geek, with the evil cunning of its kind, turned to flee the blade. He was too slow; the steel of it buried itself in his back. But of course he didn't die; geeks had no hearts, so stabbing one in the heart wasn't properly effective. But the puncture did cause some discomfort, and the creature fell out of the tent.

Okra leaped to her feet to pursue him, for if she didn't finish him off he would only return for more mischief. She strode out of the tent, and paused in dismay. There was a slew and a half of geeks climbing all over her oxblood boat, and luna-ticks were trying to suck the ox blood from it.

Outraged, Okra advanced on them. She had forgotten to recover her knife, but her fists would do. "You ridiculous geeks, what are you doing on my boat?" she demanded.

They looked at her. "We want to talk you into coming with us, of course," one said. Geeks were not the smartest of creatures; in fact some were rumored to be almost as stupid as ogres. So it didn't occur to them not to answer a question. "Once we have you, we will tie you up and hit you, for no reason at all, until your willpower is gone and we can start work on your won't power. When you finally give us the pleasure of dying, we will feed your carcass to our hungriest luna-ticks." He had an oily, stinky voice and the smell of a dung beetle; those were his better aspects.

"But you geeks don't know how to row a boat," Okra protested, for the moment being almost as stupid as they. It was expected of an ogre, after all.

"We will make you row it to our hideout, where there are many more of us. We will take the merwoman along too; she looks luscious enough to give us some pleasure before we take all her blood."

Okra didn't know quite what he meant by that, but was sure it wasn't anything nice. She had heard enough; it was time to act. So she waded in, forming her best emulation of ham fists and knocking geeks every which way. She was the smallest and weakest of ogres, but these were only geeks. Soon she had scattered them to a suitable degree; they would not bother her for a while.

Then she picked up her knife and returned to the tent to check on Mela. The geek had set several ticks on her, and they were already gorging. There were scarlet ribbons of blood on her face, hands, and breasts. The worst of it was that she remained asleep; the bites of the ticks were painless, so Mela didn't even know how she was being drained.

"Mela, wake up!" Okra said urgently.

Now the merwoman woke. She felt the ticks on her body, looked down at them, and exclaimed "Yeeeech!!!!"

Okra was startled. She had never before heard a four-point exclamation, but the exclamation points were definitely there, just like little clubs. Then she got into action, pulling the ticks off Mela and squishing them with blows of her mini–ham fists.

Then Okra donned her knapsack and led Mela out. The merwoman remained weak and dizzy, having expended much of her remaining store of energy in the production of that excellent exclamation. She would need further attention, but first they had to get to a safer place.

Mela blinked as she stepped out and looked around. "Ek," she said, managing a quarter point scream that was hardly audible. "What are those things doing draped across the branches of trees, and with their heads rammed through knotholes, and with their feet sticking up from the mudbank?"

"Those are geeks," Okra explained. "I asked them to get out of our way."

"Oh." Then Mela's eyes fastened weakly on the boat. "Eek." That scream was a little better formed and more emphatic than the last, but still not in the same universe as the first exclamation.

Okra picked up the boat and shook it, dumping the luna-ticks into the water. Mela relaxed.

They left the dangerous bay behind them, going out onto deep water. There was no sign of Fracto, fortunately; the late afternoon was beautiful.

Okra shipped the oars and dug in her knapsack for her medical kit. This was yet another unogreish artifact she had picked up; most ogres took no note of pain and less of injury. She dabbed at the tick bites with unguent, but didn't accomplish much. Mela had lost too much blood.

Even the twin firewater opals she wore on the chain around her neck looked listless.

So Okra did the best thing she could think of: she rowed back to the island. There she avoided the sand trap and hauled Mela to the hot pool and washed her off. Then Mela began to revive, for a hot bath had a magical effect on any woman. Her listless straw hanks of hair began to turn to golden tresses, which turned a pretty green under the water.

Okra found a timely thyme plant, and a medicinal mint herb. She dipped them in a mug of the hot water, concocting first one tea and then two teas. She gave these to Mela to drink, and these teased her into further improvement. Then Okra set her on pillows and sang ogreish songs until Mela faded away to sleep. Unfortunately the only one she could remember was "Happy Birthday."

A rare blue moon came up. Okra admired its color; this was the first time she had seen this hue on the moon. She wished she could get some blue cheese from it, but couldn't reach that high. Then she slept, especially lightly, ready to wake at any sign of trouble.

In the morning Mela felt better, but Okra felt worse. She was hardly able to get into the boat to resume rowing. Yet she wasn't wheezing. What was the matter with her?

"Let me check this," Mela said. "Take off your knapsack." She helped Okra remove it. "Ha! I thought so. There's a tick on you."

Indeed, the tick was on Okra's back, hidden by the knapsack, which she had not removed overnight. It must have crawled into the knapsack while Okra was dealing with the geeks, then gotten on her while she slept.

Mela took pleasure in drowning the tick in the hot pool. Then she took care of Okra, the way Okra had taken care of her, and by the end of the day Okra was feeling better. They had a meal of fresh coconut cocoa, breadfruit, and a variety of butters from beach buttercups.

The following morning Okra rowed them back across to the western shore. Mela used her opals as searchlights to find a safe path that would guide them across a mountain of sand dunes and down into a huge cave with magic springs, an underground stream, and a colony of freshwater merfolk. She had a little manual in her invisible purse that described the locations of the various merfolk tribes, and there was supposed to be such a colony here. For she depended on these cousin creatures to give her directions to reach the castle of the Good Magician. The freshwater folk had little association with the saltwater folk, but merfolk were bound to support merfolk.

However, there were details that Mela's manual didn't mention. After topping several sandy dunes, they stopped by the pathside in the shade of a mixed forest of beach umbrella trees, bagpipe bushes, clove trees, and ladyfinger and palm trees. The umbrella provided shade, the bagpipes played skirly music, and the ladyfingers made delicate gestures that caused the palms to sweat. Okra's own palms were sweating, for she was carrying her oxblood boat and the higher they climbed, the heavier it got. That was part of the magic of heights, of course: they made things heavier.

They found a health spa spring and drank from it. Then the path became narrow, and they had to leave the boat at the spring and follow the winding rocky magic path as it became a white marble chip path. They reached a charming antique garden, where they settled down to rest. Mela could not resist plucking a silvery platina lace shawl from a nearby Spanish shawl bush, and Okra nibbled bits and pieces from the pink peppermint candytuft tree. It seemed that they had lost any cares they had ever had, and were now carefree.

Mela knew a song, which she taught Okra: "The Saga of the Sleeping Dragon." The sun seemed to slow its journey overhead, listening. Then they saw thyme plants growing near, and realized that the presence of a number of these could slow time here and make the day longer. It wasn't just their imagination. They could relax here as long as they wanted, and only a little time would pass outside the thyme garden.

But soon they moved on along the path, realizing that the slowed time was also a good way to get more rapidly where they were going. They walked on through the glorious colors, symmetries, music, tastes, smells, and feelings of this region. It appealed to all their senses.

"Ahhh, ohhh," Mela sighed as they came upon a crystal rock garden filled with sweetly scented white rock roses, tiny paper narcissi, and softly baa-aa-aaing white phlox. Even Okra, untrained as she was in the appreciation of loveliness, was rapidly learning it. A small crystal spring bubbled and sang from the top of the miniature crystal mountain to tumble down, down the little crags into a crystal pool below. It was perfect except for one small detail: the small frozen figure of a young human woman encased in a large block of crystal that was being used to prop open the door of a garden shed.

They entered the shed, which turned out to be a cave with dusky recesses. They gazed at the figure. She was a fairly pretty creature, wearing pale water-washed aqua blue chiffon dress and golden filigree sandals.

"I don't like the look of this at all," Mela whispered, grabbing nervously at Okra's arm and shivering. "Suppose you and I also fall into that crystal and remain here as prisoners of thyme forever? We must hurry away from here!"

"But what about that poor trapped girl?" Okra asked. "Is it right to leave her here?"

Mela frowned. "You would have to think of that! No, it's not right. We shall have to try to help her."

Mela lifted her two firewater opals and approached the crystal. Watery fire shot out and bathed the block. It shimmered, and its corners melted, but the girl inside remained frozen. The opals were not strong enough for this job.

"Maybe I can carve her out," Okra said. She drew her knife and attacked the crystal. Fragments flaked off and fell to the floor. But soon the knife dulled, and the main bulk of the crystal remained.

"Maybe my siren song can do it," Mela said. She opened her mouth and sang her lovely, weird melody. The crystal shimmered, and rainbow glints of light radiated from it, but it did not fracture or dissolve.

Mela gave up. "Maybe your voice can do it," she said. "Try singing ogre loud."

Okra opened her mouth. A strange feeling came over her. She sang a note, and then a higher note, and then more higher notes in a stair-step pattern. The notes rose to high C, and above, until they disappeared through the roof and could be heard no more. There was silence—but Okra was still singing.

"That's your magic talent!" Mela exclaimed. "You have an ultrasonic voice!"

The crystal block shivered and cracked. Suddenly it burst apart, and the young woman stood there, free, shaking her head and blinking her eyes.

But now the heavy stone door to the garden shed was closing, having lost its doorstop. "Get out!" Mela cried, alarmed.

The young woman merely shook her head, confused.

Okra acted. She charged through, picked up the girl, and carried her out before the door shut them in. Mela followed her out. The three of them stood breathing hard as the door crunched into place behind them.

Okra set the young woman down. "What's your name?" Mela asked her.

The young woman took a breath, and at her bosom the material of her dress shimmered into a silvery Aegean blue green which exactly matched her pale jade green hair and aqua green eyes. "I da—don't—"

"Ida?" Mela asked.

"Know," she finished.

"Oh." The merwoman considered. "Well, let's just call you Ida, then. I am Mela Merwoman, and this is Okra Ogress. We just rescued you from a cruel imprisonment."

"H-hello," Ida said. "Thank you."

"Now we must learn all about you," Mela said. "So we can help you. Where are you going?"

Ida shook her head. "Going?" she asked blankly.

"Well, then, where have you been?"

Ida spread her hands. "I'm not sure."

Mela looked at Okra. "I think we have a problem."

But Okra had an idea. "Maybe she wants to go to see the Good Magician, just as we do, to get her life straight."

"Is that the case?" Mela inquired.

"Yes, I think so. If I can find the way."

Mela smiled. "As it happens, we are in the process of finding the way. So you can come with us, and the Good Magician will know what to do."

Ida nodded. "Yes, I'd like that."

"But the path is closed off now," Okra pointed out. "The door closed when we took out the block. Now we can't reach your merfolk cousins and get directions."

"Maybe there is another route," Mela said. "We shall just have to go back and see."

So they started back. Mela led the way, and Ida followed, and Okra was last. Once again her thoughts started galloping around inside her skull, bouncing off the bone and getting all mixed up. What a strange thing, to meet such an elegantly garbed young woman, sealed up in a crystal!

Chapter 4. Che

Castle Roogna was protected by its great orchard. Che knew about this, of course; it was part of the Centaur Lesson Plan. "We have to make sure that the trees know we are friends," he said. "Otherwise they will move their branches to block us."

"Oh, pooh!" Jenny said. "Trees don't move their branches unless there's a strong wind." She marched ahead along the path.

Branches swung down from the left and right, barring her way.

"Then again, maybe they do," she said, stepping back. "I forgot that this isn't like the place I came from."

"How do we let them know we are friends?" Gwenny asked.

"We identify ourselves and state our mission," he said. "Once they know us, they won't bother us again."

So the goblin girl approached the crossed branches. "I am Gwendolyn Goblin, heir to the chiefship of Goblin Mountain, on the way to consult the Good Magician about something I need if I am to succeed in becoming the first female chief among the goblins."

The leaves of the trees rustled. After a moment the two

61

big branches lifted up, letting her pass. But they dropped back into place behind her.

Jenny stepped up again. "I am Jenny from the World of Two Moons. I'm Gwenny's friend, and I want to help her."

The leaves rustled again, and then the branches lifted, letting her pass.

Che stepped up. "I am Che Centaur, Gwenny's companion. I may be destined to help change the course of the history of Xanth."

The trees let him pass also. "Thank you," he said.

They moved on through the orchard, where all manner of trees grew with their fruit. There were cherries in varieties ranging from chocolate to bomb, and pies ranging from lemon to cow, and footwear trees ranging from boot to lady's slipper. They looked at these, sorely tempted, but knew that they had to present themselves at Castle Roogna before touching anything.

Then the castle itself loomed up forbiddingly, surrounded by a deep moat. A serpentine moat monster lifted its head to stare at them. But it recognized them, and relaxed. They had, after all, been here before. They just hadn't come by foot, then.

There was a scream from inside. In a moment a young woman in blue jeans and shirttails dashed out, her braids flying. "Che! Gwenny! Jenny!" she cried.

It was Electra, the first princess of Xanth to wear such informal clothing. They had been at her wedding, two years before. She was actually twenty years old, but looked sixteen. That was fine, because her husband Prince Dolph was seventeen, and women were supposed to be younger than men, and if they weren't, they had to fake it. Che wasn't sure of the origin of that particular rule, but it was in the big book of rules somewhere.

Electra hugged them all and ushered them into the castle. She took them to the nursery to show off the twin girls the stork had brought her, Dawn and Eve. It was hard to

imagine this girlishly freckled person as either princess or
mother, but she was, and evidently quite happy to be so.

They were given a room to share, and Che gazed out
the window while the girls took baths and changed clothing. Centaurs did not have the same conventions as the
human folk, but honored them when in human company.
So he did not try to sneak a peek at anyone's panties,
tempting as the prospect was.

Then they were escorted to the main dining hall for
dinner. Now they met King Dor and Queen Irene, who
were gracious. Prince Dolph was also present, looking
somewhat gangly. Then Electra appeared, and for a moment Che did not recognize her, for she had been trans-
formed.

She wore a pale green gown speckled with golden
motes, and a tiara in her hair, and her feet were dainty in
lady's slippers. Her face remained freckled, but now it
was adult and beautiful. She looked almost as wonderful
as she had on the day she married Dolph, when the magic
wedding dress had changed her from nothing to lovely.

"You seem surprised," Queen Irene remarked. Che
glanced guiltily around, and realized that she was speaking to Gwenny and Jenny, whose mouths had sagged open.
That was a relief; Che's mouth had almost done the same.

"Electra's so different," Jenny said. "Just a moment
ago she was in blue jeans."

"We have learned the art of compromise," Queen Irene
said. "By day, and in informal situations, Electra dresses
and acts as she pleases. In the evening, and when formal,
she dresses for the part. She is after all a princess now."

"I wonder if I will ever be like that," Gwenny murmured, awed.

"Surely you will, dear, when you are chief," Queen
Irene said. "Your mother is excellent with clothing and
manners."

Actually, she was not far from it now, Che reflected.
Gwenny, like all goblin females, was petite and pretty, and
in the dress she was wearing at the moment she was win-

some. But she did not know it, which was surely part of her appeal.

They ate well, for all the fruits of the orchard that had tempted them were served. There was even a nice plate of cat treats for Sammy. Che realized that Queen Irene had noticed, and made sure to please the guests.

Yet why should the Queen have gone to such trouble? They were merely three creatures on a private mission, hardly worthy of royal treatment.

No, that was not correct. They were special people. Jenny was a representative of a species of elf never before seen in Xanth, whose story was as yet incomplete. She had pointed ears and four fingers, and her folk, in their own realm, had the ability to communicate mind to mind. Gwenny had the chance to be the first female chief of a goblin tribe, and that could transform the relations of goblins to other species as dramatically as the change of clothing had done for Electra. And Che himself was supposed to change the history of Xanth, though the way of that was not yet clear. Perhaps he would be instrumental in helping Gwenny achieve the chiefship, or perhaps it would happen in some other manner. So the three of them, though young, were not ordinary, and Queen Irene was well aware of that. Possibly his sire and dam had notified the Queen that they were coming; centaur adults left little to chance. Still, he appreciated the courtesy which was being extended, and knew that the girls did too.

After the meal, Electra invited them to join her and her daughters in Princess Ivy's old room to see the magic Tapestry. She carried the twins in a large bassinet. "They like to watch it," Electra explained. "So we watch it before they go to sleep for the night. It is always interesting."

The Tapestry turned out to be a big woven picture of Castle Roogna hung on the wall. It had been made back in Electra's time, almost nine hundred years ago, by the Sorceress Tapis. The Sorceress had given it to the Zombie Master in the form of a puzzle, and he had not appreciated its nature until he had assembled it. Now the Zombie Master lived in the present, but had elected to leave the Tapestry where it was most useful at Castle Roogna. It had helped educate Princess Ivy and Prince Dolph, and any number of other folk.

For the picture on the Tapestry was not fixed. It constantly changed, showing facets of the history of Xanth or contemporary events. It was possible to spy on others, using it, though of course good folk would never do that. Still, that did make it a most interesting item.

"What would you like to see?" Electra inquired. "The twins don't mind what is on; they're too young, yet, to be choosy." Actually, at the moment the twins weren't looking at the Tapestry at all; they were watching Sammy Cat, who had joined them in the bassinet. He was playing with a loose thread on their blanket.

Gwenny shrugged, but Jenny looked concerned. "Do you think it might show Okra Ogress?" she asked hesitantly.

Immediately the picture changed. It showed a strange crystal rock garden with white rock roses and sheeplike white phlox. A crystal spring flowed from a little crystal mountain, making miniature waterfalls until it formed a pool below. The scene was beautiful.

But there were no figures in it, ogre or otherwise. Only a block of crystal which propped open a door.

Then a figure appeared: a rather large human woman, heavy boned and lightly furred. Her strawlike hair flared outward from her head and down her back in knots and tangles. With her was a smaller but more voluptuous woman, wearing slippers and nothing else. Her hair was the same yellow color, but the tresses were glossy and silky rather than crude and ropy.

"That's Mela Merwoman!" a voice said from the doorway. It was Prince Dolph, who had stopped by for a moment.

"That's right—Nada said you knew her," Electra remarked without enthusiasm.

"Uh, yes," he said, staring at the image. "Of course I didn't want to marry her."

"Because you were nine years old at the time," Electra retorted.

"But I must admit that she has very nice—"

"Never mind!" Electra snapped. The picture fuzzed in the region of Mela's torso, so that whatever he thought was interesting was no longer so.

Prince Dolph's eyes were freed from what had held him like the peephole of a hypnogourd. "Oh, to be nine again," he murmured as he departed.

Gwenny and Jenny exchanged a glance, which Che intercepted. He knew their thought: was this what marriage did to a relationship?

Then Electra got up. "Do you mind keeping an eye on the twins for a while? I have something to do."

The girls, in the manner of their kind, were glad to keep an eye on the twins. All girls loved all babies, in Che's observation. Electra hurried out.

"I wonder what she has to do so urgently?" Jenny said musingly.

"I suspect she means to apologize to Prince Dolph," Che said.

"Apologize? For what?"

"For being jealous," Gwenny said.

"Oh." But Jenny wasn't quite satisfied. "Couldn't she have just said she was sorry, here?"

"Perhaps she had a gourd realm apology in mind," Che said, smiling.

Jenny's brow furrowed. "That's different?"

This time it was Gwenny and Che who exchanged the glance. "You don't know about apologies among the brassies?" Gwenny inquired.

"An apology's an apology, isn't it?"

"I see we shall have to show you," Gwenny said, with an obscure smile. "Che?"

The naughty girl! Che approached her. He was seven and she was fourteen, but he was of a larger species, and his human portion was somewhat taller than she. "Who apologizes to whom?" he inquired.

"I'll apologize to you," Gwenny said. "The way Electra will do with Dolph."

"Very well. Proceed."

"I don't understand—" Jenny started.

Gwenny embraced him. "I apologize, Che," she said winsomely. Then she drew herself close and kissed him on the mouth.

"What are you doing?" Jenny asked, amazed.

"Do you accept my apology?" Gwenny asked.

Che grimaced. "I'm not sure," he said with a smile, playing the game. Actually, Gwenny was very nice to have so close; her body had become rounder and softer in the past two years. But that was surely irrelevant.

"Oh, you're not?" Gwenny breathed. "Then I shall just have to try harder." She removed her spectacles and brushed back her hair with her hands. Then she embraced him again, more closely, so that there was no space between their bodies. She reached up and hauled his head down, mussing his hair, and plastered him with Xanth's sloppiest kiss. *"Now* are you sure?" Her face was serious, but he knew she was trying to stifle her laughter. It was a favorite game, to imitate the foolish things adults did.

He stifled his own mirth. "Well—"

"Enough!" Jenny cried, giggling. The twins seemed to be smiling, too, watching the apology instead of the Tapestry. So was Sammy. "You mean that's what Electra and Dolph are doing now? Kissing?"

"More than that, I think," Gwenny said with mock gravity as she recovered her spectacles so that she could see clearly again. "But I'm not partial to the Adult Conspiracy, so I don't know what. I suppose they enjoy it, though."

"That Adult Conspiracy is such a bore," Jenny said. "What is it they think should be such a big secret?"

"I'm sure I don't know," Gwenny said. "But it seems

to relate to why men like to look at creatures like Mela Merwoman.''

They looked at Mela again in the Tapestry, whose body was no longer fuzzy. But no matter how hard Che stared, he couldn't fathom why men would prefer to look at the merwoman rather than at something interesting, such as a dragon or pie tree or mathematical equation.

Meanwhile, the action proceeded in the picture. Mela and the other woman were trying to get the block of crystal to break open, for it seemed that there was something inside it that they wanted. They weren't having much success.

"But we were supposed to see Okra Ogress," Jenny said plaintively.

Che suffered a realization. The room brightened momentarily as an invisible bulb flashed above his head. "That big woman—*that's* the ogress!"

Gwenny and Jenny stared. "But she's not big enough or ugly enough!" Gwenny protested. "She's mostly like a big human woman."

But now Che was orienting on particular features. "I do believe she is an ogress," he said. "The patterns of her bones, her way of moving—these indicate ogre stock. But she must be the smallest, weakest, and least ugly of all ogresses."

"Maybe she had a bad illness," Gwenny said. "So she doesn't measure down to ogre standards, and got booted."

"Maybe she should have gotten the part, then," Jenny said. "Maybe she should have become the major character, so—"

"And where would you be, now, if that had happened?" Gwenny inquired sharply.

"Back in the World of Two Moons," Jenny said. She began to cloud up. "With my family, and the ability to send—"

"Without your spectacles," Che said quickly.

"Or your new friends," Gwenny added.

Jenny brightened. "That's true. But still, it wasn't fair to exclude—"

"We don't know why you were chosen to come here, or by whom," Che said. "But there must have been good reason. One day we shall learn it. Until then, we can't judge it."

"I suppose you're right," she agreed. She looked again at the picture. "Is this what is happening right now, there?"

"I don't think so," Che said. "I understand that the Tapestry normally orients on events of the past, so this may have happened a few days ago. But it is now night; it may be that the ogress is sleeping, so the Tapestry showed her a few hours ago, when she was active."

"I wonder what's in that block?" Gwenny remarked.

"If we knew how to manage the Tapestry, we could change the orientation of the picture," Che said. "We are seeing the block from behind. But it looks as if there is a person inside it."

"How weird!" Gwenny exclaimed.

Then Electra reappeared, looking slightly disheveled but happy. She was back in blue jeans. "Thank you," she said, going to the twins.

"Did he accept your apology?" Jenny asked.

"What?" Electra asked blankly.

Gwenny stifled a giggle. "We thought maybe—but obviously we were wrong. The twins are fine. Do you know their talents yet?"

"As a matter of fact, we do. The Good Magician told us. Dawn will be able to tell anything about any living thing, and Eve will be able to do the same for any inanimate thing. He says those are both Magician-class talents."

"Wow," Gwenny said, awed.

"Well, it's not really coincidence. Every one of Grandpa Bink's descendants has Magician-class talent. I'm not sure why, but it has been true so far. I was just lucky I married Dolph, so that my children are blessed."

"That's great," Jenny said. "Those talents will be very useful, when they get old enough to use them."

Electra picked up the bassinet and carried it away. Sammy jumped down, losing interest. Che went with Gwenny and Jenny to their room, where the girls changed into nighties and he lay down on the floor among cushions. Sammy joined him. Then Jenny sang a song, and soon they were all in the magic dream that formed. There was a trick to sharing Jenny's dreams: they had to divert their minds to something else first. But they had learned how to do that, and so had Sammy. So they found themselves sharing a dream of friendly dragons, unicorns, and centaurs in an orchard much like the one around Castle Roogna, with pleasant skies. Then they lay down on the soft sward and fell asleep. Somehow it was always more fun to go to sleep in a dream than it was in reality.

On the morrow they resumed their trek to the Good Magician's castle. There was an enchanted path leading directly there, so they knew that that part would be easy. But they also knew that getting into the castle would not be easy. There were always three challenges, and if the querent succeeded in getting by them, she still had to perform a year's service for the Good Magician. In short, frivolous Questions were discouraged. Thus their mood was not light as they set out.

The air fuzzed before them, and the Demoness Metria formed. "You must be really excited," she said.

"Our anticipation knows no bounds," Che agreed tersely.

"Especially considering that the Good Magician has arranged to hit you with the most intriguing possible challenge," the demoness continued. "I have never seen him use this one before in the century or so I have known him."

She was of course trying to fluster them. Che knew better than to let her succeed. "No doubt the other challenges are even worse."

"No, there is to be only one challenge this time."

"But there are always three! And we are three people, so we may have more."

"Not so. The Good Magician has made a freedom in your case."

"A what?"

"Privilege, manumission, deliverance, emancipation, liberation—"

"Exception?"

"Whatever," she agreed crossly.

"But why? We are just ordinary supplicants, not deserving of any special treatment."

"True. Therefore it is a mystery. How I love a mystery!"

"Why don't you ask a Question of the Good Magician yourself, then?"

"Because it is his business to resolve mysteries, not to generate them. Anyway, Dana doesn't like me to get too close to him."

"Who?"

"The Good Magician. Who else?"

"I mean, who is Dana?"

"His wife. I told you about that before."

"Oh." She hadn't told him, but probably had told someone and misremembered whom. Her memory was like that. Che had heard about the matter: the Good Magician had had five and a half wives in the course of his life, and now they took turns being with him. Dana must be the one who was a demoness. So it seemed that one demoness could be jealous of another. That was interesting. They did have some human emotions.

Then he thought of a way to get rid of Metria, for a while. "Why don't you go ahead and wait for us to arrive at the castle, instead of watching our boring walk there?"

"Are you trying to get rid of me?"

"Of course."

"That means you don't want me there. You are trying to fake me out."

''Of course.''

''Good idea. I'll do it.'' She vanished.

''You faked her out!'' Jenny exclaimed. ''How did you manage it?''

''I locked her into an either-or mode,'' Che explained, pleased. ''She thought she had to be either here or there, and chose there as more interesting. It didn't occur to her that she could have done both.''

''You're smart!''

''I am a centaur,'' he said modestly.

''Maybe by the time we get there, she'll have forgotten us,'' Gwenny said.

''That is my hope.''

The path enabled them to travel rapidly. Nevertheless it was more than a day's walk. ''Maybe we should look for a place to camp for the night,'' Jenny said.

Sammy ran ahead of them. As always, she followed, because the cat was almost as good at getting lost as he was at finding things. Che and Gwenny followed her.

Sammy took a side path they wouldn't otherwise have noticed. It led to a little park. They found a nice umbrella tree, conveniently placed for just such travelers as themselves, with nearby fruit and nut trees and a big pillow bush. So they dined on breadfruit with butternuts and drank vanilla milkweed pods, with candy canes for dessert.

''Do you think we'll stop liking such things, when we turn adult and join the Conspiracy against fun?'' Gwenny asked.

''Oh, I hope not!'' Jenny exclaimed.

''Yet somehow it seems that everything changes, when a person grows up,'' Che said sadly. ''Look at Electra.''

''Actually, she's not so bad,'' Gwenny said. ''She still wears blue jeans by day. Maybe she didn't really join the Conspiracy.''

''She summoned the stork,'' Che pointed out.

''Maybe it's possible to learn how to do that, without

adopting the bad parts, like spinach,'' Jenny said hope-
fully.

"Let's agree that we'll subscribe to only the good parts
of the Conspiracy,'' Che suggested. "We'll be different,
when we grow up.''

"Yes!'' Gwenny agreed. The three of them clasped
hands, sharing the oath.

They settled down for the night, moving into a dream
and then into sleep, as usual.

Che suffered a bellyache during the night. He wished
he hadn't eaten quite so many candy canes; they now had
a distressing aftertaste. He heard the girls tossing restlessly in their sleep, and knew that they had the same
problem. It was of course impossible that a person could
ever get too much candy; still, there was something.
Maybe there had been a curse on some of them.

In the morning they marched the rest of the way to the
Good Magician's castle. None of them had been here before, so it was more daunting than Castle Roogna had
been, despite being smaller and without the tree guardians. Well, technically Jenny had been here, but only
briefly; she had been allowed to inquire about the way
back to the World of Two Moons, but then had changed
her mind before getting the Answer. She had decided that
she wasn't ready to leave Xanth yet, to Che and Gwenny's
relief. But since the Good Magician's castle was different
each time anyone visited it, that hardly counted. Now it
was just a somewhat dilapidated stone edifice surrounded
by a small moat. It seemed undefended: there was no moat
monster, and the drawbridge was down. No person was in
sight.

As they came closer, they saw that their first impression
had been deceptive. This was not an ordinary castle at all.
It was made of pastry and candy. The walls were not stone,
but fruitcake with large stonelike sections of fruit. The
roof seemed to be peanut brittle. The drawbridge was gingerbread, and the moat fizzed like pop from Lake Tsoda
Popka.

They managed to exchange a three-party glance. "Why don't I trust this?" Gwenny inquired.

"Because it is not trustworthy," Che replied. "The Good Magician always knows when a querent is coming, and is always prepared."

"Querent?"

"Supplicant, petitioner, beggar, moocher, sponge—"

"Oh, stop it!" Gwenny said, laughing. "You mean folk like us, who come to ask a Question."

"Whatever," Che agreed, scowling. But he couldn't hold it more than a moment, and had to smile. At least it broke their tension, or dented it somewhat.

"There must be something we don't see," Jenny said. "Since I will ask the Question, so that I can do the year's service, I might as well lead the way." She started toward the drawbridge.

"Wait!" Gwenny protested. "There may be danger. I should go first, even if I'm not going to actually ask the Question."

"No need to quarrel, girls," Che said, putting on a superior smirk. "First, we can be reasonably sure there's no danger, because the Good Magician wouldn't want to hurt us, and the winged monsters wouldn't allow it anyway."

"But the winged monsters aren't watching at the moment," Jenny said, looking around.

"Certainly they are," he said, maintaining his superior smirk.

"Oh? Where?"

Che pointed to a purple dragonfly perched on a nearby bush. "There."

She looked. "But that's only a bug!"

"That's a winged monster. He will report to the others if anything happens, or take care of it himself."

"I don't believe it," Jenny said.

"Ixnay," Gwenny murmured warningly.

She was too late. The dragonfly had taken umbrage. It jetted into the air, leaving a trail of sparks and a contrail of vapor. It zoomed away. In a moment it returned, leading a phalanx of dragonflies. Now the sound of their wings was audible. They swung around in formation and oriented on Jenny Elf.

"Duck!" Che cried. "It's a strafing run!"

The three of them threw themselves to the ground. Little streaks of flame passed over them and burned the nearby foliage. The dragonflies flew on out of sight.

They picked themselves up. "They weren't shooting for effect," Che said. "If we hadn't ducked, they would have held their fire. I think."

"I guess they made their point," Jenny said. "I'm sorry I doubted."

The purple dragonfly reappeared and perched on her shoulder. "He accepts your apology," Che said.

Gwenny laughed. "But you don't have to kiss him."

Jenny was serious. "Still, they can't help us with the Good Magician's challenge. It's not allowed."

"Maybe Sammy can find a safe way in," Che suggested.

Immediately the little cat bounded across the gingerbread drawbridge. Jenny ran after him, as she always did. "Wait for me, Sammy!" she cried.

Gwenny rolled her eyes. "You're my two best friends, but sometimes I do wonder about both of you," she said. "You should know better than to suggest that Sammy find something, and she should know better than to dash madly into a strange castle."

"We should," Che agreed apologetically. "But we don't."

"I just hope there's not a mean witch in there."

They hurried after Jenny, who was by this time across the drawbridge and coming to the main entrance gate of the castle. The drawbridge surface was slightly spongy, but solid. The gate was open, and the cat was scampering on in.

They almost banged into Jenny, who had suddenly stopped just inside the gate. She was staring up.

Che looked in that direction. There was a giant. More correctly, a giantess: a huge human woman.

Sammy, no help in this crisis, had curled up for a snooze under the giant's chair.

"Come in, children," the woman said, her voice boomingly dulcet.

"She doesn't *l-look* like a witch," Gwenny said faintly.

"No, I am not a witch, dear," the woman said. "I am the archetypal Adult. I am here to initiate you into the Adult Conspiracy."

"No!" Gwenny cried, affrighted.

"We're too young," Che protested in what he hoped was a reasonable tone.

"Two of you are on the verge, and one of you is of a culture that recognizes another standard," the Adult said, gazing down at Che.

"But I'm with those of human derivation who honor the Conspiracy," Che said. "So I honor it too."

"I have a question for each of you," the Adult said. "Each will answer in turn. If any of you fail to answer, or answer incorrectly, none of you will be admitted to the presence of the Good Magician. Is that clear?"

Che opened his mouth to protest that the rationale wasn't clear, but the Adult's gaze bore down on him with such severity that he was daunted. He realized belatedly that it had been a rhetorical question: one that allowed only the answer desired by the one who put the question. He scuffled his front hooves. "I guess so," he said reluctantly.

The gaze moved across to the girls. Then they too fidgeted and mumbled their agreements.

"You," the Adult said, fixing imperiously on Gwenny. "Identify yourself."

"I—I'm Gwendolyn Goblin, from Goblin Mountain. I'm here to—"

"That is quite enough. Gwendolyn, what is the Adult Conspiracy?"

Gwenny was taken aback. "That's my question?"

"No, dear. That is my question to you."

Che clenched his teeth. This Adult was so adultish that it was painful. They were always so sure of themselves, and so obnoxious about it. But a child could never tell them that, because they always twisted it around to make it seem that the child was the obnoxious one. It was impossible to reason with an adult, because the mind of any adult was set, like old cement.

"Well, everyone knows that—" Gwenny began.

"No, dear. I do not want anyone's answer. I want *your* answer."

Gwenny began to show a bit of righteous rebellion. "My answer is that it is a conspiracy by adults to make children miserable!" she said. "Because—"

"No, do not tell why. Just what."

"Anything that really interests children, the adults deny. Like all the good words that can make plants wilt and dry grass burst into fire, and the ones that curse-burrs respect. And anything about how to summon the stork. And they make children eat awful things, like castor oil and broccoli, instead of the good things like cake and candy. And they won't let any boy child see anyone's panties, even if they're really pretty panties. Or any girl child see what a boy's got instead of panties. And they make children go to bed early, when they're not sleepy. Things like that."

The Adult nodded with distant tolerance. That reminded Che of another adultish annoyance: they seldom praised a child's efforts unless it was insincere, such as saying "Very good!" when the child succeeded in choking down a nauseating brussels sprout. She turned to Jenny. "Identify yourself."

"I am Jennifer Elf from the World of Two Moons."

"Jennifer, why is the Adult Conspiracy?"

"What?" Jenny asked, startled.

"Not what, dear, why." The Adult was insufferably patronizing, but that was normal.

"I don't know why adults want to make children miserable!" Jenny exclaimed angrily. "Maybe they're jealous of our open minds and sunny dispositions. It's not that way where I come from.''

The Adult frowned. ''You can do better than that, dear, I'm sure.''

There it was again, Che thought: the Adult was twisting things around, not accepting the obvious answer. Adults always preferred to be devious.

But Jenny tried. ''Well, I can tell you why it might be, if adults really cared about children. There might be something dangerous that might hurt children, so the adults try to keep children away from it. Like maybe those words of power: if a child said one in a straw house, it could set the house on fire, and the family would lose its home.''

Che and Gwenny looked at her, astonished. She was making sense! There might actually be reason for a small part of the Conspiracy, though of course that did not justify the rest of it.

''And?'' the Adult inquired in that uncomfortably prodding way they had.

''And about eating the bad stuff—it's supposed to be nutritious,'' Jenny continued. ''Candy—it tastes good, but after a while it can pall, and maybe it is not as good for the body as it seems.'' She was evidently remembering their tummyaches of last night. ''So the adults try to keep children from getting into trouble by eating too much of the wrong things. And about going to bed early— I did feel better when I got a good night's sleep, instead of when I didn't get enough because of staying up late pillow-fighting.'' She looked apologetically at the other two. ''And about not knowing how to summon the stork—I suppose there could be a problem if children started doing it, because they wouldn't be ready to take care of babies. I mean, it's fun seeing a baby once in a while, but I wouldn't want to have to take care of it all the time. And suppose a child got a baby, just for fun, and then got tired of it? That would be pretty bad for the baby.''

Che was amazed. Jenny's alien upbringing in the World of Two Moons must be telling; she had actually made it seem as if there were a sensible reason for the Conspiracy. Still—

"And the panties?" the Adult prodded.

"Well, I really don't know about them, but maybe they have something to do with the stork." Jenny paused, trying to work it out. "It seems that adults maybe really like summoning the stork, and they feel more like it if they see panties, and maybe children would feel like it too if they saw panties, and they might stumble onto the secret, so they have to be protected from that too."

"That will do, Jennifer." Again that contemptuous dismissal. The gaze swung across to pin Che again. "Identify yourself."

"I am Che Centaur, of the Winged Monsters."

"Do you agree with the Adult Conspiracy?"

Che knew that the correct answer was Yes. But he was tired of being browbeaten by adult attitudes. It was time to make a stand. So he ventured into dangerous territory. "No."

"Elucidate."

If the Adult thought he wouldn't know the word, she would be disappointed. She wanted his reasons? Well, he might as well get into a lot of trouble, as long as he was traveling that route. "Maybe the adults think they have a reason for keeping things from children and making them do things for their own good. But I think that's the wrong way to do it. Children should get good information and good experience, so they can grow to be responsible when they finally have to be adults. If saying a bad word starts a fire, then they should be warned about that, so they know not to set the house afire. And if too much candy makes a bellyache, they should be told, and allowed to try it, and after they see that it's true, they won't do it again. If not getting enough sleep makes children feel bad the next day, they should be allowed to try it until they find out how much sleep is best. They don't need to have adults deciding for them all the time.''

He paused, afraid the Adult was going to lift her monstrous foot and squish him to nothing. But she merely sat there listening. ''And?'' she prompted.

''And about summoning the stork—well, I think that even a small child wouldn't want to hurt a baby. So if children were taught how to summon the stork, but also told how important it is to take care of the babies, and that they would have to do that instead of going out to play whenever they wanted to, I think most of them wouldn't do it. The few who did do it—well, my sire says that folk do have to take the consequences of their actions, and I think that's fair for children too. So I think children should be educated completely, about both actions and consequences, and then allowed to do what they wish. I don't think any Adult Conspiracy is needed—if adults take the trouble to teach their children properly.''

He stopped talking, waiting for the dread verdict that he had answered incorrectly, so that they would not be allowed to see the Good Magician. Yet it wasn't in him to falsify; it wasn't the centaur way.

The Adult's gaze seared across the two girls. ''Do you agree?''

Gwenny and Jenny exchanged yet another glance. They fidgeted.

''Well?'' the Adult demanded in that warning tone.

''Well, yes, I guess,'' Gwenny said with understandable reluctance.

''You actually approve of giving such information to children?'' the Adult said with that this-is-your-last-chance attitude.

''Yes,'' Jenny agreed. ''I don't care what you think, he's making sense.''

''And you too, Gwendolyn?'' It was the verge of doom.

''Yes!'' Gwenny said recklessly.

''And you are prepared to face the consequences of your

attitude?'' The gaze managed to transfix all three of them simultaneously.

They were in too deep to escape. They nodded with foolhardy bravery.

''Then you are about to join the Adult Conspiracy,'' the Adult said. She reached somewhere far away and brought back two dolls. Each was the size of one of the girls. She set them down on the floor before the three of them. ''Show me how these figures would summon the stork.''

''But we don't know that!'' Gwenny protested.

''Don't you?''

''Of course we don't!'' Jenny said.

''Are you sure?''

The girls looked wildly at Che. ''I think she wants us to figure it out,'' he said. ''It's our punishment for agreeing that we don't agree with the Adult Conspiracy. My punishment, really, only since you support me, you must share it.''

They glanced up at the Adult, but she remained impassive. Somehow that was more frightening than whatever they had expected from her. They glanced at the dolls, which were male and female.

''Well, if I want to be chief, I'd better learn how to figure things out,'' Gwenny decided. ''I think I do have half a hint about it—maybe I mean half a brother. My little brother Gobble Goblin is—well, my father Gouty got together with a woman who wasn't my mother to summon the stork, and the stork brought Gobble. So from that I know that folk don't have to be married to do it; they can do it even when they're not married, and when it's wrong. They don't have to be in love, either; my father never loved anyone. Just so long as there's a male and a female. It must be a purely physical thing.''

''Yet there should be love,'' Jenny said. ''I don't think the World of Two Moons is different from Xanth in this respect. We don't have storks bring the babies, but I never was clear on the exact delivery system. I just knew that if two people love each other enough, a baby could come. I think that if they can't love each other at least some, they can't get a baby.''

"I have of course seen centaurs mate," Che said. "Our kind does not use storks, I think because our foals are too heavy for them to carry. Yet we have partial human heritage. I wonder whether the human mode of summoning the stork could be parallel in any way?''

Gwenny picked up the girl doll, who didn't have any clothes. "If these were centaurs, what would they do to get a baby?''

Che picked up the similarly bare boy doll. "I think they would get close together, like this." He put the male doll beside the female doll.

"But we were closer than that when we pretended to apologize," the goblin girl pointed out.

"Not in one detail," he said.

"What detail?" Jenny asked.

He poked around with the dolls. "This one, I think.''

The two girls stared. "But—" Gwenny said.

"But—" Jenny echoed.

"Maybe it *is* different, with centaurs," Che said.

"It's disgusting," Gwenny said.

"Not to centaurs." But he was shaken. Could it be?

They stared some more. "Maybe it is possible," Gwenny said. "But can that be all?''

Che shrugged. "With centaurs, it seems to be enough.''

"No wonder they keep it secret!" Jenny said.

"No wonder!" Gwenny echoed, giggling.

Then they were all laughing. But it was the mirth of embarrassment tinged with shame. They had never suspected that the Adult Conspiracy concealed something like this.

"I think we had better keep the secret, after all," Che said after they subsided.

The two girls nodded. Both were blushing, which suggested that they were just as uncomfortable about this as he was.

The giant Adult faded away. Where she had been was an open hallway leading into the main part of the castle.

Sammy got up and stretched, his nap done.

It seemed that they had surmounted the challenge, and could now meet with the Good Magician. But at what a price? Their innocence was gone.

Chapter 5. Ida

Ida was a foundling. She appeared as a baby one day near Faun Mountain, and a nymph carried her back to Nymph Valley. The other nymphs made a great fuss over her, and brought her milkweed pods to nurse on, and set her in a nice bed of leaves and flowers.

But it was evident that she was not a nymph. She was a human baby that the stork must have misdelivered or lost. A neighboring otterbee spied her there, and swam back to his fellows. "She otterbe with us for the night," he said. "So she won't forget, the way the nymphs do."

They agreed, for otterbees were good creatures who never shirked a task. So as dusk closed and the nymphs lost interest, they took the baby and swam with her across the marsh to their warm nest, and made her comfortable there. In this manner they protected her from the night magic of the nymphs and fauns, and allowed her to remember her prior days.

However, some damage had already been done, and the baby did not remember very much anyway. But after several years her memory improved, and as she grew through normal child and girl and young woman stages she was able to remember most of her life back to about the age of three or four. Now she understood that she must not stay the night in Nymph Valley, though she enjoyed spending her days there. Of course because she was not a nymph she did not indulge in nymphly activities with fauns. She was satisfied just to watch them having their fun. She did however swim with the otterbees, who were creatures of the water and shore who also were happy in their fashion.

"She otterbe educated in the human fashion," the otterbees decided. So they prevailed on an itinerant centaur named Cerebral to give her lessons in the human mode. (For some reason centaur scholars did not wander, they were itinerant, but it meant much the same thing.) In this manner Ida learned to speak human speech, and to don human apparel, and to brush her hair. She no longer ran around bare the way the nymphs did. She regretted that, but the centaur tutor was very firm about the importance of maintaining the conventions of one's kind, and he knew more than all of the fauns, nymphs, and otterbees combined, so she had to do it.

She came to appreciate the liabilities of nymphly status. Some other creatures preyed on fauns and nymphs. Sometimes an ogre would stomp by, pick up a screaming nymph, and bite off her head. That stopped her screaming, and he would then carry her away for a more leisurely repast, chewing as he went. Nymphs did not like that very well. Sometimes a dragon would slither through, chomp a faun in half, and swallow the pieces. If it happened to be a fire-breathing dragon, it would toast the faun first. Fauns were not too keen on that. But the following day it was as if nothing had happened; the fauns and nymphs frolicked as before, never missing the chomped ones. Ida tried to tell them about such events, but they did not believe her, because they could not remember anything beyond the one day. After a while Ida realized that they were perhaps better off that way. What was the point in moping about bad memories? Still, it bothered her. "There otterbe a better way," she muttered.

"There *is* a better way," Cerebral informed her. "The human way. Fauns and nymphs are chained to the present,

as are animals, creatures of the moment. But humans remember and reflect, almost in the manner of centaurs, and
are therefore superior. Remember that, for there will be a
pop quiz.''

Thus did Ida learn what set her kind apart from other
creatures. She did remember, and she passed the quiz, and
was duly rewarded with some pop from Lake Tsoda Popka.
Cerebral believed in the salutary effect of incentives. This
meant, in normal terms, that good things came for learning. Ida would never admit it, of course, but she found
learning fun for its own sake. There was just so much to
know, and it was fascinating.

When she came to be twenty-one years old, according
to the judgment of the centaur, who had looked at her
teeth, the otterbees decided that she otterbe on her way to
find her destiny. ''We love your company,'' they told her,
''but we are only animals, while you are a human being.
You deserve better things.''

Ida wasn't sure about that, for the otterbees seemed like
very deserving creatures to her. So she asked Cerebral.
''Unfortunately it is true,'' he replied. ''You are no more
an otterbee than you are a nymph, and you must not allow
your horizons to be limited by theirs. You must seek your
destiny among your own kind.''

''But I don't even know where my kind are!'' she protested. ''Where is there a Man Mountain or a Woman
Valley?''

''I know of no such artifacts of terrain,'' the centaur
admitted. ''Perhaps you should seek instead the castle of
the Good Magician, who I understand is back in business
at this time, and inquire about your destiny.''

''He was out of business?'' she asked, slightly curious.

''For several years. But then the castle became active
again, under new auspices. Of course there may be a certain difficulty locating and entering it, and you may be
required to do a year's service for the Magician in return
for an Answer to your Question. However, there are those

who believe this to be worthwhile despite the difficulty and cost.''

Ida had learned that the Cerebral was not necessarily expressing the opinions he seemed to be. He had the didactic manner she assumed was common to his kind. Didactics never spoke directly and simply. ''Do *you* believe this to be worthwhile for me?''

He considered, for he was never so incautious as to express a thoughtless opinion. He had once suffered a bout of hoof-in-mouth disease, and been exiled from centaur association. That was why he was available for tutoring her. He no longer put his hoof in his mouth, but remained excruciatingly careful. ''Yes, other things being equivalent, I suspect it is.''

So Ida set out for the Good Magician's castle. She carried with her a small magic purse the otterbees had given her, which contained her formal clothing, a hairbrush, and a change of unmentionables as well as a magic sandwich in case she got hungry. She wore a bracelet which protected her from harm by any other creature. These were things the fauns and nymphs had found, and the otterbees had rescued from being forgotten. The otterbees were not covetous; they merely saved things until they could be used as they otterbe.

She bid a sad farewell to the otterbees, fearing that she would never be as happy away from these good creatures as with them. She knew she would always have a liking for ponds and mudflats and sandy shores. Then she set foot on the path leading to unknown Central Xanth.

At first the way was reasonably familiar, because she had poked all through this region during the past two decades or so. She knew which side paths to avoid because they led to tangle trees or dragons' lairs, and which fruits not to eat, such as choke cherries. But the farther she went the less familiar things became, until she was in strange territory.

She came to a fork in the path. Which way was best? She couldn't decide, but she didn't want to dawdle. She was no longer in Nymph Valley, where dawdling was a way of life. Furthermore, she needed to pause for an unmentionable function and wasn't sure whether that counted as dawdling. One of the odd things about the centaur tutor was that he handled his own functions in a completely open manner, yet insisted that she as a human being should pretend that no such functions existed. This was the human way, he said, and she had to emulate human ways so as to be able to associate with her own kind, in due course.

Then a goblin came down one of the forks. Ida had an idea. Goblins were not the nicest of folk, but they could be helpful if approached in just the right manner. Maybe she could ask him where the best place for the unmentionable was, and if he gave a good answer for that, she could ask him which fork was best.

"Hey, burp-nose, where's the worst place to do something unmentionable?" she asked.

The goblin looked at her, then around at the scenery. "Over behind that bush," he said, pointing.

So Ida went behind the bush. Then something happened. "Eeeek!" she screamed in the manner the centaur had prescribed for maidens, which was how he classified her.

She marched angrily back to the path, where the goblin stoically waited. "That bush tickled me!" she said.

"Naturally. It's a tickleberry bush!"

"But I asked you the worst place to go. You were supposed to lie," she said indignantly.

"I *did* lie," he replied. "The worst place is that gooseberry bush over there."

Ida thought about that, and decided that the goblin had after all been true to his nature. "Then what's the worse path of these two?" she asked, indicating the fork.

The goblin considered. "That's hard to answer."

"Why? All you have to do is lie about the better path."

"But they are equally bad."

That meant equally good. "Very well, I withdraw the question. Get lost, snot-head."

The goblin, evidently charmed by her courtesy, resumed his walk down the path.

So her idea had worked out. Often they did. But probably she owed most of whatever success she achieved to Cerebral's apt instruction. She had had the idea that he would be the best possible instructor when she first saw him, and that had been amply vindicated. In ordinary words, that meant he had been good.

She set off down the right path, because she didn't want to take the wrong path. She had confidence that it would take her where she was going.

Indeed, it took her to a quaint little old cottage, just as dusk threatened to overtake her. Maybe there would be a sweet little old housewife inside who had a room to spare for the night and a warm pot of stew on the hearth.

Ida knocked on the door. It opened, and there was the grandmotherly woman. "Why, I was hoping for a nice young traveler to use my spare room tonight," the woman said. "Come in, dear, and have some warm stew."

Ida came in, gratefully. "Your house was in just the right place," she said. "I was hoping I wouldn't have to sleep out in the forest."

"Are you a quiet sleeper?"

"No, I toss and turn all night. I'm hyperactive." That was the centaur's word for her restlessness.

"Wonderful!"

It turned out that the old woman's old husband had gone on a trip to the market, and would be back with a basket of beans on the morrow. Meanwhile the house was quiet, and the old woman wasn't used to that. She wanted to be able to hear that there was someone else in the house with her, especially when it was dark.

After supper they sat by the fire and exchanged news. Fortunately the old woman never left her house and yard, and Ida had never been away from her home vicinity before, so neither of them had very much news to exchange. Ida was tired and the old woman never stayed up late, so they both went to their rooms to sleep, contented.

But as Ida changed into her nightdress and lay down, she suffered a qualm. Qualms were clamlike thoughts that lay at the watery bottom of consciousness and only showed up when the water got very quiet and clear, as happened when a person was trying to drift off to sleep.

Suppose, the qualm inquired, all was not quite as it seemed? Could the nice little old woman have some un-nice secret she wasn't telling that would make mischief for her guest? Ida didn't like that notion, but couldn't quite expunge it. (Expunge, in human terms, meant to get rid of something. Sometimes she mopped up spilled milk with an old expunge.) She was concerned about what the dark-ness might reveal.

Sure enough, the moment she blew out the candle a ghost loomed up. "Hoooo!" it cried airily, flapping its sheet tails.

Ida squirmed down under the covers. "It's only meeee," she replied apologetically.

The ghost seemed embarrassed. "I beg your pardon! I mistook you for the dirty old man."

"Dirty?"

"He never washes his feet. They get the sheets all messed up. I can't stand to see sheets abused. So I haunt him." The ghost reflected for a moment, before the mir-ror. "How are your feet?"

"My feet are clean," Ida said. She poked a foot out from under the sheets. "Maidens are supposed to have dainty feet, so I try to conform."

The ghost examined them. "You're right. Those are very clean, dainty, maidenly feet. When will the dirty old man be back?"

"Tomorrow, I think."

"Then until tomorrow—" The ghost faded out.

Relieved, Ida settled down to sleep. She was so glad it had turned out to be a nice ghost.

In the morning she mentioned the matter to the old woman. "Did you know you have a ghost?"

"A ghost? I thought it was a hussy! He's a dirty old man, you know."

"Yes. His feet get the sheets dirty, and the ghost doesn't like that."

"Well, I'll make him wash his feet!" the old woman said. "I don't like dirty sheets either."

After a nice breakfast of beans porridge, Ida resumed her walk along the path. She wondered what she would have encountered along the other path. She was almost tempted to go back and take the other one, just to find out, but restrained herself. After all, the sooner she found the Good Magician's castle, the sooner she would know her destiny. She hoped it was a nice one, for she was a nice girl.

The path did not lead directly to the castle, however. It led to a dragon's lair. Ida almost stepped into it before she realized.

She backed away. As a general rule, dragons' lairs were not good places to be, for those who were not of the dragon persuasion. Now she would have to return to take the other path, though it was a rather long walk. At least she would satisfy her curiosity about it.

Then the shadow of a dragon fell, and after it the dragon himself. He had coincidentally cut off Ida's escape. "Well, now," the dragon said. "Allow me to introduce myself. I am Dragoman Dragon. What have we here?"

"Nothing but a delicate maiden," Ida replied truthfully.

"And do you know what I do with delicate maidens?"

Ida had a notion, because of her memories of the dragons who had poached nymphs from Nymph Valley. But she knew that her magic bracelet would protect her from harm. "I think you shall have to let this one go, for you cannot harm me."

The dragon squinted down at her. "Oh? Why not?"

"Because I have a charm that guards me."

"You are surely most charming," Dragoman agreed. "But as it happens, I collect winsome maidens."

"No, I didn't say that I was charming, though that may be true. I meant that I wear an amulet."

"Hm." The dragon considered. "That does require some interpretation. May I see it?"

"Certainly." Ida removed the bracelet and handed it to the dragon.

Dragoman inspected it closely. "You are correct. This charm is effective against all comers. No creature can harm she who wears this."

"Yes, so I was informed. May I have it back, now, please?"

The dragon puffed a small puff of smoke. "There is something I feel constrained to clarify for you. You are not wearing the charm now, so I may do what I wish with you. If I return the charm to you, I will not be able to harm you. Somehow I doubt that my interests would be well served by giving you back your charm."

Ida realized that she had made a mistake. But she had an idea how to proceed. "It is true that I am unprotected now. But I was protected when you asked for the charm. This means that it was protecting me from you. If you now were to harm me, that would mean that it failed to protect me. That would be what my centaur tutor would call a paradox. A paradox is not a good thing."

Dragoman puffed more smoke, pondering. "I enjoy problems in logic," he admitted. "I shall have to think about this."

"Certainly. May I have my bracelet back while you ponder?"

"As you wish." The dragon handed it back to her, distracted by the intellectual problem.

"Thank you." Ida placed the bracelet firmly back on her wrist.

After a moment Dragoman came to a conclusion. "I think you are correct: you would not have been able to give me the bracelet had I intended to harm you. Since I have no harmful intent, there was no problem, and no paradox."

"That's nice," Ida agreed.

The dragon reached out and grabbed her. "However, I never did tell you what it is I do with delicate maidens."

"Eeeek!" Ida screamed, for that seemed appropriate at this stage.

Dragoman picked her up. "So nice of you to inquire. I collect them. I take very good care of them; in fact I keep them perfectly preserved. So, you see, I intend no harm to you, and your bracelet has no need to be concerned." He spread his wings and lofted the two of them into the air.

He took her to a crystalline cave. It was beautiful. All around it were giant crystals, and in each crystal was a lovely young woman, frozen still, looking exactly like a life-sized doll.

"But I don't want to be preserved in stone!" Ida protested.

"You don't have a choice," Dragoman said.

"I don't?"

"You don't. You are destined to be preserved in all your prettiness until someone happens to rescue you. With luck it will be a prince, but it's as likely to be nobody of interest. Now change into your nicest raiment."

"What?"

"Raiment is clothing."

"I knew that. It's the kind of term centaurs use. What I meant was an exclamation of indignity. Why should I cooperate with you?"

"Because you are less likely to be rescued if you look like half-chewed dragon bait."

Ida considered that, and realized he was correct. So she changed into her best dress, the blue chiffon, and donned her display sandals so that her dainty clean feet showed.

Meanwhile the dragon was fretting. "I'm going to have to enlarge this chamber," he said. "It is getting too crowded. I'll just have to stack you in the shed, for now, until the renovation is complete."

"The shed!" Ida exclaimed. "Don't I deserve better than that?"

"Of course you do," he said consolingly. "And I promise I'll move you to a better place, the moment I can."

She was not as satisfied by this as perhaps she should have been. But since she didn't have much choice, she did not complain. Anyway, she noticed that the shed wasn't really a shed, but a shed door leading out to what looked like a nice garden. At least she would have a nice view there. She brushed out her hair, and was ready.

"Ah, you look divine," the dragon said. "Step right up here on this pedestal, please."

Ida stepped, resigned to her maidenly fate.

Dragoman breathed a cloud of thick vapor at her. It coalesced, encasing her, and suddenly everything changed. Dragoman was gone, and a voluptuous merwoman wearing legs was yelling at her. "Get out!"

What had happened? Where was the dragon? Ida shook her head, confused.

Then someone charged in from the side, picked her up, and carried her out of the shed before its door swung closed.

The second person, who turned out to be a big young woman, set her down. "What's your name?" the merwoman demanded.

Name? She had never had a name. None of the Fauns, Nymphs, otterbees, or monsters had names. Only Cerebral Centaur and Dragoman Dragon. "I don't know," she said, having difficulty speaking.

"Well, let's just call you Ida, then," the woman said. "I am Mela Merwoman, and this is Okra Ogress."

An ogress! Ida gazed at her in surprise. Then she realized that she had never seen a female ogre. It was possible that they were much less ugly than the males, as was the case with goblins.

Mela continued to question her, but Ida was at a loss for answers. She had sought her destiny, and her destiny had turned out to be crystallized. Apparently that had occurred, and these were the folk who had rescued her. She had no idea how much time had passed or where the dragon was now. But the name they had given her was settling in, and now it seemed that she had always been Ida, and that anyone who might have talked or written about her would have been calling her that. The centaur would have alluded to it as retrospective nomenclature, but probably it was just back-dating the text.

The folk who had rescued her seemed nice enough. Possibly they were on a mission of their own. It would be really nice if they were going to see the Good Magician.

It turned out that the merwoman and the ogress were indeed going there. So Ida decided to join them. It seemed that their path led through the garden shed, and was closed off when they removed the crystal block containing Ida, so they had to find another way. She was sorry to have interrupted their journey, but had not been aware of what was going on until they freed her from the crystal.

Mela led the way, and Okra was last, with Ida safely in the middle. They reached a health spa spring and had a drink. Then Okra picked up a red boat she had evidently left there before, and carried it over her head with the strength of her kind. They finally came to a big lake. This was, it turned, out, Lake Kiss-Mee. They got into the little boat, and Okra rowed them vigorously across to an island. "It isn't really safe on the shore," Mela remarked. "It's not safe on the island either, but we know what the dangers are, so we're more comfortable here.

Indeed it was comfortable, for there was a wonderful hot pool. Mela explained that she was not at all partial to fresh water, but had learned to appreciate this pool, as it was firewater. She had a set of firewater opals that seemed to glow more brightly as they neared this pool. The three of them soaked in it and compared histories. Ida told her story up to this point; and Okra told hers, and how she hoped to become a Main Character and maybe lose her asthma; and Mela said that her story was too long to cover, as she was older than she might appear, being one of the long-lived sea monsters, but that she was now in search of a suitable husband. She really was not choosy; any handsome, thoughtful, intelligent, gentle, and manly prince would do, especially one who happened to like well-endowed merwomen.

Ida was not conversant with the tastes of princes, but she suspected that any who were manly would like Mela's endowments, which were trying their best to float to the surface of the hot water.

Okra had a question. "How is it that you understood the speech of the dragon?" she asked Ida.

Ida was taken aback. "Wasn't I supposed to?"

"But human folk don't understand the languages of other creatures, do they? I mean, they understand creatures of human stock, so you can talk to the two of us, but dragons are different. To us, their speech is just roars and growls."

"Oh, I didn't realize that," Ida said, chagrined. "I have been talking to animals all along, never realizing that I wasn't supposed to. The otterbees are friendly furry animals who like to swim and eat fish. Shouldn't I have talked to them?"

"Of course you should have," Mela said. "We are just surprised that you have that ability. Maybe it's your talent."

"My talent?"

"Every human person has a magic talent. Didn't you know?"

"No, I didn't. The fauns and nymphs didn't."

"They aren't quite human enough, I think," Mela said. "Some of us part humans have built-in magic, such as being able to breathe water."

"I never thought of it as magic. I just spoke to anyone who spoke to me."

"Well, we can check it the next time we meet a dragon or other monster," Mela said. She went off to find some ripe pies for supper. Ida hurried to help her, for she had always been used to finding her own pies.

After supper they discussed their plan of travel. Mela

had a map, which indicated that the Good Magician's castle was to the west. It had shown a path that went that way, but that was the one now blocked off, so they had to find another.

They pored over the map, and discovered what Mela had not seen before: there was an invisible river flowing from Iron Mountain through Poke country to Lake Kiss-Mee. The only way to find the river was to spot the faint reddish flecks of rust in it, from the mountain.

Heartened, they decided to try that in the morning. Then they settled down for the night.

But Ida had one question. "Do you happen to know why this is called Lake Kiss-Mee?"

"It was once a very friendly lake," Mela explained. "So was the Kiss-Mee River which flows from it. But then the Demon Corps of Engineers pulled the river straight, and it lost all its charm and became the Kill-Mee River. They finally had to put it back the way it was, but neither the river nor the lake has yet fully recovered from the shock. That may be just as well, because we don't want to be compelled by their magic to be forever kissing them and each other."

Ida had to agree with that. She had never kissed anyone herself, but had seen the fauns and nymphs doing it all the time. They had never stopped at kissing. So if kissing was one step in an ongoing process, Ida was not yet ready for it.

In the morning Okra rowed them back across the lake. Ida wore her dull ordinary dress, for she was no longer on display. This time they explored the shore, looking for the invisible river. It occurred to Ida that she might be able to spy it if she squinted, because that changed the way things looked. Sure enough, soon she spied a faint wave pattern of air with flecks of reddish brown. Only if it was what she hoped it was, it wasn't air, but invisible water. The water was invisible, but not the sediment it carried along. "I think I see it," she announced pointing.

Okra was facing back so she could row, but since Ida

was in the rear end of the boat, the ogress could see her. So Okra guided the craft in that direction, and soon Mela also spied the specks of rust. "It looks just like wind," Mela said doubtfully.

But Okra's oars made splashes as they encountered the invisible water. So she rowed right into the river, leaving the lake behind. The current was slow, so there was no trouble going against it; still, Ida was impressed with Okra's strength and endurance. This river flowed not in a regular riverbed, but across the varied landscape. Apparently (despite invisibly) it did not disturb the land it passed over, and kept to itself until it reached the lake. It maintained its elevation, winding back and forth to avoid hills and holes, so they got a fair tour of the surrounding land. It was mixed countryside, with trees of many kinds and bushes of a few kinds and herbs of one kind.

A swirl of vapor appeared above the boat. Curious, Ida stared at it. Was it another branch of the invisible river? But it didn't seem to be flowing, just hovering.

Then a mouth formed. "What are you staring it?" it demanded.

"It talks!" Ida cried, affrighted.

"Of course it talks," the mouth said. A pair of eyes formed, focusing on her. "What did you expect, a belch?"

"But you're a cloud!" Ida protested. "Clouds don't talk. Do they?"

"Of course clouds talk. Just not in a language humans understand."

"Oh, you mean the way dragons do?"

"Cardinally."

"What?"

"Intrinsically, inherently, fundamentally, elementarily, primarily."

"Essentially?"

"Whatever," the vapor said, clouding up.

"That's the Demoness Metria!" Mela exclaimed, looking back.

"However did you know?" the cloud asked, forming

into the shape of a woman almost as shapely as Mela herself.

"It was a lucky guess. There's nothing of interest going on here, Metria, so we shouldn't waste any more of your time."

"But isn't this Ida?" Metria asked. "She's the most interesting person in Xanth."

"I am?" Ida asked incredulously.

"She is?" Mela asked. "Why is that?"

"Because of her destiny. There's never been one quite like it before."

"But my destiny was to be crystallized by the dragon," Ida said.

"That may have been what the dragon claimed," Metria said. "But dragons are notorious liars."

"I didn't know that."

"Well, you haven't had much experience with dragons."

"That's true," Ida agreed. "I didn't even know that humans couldn't talk to dragons."

"That's what comes of an isolated upbringing," the demoness said.

"Unless maybe my magic talent is to talk to monsters."

Metria laughed. "What an interesting way to put it! But your talent is hardly that."

"You know what my talent is?"

"Of course I know!"

"Will you tell me?" Ida asked eagerly.

"I might, if you asked."

"What is my talent?"

"Then again, I might not." The demoness faded out.

"I should have warned you," Mela said. "She likes to tease mortals. She probably doesn't know your talent anyway."

"You mean demons are like goblins?" Ida asked. "You have to treat them discourteously?"

"Not exactly. But they don't mean to do you any favors. Metria isn't bad, as demons go; she merely is bored and likes to entertain herself by watching what mortals do. But she has a problem finding the right word sometimes, and that gives her away.''

"I noticed."

Now Okra spoke. "Why does the demoness think Ida is the most interesting person in Xanth?"

"I'm really not very interesting," Ida said with maidenly modesty.

"She said it was because of her destiny," Mela said, remembering. "I must say that though Metria can be annoying, she does seem to tell the truth. There must be something very special about Ida."

"Maybe we'll find out when we reach the Good Magician's castle," Okra said.

They continued on up the stream. It was definitely slanting uphill now; the current was stronger, and the flecks of rust were thicker.

"Aren't you getting tired?" Ida asked the ogress. "You've been doing all the rowing."

"I suppose I am," Okra agreed. "I hadn't noticed until now."

"Let's see if we can pull to the side, without falling out of the water," Mela suggested.

They did so, cautiously, and were able to come safely to land. They got out of the boat, and Okra lifted it out of the water and sat down to rest. Mela and Ida went looking for food, and found some cupcakes for Ida and some watermelons for Mela. But what would Okra like? They saw some okra plants growing, and knew that their fruit would be perfect for the ogress.

As they ate, Ida saw a plant growing pretty red caps. "One of those will be fine to protect my delicate hair from the sun," she said. She went and picked a cap and put it on, and it fit her perfectly.

Mela stretched. "We should get moving," she said.

"Who says?" Ida snapped angrily.

"Why, I just thought—"

"So don't think!" Then Ida went and kicked the boat, startling the ogress. She was furious.

Mela stared at her a moment. Then she sought her purse and brought out a little book. She leafed through its pages. "That's it!" she cried, finding her place.

"That's not it!" Ida snarled.

"What is?" Okra asked.

"It's a madcap," the merwoman said.

"Stop insulting me!" Ida screamed.

"Please take off that cap."

"I will *not!*"

But Okra, behind her, reached out and lifted the cap from her head.

Ida was immediately appalled. "What was I saying?"

"It wasn't you," Mela explained. "You happened to pick a madcap. See, here it is in my manual. The moment you put it on, it made you mad."

"Oh." Ida felt herself blushing. "I would never act like that. I mean—"

"I knew something was wrong, and since the cap was the last thing that changed, I checked it. It wasn't your fault."

"Oh, throw that awful thing away!"

But Okra considered. "It might be useful sometime." She folded it and tucked it into a pocket. That startled Ida, because she hadn't known the ogress had any pockets, since she wasn't wearing anything.

They put the boat back in the invisible river and climbed in. Okra, rested, rowed it more swiftly upstream. Ida could only marvel at the girl's strength. But of course that was the ogre's talent. Ogres were strong, ugly, and stupid, and it seemed Okra had one of those traits.

They came to another lake. This one was smaller than the last, with a smooth surface on which little footprints showed. "I'd better check this," Mela said, getting out her manual. In a moment she had it: "This must be Lake Wails. We had better portage around it."

"Why?" Ida asked.

Then a huge creature appeared, running along the surface of the water, wailing. "Because we don't want to run afoul of the wails," Mela said. "I understand they get very upset if their prints are erased."

"The prints of wails?"

"That's right. They are unhappy enough as it is."

Ida had to agree. So they got out of the boat and walked around the lake. At one point they encountered a multi-headed serpent. "Hello, serpent," Ida greeted it. But the thing only hissed several times at her simultaneously.

She realized that Mela had been right: she couldn't talk to monsters. However, she doubted that the serpent had anything to say that she really wanted to hear.

They found the river on the far side of the lake, and resumed their travel.

Then the tip of the Iron Mountain came into sight. It was solid metal, poking high into the sky. The closer they came, the larger it loomed, until it towered above them. The river did flow from it, but not gently; it issued from a coiled spring in the side and plummeted through a waterfall.

They parked the boat and started up the mountain. The way was steep, but there were iron steps and an iron guardrail, so it was all right. It seemed that they were not the first to come here.

But when they were halfway up, walking along an iron ramp with a sheer cliff above and below, a dragon appeared in the sky. Ida looked, and her worst fear was realized. "That's Dragoman, the dragon who crystallized me!"

"Well, we can't let him take you again," Mela said.

"But we're helpless here! He can pick us all off, and probably will." Her fear was growing into a deadly certainty.

"No, he won't," Okra said.

"He won't?"

"He won't?" Mela echoed.

"Trust me."

So Ida trusted her, since she had been asked to. Her deadly certainty faded back into weak-kneed uncertainty. There must be something Okra could do to dissuade the dragon from its fell purpose. Otherwise she would not be so confident.

The dragon gave a harsh cry and swooped down at them, its dread talons extended. Ida did not understand what he was saying, but she could guess. He was angry that she had gotten away from his showcase.

Okra fished out the madcap and put it on. She scowled. Then as the dragon made a grab for Ida, Okra made a ham fist and swung it furiously. It bashed the dragon on one leg and sent it spinning out of control.

"Oh, lovely!" Mela breathed. "If there's one thing that can stand off a dragon, it's a mad ogre."

So it seemed. But the dragon had not yet caught on that one of the three maidens was an ogress. He righted himself and came diving in again.

This time Okra didn't bash his foot, she made a swipe with her ham hand and caught it in an ogre grip. She hauled the dragon in. Then she bashed him in the snoot with her other ham fist. "Don't fool with us, bezoar-breath!" she roared, and hurled him away.

Now at last he caught on. He pulled out of his tailspin and circled, out of sorts.

Then he reoriented and came in again. He might be up against an ogress, but after all, he was a dragon, and she was a rather puny example of her kind. He looked as if he had something new in mind. He opened his mouth.

"He's going to crystallize us!" Ida screamed. "Don't let that vapor touch us!" Of course it seemed doubtful that they could stop the dragon from breathing on them, but Okra had said to trust her, so Ida did.

The dragon loomed close. A jet of vapor came out.

Okra opened her own mouth and breathed back at the dragon. There was an awful stink.

The dragon's breath and the ogre breath collided. They formed into the ugliest crystalline cloud imaginable. Then the crystal melted and dropped like the foul stone it was. The ogre breath had nullified it.

The dragon took a look at this, shrugged, and flew away. His worst weapon had been thwarted, so he was doing the sensible thing and retreating.

Okra turned toward the two of them. Her face was swollen and horrible. She inhaled.

"Take off the cap!" Mela and Ida screamed together.

Snarling, Okra swept off the cap. Then she looked appalled. Ida knew exactly how she felt. "You did wonderfully!" she said. "You got rid of the dragon and saved us all from a fate worse than—well, I don't know what it's worse than, but I'm glad you saved us."

"I guess I did," Okra said. "I've never been ogre-mad before, but it seemed to be a good time for it."

"It certainly was," Mela agreed warmly.

Then they resumed their trek up the mountain. Ida thought about what had just happened. It seemed to her that Okra had a reasonable chance to achieve her dream of becoming a major character. She had certainly acted like one.

Chapter 6. Jenny

Jenny was still shaken by the revelation of the content of the secret of the Adult Conspiracy. But there was no time to ponder that, because the way was open and she had a Question to ask the Good Magician. Sammy Cat was already bounding into the main part of the castle.

Actually, she had been here once before, but that was almost like a dream, and the castle had looked different. So it was just as unfamiliar now to her as it was to her friends.

A young woman appeared. She had long fair hair with a tinge of green. "Princess Ivy!" Jenny exclaimed. She had met Ivy at the wedding of Prince Dolph and Electra.

Ivy hugged them all, then ushered them into the main chamber where Magician Grey sat. "You're just in time for lunch," Ivy said brightly.

Jenny started to protest, but realized that she was hungry, and the others surely were too. Sammy had already found the dish of milk that must have been set out for him. So they joined Grey at the table. He was nondescript, and not at all like Jenny's impression of someone from Mundania. But of course she had never been to Mundania, so couldn't judge the dull folk there.

"Didn't I see you here before?" Grey asked Jenny.

"Yes. When I came to ask the Good Magician how to return to the World of Two Moons." Jenny laughed. "It happened to be Portrait day, and all five and a half of the Good Magician's wives were here for the occasion. They were all beautiful; I think each one was prettier than the others. But then I changed my mind, and decided to stay in Xanth for a while longer."

"You have friends here," Ivy said.

"Yes." That counted for a great deal.

A maid brought in a huge shoefly pie, and served them each a slice. Jenny was glad to discover that the shoes were really pastry in the form of footwear, and their little wings were leaves of lettuce.

"We expected three challenges," Gwenny remarked. "We were surprised."

"One might even say dismayed," Che added.

"Here in Xanth, so much is made of the Adult Conspiracy," Jenny said.

All three of them waited expectantly.

"We were surprised too," Ivy said. "But the Good Magician Humfrey always knows what he's doing. He said you had to be inducted into the Conspiracy, or he wouldn't be able to help you."

"But we have such a simple Question!" Jenny protested. "I'll ask it, but it's for Gwenny. It has nothing to do with—"

"When he answers it, you won't be able to benefit unless you belong to the Conspiracy," Grey said. "I thought it was strange, though things are more confused in Mundania and I'm not sure I agree with the Conspiracy any more than you do. But it seems that Gwenny must belong, and since you three are working together, you all must know. Humfrey said he wouldn't have done it if the matter weren't so important. There's no telling what harm this early knowledge may do to you. But the alternative is to deny you, Gwendolyn, your chance to be chief of Goblin Mountain, and that was unacceptable."

"I suppose it would be hard to be chief without knowing such things," Gwenny said distastefully as the maid brought dessert: eye scream sandwiches.

Jenny changed the subject. "Which wife does Magician Humfrey have now?"

Ivy laughed. "She's right here! Didn't you realize?"

Jenny accepted her sandwich from the maid. She peered at it, and its big green eye peered back at her. She wondered whether it would scream as she ate it. "No, I didn't see her."

Sammy was rubbing against the maid's leg.

"The maid!" Che exclaimed, catching on.

The features of the maid changed. Her drab dress became bright, and her body turned buxom. Now Jenny recognized her as one of the beautiful Portrait brides. She could of course assume any likeness, so was as lovely as she chose to be. Jenny realized that this was probably an asset in a marriage. "Dana Demoness! I didn't know you in costume!"

"You didn't recognize me as the Adult, either," the creature murmured.

"Ooooo, so I didn't!"

Gwenny squinted at the demoness. "How can Humfrey trust you, if you don't have a soul?"

"Demons can be trusted to do what suits them. My husband knows that when I had a soul, I loved him, and I made him ludicrously happy, and gave him a son. When I lost my soul I left him, and then I was horribly bored. Now for a month things are interesting again. If I act soullessly, I will instantly lose my place to the next wife on the roster. So I act just as if I have a soul, for the sake of the game."

"You had a son?" Che asked.

"Dafrey Half-Demon. That was back in nine hundred fifty-four, a hundred and thirty-seven years ago. He grew up and married in the normal human manner, and had a son of his own, and *bzzzzt!* he was gone, having passed the soul on to his offspring. I lost track of him after that.''

"Nine hundred fifty-four?" Jenny asked. "That's a date?"

"That's a date," Che assured her. "Don't you remember our history lessons? The year is now one thousand ninety-one, dating from the onset of the First Wave of human colonists in Xanth."

"I guess I wasn't paying attention," Jenny confessed. "All those numbers—I never did get along well with numbers."

"Perhaps you will learn to count the days of your year working for my husband," Dana said.

"Maybe I will." For Jenny really did not relish that upcoming year. She would much prefer to remain with Che and Gwenny and the centaurs. But she would do what she had to do.

"Speaking of which," Ivy said, "it's time for your appointment."

Jenny got up. "Can—can the others come too?"

"Yes. But they can't ask Questions."

They followed Ivy up a winding stone staircase to a crowded little chamber. There sat the gnomelike Good Magician before a monstrous tome. He looked at least a hundred years old, though Jenny knew that he had youth elixir to make him as young as he chose to be. Apparently he liked this age.

Humfrey looked up. "Well?" he said grumpily.

"Ask him," Ivy whispered.

"Wh-where can we find a pair of contact lenses for Gwendolyn Goblin to wear, so she can—"

He probably frowned, though his face was so set and lined that it was hard to be sure. "There is only one pair available, and they are problematical."

"We—she has to have them, because—"

"In three respects. First, there is danger in their vicinity."

"But there is danger if she doesn't have them!"

"Second, they are in the realm of dreams."

"In the gourd? But—"

"They are intended for use by vision-impaired night mares. Herein lies the third problem. They will enable the wearer to see dreams, as the night mares do."

"But that's not a problem," Jenny started. Then she had a second thought. "Bad dreams?"

"All dreams. Including those in violation of the Adult Conspiracy."

"Oh!" Gwenny exclaimed behind her.

Now it made sense. Gwenny could not use those lenses unless she was in the Conspiracy. Anticipating this, the Good Magician had inducted her into it, distressing details and all. He had had to finesse it in a couple of ways, because he would have been in trouble if he had violated the Conspiracy by simply telling her. In fact, he had told her nothing; he had assigned the job to Dana Demoness, whose lack of a soul and conscience had enabled her to force the children to assume part of the dread mantle of Adulthood.

"I will give you instructions so that you can enter the realm of the gourd and locate the lenses," Humfrey said. "Even so, you will find it difficult. The winged monsters will not be able to protect you there."

"We'll do what we have to do," Gwenny said. "Thank you, Good Magician."

Jenny turned to her, feeling sad. "I wish I could go with you. But now I have to serve the Magician."

"Not till you help her get the lenses," Humfrey said. "Your year commences after the completion of your mission."

"Oh, thank you, Good Magician!" Jenny exclaimed, delighted.

"The route to the lens bush will be marked by mock lenses," Humfrey continued gruffly. "See that you do not lose the way, because they will fade out after you pass them. You must find them within one day, because after that we shall have to rouse you."

"Rouse us?" Jenny asked.

"We won't go physically into the gourd," Che explained. "We'll look in peepholes. When someone outside interferes with our line of sight to the peephole, we emerge."

"But why only a day?" Gwenny asked. "It might take longer."

"Because I promised your mother and Che's dam, who spoke also for Jenny Elf."

The three exchanged a look which was a good glance-and-a-half long. So the parents had known about this! But it could not be helped; it was the only way.

"I will show you to the gourds," Ivy said.

Jenny looked again at the Good Magician, but he had already returned to the tome, having forgotten them.

Ivy had set up a pile of pillows for them to lie on. There were four greenish gourds, their peepholes covered over with tape. They got comfortable, then linked hands. Jenny held on to Sammy's paw. They had to be touching when they entered, or they would find themselves in different settings. Ivy checked the alignments, making sure that each of their heads were braced right before the peepholes. "Are you ready?" she asked.

They agreed they were ready. Jenny tried to conceal her apprehension; she had never done this before, and dreaded it. But she wouldn't leave her friends to face it alone, now that the Good Magician had given her the chance to be with them. At the same time, she was afraid it wouldn't work. What kind of sense did it make to enter into a growing gourd, without one's body?

Ivy pulled the tape from Gwenny's gourd. Gwenny looked, and froze, fascinated. Then Ivy did the same for Che's gourd, and Che also froze. Finally she came to Jenny's gourd. Just then Jenny had a perilous thought: how could dream lenses do the physical Gwenny any good? Surely they would be left in the dream realm when Gwenny

woke. All this might be for nothing! She opened her mouth
to say something to Ivy.

But as she did so, her eye saw the exposed peephole—
and she found herself in a chamber with a flat floor and a
deep drop-off ahead. Alarmed, she stepped back, and
banged into Che. Then she saw Sammy pop into existence
beside her.

"We're all here," Gwenny said, sounding relieved. "I
was so nervous when I arrived here alone, but then Che
appeared, but then it seemed like forever before you
came."

Jenny decided not to voice her doubt. What was the
point, at this stage? She would just have to hope that the Good
Magician had taken this into account, and that the lenses
would work in the real world as well as in the gourd. After
all, the night mares operated outside the gourd; that was
where they needed to see the dreams they brought, to be
sure they were working properly.

"All three of us," Che agreed, also sounding relieved.
Jenny remembered that however mature he might seem,
because he was a centaur, he remained only his real age
of seven emotionally.

Suddenly there was a crowd of people in the chamber.
Jenny stared. They weren't just any people; they were
Gwenny and Che. Three of each. And two others—who
she realized were elves. Jenny Elves! There were three of
her, too! And three cats.

They exchanged a nine-way glance. Then one of the
Gwennys blinked. "I'm looking twice, but I still—"

"See another me," a new Gwenny exclaimed, chiming
in. Now there were four Gwennys.

"I'm looking tw—" Jenny started. But before she could
finish saying "twice too," one Che interrupted her.

"Don't say any more!" he cried. "This is a multiplication table!"

Jenny shut her mouth. She had never trusted multiplication tables; indeed, the whole subject of math
was somewhat alien to her. But she had not thought

that it worked quite this way. She could see that the two other Jennys and all three Sammy Cats were just as confused.

"Look," another Che added, pointing to the drop-off. "That is the edge of the table. See the corners, and the other sides."

The three Jennys looked, and sure enough, it was one big table, of the scale that would have been suitable for the huge Adult in the Good Magician's castle. Now she saw that there were markings on it: numbers along the edges, and numbers in the center. That much she understood: the numbers in the center represented the results of the numbers at the edges. She could never remember whether six times seven had a sum or a product or a total, or whether that result was supposed to be thirty-six, or forty, or forty-two, or maybe forty-five. Probably none of the above. As far as she was concerned, the world would be a better place if numbers just went away. The very last place she wanted to be was in the middle of a multiplication table.

And maybe that was the point of it: this was her bad dream. This was the place of the night mares, after all.

"Whenever we speak a number, it multiplies us by that number," the third Che concluded. "When I said—what I first said—it multiplied us by that number. When Gwenny said what she said, it multiplied her by that number. I had said 'us' so it multiplied us all; she said 'I' so it multiplied only her. Now we have a problem."

The four Gwennys and three Jennys nodded, afraid to say anything. The problem was that there were too many of them.

"I suspect that each of us feels that he or she is the original person," the first Che began carefully.

"And not one of us wishes to give up his individuality," the second continued. "The word 'one' is probably safe to use, because the multiplication leaves that person unchanged."

"Yet it is surely necessary to revert to our original states before proceeding farther into this region,'' the third concluded.

The seven girls nodded, still afraid to speak, because none of them had the centaur's brains.

"Perhaps if we perform an act of division—" the first Che started.

"But this is a multiplication table!" one Gwenny said.

The second Che smiled. "The two functions are related. We have merely to multiply by a fraction."

"Will it work?" a Jenny asked. Jenny was no longer sure which one was herself.

The third Che nodded. "I think our best approach is to reduce the Gwennys to the same number as the others, then do an overall multiplication on the group."

All four Gwennys looked nervous. "Will it hurt?" one asked.

"I don't think so," the first one said.

"I need merely speak to you the fraction three quarters," the second Che continued.

One of the Gwenny disappeared. Now there were three of them, all looking alarmed.

"Did that hurt?" Jenny asked.

"I don't know," a Gwenny said. "I wasn't the one who was disappeared."

"I doubt that it hurts, either way," the third Che remarked.

"I suppose we have to do it," one of the Jennys said with resignation.

"Yes, I suppose," one of the Gwennys agreed unhappily.

"Then I hereby multiply us by one third," the first Che said.

Suddenly there were three of them: one Che Centaur, one Gwendolyn Goblin, one Jenny Elf, and one cat. They exchanged three thirds of a glance, as nearly as Jenny could make it. She felt the same as she always had.

Silently they walked to the edge of the table and peered over. There below were assorted plants. One of them leaned toward them, showing a deep cuplike center. A branch swung toward Jenny.

Che pulled her away from it. "Beware," he said. "I think that's a pulpit. It will pull you into its pit."

Jenny quickly retreated, horrified. She went to another side of the table. There was a big bee buzzing among flowers. But the bee wasn't gathering pollen; it was cutting the heads off the flowers. "Now what's the matter with that bee?" she asked, dismayed.

Che looked. "I believe I recognize that species. That is Attila the Hunny Bee."

"Oh, I wish we could find a safe way away from here!" Gwenny said.

Sammy marched to another side of the table. "What about that plant?" Jenny asked, pointing at one with very large transparent leaves, right opposite the cat.

Che brightened. "I believe those are leaves of absence. They will probably conduct us away from here. And see— there is a lens!" For dew was sparkling on one of the leaves in a way that focused the light. That was their sign of the way.

"Then let's get conducted!" Gwenny said.

They linked hands, and Jenny picked Sammy up and set him on her shoulder, then reached out to touch one of the leaves. Immediately they found themselves in another place.

This one did not seem much more promising. There were wilting bushes and sad-looking trees with fallen fruit at their bases. Flies buzzed from bush to fruit and back again. The smell was awful.

"Ooo, ugh!" Gwenny said, wrinkling her nose.

"No wonder!" Che said. "Those are putriflies! They make things rot faster."

They walked quickly on, and left the wilting things behind. But there was more mischief ahead. They encountered a figure which looked less and less manlike the closer it got. It had two legs and two arms, but its body was made of gray metal, and its neck was a projecting tube with no head, just a hole.

"What is that?" Jenny asked, perplexed.

Just then the creature bent forward, and its hollow neck came to point directly at her. There was an ominous click.

"No!" Che cried, catching her arm and yanking her to the side. As he did so, there was a loud bang, and something whistled past the place she had just been. Smoke poured out of the creature's neck, and there was the smell of brimstone or something similar.

"Something hit a tree," Gwenny said, looking back. Jenny looked and saw a hole in the tree, just about the size of the creature's hollow neck.

"Now I recognize it," Che said. "It's a gunman! I thought they existed only in Mundania!"

"A gunman?" Jenny asked, still confused. "All I see is a metal thing with no head."

"A gun is one of the bad dreams the Mundanes have," he explained. "It exists only to hurt other creatures. It shoots out slugs of metal, and they lodge in the flesh of others, or make holes in them."

The gunman bent forward again. Che dived for it, grabbing at its body. "No!" Gwenny screamed.

But nothing happened. The gunman staggered back without firing, then turned around and ran away.

"What happened?" Jenny asked, hurrying forward to help steady Che.

"I put on its safety," the centaur said. "It couldn't fire, then."

"I won't even ask what a safety is," Gwenny said. "The Mundanes must be terribly afraid of guns."

"No, I understand they like them," Che said.

"I never want to go to Mundania!" Jenny said fervently.

"Nobody does," Che agreed. "It's an awful place."

"So where do we go now?" Gwenny asked.

Jenny looked around, and spied another sparkling lens. "Look! That way!"

They hurried along a path to the side, passing through the mock lens. The path wound around and down into a glade where there seemed to be more figures moving around. As they got closer, they saw that these were fauns and nymphs. But not ordinary ones. "They have wings!" Che exclaimed.

So they did. The creatures were not merely running around, they were spreading their wings and flying. Otherwise they were normal, for their kind: all of them were naked, the fauns were chasing the nymphs, and the nymphs were running away and screaming. This was their idea of fun.

"I wonder if there are any centaurs among them?" Che murmured musingly. Jenny realized that he was thinking of the lack of any others of his own kind. His parents were the only adult winged centaurs in Xanth, and he was the only winged centaur foal. Jenny herself had a notion what it felt like to be unique in Xanth: it was lonely.

"I never heard of winged fauns in Xanth," Gwenny remarked. "So why are they in the gourd?"

"Maybe the regular fauns and nymphs have bad dreams about them," Jenny suggested.

"But regular fauns and nymphs live only for the day; they can't remember prior days," Che said, "so shouldn't have bad dreams about them."

"Well, let's ask," Jenny said. She approached a pair of them who were lying in the flowers at the edge of their glade. Then she halted. "Oops."

"What's the matter?" Gwenny asked.

"Adult Conspiracy. I recognize it now."

"You mean they're—?"

"I think so."

"That *is* what fauns and nymphs do," Che said. "Once they catch each other."

They stood and watched. "I don't want to interrupt them," Jenny said. "Do you think they'll be through soon?"

"They look as if they're having fun," Gwenny said, surprised.

"I suppose it should be fun, or folk wouldn't do it," Che agreed dubiously. "I confess that it seems to me that a pillow fight would be more fun."

"Or a tsoda popka fight," Jenny said.

Gwenny shook her head. "It must be a terrible thing to become adult and lose interest in the fun things, and have to settle for dull things like this."

The others could only agree.

Then the faun and nymph finished their business. They looked up. "Eeeek! Strangers!" the nymph shrieked.

"Run!" the faun cried.

"Wait!" Jenny exclaimed. "We only want to ask you a question."

The two considered, then decided to wait a moment. "But no more than one moment," the nymph said firmly. "We can't spare two moments."

"Why are the winged fauns and nymphs here in the gourd," Jenny asked quickly, trying to stay within the moment, "when there aren't any in Xanth?"

The faun's eyes went round. "We don't remember," he said.

Then the two were up and away. She leaped into the air, spread her wings, and flew around a tree. He pursued her. "Eeeeek!" she cried as he caught her.

"Ask a foolish question, get a foolish answer, I guess," Jenny said. "If they can't remember any prior days, they can't remember about why they're here, either."

They walked on. There beyond the tree were the same faun and nymph, lying together on the ground.

"But they just did that!" Jenny said, surprised.

"They must have forgotten," Gwenny said, laughing with more than a tinge of embarrassment.

Then they saw another mock lens, marking another offshoot trail, and moved on along it.

This one led to a blank wall, but when they touched the wall, they discovered that it was illusion. They stepped through it, and were in a region as gloomy as the other had been pleasant. It was night, with a huge gibbous moon hovering suspiciously low. Ahead were somber grave-stones.

"Oops, *now* we're in one of the scary sections," Jenny said. "Let's hurry through."

They broke into a jog to follow the path through the center of the graveyard. But the sand crunched under their feet and made a horrible scratching noise. Then the soil of the graves stirred.

"Eeeek!" Gwenny screamed, sounding exactly like the nymph.

They stopped, for there before them a bony arm and hand were poking up from the ground. It moved as if casting about for something, such as maybe an ankle. Sammy hissed at it and backed away.

They tried to retreat, but two things stopped them. "First," Che said, "the path isn't marked the other way, and we'll lose it."

"Second," Jenny said, shivering, "bones are appearing behind us, too."

"Third," Gwenny said, "we're—"

"You can't say that," Che reminded her. "There are only two."

"Oh." She looked around. "Then I have only one thing to say."

"What is that?"

"EEEEEEEEK!!" she screamed, twice as long and loud as before.

Che nodded. "I believe that covers it."

They huddled together for support against the fright while all around them things hauled themselves out of the ground. Soon there were a dozen horrendous figures.

"The walking skeletons!" Che exclaimed. "Like Marrow Bones and Grace'l Ossein!"

"Who are they?" Jenny asked.

"They are friendly refugees from the gourd," he explained. "Marrow got lost, and Esk Ogre brought him out. Then Grace'l got in trouble for ruining a bad dream, and was kicked out. Now they're a couple. They may even have summoned the stork, or whatever it is they do. Maybe they simply assemble a baby skeleton from small bones. At any rate, such folks do scare people in dreams, but that's just their job. I understand they are nice when you get to know them personally.''

"M-maybe we should make the effort," Gwenny said. Then she turned to the nearest skeleton. "H-hello. Are you f-friendly?"

"Why, I never thought about it," the skeleton said. "I never tried to be friendly with a monster."

"Monster?" Gwenny looked fearfully around. "Where?"

"He means you," Che said. "Us. Because we're different."

"Me?" Gwenny was amazed. Jenny understood why. Though Gwenny was not vain, she was a very pretty goblin girl, and could hardly be ignorant of that fact. "Maybe it's my spectacles."

"No, it's your grisly flesh," the skeleton said. "I see that you have tried to cover it up, but enough shows to make you a truly frightful creature. Are you from another section of the dream establishment? You must be very good at terrifying dreamers!"

"No, I'm just visiting. I'm looking for the contact lens bush. I don't suppose it's near here?"

"As a matter of fact, it is," the skeleton said. "I understand it's the last one growing. The night mares come to it when they have trouble seeing well. I suppose going out into that horrible other realm is bad for their eyes."

"That must be the case," Gwenny said, evidently gaining confidence. "Just let me go and get a pair, and we'll leave this area so you won't have to be appalled by the sight of us."

"That will be much appreciated," the skeleton said, and the other skeletons nodded. "We don't mean to be impolite, but it is hard to be close to freaks like you without spooking.''

"I understand perfectly," Gwenny said.

They walked on along the path, the skeletons making wary way for them. There in the center of the graveyard was a glittering bush—and there on the bush glittered a single pair of tiny lenses.

"Oh, I can hardly believe it!" Gwenny said.

They stood around the bush. "But how do I put them on?" Gwenny asked after a moment.

"I think you just look straight ahead, and set them on your eyes," Che said. "Maybe I can help you."

"I think I have to do it myself," Gwenny said. "So that they will work for me. If you touch them, they might decide to work for you instead."

"Good point," he agreed, stepping back.

Gwenny reached out and very gently took a lens. It dropped into her hand. She removed her spectacles, put them in a pocket, and brought the lens to her face—and it jumped onto the right eye. "Oh!"

"Is something wrong?" Jenny asked, alarmed.

"No, it's right! I can see clearly with my right eye, and fuzzily with the left. It's as if I have only half my spectacles on."

Then she took the other lens and put it to her left eye. She blinked. "Oh, it's wonderful!"

Jenny tried to imagine what it would be like to have such lenses. She pictured herself with a pair, walking around without her spectacles. She would feel naked, just as if all her clothes had dissolved, because she had used the spectacles ever since coming to Xanth.

Gwenny's gaze swung around to Jenny. "Oh, you're naked!" she exclaimed.

"No, she remains clothed," Che said, surprised.

Jenny jumped. "You saw my daydream!" she exclaimed.

"Oh, now you're clothed again," Gwenny said. "I—your dream?"

"I was daydreaming," Jenny said. "And you saw it—just as the Good Magician said you would."

"That is an excellent sign," Che said. "It means the lenses are working exactly as they are supposed to."

"But actually seeing dreams—is that polite?" Gwenny asked.

Jenny smiled. "That must depend on the dream."

"Oh—and some folk will be dreaming Adult things," Gwenny said. "I wish there had been some other lenses."

"Actually, these may be worthwhile," Che said thoughtfully. "You will face a difficult situation at Goblin Mountain. If the daydreams of people indicate their real feelings—"

"You might be able to tell when they're not telling the truth!" Jenny said.

"But of course folk would tell the truth," Gwenny said.

"Goblin males?" Che asked pointedly.

"Oh." Because male goblins were just naturally the worst of folk, being the opposite of goblin females. "But I wouldn't want to spy on anyone!"

"Now look, Gwenny, a chief has to know what's going on," Che said. "You know that goblin males are always conspiring to do mischief. How long do you think you will last if you don't know what they're thinking?"

"He's right," Jenny said. "You will be chief over the meanest male folk, as well as the nicest female folk. Maybe if you were an ordinary goblin girl, you could just be your nice self. But that's not your destiny. If you can't be mean, you'll have to be knowledgeable."

Gwenny still looked doubtful, so they worked on her some more. "You should practice using those lenses now," Che said. "So you'll be able to know folk's dreams and tell whether they're your friends or your enemies."

"And so you won't blush when you see an adult dream," Jenny added.

"But what can I practice on?" Gwenny asked without enthusiasm. "The folk here *are* dreams." Then she had a second thought. "How was I able to see Jenny's daydream? I mean, she's right here in dreamland, so how could she be dreaming?''

That set them back. But then Che came up with the answer. *"We* aren't dreams. We're just visiting. Our real bodies are lying in the Good Magician's castle. So we can still have dreams, through those bodies.''

That seemed to make sense. So Jenny tried to make another dream, but she couldn't. The more she concentrated on it, the more she paid attention to their here and now, rather than wandering to something else.

"Sing,'' Che suggested.

Maybe that would do it! So Jenny sang, imagining a pleasant landscape not at all like the graveyard here. It worked! Soon the landscape became real for her. Then Sammy appeared in it, preferring it to the "reality" of this dream realm. After a moment Che appeared in it too. Finally Gwenny appeared.

Then they walked through the field of flowers toward the brilliant sunset. And beside them walked some of the skeletons, who seemed surprised.

"But I'm not seeing your dream,'' Gwenny protested. "I'm *in* it!''

"And so are the skeletons,'' Che said. "I think Jenny actually changed the scene here.''

So it seemed. "I guess we'll have to practice outside the gourd,'' Jenny said. "But we might as well wait here where it's nice until we are recalled to reality.''

So they settled down for a nap, inside Jenny's dream.

Then Che had a notion. "Jenny, if you are able to bring us all into your dream here, including the skeletons—what about the Good Magician's castle?''

"His castle? But we're already there, really.''

"That's what I mean. Can you dream us back out of the gourd, awake, so we don't have to wait here anymore?''

Jenny thought about it. "Why, I really don't know. My dreams always end when some outside disturbance interrupts them. Just the way the gourd visions do. Or when I stop singing.'' That brought another realization. ''But I'm not singing now! So why didn't this vision end?''

''Probably because this *is* the dream realm,'' Che said. ''When we shift from one dream setting to another here, we have neither slept nor awakened; we have merely moved within the larger dream. So your singing just facilitates that movement. But what I'm thinking of now is whether you could make a dream of us back awake in the castle, and have *that* come true. Because if that worked, you would be able not only to change dreams, but to get out of the dream realm on your own. That would be truly remarkable.''

''Why, I don't know,'' Jenny said, intrigued. ''I suppose I could try it.''

''If it doesn't work, we'll be rescued anyway in a few more hours,'' Gwenny said. ''Still, I don't want to stay here any longer than I have to.''

So Jenny sang again. This time she imagined the chamber in the Good Magician's castle, with the three of them lying on their cushions and looking into the gourds. Then she had herself look away from the peephole—and she was there. She quickly covered the peephole with her hand, then turned the gourd around so that she could not accidentally look at it again.

But the others remained locked to their gourds. She tried to imagine them looking away, as she had done, but they did not. Then she put her hand between Che's face and his gourd, and he snapped out of it.

''It worked!'' he exclaimed.

But Jenny had a nasty thought. ''Suppose it didn't work? Could this just be a dream of us waking, and we didn't wake at all, but only thought we did.''

He put his hand before Gwenny's face, waking her. ''No, I don't think so, because I had not yet entered your reality dream. I had not yet become distracted, so I was still in the flower valley. I woke from there to here.''

Gwenny sat up. "Are we out?" she asked, blinking behind her spectacles.

"I think so," Jenny said. "Except—oh, no, I forgot to include Sammy!"

"Sammy's here," Che said, turning the cat's gourd around.

"But when I pictured this chamber, I didn't picture him in it! So he should be missing. Why isn't he?"

"Because this is *real,*" Che answered. "What you pictured of the rest of us had no relevance; we must enter your dream ourselves. You pictured me, but I wasn't there in your dream."

"But you had to be, because I woke you!"

"No. *You* were in it—and since your dream was of reality, you saw reality. You may have forgotten to imagine Sammy here, and he may not have come in by himself, but since this is not a dream but reality, he *is* here."

"I suppose you're right," Jenny said, her head spinning because surely if it were just her imagination, Sammy would not be here. That seemed to be the proof of it. But she wasn't quite sure.

Then her uncertainty found another focus. "But the lenses! Did they come through?"

Gwenny removed her spectacles, which were back on her face, here in reality. She looked around. "I can see everything! Better than before. Only no dreams."

"That's because none of us are daydreaming at the moment," Che said.

Then Gwenny's gaze fell on the cat. "Now I see a chocolate mouse!" she said.

"Sammy does like them," Jenny said. "So he must be dreaming of one now. So the lenses do work here."

"Well, let's go down and surprise the others," Gwenny said, delighted. "They think we're still locked into the gourd."

"That's right!" Che agreed. "We may be the first to have found a way to escape the gourd by ourselves. Actually, Jenny's the only one who can do it, but it remains a valuable discovery. We can never be trapped in the gourd, if she's along.''

''Then we had better remain friends with her,'' Gwenny said, laughing.

Jenny picked Sammy up, and they headed out to surprise the others in the castle.

Chapter 7. Panting

Mela's legs were really getting tired as they neared the top of Iron Mountain. She had never used them this hard before, and she wished she could rest them. Legs were so inefficient, compared to a tail! But this was the route to the Good Magician's castle, according to the map, so she just had to suffer through.

Finally they reached the top. It was bare; trees just did not seem to grow well on solid iron. Not even ironwood. But the view was terrific. They could see Xanth spread out all around them.

But that did not help much, because they couldn't actually see the Good Magician's castle. From this vantage, one part of Xanth looked much like another.

It did not even seem to be a very good place to camp for the night, yet they were too tired to make the arduous trip down the west side on this day. What were they to do?

"I wish I had a nice soft moss bed to lie on," Ida said.

"I wish I had a nice hardwood pallet to lie on," Okra said.

"I wish I had a seawater pond to float in," Mela said.

Smoke formed before them. It swirled and became a female figure. "Are you travelers in distress?" she inquired.

126

"Oh, hello, Metria," Mela said without enthusiasm.

"I'm not Metria," the demoness said.

"Well, whoever you are, we aren't looking for trouble, and we hope you will go away."

"I'm Dana, the Good Magician's wife. I have no soul, but I try to emulate a souled person by doing a good deed every day, if I can find one to do. I thought perhaps I could help you in some way."

Mela did not quite trust this, but did not want to annoy the demoness, because that could lead to worse mischief. So she tried to avoid disagreeing directly. "I had thought the Good Magician was married to the Gorgon." Mela had recently been told otherwise, but she distrusted the source of that information.

"He now has six wives, counting MareAnn. We take turns with him, while the others remain in Hell. This is my month of delight."

"The demoness Metria did say he had married other wives," Mela agreed. "But she also said that he was once a king. I find such things difficult to believe."

"Oh, yes, he was the king of Xanth when I married him. I had a soul, then, but knew I could get rid of it only by marrying a king. Now I wish I had a soul again, though I blush to confess it." She turned an attractive pink. "But please, if there is any good deed I can do for any of you, let me do it, so that I can pretend to have a soul."

Mela exchanged two glances with Okra and Ida. "As a matter of fact, we were making some wishes."

"Oh, I thought I heard something like that! What were they?"

"I wanted a seawater pond to soak my tail in."

Dana gestured. A depression appeared in the iron surface, filled with water.

Mela dipped a toe cautiously in it. "Oooo! It really is salt!" She converted her legs to tail and plunged in. It was wonderful.

Soon Okra had her hard pallet and Ida had her soft moss. All three made sighs of satisfaction.

"How can we thank you, Dana?" Mela inquired blissfully.

"Oh, no," the demoness protested. "You must not thank me! This is my Good Deed for today. I feel almost as if my soul is back."

"Wouldn't it be nice if souled folk did good deeds too!" Mela said. "If we can't thank you, at least we can hope to see you again soon, when we reach the Good Magician's castle."

"Oh, you are going there? Do you know the way?"

"We have a map, but it hasn't been easy to find the route."

"I will come again tomorrow morning and show you the best route. That will be my good deed for that day." Then the figure turned smoky, clouding up. "Oh, I forgot; this is my last day! At midnight I must exchange with my successor, the Maiden Taiwan. Oops, I mean the Matron Taiwan; she's not exactly a maiden anymore. Or maybe Sofia. I will not be able to guide you."

"Well, it was a nice thought," Mela said. The feel of the salt water on her tail was so good that nothing could upset her at the moment.

"I know," Dana said. "I'll have Metria do it."

"But Metria is full of mischief," Mela objected.

"True. But she is bored, and if I tell her that you will be doing something interesting, she will help."

"Something interesting? Such as falling off the mountain?"

"No, nothing like that. But if you are to appear at my husband's castle, you will have to put something on."

"Something on?"

"All three of you," Dana said firmly. "The Matron Taiwan will insist on it."

"But I'm a merwoman!" Mela protested. "I never wear clothing."

"And I'm an ogress," Okra said. "Ogres don't wear clothes either, except for special occasions. Fur suffices."

"Dana's right," Ida said. "I understand that all human folk wear clothing, so they probably expect it in others."

"The matron is very concerned about protocol," Dana agreed. "You are not nymphs; you cannot run around bare bottomed. So I will have Metria guide you to the pantry."

"The pantry?" Mela asked.

"That's where you start. Well, I must be off; I have only half a night to make Humfrey deliriously happy." She disappeared.

They made a meal of Ida's magic sandwich, which expanded enough to feed all three of them, with enough left over for another meal. Then they slept comfortably on or in their respective gifts from the demoness.

At the first crack of dawn, the Demoness Metria appeared. "Up, you lazy bones! We don't have all aurora!"

"All what?" Mela asked sleepily.

"Sunrise, daybreak, cockcrow, dawn, grief—"

"Grief?" Okra asked.

"Morning!" Ida exclaimed.

"Whatever," the demoness said crossly. "Dana told me to get you to the pantry if I wanted to see something interesting, so let's get on with it."

They got off or out of their assorted sleeping places, which promptly disappeared. Mela flexed her legs, which felt marvelously restored after the night's rest in tailform. They snatched another bite of magic sandwich, then followed Metria down the steep iron path to the west.

In due course they arrived at the pantry. This was a huge tree in the shape of a pan. Metria opened a door in the trunk, and they walked into the interior, which was one big chamber. All around its circular wall were displayed its hidden fruits.

"Panties!" Ida exclaimed. "How marvelous!"

"We have to put on panties?" Okra asked, not pleased.

"Yes. This should be most interesting."

They walked around the circle, gazing at the assorted panties. Mela had been diffident about this matter, but found herself getting interested. She had never dreamed that there could be such an array to choose from. There were panties of every type and description, from blah to fantastic and all the shades between.

But something nagged her. She finally put her mental finger on it. *"Why* should this be so interesting?'' she asked the demoness.

''Because of the— Oh, you mean you really don't know?''

''I really don't know. But I'm sure that you must have good reason to be interested, and that may not be what interests me.''

''Indubitably.''

''In what?''

''In doubt, suspicion, distrust—'' Metria paused. ''Hey, wait! I had it right the first time. It means *not* to be doubted for even a tiny instant.''

Had Mela not been a fair-tempered creature, she might have thought of being annoyed. ''Thank you. What is that not-to-be-doubted-for-a-tiny-instant reason for your interest?''

''Last year Good Magician Humfrey was dickering for his wife with the Demon X(A/N)th, and to get her back he would have to answer a question that couldn't be answered. That put him in a picklement, as you might imagine. But he managed to wangle a compromise, so didn't have to answer the question.''

''Which wife?'' Okra asked. ''Dana?''

''No, Rose of Roogna. You don't know her.''

''What has any of this to do with me?'' Mela demanded, mentally dousing her temper in chill seawater to keep it from warping.

''Why, it has everything to do with you,'' Metria said. ''You are the central figure.''

''I am?''

''Or maybe your center is to be figured. The greatest mystery of Xanth is about to be solved.''

''Something I'm doing will solve a mystery?''

"Yes. It will answer the unanswerable question. That's why it's so interesting."

"*What* question?" Mela demanded.

"The question the Good Magician couldn't answer."

The temper was definitely fraying. "And what is that?"

"The color."

"The what?"

"The color of your panties."

Mela digested that. "The Good Magician can't tell the color of my panties?"

"That's right."

"But I never wore any!"

"That's what makes it such a challenge."

"But that's not a fair question."

"Yes it is. Because you are about to don panties, and they will surely have a color, even if that color is transparent, and then there will be an answer."

"But surely he already knows that color, since he knows everything."

"Ah, you see it is more complicated than that. The Demon $X(A/N)^{th}$ did not want to free Rose, so he planned to change the color you chose, to make Humfrey's answer wrong. He has the power to do that sort of thing, and Humfrey could not oppose it. But the cunning mortal managed to get around it with a plea bargain, and so the question remained unanswered. Not that it matters; now it is merely a curiosity. But I am very curious. That's why I brought you here."

"To find out what color my panties will be?"

"That's right. I've never had the answer to an unanswerable question before."

"Then maybe I won't don any panties!"

The demoness shook her head. "They'll never let you into that castle bare nude. You look way too much like a woman. You have to choose."

Mela sighed. She did want to find a good husband, which meant she had to see the Good Magician, and if getting panted was part of the price of that, then she had to do it. Even if it gave the demoness satisfaction. Besides, she was really quite intrigued by the variety of panties offered. The right panty might do wonders for her midsection, and possibly even enhance her chance of catching a husband.

So she lifted a panty from its hook and flattened it against her. It was plain white. "I don't think this does much for me," she said.

"That's no way to judge," Metria said. "You have to put them on. Take them into the changing chamber." She indicated a curtained region in the center of the pantry.

"I don't need a chamber," Mela protested. "I can try it on right here."

"No you can't," the demoness said. "That's not the way."

"Yes I can." Mela bent forward and lifted a foot. But the moment it approached the panty, the material wrinkled and writhed away and got all twisted up. She couldn't get her foot in it.

So with ill grace she stepped into the chamber. Then the panty behaved, and she was able to put first one foot and then the other in. The garment fit her perfectly, and she realized that this was part of the magic of the pantry. All of its wares would fit any woman who came here.

She stepped outside. The other three were now seated on stools in a semicircle. "Turn around," Metria said.

"Why?"

"Because that's the way it's done. If you're going to model panties, you have to do it properly."

"Suppose I don't?"

At that point the panty started twisting up again, and uncomfortable wrinkles pressed into her tender flesh. So she turned around.

"Oh, they look much better now," Ida said. "Your bottom looks so much more interesting."

This, too, did not fully please Mela. She had been under the impression that her bottom had always been sufficiently interesting. But she spied a set of angled mirrors, which magically showed her from behind as well as in front, and had to admit it was true: her midsection was enhanced by the panty. There was a certain glossy mystery about it now. Was this the mystery that was about to be solved? She wasn't sure that she liked the notion of the attention of all Xanth on her posterior. But she also wasn't sure she didn't like the notion. It depended on the panty, and her mood.

Still, plain white was not her favorite color. She would try on something else.

She retreated into the changing chamber and removed the panty. It hung limply, depressed about being rejected. She took it out and hung it back on its hook. Then she took another panty. This one was lustrous black.

In a moment she was in it and doing her turn before the little audience. "That's nicer," Okra said. "It makes your bottom ripple when you walk."

Mela checked the mirror, and saw that it was true. Her walk was definitely more intriguing than it had been. Still, she hoped to do better.

She tried a lovely sea green panty. That was better yet, for the currents of the ocean seemed to flow across it as she walked, but it still lacked something.

"Enough with the simple stuff," Metria said impatiently. "Let's see some fancy pants."

"Then you pick them out," Mela said shortly.

"Gladly." In a moment the demoness brought a shimmering peacock blue silk panty oversewn with a golden net. Within the net hung glowing fireflies. Mela was amazed; she had not realized that anything this fancy existed.

She put it on and stepped out. The room lit up. "Oooh, I like it!" Ida exclaimed.

Mela was tempted, but now was getting into the delight of panting. There might be even better panties coming. She would find the very best panty for her, and that was the one she would wear. After all, if the fate of the Good

Magician Humfrey had once depended on what she wore, she owed it to Xanth to choose carefully.

The next panty was royal deep purple satin, embroidered with woven golden ribbons edged with golden threads hung with little golden bells. With each step she made music, and when she twirled she tintinnabulated.

"You what?" Metria asked.

"I can't pronounce the word," Mela said. "I can't even think it properly, when I try to. It means the way I made the bells ring."

"Tin-can-ambulate?" Okra asked.

"Close enough," Mela decided, going for another change.

The next panty was hand-knitted pink, with matching stockings of pale rose hue, as gossamer as a spider's web on a rose bush. They made her legs feel impossibly slender and smooth. They seemed almost as nice as a tail.

"I always wondered why pink panties are supposed to be so magically wonderful," Ida said. "Now I know. Those are so—so—"

"Only a man could find the word," Metria said.

"A man?" Ida asked. "Why?"

"Because only a man would say that panties are not the best thing in Xanth, just next to it."

"I don't understand."

"That's because you are a nice girl. I, of course, understand all too well."

"Would this snare me a husband?" Mela asked, gazing at her slick bottom in the mirrors. Ida was right: the effect was just so. She twitched a muscle and watched the panty surface flex fascinatingly.

"I'm not sure. I don't think any man has seen those. No men are allowed in here, of course. They would totally freak out."

Mela decided to keep looking. The next panty was country style, with creamy cool white cotton gauze with saucy white linen rosettes and garters.

"Garters?" Okra asked. "What are they for?"

Metria looked at the little snakes. "They are to hold up stockings. They bite down onto them, and then the stockings can't fall. Probably the Gorgon uses them, since she already has snakes on her head. But I fear it might be awkward feeding the snakes, to keep them healthy."

Mela agreed. This was a nice panty, but she wanted nothing in it except herself. She went for the next.

This was another country-style effort. Stone-washed, water-washed bonjour blue cotton denim, with an easy comfort button on the back. Serviceable, but Mela was becoming jaded.

So she tried on a jade panty. It was a deep blue-green with glowing waves which rippled when she moved, reminding her so strongly of the sea that a drop of seawater leaked from her eye. How she missed the deep salt ocean! She couldn't wear this, wonderful as it was, because it would make her forget all else in her longing to go home. She couldn't go home until she had found a prince to take home with her.

"This is special," Metria said as she brought the next panty.

Mela donned it. It was made of milk pods interspersed with stripes of mint, peach, and peppermint. It was nice enough, but somewhat heavy. "How is it special?" she inquired as she stepped out to model it.

"It's edible," the demoness explained. "If you get lost in the woods with no pie trees in sight, you can eat your panty. Or if you nab your man, and he gets hungry—"

"I think I'll try another," Mela decided. It was an intriguing notion, but she didn't want to risk getting eaten by some ardent fool who didn't know where to stop.

The next was a colorful contrast. It was a rainbow moon panty, in several variants, with colors of azure, beach sand, clay, heather, and other. That last color was really special, but she feared it would call so much attention to itself that she herself would be neglected. That did not seem to be the best strategy. A potential husband might decide to marry the panty instead of the merwoman.

Then there was a gossamer silk Bluebeard's blue mist panty, shot through with shimmering silver threads among the gold, sporting sparkling green peridots in pairs of dots all over. But there was some kind of association with the notion of Bluebeard that she didn't quite like.

And assorted hot-pants panties. But the day was already warm enough, and these were threatening to make her break out in an unladylike sweat. Indeed, steam was rising from them before she managed to get them off.

There was a feather panty to tickle her fancy. Unfortunately the feathers tickled more than that. She didn't want to go into a giggling fit the moment a man came near. There was a Queen Anne's lace panty, with exquisite white lace sporting milkweed flower trim with seed pearl centers. The center panel shimmered with a faintly greenish glow from green witch stitchery. There was a spellbinding black lace panty, the lace embroidered with gold thread "rack and runes." The matching lace net stockings had golden zodiac clocks. But who wanted to keep time?

The next was a timepiece of another kind: it was fashioned from sprigs of thyme. "Part of you will never grow old, in this," Metria said.

"But what about the rest of me?" For it occurred to Mela that a man just might want to look at the rest of her, too. In fact, she rather hoped he would.

Next was a knot-so-fast panty made of knotted macrame lace, designed to tease the life out of any male lucky enough to catch a glimpse. And a panty to wear up a gum tree: trimmed with a pocketful of gum drops. But she worried about the drops; she might land too hard, and get gummed up in an exceedingly awkward manner.

There were several scented panties; when she modeled them there was the smell of rose, lavender, heliotrope, and jasmine for evening use. And a cowgirl panty, trimmed with lotsa moolah. An an almost transparent panty, shot through with radiant metallic copper and platinum threads. Now this was tempting, because in shadow it would be practically invisible. She could qualify as wearing it without seeming to. Still, if she was going to wear anything, she might as well show it off.

"This, then," the demoness said, handing her something else. "It is a violet d'amore—elixir of love—panty." It was black velvet embroidered with silver spiderwebs shimmering with "dew": tiny diamonds sewn with translucent thread. Ida oooh'd and Okra aaah'd when they saw that.

But Mela still wasn't quite satisfied. None of these seemed to be quite exactly precisely devastatingly *her*. The demoness frowned, then brought out some truly fancy stuff.

There was the gold coast gold lace panty, trimmed with long chains of tinkling goldfish. When Mela walked or swayed there was gentle music. And the royal midnight blue panty, with a small silver moon complete with tiny moon moths and shining silver stars woven in. As she walked, the stars progressed across the flexing heaven, and the moon waxed and waned mysteriously. That almost satisfied her, but she was concerned about wearing it in daylight. The stars might fall out in the heat of the sun.

She tried a love lace panty, with cotton gauze trimmed with silver filigree fringe studded with heart-shaped amethysts and tiny see shells. And another hot panty, gold lamé fire opals on scarlet lace, and spectacularly long floating panels of flame-colored chiffon. Also a metallic mail panty, proof against any attack, trimmed with horrific golden goblin teeth. But she was afraid it would also be proof against the right male.

There was a panty with plain background, embroidered with the words THE ONE I LOVE IS UNTRUE—BEWARE SHE WHO DANCES WITH DEMONS. But she was afraid it might give the one she loved a bad idea, once she found someone to love.

Then there was an ethereal panty: blue green silk, foaming white lace shimmering with pearls, with a faint clinging scent of sea lilies. That very nearly satisfied her, but again she knew that she could not afford to think of the sea too much, lest she lose her stamina and give up on her quest. So that, too, she reluctantly doffed.

There was a pause. She looked up. Why hadn't Metria brought her the next panty?

"You have tried them all," the demoness said, amazed. "We have been here all day. I hardly noticed."

Tried them all? Mela had somehow thought the parade of panties would go on forever. She, too, had not been aware of the time passing. It had been such a blissful experience! But it was all too true; the pantry was darkening.

But now she had to choose from among the myriad she had modeled. Which one? Still she could not make up her mind. They were all so pretty! Yet no single panty had been just purely totally utterly right.

"Aren't there any more?" she inquired plaintively.

Ida and Okra got up and looked through the hanging panties. "There must be just one more," Ida said. "There must be one that's completely right for you."

"Must be," Okra agreed.

Metria sighed. "Very well. I will distill again."

"You will what again?" Mela asked.

"Condense, digest, summarize, refine, search pattern—"

"Seek?"

"Whatever." The demoness disappeared crossly among the panties.

"I think I found one!" Ida cried. She hurried forward, carrying a bit of cloth. "It had fallen down behind another."

Mela took it. It was a dust-covered mass, hardly promising. But she shook it out and took it into the changing chamber. It was comfortable, but lacked any spangles or embroidery. It was just an ordinary panty.

She stepped out and did her little walk and turn. "Ooooh," Ida exclaimed. "That's perfect!"

"Yes, it is," Okra agreed.

"This little nothing?" Mela asked. She suspected that they just wanted her to take it so that they could get out of here. But she looked in the mirrors.

The mirrors made their region brighter. Now Mela saw the full color of the panty. It was a crossbarred pattern, with many hues cunningly interwoven.

"Why that's skirl!" Metria exclaimed.

"That's what?" Mela asked, peering at her full bottom contained in the panty.

"Bagpipe, highland, blanket, Scotch tape, kilt—"

"Skirt?" Okra asked.

"Whatever," Metria agreed crossly. Then she uncrossed. "No, wait, that's not it. Cloth, material, crisscross, distinctive, scarf, tartan—"

"Plaid!" Ida said.

"Um," the demoness agreed, recrossing.

Plaid! Mela hadn't thought of that, but she did like it. She turned around again, watching herself. The plaid flexed and shifted aspects most gracefully. The more she saw of it, the better she liked it. It was conservative without being dull, and its detail was interesting.

Still, she wasn't sure it was perfect for her. Maybe she would be better off in the one with the moon and stars. Or maybe there was one with the sun and blue sky, that would dazzle anyone who gazed directly at it. That would serve the gazer right!

She started toward the changing chamber. "What color is plaid?" Okra asked.

"Why, it's—" Ida started. "That is—"

"It's not exactly a color, it's a pattern," Metria said. "A design. Each one is unique to itself, with its own history."

Now Mela saw that the colors and ratios were indeed shifting with her motions, so that the exact display could never be fixed. That was intriguing. A person could get lost amidst the shifting lines, especially when she was walking, and never be able to say exactly what he had seen.

She decided that she liked this panty. "I'll take it," she said.

Ida went back to where she had found the panty. "There must be spares, to use when the first gets soiled."

"Soiled?" Mela asked sharply.

"Dirty, defiled, polluted, foul, filthy—" the demoness said helpfully.

"Pooped?" Okra asked.

"Whatever." Metria wasn't cross this time, for some reason.

"Whatever!" Mela echoed indignantly. For some other reason, she was now the cross one.

"Wait, I didn't mean that!" Ida protested. "Just that they can get smudged if you sit on the ground, or—ah, there they are!" She fished out two more plaid panties.

Now Mela had not just one panty, but three panties. She was thrilled. She put the two spares in her purse.

Meanwhile, Okra picked up a pair of furry black panties in the ogre style, donning one and saving the other. Since they matched her fur, they didn't show, which evidently satisfied the ogress. Ida took plain white and plain pink and yellow tinged with green panties, matching her hair, but did not put any on; she was already clothed. This was merely a reserve, in case of soilage, or whatever. They were ready to go.

Outside it was dusk. They considered, then decided to spend the night in the pantry, where it was surely safe from monsters. They went out just far enough to take care of private business and forage for food, and Mela was lucky enough to find a pie bush with a plaid-crusted pie on it. She stared, amazed, until Okra joined her, and found a black furry cherry pie beside it. Then Ida came, and found a pink meringue pie. The pies matched their panties! That was the magic of this place.

In the morning they set out again. Metria remained with them, which made Mela wonder; surely the entertainment was over, since the great mystery of the color of her panties had been resolved. It couldn't be because of the goodness of the demoness's heart, because the Metria had no goodness and no heart. But it wouldn't do to ask her, because that could remind her to do some mischief. Maybe the demoness had simply forgotten that the fun was done.

The path wended its way westward in the manner of its kind, through woods and vale, through fields and hills, and through some interesting regions and more boring ones. They had found an enchanted path, so were reasonably safe from molestation. At one point they spied a dragon snoozing nearby. He was a big lusty masculine reptile.

The three mortals paused. "Are you sure—?" Mela asked.

"Can't touch you," Metria assured her. "Can't even breathe fire on you. These paths are absolutely vermin free. All he can do is watch and salivate. You might as well relax and enjoy teasing him."

The demoness always told the truth, so it should be safe. Mela forced herself to breathe normally and led the way onward.

The dragon opened an eye. He blinked. His pupil expanded awesomely. Then he rolled over as if dead.

"What's the matter with him?" Ida asked.

"Routine freak-out," Metria said. "He'll recover in due subject."

"In due what?"

"Study, orbit, flow, process, mode—"

"Time?"

"Route, bearing, direction, trend, course—" The demoness did a double take. "Course! I got it! In due course!"

It seemed to Mela that her suggestion of time would have sufficed, but the case was not worth arguing.

They went on. They passed a goblin cave. Three ugly mean goblin males stood outside it, staring malevolently at the approaching party. They looked as if they would like nothing better than to swarm over innocent maidens and do unmentionably horrible things to them. But, reassured by the dragon's inability to bother anyone on the enchanted path, Mela strode onward.

The goblins' eyes fixed on her. Then, in turn, they fell forward on their faces and remained that way.

"I never saw a goblin do that before," Okra remarked.

"Another routine freak-out," Metria said. "Think nothing of it."

Later they passed a small human village. It contained three and a half houses. Three bold men and a boy stood watching the path. But Mela figured that its enchantment should be effective against them, too.

The human males stared. Then one fell to the left, another to the right, and the third on his back. Only the boy remained standing, but his face was slack.

"What *is* it with you?" Mela demanded.

The boy's mouth opened with an effort. "P-p-p—"

"Plaid," Metria said. "Let's move on."

Finally they came into sight of the Good Magician's castle. It looked perfectly ordinary from a distance, and more so as it got closer.

There was a young man walking on an intersecting path. "Why that's Magician Grey Murphy," Metria said. "This should be really interesting."

Mela still distrusted the demoness's attitude, but couldn't fathom it.

The man saw them and paused. "Why, hello, Metria," he said. "What mischief are you up to at the moment?"

"I am bringing three querents to see you or Humfrey," Metria responded.

"Queer whats?" Mela demanded suspiciously.

"Odd, strange, peculiar—no, wait, it's the right word. It means questioners."

"She's right," Grey said. "Those who come to the Good Magician are querents."

"Let me introduce them," Metria said briskly. "Here is Ida Human."

Ida turned suddenly shy, for she had never before formally met a man of her species. "H-hello," she managed.

He squinted at her. "Have we met before? You seem somehow familiar."

"I don't think so," Ida said. "I have lived apart from human folk all my life."

"This is Okra Ogress," Metria said.

"Hi," Okra said, hardly less abashed.

"You don't look like an ogress," he remarked.

"I know," Okra said, ashamed.

"And this is Mela Merwoman."

"Hello, Mela. I have heard much about you."

"I almost married Prince Dolph," she said.

"I remember. However—" Then his eyes, which had been fixed on her upper section, happened to drop to her midsection. They widened. Then they narrowed. "So *this* is your mischief, Metria!" he said severely.

"Oh, river blockage!" the demoness exclaimed.

"You mean a dam?"

"Whatever. I thought you'd freak out, the way the others did."

"You forget my talent. Begone, Metria, or I'll null you." He reached toward her.

The demoness instantly faded away.

"But why would you freak out?" Metria asked.

"She didn't tell you, of course. It's that magic panty. On a body like yours, it is guaranteed to freak out any male who sees it. Except that I can nullify magic, so can resist it. Nevertheless, you should put on some clothing before you proceed farther."

"But I have some clothing on!" Mela said. "Just as Dana said I should. This is all I have."

"She meant more than a panty. Nude, you can be mistaken for a well-endowed nymph. Clothed you would resemble a buxom woman. But panties alone are dangerous. You are in violation of the Adult Conspiracy."

"So that's what Metria was waiting for!" Ida said. "To see if the plaid panty freaked out the Magician!"

"Precisely. I suppose you should proceed to the challenges now, and Sofia will see to some clothing for you once you are inside. I must go now; I wish you well."

"Thank you," Mela said faintly. Oh, that demoness!

Chapter 8. Godiva

Gwendolyn Goblin was thrilled with and nervous about her new lenses. They worked perfectly, but this business of seeing dreams was daunting. Would the bad dreams of others frighten her? She hardly wanted to find out.

She also felt guilty about letting Jenny Elf serve for Gwenny's Answer. How could she ever repay Jenny for this? If she managed to become chief, she would not be available to return the favor by serving a year for an Answer for Jenny. Her responsibility to her tribe would come first. She was likely to be stuck with this considerable favor owing.

Dana Demoness was surprised to see them. "But who freed you early from the gourd?"

"Jenny did," Che said. "Her talent makes her able to escape the dream realm."

Dana nodded. "That is more of a talent than it seems. I suggest that you keep Jenny close by you, and that you do not tell others about this."

Soon Ivy and Grey Murphy were there. "They have the lenses, so there wasn't any point in remaining in the gourd longer," Dana said.

Ivy seemed nonplused. "Of course. But—"

"Let it pass," Grey told her. Perhaps he had caught on; he had an understanding of how magic could be canceled magically, or perhaps he had seen it in the Book of Answers.

"Will you be going directly to Goblin Mountain now?" Dana inquired.

"Yes, I think I must," Gwenny said. "The longer I'm away, there more mischief there may be." She looked at Jenny. "It may be dangerous. Maybe it would be better if you stayed here, to do your year's service."

"No, I will see the mission through," Jenny said firmly. "I want to see you be chief. Then I'll return here."

"But if something happened—you know how mean goblins can be—"

"That's why I have to be there to help you."

"She's right," Grey said. "There will be time for her service."

Gwenny remained frustrated. She just couldn't seem to do anything good for Jenny! Yet at the same time she was relieved that Jenny would remain with her. They had been friends for two years, the best years of Gwenny's life, and she wished that could continue forever.

"You will need a pass for the Gap," Ivy said. "I'll write one out."

"A pass?" Gwenny asked blankly.

"The shortest route from here to Goblin Mountain is a straight line. You won't want to take the longer route to cross the bridge over the Gap Chasm. That means you have to go down into it. The pass is so that my friend Stanley Steamer, the Gap Dragon, will know not to eat you."

"Oh." Gwenny was not thrilled with the notion of going down into the Gap. But unless she wanted to accept a lift from the winged monsters, that was the way she would have to go. "Thank you."

"I did not realize that the dragon could read," Che remarked.

"He can't," Ivy said. "But the paper and ink smell of

me. He won't chomp anyone with this.'' She handed it to Gwenny. ''Just don't lose it!''

''I won't.'' Gwenny tucked the paper into her pocket.

Soon they were on their way, following an enchanted path northeast. There were several bypaths which surely led to interesting things, but they were determined not to be distracted, so hurried on along the main path without pausing at any of the diversions. Just to be sure, Jenny had Sammy Cat pick the route at each intersection, because Sammy knew they were looking for the fastest way to Goblin Mountain, and he could always find the right path.

Nevertheless, they noticed some of them. One side path was marked STOCK MARKET—SEE THE BULLS AND BEARS. Gwenny was extremely curious about those animals, for she had never seen either variety in Xanth. They could hear an occasional noise, as if big creatures with hard feet were stampeding, alternating with depressing growls. Whatever could be going on there? Another side path was marked COM-PEWTER—THE NICE MACHINE. Gwenny didn't quite trust that either. A third path was marked THE BIG TOP; they were able to see the upper surface of a mountainous spinning top beyond the trees.

Then they encountered someone going the opposite direction. It was a young human man and an odd dog. The man was perfectly ordinary, but the dog was made out of stone. The two came to a halt as they saw the three.

''Oh, hello,'' the man said. ''Are you looking for the Good Magician's castle? Because if you are, you're going the wrong way.''

''No, we just came from there,'' Gwenny said. ''We're going to Goblin Mountain.''

He peered down at her. ''I say! You're the prettiest goblin I've seen!''

At that point, by sheerest coincidence, a shy fly came by and smacked her right in the face. Gwenny started blushing too badly to speak.

Che stepped forward. ''Perhaps we should exchange introductions before we part," he said. "I am Che Centaur, and this is Gwenny Goblin and Jenny Elf. And Jenny's cat, Sammy." Sammy was sniffing noses with the stone dog.

"I am Alister," he said. "And this is my dog Marbles. We're going to ask the Good Magician about finding a magic talent for my father. My talent is finding things. I can find anything except an answer."

"That's Sammy's talent!" Jenny exclaimed. "He can find anything except home."

Alister was surprised. "I thought no two people ever had the same talent."

"Sammy's an animal."

"Oh. Then it must be all right. I was afraid we were in the wrong time, or something."

"Stranger things happen," Che said.

"Actually, I was amusing myself on the way, because I know this path leads to the Good Magician's castle. I was seeing whether I could find special things along the way, without deviating from the path. This time I had decided on the prettiest girl in the region. I can see my talent is in good working order." He glanced again at Gwenny.

And she had the tremendous misfortune to get stung by another shy fly just at that moment. Again, her blush drowned out her effort to speak. Oh, how that embarrassed her!

Then they resumed their walk to the northeast, and Alister and Marbles continued southwest. Gwenny wondered whether they really could be in the wrong time. Wouldn't that be odd, meeting folk who were there some other time!

"Actually, the soldier Crombie finds things, too," Che remarked in an afterthought. "I understand that he closes his eyes, whirls around, and points, and whatever he is seeking is in that direction. But he's pretty old now, so maybe he doesn't do it anymore."

Gwenny finally recovered from her shy attack. How embarrassing to have it happen just then! He had seemed like a nice young man, for a human being. "Maybe it isn't finding that's the talent that can't be repeated," she said. "Maybe it's *how* a person finds something. Crombie whirls around, and Sammy just runs; Alister must have some other way."

"That is surely it," Che agreed.

"Meanwhile we had better find a place to camp for the night," Jenny said.

Sammy bounded ahead. Jenny ran after him, as she always did. "Wait for me, Sammy!" she cried, as she always did. But he didn't wait, as he always didn't.

Gwenny and Che were used to this. They ran along after the two. Soon they came to a pathlet to the side, and ran down it. It led to a large spreading tree. Its branches formed a big cuplike center covered by broad mottled leaves. Sammy jumped right up into this cup and stopped.

Gwenny examined one of the leaves. She discovered to her surprise that the mottles were in the form of legible print. I AM THE MINISTREE. WELCOME TO MY BRANCH.

"A ministree?" Jenny asked. "Sammy, are you sure—?" But the cat was licking his paw, ignoring her.

So they all climbed into the center cup. One of the branches extended down to the ground so that Che was able to walk up it without much trouble.

They discovered good fruits on the tree, and found that the bark of the branches was spongy and comfortable to settle down on. A number of the big leaves hung low. Gwenny picked another and read it.

HAVE YOU CONSIDERED PROTECTING THE TREES OF XANTH?

She picked another. OUR MOST PRECIOUS HERITAGE IS OUR PLANT LIFE.

Hm. Were there random messages, or was there a pattern? She picked another leaf, randomly, and read it. WE URGE ALL FEELING CREATURES TO CONSERVE THE VEGETABLE KINGDOM.

"I think this tree is trying to tell us something," Gwenny said, showing the leaves she had picked.

"Well, it seems to be ministering to us," Che said.

"That is consistent with its identity. Perhaps it is also ministering to the environment of Xanth."

Gwenny thought about that, and decided it was all right. "Sammy was right," she said. "This is a good place to stay. And we should try to preserve the good plants of Xanth."

She picked another leaf. THANK YOU, it said. PLEASE REMEMBER NOT TO LITTER.

"We won't litter," Gwenny promised.

Che picked a leaf. REMEMBER WHAT THE DEMONS DID TO THE KISS-MEE RIVER it said.

"That was a terrible thing!" Che agreed. "We hope the demons learned their lesson."

The tree's leaves rustled with appreciation. It was satisfied that its ministry was effective.

In due course they settled down to sleep, each nestled comfortably on a broad branch. Gwenny took one last look around before closing her eyes.

Che, the youngest of them, was already asleep. Gwenny saw his dream. It formed in the air around him, like a picture projected on him, so that he was both lying quietly on the branch and being active in the dream. In the dream he was spreading his wings and flying up into the sky. Up, up he flew, gloriously, spiraling in the sunlit air, for it was full day in the dream. He sailed over the ministree and on over the Gap Chasm, which was close by to the north. He felt wonderful; there were little lines of joy and excitement around him, showing his feelings.

Then he looked down and back, and saw the cup of the ministree, where his two friends remained. "I can't desert them!" he exclaimed. He began spiraling down as the dream faded out.

Gwenny was touched. The young centaur had personal aspirations, but he also had loyalty. His dream had shown that more perfectly than words would have.

She looked at Jenny Elf, who had now drifted to sleep. In her dream she was standing on the ground, holding her cat. "I wish I knew the way home," she said.

Then Sammy jumped from her arms and bounded away. "Wait for me, Sammy!" she cried, chasing after him. "You'll get lost!"

The cat leaped through a shimmer in the air and landed in a strange scene beyond it. Jenny followed. It remained fairly dark; the night had not changed to day. They charged through a weird un-Xanthian landscape, where trees were subtly and unsubtly different and bushes were simply not the kind that grew in Xanth. There were two moons hanging in the dark sky. Jenny and Sammy ran up to a huge tree, where several big canine animals lounged. "The Holt! The wolf-friends!" Jenny cried joyfully. She threw herself among them without fear.

People came down from the tree. No, they were huge elves, with pointed ears and four-fingered hands like Jenny's. They embraced her joyfully. "Jenny! We thought you were lost! We feared that something terrible had happened to you! We feared you were dead or cruelly hurt!"

"No, I'm all right, I'm all right!" she replied. "I've had the most wonderful adventure!"

"But what is that thing on your face?" one of the adults asked.

Jenny put a hand to her spectacles. "Oh, I got these in Xanth! They help me to see clearly!" Then she stood still. "Xanth! My friends! I can't leave them! Not while they have such important things to do! And the Good Magician—I have to serve—I promised—"

Then her dream faded out. She was back in the ministree. She, too, was loyal, even in her sleeping fancy. She wanted to go home, but wouldn't until she had met her commitments.

Gwendolyn Goblin closed her eyes, but she felt the tears squeezing out anyway.

Next day they thanked the ministree for its hospitality, promised to treat plants and trees with respect, and set out refreshed. By noon they reached the Gap Chasm. It was as awesome as it had been from the other side.

"But how are we going to get down this clifflike slope?" Gwenny asked, appalled at the magnitude of the challenge.

"I can make us light enough to handle the climb safely," Che said. "All we need to do is find a section where there are sufficient handholds. It may be tedious, but feasible."

"Why not just jump?" Jenny asked. "It would save us time and scratches."

Gwenny laughed. "That far? We're not crazy!"

"But if we are light enough, we wouldn't land hard enough to hurt, would we?" Jenny asked.

Gwenny's outgoing glance collided with Che's incoming glance. The elf might be right!

"Perhaps we could verify it," Che said.

"How?" Gwenny asked, not at all easy about such a descent.

"We could make the C-A-T light, and inquire the fastest and safest way down. If he were to J-U-M-P—"

Jenny looked at Sammy. "You aren't fooling him. He's been listening in on all our lesson sessions, and probably can spell as well as we can."

"But he's an animal," Che said.

"Sammy, find C-H-E," Jenny said, facing away from the little centaur.

The cat leaped onto Che's back.

It seemed that the centaur had been stung by a shy fly this time. His face, neck, and shoulders turned red. Gwenny knew how he felt. Sammy, however, looked smug.

They decided to try it. After Che cooled off, he flicked each of them several times with his tail, making them so light that they had to pick up stones for ballast. Then he flicked Sammy similarly.

"Sammy, find the fastest and safest way down into the Gap Chasm," Jenny said to the cat.

Sammy ran along the brink of the chasm. They followed. He came to a smoothly slanting face of rock where a small river crossed on the way down. The river found a rounded channel farther down and happily coursed along it.

Sammy ran away from the river. He stopped at a tree with leaves as big as any member of their party. They were glossy and looked slippery and tough.

"A toboggan tree!" Che exclaimed. "We must pick leaves for ourselves and Sammy."

They did so, carrying them back to the brink.

Sammy jumped onto his leaf, which then overbalanced and slid into the river. The cat rode the leaf down across the rock face and into the channel.

Jenny jumped after him, riding her leaf. Gwenny was next, and then Che. They were all in the small river, sliding down. It was fun, in its way, but scary, for they were moving very fast despite their lightness. It was the current of the river that was carrying the leaves along at its own pace, not that of their bodies. They clung to their leaves.

The river twisted around, seeking what seemed to be the most devious possible route. It shot through a narrow channel, then paused in a brief pool, then set out again across another slanting stone face. Then it leaped gleefully out into space. "Ooooo!" Gwenny cried with mixed joy and horror. But the leaf landed gently on another slope, and continued down.

Suddenly the river curved and spread out. The world seemed to be set on right angles. Then Gwenny realized that they were at the bottom; it was the normal level land that seemed strange, after the long slide down the side.

They got off their floating leaves and waded to the bank of the river. They were wet around the edges, but were safely and swiftly down. Sammy had indeed known the way.

The base of the chasm was almost level here. There was green grass and a number of bushes and even small trees. There was also a beaten track down the center. They knew what used that: the Gap Dragon.

Indeed, as they spied the track they felt a shudder in the ground. The dragon was coming!

"Get out your pass, Gwenny," Che reminded her. "We don't want the dragon to get confused and eat us."

Gwenny reached for her pocket—and stood appalled. The pass was gone! It must have fallen out during their wild ride down the slope.

"Oh, no!" Jenny said, looking at her and understanding her expression. Then: "Sammy, find the pass!"

The cat headed back the way they had come. But he stopped at the base of the slope. It was too steep for him to climb. The pass must be somewhere up the side of the chasm—and they could not reach it.

Meanwhile the shuddering was intensifying. Now they could feel a distinct whomping pattern to it. The dragon was definitely bearing down on them.

"Oh, what are we going to do!" Gwenny cried, terrified.

"Sammy!" Jenny called. "Find the best place for us to hide from the dragon!"

The cat did something strange: he hesitated. He took a few steps toward Che, then away, seeming not to know where to go. That suggested that there *was* no good place to hide from the dragon. This was the bottom of the Gap, his hunting ground; it was to be expected that he would have everything covered.

A column of vapor showed above the bushes to the east. That was the steam of the steamer! In a moment the dragon himself would come into sight, and in another moment he would be upon them.

If there was no place to hide, what was their best course? Was there any way for them to save themselves? Gwenny cudgeled her mind, trying to think of something. But her head was too jam-packed with fright to let any positive thoughts through. She saw Jenny and Che similarly petrified.

The dragon appeared. He was long, low, and sinuous, with six squat legs, vestigial wings, big teeth, and a lot of puffing steam. His front set of legs would lift and jump forward, and then the middle set, and finally the end set, proceeding by rapid whomps, so that his motion resembled that of a racing caterpillar more than that of a serpent. He was moving far too swiftly for them to outrun, however.

She saw Sammy standing there. Too bad she couldn't ask him what they should do! But the cat didn't solve problems, he just found things. When they weren't hopelessly out of reach, like their safe-conduct pass.

The dragon turned to whomp straight toward them, his scales glistening green. Jets of steam shot forward from his nostrils, singeing the foliage of the bushes on either side. The three of them would be steamed and cooked before they ever got chomped.

Then half a thought squeezed through her mind, perhaps shoved from behind by the overload of fright thoughts. "Sammy!" she cried. "Find the best thing for us to do!"

The cat bounded toward Che Centaur and leaped onto his back, digging in his claws. Che, startled out of his stasis, jumped forward—right toward the onrushing dragon. He passed Gwenny and Jenny and came to a stop, petrified again. His little wings fluttered pitifully. Gwenny remembered his dream of flying; in the dream his wings had fleshed and feathered out, but in life they remained inadequate. They were simply too small with too few flight feathers. He could not fly away, even if he made himself light enough to float like a bubble in the air; the wings just weren't ready.

Could Sammy mean for Che to flick them all again with his tail, making them all air light so that they could jump too high for the dragon to get? If so, it was already too late, for Che would be the first one chomped. Anyway, unless there came a good wind, they would just drift back down to the ground where they jumped from, and the dragon would be waiting to snap them up. There weren't even any good-sized trees here that they might hide in, out of reach of the dragon. The chasm was a trap, sure enough.

The dragon whomped up to Che—and stopped. His horrendously toothed mouth opened. His tongue came up. He licked the centaur on the face.

Then Gwenny caught on. "He's a winged monster!" she cried. "Even if he can't fly, he still has wings. Just as you do. And no winged monster—"

"Will hurt me!" Che finished. "How could I have forgotten!"

The dragon eyed Gwenny. He oriented his snout toward her. "Tell him I'm your friend!" Gwenny cried. "And Jenny too! And Sammy!"

"They're my friends, Stanley," Che said quickly. "We are traveling together. We had a safe-conduct pass from Ivy, but we lost it."

The dragon nodded. It was evident that he recognized Ivy's name. Now it was all right.

Gwenny felt her knees turning to wet noodles. She hoped they didn't look too bad. She was glad that Sammy Cat had known what to do. If Jenny had not come along, then neither would the cat have come, and then Gwenny herself might have been steamed and eaten before Stanley realized she was with Che. That thought made her noodle knees turn to mush, which was even worse. Steam had that effect.

Not only did the dragon not eat them, he turned out to be quite friendly, now that he knew they were all right. Maybe he missed his years of growing up with Ivy, who by an odd coincidence had once been the same age that Gwenny and Jenny were now, fourteen. In fact, by an almost unbelievable coincidence, she had also once been Che's age of seven. So the dragon might have a fond memory or two left in his hot skull of young folk. In fact, Gwenny caught glimpses of steamy daydreams he had, of cute little Ivy playing with him, enhancing his scales until they shone like mirrors, and kissing him on his ear. An offshoot dream memory was of him losing an ear, a long time ago, to an ogre, but he had grown it back when he got rejuvenated. Dragon ears, Gwenny knew, were very special things, with magical properties. That was one reason dragons didn't like to lose them.

Stanley guided them to a place where a walkable path climbed up the north slope of the chasm. There had been others, but the dragon had passed them by, perhaps knowing that they led only to caves or just petered out, getting tired long before reaching the top. The dragon knew exactly which ones offered no hope of escape, of course, because he caught and steamed and ate any creatures who tried to flee on them.

"Thank you, Stanley," Gwenny said as they were ready to part. Then she did something daring and naughty: she leaned down and kissed his ear, the way his memory daydream had shown Ivy doing. By yet another unbelievable coincidence, a shy fly stung him at that very moment, and the dragon's scales blushed burning red. Even his steam turned pinkish. But he did not look unhappy.

They started up. Sammy led the way, because he had been told to find the safest path, with Jenny following. Then Gwenny, and Che bringing up the rear again. That was because, as he explained, centaurs had better rears than other folk did. Also, if one of the others slipped and fell, he would be better able to catch and hold that one, making her light so that they did not both go tumbling down into the chasm. Che himself retained most of his full weight now, because it gave him better traction.

The path did try to trick them by sending off occasional offshoots that led either to cliff brinks or nowhere. One offshoot started out nicer than the true path, but they could see how it then turned and tried to go straight up a cliff. That was a mean-spirited path! But Sammy didn't even think about being fooled; he pattered right on up the correct path every time.

It was a wearying climb, despite the way Che lightened them when they came to brief landings where his tail could reach them. Then a cloud appeared and eyed them.

"Oh, no," Gwenny breathed. "I hope that isn't—"

"Fracto!" Jenny finished, her dread echoing Gwenny's own.

"It isn't," Che said. "That's an ordinary cumulus humilis cloud. They don't mean any harm to anyone. They're just curious about landbound activities."

"Fun loving?" Jenny asked. "I'm not sure we'd like a cloud's idea of a joke."

Che smiled. "That's humilis, as in humility, not humorous. No joke."

Gwenny felt her knees softening again with relief.

"Hey, stiffen up your knees," Jenny said warningly as she glanced back. "They look like bread dough."

"Noodle dough," Gwenny said.

"Pasta," Che corrected them.

"Past what?" Jenny asked.

"Past a bit of dough, but not beyond spaghetti," he explained.

Gwenny concentrated, stiffening them, and managed to maintain her pace.

As they neared the top, the day was fading. It was still bright above, but the depths of the Gap were in deepening shadow, so that they could no longer see the bottom. Gwenny was glad they were going out of it instead of into it; it was gloomy, though she knew that there was no longer much danger down there for them. Unless they fell.

She shuddered, and kept her eyes on the path ahead.

At last they emerged. They walked a reasonable distance from the awesome brink, then dropped to the ground, feeling faint with relief.

"I'm glad I'm not adult," Che said. "Because then I would have had to face that without being afraid."

"Actually, we may be adult," Gwenny reminded him. "We were inducted into the Adult Conspiracy, remember."

Jenny laughed. "That's like the Gap Chasm! Deep and dark and wearisome, and not a lot down there once you see it."

They all laughed, but there was too much truth in it to sustain the laugh for long.

Then they had Sammy find them the best place to camp for the night, and they dined on the wonderful assortment of pies that grew in this region. They even found an old tent left by tent caterpillars; it made a perfect place to sleep, because it was silken throughout, with a layer on the ground to shield them from bugs, and silk hammocks hung from the branches of trees beside the tent.

So they slept in fairly good comfort, and they really needed that after their arduous day's trek. Gwenny didn't see any of the dreams of the others, because she fell asleep as fast as they did and sank down almost as deep as the Gap Chasm. In fact she probably dropped below the dream realm, because she didn't remember having any dreams.

In the morning they discovered that their tent was close to a village. "That would be the Gap Village," Che said, consulting his memory. "I believe there is also a goblin village to the east, if you wish to—"

"No, I think not, thank you all the same," Gwenny said quickly. "It would be run by goblin men, and you know how they are."

"Unfortunately I do, no offense."

"But when Gwenny becomes chief, all that will change," Jenny said brightly. "Because they aren't so bad, when they have proper leadership. In fact, Idiot, Moron, and Imbecile are sort of fun. Remember how they brought us tsoda popka, and we had a squirt fight?"

Gwenny had to smile. "That was when joy came into my life, in the form of the two of you. I must confess I am uneasy about returning to Goblin Mountain." That was the understatement of the year!

"We are here to make you less uneasy," Che said.

"Oh, you are doing it!" Gwenny exclaimed. "Let me hug you!" And she hugged each of them in turn, just so glad to have them both with her.

"Meow," Sammy said.

"You too!" Gwenny agreed. She picked up the cat and hugged him carefully, and kissed his whiskers.

Then they wrapped up their business and proceeded to Gap Village. It was a small one, and the folk did not seem to be unduly curious about them, though it was surely not every day that an elf, a goblin, and a winged centaur passed through.

They caught a path in the center of town, and took it north toward Goblin Mountain and the regions between. But soon they reconsidered. "Do we really want to pass through dragon country?" Gwenny inquired. "Even if the path is enchanted to be safe, I'm not sure how far it extends in that direction."

"We could cut across to the Sane Jaunts River," Che suggested. "And make another raft, and float down toward Goblin Mountain."

Gwenny grimaced. "We did not have exactly the best experience the last time we made a raft," she said.

"But we can't get blown out to sea, on a river," Jenny said. "And it would allow us to travel while resting our legs."

Gwenny looked down at her legs. They were not turning into pasta at the moment, but the prospect of resting them was appealing.

So it was agreed. They took the next side path east, and in the afternoon came to the big river. It seemed far too wide to have originated north of the Gap, but Che had the answer to that: "I understand it crosses the Gap. It flows down the south side, and up the north side. I suspect it has to use magic to make the climb, but rivers always do what they need to to get by. Every one of them knows where there is the sea or a lake, and winds toward it unerringly. It is part of their water magic."

They foraged for suitable wood, and for vines to lash the sticks together, drawing on their prior experience. By nightfall they had a big unruly raft. But they were satisfied with it, because any water dragons who tried to chomp it would get a mouthful of messy branches, and would probably give up the effort before causing any real damage. A fire dragon could set the wood on fire, of course, but it was unlikely that any fire breathers would be on the river. They stocked the raft with many pillows and towels, so as to have comfortable beds and masks against smoke and steam, just in case. And of course they stocked a pile of assorted pies, together with many milkweed pods.

They floated down as the night closed. Che had assured them that his geography showed no waterfalls on this river. They might get hung up on overleaning tree branches, but that would merely delay them, not hurt them. Progress might be slow, because the current was easygoing, but they would be able to keep moving day and night, which was nice.

Indeed, it seemed that the river dragons were not paying attention, because they passed the night unmolested. In the morning they were well along the river, significantly closer to Goblin Mountain. Then Gwenny glanced up, and saw a flying dragon circling overhead. Oh: the winged monsters were still watching, and must have let their river-dwelling cousins know that this raft was to be left alone. That was the advantage of having Che Centaur in their party.

In two days they drifted about as close as the river cared to go toward Goblin Mountain. Gwenny could understand why it preferred to stay clear. They left their big raft with a certain regret and resumed their foot trek.

Now they walked west toward the mountain, which loomed in the distance. It was Gwenny's true home, but she had seldom seen it from the outside, and it looked awful. In the past two years she had developed an appreciation for the open outdoors, and for the surface cabin of the centaurs. When she had visited home, the centaurs had normally carried her there through the air, and she hadn't worn her spectacles, so that she had not seen it clearly. That had been more of an advantage than she had realized at the time.

But worse was her dread of the even uglier goblin politics she knew she would encounter therein. She had been protected from that sort of thing by her mother, but now she knew that she would face the worst of it, and Godiva could not shield her from very much. But maybe with the help of her friends she could find her way through that morass too. She hoped.

A goblin guard noticed them. He had of course been snoozing on the job, but now he jumped up and waved his club. "Get out of here, you freaks!" he yelled politely.

"Oh, don't be silly, Hawkspittle," Gwenny retorted. "Go tell the Lady Godiva her daughter's here."

Hawkspittle rubbed his eyes. "Oh, it's you, Gwendolyn," he said, recognizing her. He turned about and went into a hole in the mountain.

In due course Gwenny's mother came out, her voluminous hair swirling with authority. She hurried to embrace her daughter. "Oh, Gwendolyn, you're just in time. Thank goodness you're here! Something terrible has happened!"

Gwenny's feeling of dread intensified. "What, Mother?"

"It involves your half brother, over whom my authority has disappeared since the death of your father. Now he is worse than ever."

"I think that is impossible, Mother," Gwenny said seriously. "What could be worse than his normal brattiness?"

"There has been a violation of the Adult Conspiracy."

Now the dread welled up like a monster from the gourd. "You mean he—he *knows?*"

"Yes. And he is threatening to tell it to every child in Goblin Mountain, if he isn't made chief by high noon tomorrow."

Now Gwenny understood how this related to her. Gobble was her only rival for chief, because he was the only other child of Gouty Goblin. But he was too young, at age twelve, except by special dispensation. With an awful threat like that, he might obtain that dispensation.

Gwenny, at age fourteen, and now legitimately in the

Adult Conspiracy, just barely qualified for the office. But she was a girl, which was two strikes against her. Her bad eyesight would have been the third. She had fixed that, but if Gobble's disgusting ploy worked, it would make no difference. Goblin Mountain would not only have another bad male chief, it would be the worst possible one—and a juvenile too. Instead of improving, the goblins would become much worse than before.

And it was her job to prevent that. She was the only one who could. If only she had some idea how!

Chapter 9. Humfrey

Okra now felt distinctly awkward in her panty, though it hardly showed on her dark body. She, too, had been deceived by the Demoness Metria. It wasn't that Metria had lied, she had just failed to clarify the truth, knowing they would misunderstand. Okra was of course stupid enough to do that. It made her feel slightly less worse to know that Mela Merwoman had also been deceived. Thus they had both uwittingly violated the Adult Conspiracy, and given the demoness her demonic laugh for the day.

Well, Magician Grey Murphy had said that there would be better clothing for them inside. That would be welcome! Now all they had to do was get inside.

The Good Magician's castle stood in the center of a circular plane. A breeze wafted out from it. As they approached, the breeze became a wind, then a gale, and finally a storm too strong to go against. Their hair streamed out behind them, and they leaned way forward, but their feet slid against the sand and they could not make further headway.

"A challenge!" Okra said.

"It must be," Mela agreed. "But since it's only wind,

maybe we can get around it and get blown into the castle from the other side."

So they walked around the edge of the plane. But the wind kept blowing at them, and when they were on the opposite side, it was still blowing them away from the castle.

"How can it be a circular wind?" Ida asked. "I mean, where is the wind coming from?"

"I think I heard of something like this," Okra said. "A story of places called the—the Propeller Plains. I wonder if this could be one of them that maybe the Magician borrowed to use as a challenge?"

Mela nodded. "Maybe my magic manual shows it." She dug it out of her purse and turned the pages. "Yes. The Propeller Plains are in western Xanth. They are big invisible blades that turn over their planes, sucking air down from above and blowing it out along the ground. You just have to go around them."

"We have been around this one," Ida said. "But the castle is in the center."

"There must be a way," Mela said. "There's supposed to be. All we have to do is find it."

Okra got down flat on the ground, to see if she could crawl under the propeller. But the wind was just as strong there. She scooped some sand out with a hand, but the wind immediately filled in the hole with more sand. She couldn't dig under it either.

"There must be something we haven't seen yet," Ida said.

They retreated to ponder the matter. Beyond the edge of the plane were bushes and trees and a shed. The shed was filled with small figures. "What are these?" Ida asked, picking up one of the figures.

"It seems to be a doll," Mela said. "With a drum."

"A toy?" Okra asked, picking up another. It did indeed seem to be a little drummer boy with two sticks to beat his drum. In back was a key. She turned the key, and when she let it go, the doll's arms moved, making the sticks strike the drum in a faint pitter-patter.

"Do you think these dolls have anything to do with the challenge?" Ida asked.

"They must," Mela said. "But how can a little doll stop all that fierce wind?"

"A doll that drums," Okra said, intrigued. "I never saw one of these before." She wound her doll. "Drum, doll, drum!"

"What did you say?" Ida asked.

"Doll, drum," Mela said. "Isn't that—?"

"Maybe it is!"

"What is?" Okra asked, perplexed.

"When the doll drums, maybe— Come on, we must try it!"

They hurried back to the plane with Okra's doll, to her confusion. "Now make it drum," Mela said.

Okra wound the key a turn and let it go. The doll drummed. The wind died.

"It works!" Ida exclaimed, clapping her hands.

"Why did the wind stop?" Okra asked, still confused.

"The doll drums make it stop," Mela explained. "Doldrums! Those are calm regions. That's how we can get through!"

But then the wind resumed. "No problem," Mela said. "We just have to wind the doll more, so it will drum longer."

"Maybe we should take several dolls," Ida suggested. "So that when one stops, we have another, and don't get blown away."

"Excellent notion!"

They gathered two dolls apiece, and wound one each. "We'll take turns," Mela said. "When mine stops, let yours drum, Ida, and when that stops, you let yours play, Okra. Meanwhile we'll each wind our other doll and hold it ready, so that the drumming never stops. We should be able to make it all the way to the castle, if we're careful."

They did so. They found that it didn't matter if two dolls were going at the same time, but if there was even a moment when none was going, the winds resumed fiercely.

So they overlapped them, and walked steadily toward the castle.

When they reached the moat, the winds stopped. They experimented, letting their dolls run down. The wind resumed, but now it was beyond them. They were inside it. They had passed the first challenge.

But the second challenge was already hard upon them. A horrendous dragon was running just outside the moat, charging toward them.

"Eeeek!" Ida screamed. "What kind of dragon is that?"

Okra peered at the monster. She had seen dragons on occasion, when ogre males got into fights with them, so she knew the basic types. They could be flying, ground, or water; fire, smoke, or steam, in any combination. This one wasn't flaming, smoking, or steaming, so it might be a rare "breathless" dragon, still dangerous. It was on the ground and lacked wings, so was landbound. Yet there was something odd about it. The scales of the back were not lying flat; some were sticking up in rows.

"A weird one," she said. "But it does have teeth, so we need to get out of its way."

"But we can't go back the way we came," Mela said. "The wind would blow us away, unless we kept playing the doll drums, and then the dragon would probably snap us up."

"And we can't go into the castle, because the drawbridge is up," Okra said.

"Then we'd better run," Ida said. "Because that thing is getting awfully close."

They ran ahead of the dragon, around the moat. But the monster was gaining. "Do we go into the wind or the water?" Okra asked. She was moving along well enough, but the other two were puffing. That was because they weren't ogres.

"The water!" Mela gasped.

So they swerved inward, and plunged into the moat. They got enmeshed in moatweed, and Mela wound up astride a thick tentacle of the stuff. "Oh, yech!" she exclaimed. "I forgot it was fresh water!" She slapped the weed tentacle, and it sank back into the murky water. "I can't change to my tail in this stuff."

Ida was no better off. Her clothing was now festooned with soggy weed, and her hair was green with moat slime. "Yech," she echoed.

But Okra's mind was on business. "The dragon's still coming after us!"

"We'll have to swim across," Mela said. "It probably can't swim."

They tried to swim, but there turned out to be a fierce current in the moat that carried them right back to shore. Worse, the dragon was entering the water—and it floated! Its raised scales formed a barrier against the water, so that its body was much like a boat. It could handle the water better than they could.

The dragon floated near them. Its toothy head loomed close. It was about to gobble them up!

"Maybe we can talk it out of eating us," Okra said without any great effusion of hope.

"That's an idea!" Ida agreed. "Maybe it will work."

Mela hauled herself upright, thigh deep in the water, and faced the monster. The creature's gaze bore down on her. There was a reflection of plaid in his eye. "I say, dragon, let's introduce ourselves. Who are you, and what is your business?"

"I am Dragon Dola," he replied. "I am going to put you in my belly."

"But we aren't very good to eat," Mela said. "I'm Mela Merwoman, and I taste rather fishy. This is Okra, and she tastes like an ogress. And that's Ida, and her soggy clothing would snag on your teeth."

Something about the dragon nagged at Okra. His name and the way he floated, reminded her of something. "His name—it means something. Something that floats—"

"I'm sure you will all fit nicely in my belly," the dragon said, cranking his jaws open.

Then Ida figured it out. "You're not a dragon—you're a gondola! A type of boat. We misheard your name!"

"Dra Gondola, at your service," the dragon agreed.

"So all we have to do is climb into your belly, and you'll carry us across the moat!"

"Exactly."

So they climbed over the upright scales and into the belly of the boat. Then Dra lifted his head high, paddled his feet, and moved smoothly across the water. The current didn't bother him, as he was mainly above it.

Okra was amazed. All they had had to do was get the dragon's name right, and he was part of the solution instead of part of the problem.

Dra Gondola reached the inner shore and crawled up onto the land. "Time to disembark," he announced.

"To do what kind of barking?" Okra asked.

"To get out before you get barked at," he clarified.

They clambered out. "Thank you, Dra," Mela said.

"I might not have helped, if I hadn't been dazzled by your panty," the dragon confessed.

"Oh!" Mela exclaimed, blushing in a plaid pattern. Okra had not known she could do that.

Dra slid back into the water and paddled back across the moat. Their second challenge had been navigated. Now all they had to do was pass the third and enter the castle.

The main gate was closed. Mela tried the latch, and the gate opened. They went in. Could this be all? No third challenge? Okra didn't trust that.

They walked on through a wide passage. The stones of the castle arched up overhead, closing it in. It was dark, but not too dark; they could see light at the end.

They reached that light—and discovered that it was the other side of the castle. They had walked right through it without really getting in.

They walked back through, looking for side passages, but there were none. It was just a tunnel through the center of the castle, going nowhere.

"I think we're in the third challenge after all," Ida remarked.

"We must have to find the entrance," Mela said. "But I certainly don't see it."

"We'll just have to look better," Okra said. She put her hands to the wall, feeling the stones. She pulled—and a stone swung out. It was a door! It seemed to open into some sort of closet.

The others crowded close. But when it was all the way open, there was a surprise. "Boo!" something cried, rattling.

"Eeeek!" Ida screamed, and Mela gasped. Okra slammed the door closed. For there in the closet was a skeleton. It was a small one, but definitely human. Every bone was bare.

Still, they had discovered that the walls of the tunnel were not solid. Where there was one door there might be another. Okra felt along more stones.

Soon she found another door stone. Cautiously she pulled it open.

"Boo!" It was another little skeleton. Okra shut the door.

So it went. There turned out to be many doors, but behind each was a rattling bony figure. There was a skeleton in every closet.

They sat on the stone floor in the center and consulted. "Maybe we could go on through a closet, if a skeleton weren't there," Ida suggested.

"How can we get into the castle proper when there's no way past those little horrors?" Mela asked. "I certainly wouldn't want to touch one!" But then she reconsidered. "They aren't all horrible. I remember now. Marrow Bones was a good creature, and so was his friend Grace'l Ossein. But they were adult skeletons from the gourd."

"From the gourd?" Ida asked.

"You don't know about the realm of the gourd? It's where bad dreams are made, for the night mares to carry out to deserving sleepers."

"Yes, I know that. My tutor told me. But I didn't know that any creatures could come out of it, except the night mares."

"Well, they seldom do. But sometimes funny things happen. Marrow and Grace'l had quite a story. They helped me, actually; that's how I recovered my firewater opal."

Okra noticed that a closet door was opening a crack by itself. Could the skeleton be listening? Maybe talk about big skeletons interested little skeletons.

Could that be a way through? If they got all the little skeletons listening, so they didn't want to yell "boo!" all the time? Okra wasn't quite sure how that would help, but it seemed better than nothing.

"Tell us about Marrow and Grace'l," Okra suggested.

"Yes, I'm curious too," Ida said.

"Well, it really isn't—" Mela started to demur. But Okra nudged her gently with a toe. Then Mela saw the partly open closet doors, and realized that something was happening. "Very well. It all started, as far as I was concerned, when Marrow brought Prince Dolph to me in a boat. Actually the boat was made up of the bones of Marrow and Grace'l; it was weird! I saw that cute prince and decided that he would do for a husband, once he came of age to join the Adult Conspiracy." She paused. "Do you suppose those little skeletons in their closets are youngsters? Then I mustn't say any more about that!"

"How many adult skeletons are out of the gourd?" Ida inquired.

"Only those two, I believe. So they made a couple." Then Mela's eyes widened. "Why, these little skeletons must be theirs! There's no other way, because any other little skeletons would still be in the gourd."

"So there can't be very many," Okra said. "Maybe only one or two, and they move around to block off any doors we open."

Mela nodded. Then she resumed her history. "So I took the little prince down to my cozy den under the sea, and fed him nutritious food. But the little mischief changed into a gourd and I got caught by its peephole. Then Marrow Bones came down to take him away. But we made a deal: in exchange for the prince, they would fetch me back my lost firewater opal. So Grace'l remained with me as a hostage, and I let the prince go."

Okra saw the doors opening farther as the little skeletons listened. There were only two of them, it seemed. That would be about right for a family of four.

"So then the prince and Marrow Bones went to beard Draco Dragon in his den, where he hoarded my precious opal together with another he had. They fought, and the prince changed into all sorts of shapes, but it was an even contest. Then they had to make a truce, to attend Chex Centaur's mating ceremony. But while they were gone, the goblins raided the dragon's nest, and only Marrow Bones was there to defend it. I must say, he behaved exactly like a hero, fighting off all those goblins alone."

The doors opened all the way, and the two little skeletons came out, fascinated by the history. They weren't nearly so frightening, now that they were acting like children instead of like spooks.

"He used all sorts of skeleton tricks," Mela continued. "He had the bats who helped guard the dragon's nest dump the gems into the water, and the fish who also helped guard the nest bit at any goblin who tried to get those gems. But in the end the goblins pulled his bones apart and put them in bags, and got most of the gems. He hid the two firewater opals in his skull, but the goblins took his skull too."

The little skeletons crept closer, listening. They were almost within reach.

"When the prince and dragon returned, they discovered the disaster," Mela continued. "So they enlisted the help of the naga folk, and Prince Dolph agreed to marry Princess Nada Naga, when they both grew old enough. Later he changed his mind and married Electra instead, but that's complicated. The naga intercepted the goblins and rescued the treasure. And Draco Dragon was so grateful to Marrow Bones for all he had done that he gave him both firewater opals, and he brought them back to me. I was so pleased! So I wish him all the best, and his offspring too.''

Then Okra caught one little skeleton by an ankle, and Ida caught the other by a wrist bone. They struggled, but they were too small to win free.

"And you must be Marrow and Grace'l's children," Mela said. "How nice you look! What are your names?"

"I'm Picka Bone," one said. "I'm Marrow's son."

"I'm Joy'nt," the other said.

"Well, you seem like two fine boys," Mela said.

"I'm not a boy, I'm a girl," Joy'nt said. "I'm Grace'l's daughter."

"Oops. I couldn't tell, without—" Mela paused, evidently concerned about the Adult Conspiracy.

"I have an extra rib," Joy'nt explained. She flicked a rib with a bone finger, and it chimed.

"And you are serving your service for an Answer," Mela said. "And you did very well. But I think now we shall be able to get through one of those closets without getting spooked."

"We just wanted to hear about daddy's great deeds," Picka said.

"And about mommy's trial," Joy'nt said.

"Well, I hadn't gotten to that yet." So then Mela told them all about Grace'l's trial for messing up a bad dream. They had evidently heard all this before, but never tired of it, in the manner of children.

And while Mela talked, she got up and checked the nearest closet. Sure enough, it now had no spook, and it led into the castle proper. They had found the way past the third challenge.

Inside they found Humfrey's Mundane wife, Sofia. She was old but brisk. "You must clean up immediately!" she exclaimed. "You have moat moss all over you! And you'll have to put on something more than panties. I fear that dressing all three of you is more than I can handle. Socks are more my specialty.''

"We're sorry," Mela said, sounding as shamefaced as Okra felt.

"I will have to exchange with Rose," Sofia decided. "She's expert with dresses."

"We don't mean to be any trouble," Ida said. "We just came for some Answers."

"Not garbed like that!" Sofia said firmly. "Suppose someone saw you? Now get in the shower, and I'll see about exchanging."

Obediently they marched into the shower. This was a chamber with a dense little raincloud floating above. The moment they stepped in, it proceeded to rain on them. The water was cold, but that couldn't be helped. They struggled out of their soiled clothing and stood bashfully bare, getting cleaned by the water.

Okra, shivering, had an idea. "Maybe if we make the cloud mad, it will heat up."

"Oh, that does make sense!" Ida exclaimed.

"So who is the best at insulting clouds?" Mela asked, bemused.

"Let me try it," Okra said. "I'm going to pretend it's Fracto." She took a breath. "Cloud, listen to me. I think you're the ugliest bit of fog I've seen."

The cloud twitched. It was listening.

"I've seen big clouds and small clouds," Okra continued. "But you're the puniest excuse of all."

The cloud developed a pink fringe. It was getting angry!

"I've seen satisfying clouds and maddening clouds, but you're far from the maddening cloud."

Little flecks of lightning zapped through the cloud. It was really getting furious. Indeed, its water was warming.

"In fact—" Okra began.

"Enough," Mela whispered. "The water's getting too hot." She was using a carved soapstone on her body. It cleaned off the grime wherever it rubbed. Okra had not seen this type of magic before, but she liked it.

"In fact, I guess you're okay," Okra said.

The rage of the little storm subsided. The water went from hot to warm. As it sank back to cool, they got out from under, having finished their shower.

They found cottonwood towels and dried themselves off. It was a job to get their hair dry and fluffed out, for all three of them had whole hanks of it. Mela's was golden in the air, but sea green when wet; Ida's was light brown above, turning green-yellow below; Okra's own was of course ogre dark.

Then Mela put on one of her spare plaid panties, and Okra put on her spare black panty, and Ida dug her spare yellow panty from her purse. Her remaining clothing was still sodden; she rinsed it out under the cloud.

They stepped back into the larger chamber. There was a new woman. She was dressed like a former queen or princess, with roses on her gown. "Oh, you must be Rose!" Okra said.

"So I am," the woman agreed. "Sofia exchanged with me. And you three are surely Mela, Okra, and Ida. Let's see about dressing you. I have a collection of clothing left behind by various parties, and I think some of it should fit you, with a few adjustments."

Rose did indeed know her business. For Okra she produced a pair of ocher dragon leather pants and boots, making her an ocher ogre, as well as stainless steel gauntlets and an umber vest and jacket lined with a golden fleece.

"I have heard so much about you," Okra said shyly.

Rose was surprised. "You have? But I have been back in Xanth only recently."

"I know Magpie, the demon maid. She said—"

"Oh, Magpie! She's the only demoness I know with a tender heart. She doesn't have a heart, of course, but she acts as if she does. I didn't know she was working among the ogres!"

"I think it amuses her. The way it amuses Metria to trick people, only Magpie never tricks anyone."

"That is true," Rose agreed.

For Ida she brought a princessly blue dress and slippers. "Oh, I couldn't wear that!" Ida protested. "It's far too fancy."

"Oh, it's all right," Rose said reassuringly. "This is one of Princess Ivy's dresses. You are just about her size. She's visiting Castle Roogna now, a place dear to my heart, but I'm quite sure she will be glad to have you borrow it."

"A princess!" Ida exclaimed, dismayed. "No, she wouldn't want a lowly person like me to touch her things!"

"Trust me," Rose said, with a subtle smile. "She is a sharing person."

Then she dressed Mela. "Sofia was right: you cannot go around showing mantraps like those," Rose said, glancing down at the plaid panty. "Any male who saw you would freak out."

"They did," Ida said, giggling.

Soon Mela was wearing a nice plaid skirt which completely covered her panty, so that if a naughty gust of wind should happen to blow it up, no one would realize that the matching panty had been exposed. That should save a number of males from risk. Above, she wore a heavy-duty halter which must have been left by a sea horse, and a blue green shirt with wave patterns on it. Okra would hardly have recognized her, if she hadn't been present for the change. Mela looked just exactly almost like a full human woman, with the accent on the full.

Then Rose showed them to a mirror wall, and Okra almost didn't recognize herself. "But I too look almost human!" she said. She had never thought that what was possible for a merwoman was feasible for an ogress. It was disgruntling, and an ogre without grunts would be in a sad state.

Rose considered. "You're right. We must do something about those gauntlets." In a moment she brought a pair of elbow-length black gloves. "Put these on instead."

"But I like the gauntlets!" Okra protested. "They are ogre style."

"Then perhaps you can wear them over the gauntlets," Rose suggested.

They tried that, and it worked. The outline of the gauntlets softened, and now Okra's hands and arms looked nearly completely human. It was embarrassing.

"Now you must be hungry," Rose said. "Sofia is better at meals than I am, so I will switch back with her."

"You can switch back and forth, just like that?" Okra asked.

"Oh, certainly. As long as there is only one of us here in Xanth at a time."

"But don't you get into any differences about whose turn it is?" Ida asked.

"Oh, no. We have known each other for a long time, and we are all friends. We have much in common."

"In common?" Mela asked.

"Humfrey."

Oh. Okra realized that it probably would be awkward for more than one wife to be here at a time.

Then a strange animal appeared in the doorway. "Eeeek, a monster!" Ida shrieked.

Rose laughed. "No, that's only Canis Major. He's from the Dog Star. He's very Sirius."

"He certainly looks serious," Mela agreed.

"He's a dog of the species transmuto," Rose explained. "Each day he is a different breed. He was invisible when our last visitors were here, so they never noticed him. Today he is nondescript; tomorrow, who knows? Let him sniff you, so he will know you."

Canis approached. He sniffed each of them in turn. Then he wagged his tail. They discovered that it was fun petting him. None of them had seen such a creature before.

"Now you must be hungry," Sofia said from the doorway.

They jumped. For a moment it seemed that Rose had changed into another species, but Okra realized that she had merely exchanged again with the other wife. This must be a strange household!

She brought them to the dining room and served them homemade shepherd's bread from a large old black iron kettle with a lid on, in the big stone oven. She sliced up the bread and made toasted cheese open-faced sandwiches served with pumpkin-seed sauce, fresh razzleberries and cream in glass bowls, fresh figs from the figment tree, and watermelon shells full of fresh water.

Okra lifted her sandwich to her mouth, and paused. Its open face was frowning.

"Just bite into it," Sofia said.

"But I'm afraid it will bite me back."

"No, I'm mundane. My food is mostly unmagical. My open-faced sandwiches aren't really alive."

Okra poked the face with a finger, and it didn't react. She realized that it was merely a molded face, not a real one. So she bit into it, and it tasted magically good.

For dessert they had cheesecake scented with key lime juice and topped by crystals of citrus rinds. There was also what Sofia called chocolate bliss: fresh chocolate cake served with a dish of white chocolate and raspberry sauce swirled together. The cake was topped with candied violents which whipped the cream.

Finally Mela protested. "You folk are being very nice to us. But we came here to ask the Good Magician our Questions. We don't deserve all this attention. In fact, we expect to have to serve our years for our Answers."

"That's no reason not to treat you courteously," Sofia said. "I spent a good many years with Humfrey, and we always treated querents well. After all, if they have the gumption to come through the challenges, they deserve some respect."

That did seem to make sense. "But we had better go ask the Good Magician and get it over with," Ida said.

"I'm afraid you will have to wait until tomorrow morning," Sofia said. "The Magician is indisposed today."

"You mean he's grumpy?" Okra asked. Immediately she regretted it, because she could tell by the reactions of the others that she had pulled another ogreish social blunder.

But Sofia only smiled. "That is his nature," she agreed. "Every decade he gets a little worse. But of course he has a lot on his mind. However, I'm sure he will see you in the morning."

Their room for the night was piled with pillows. Okra sniffed the air with her sensitive ogre nose. "Someone has been here," she said.

"Well, of course," Sofia said. "This is our guest chamber. I wasn't here, but I understand that the last group of querents visited during Dana's watch. A goblin, an odd elf, and a winged centaur foal. They have been the objects of some interest among those of us who now reside down in Hell, as have you three."

"Us?" Ida asked, startled.

"Of course. All of us were curious about the color of—"

"My panties!" Mela said, seeming not entirely pleased.

"And about the identity of Ida, who it seems was lost by the stork near Nymph Valley. And Okra, who it seems was displaced by Jenny Elf."

"Displaced?" Okra asked, as startled as Ida had been.

"Oh, didn't you know? There was to be a Jenny character, and the choice was between an elf girl and an ogre girl, and the elf was chosen. So she is Jenny Elf, and you are a minor character."

"I was supposed to be a major character?" Okra asked, a strange emotion coursing through her.

"Well, only if you were chosen. But you weren't, so it doesn't matter. Well, good night." Sofia departed.

Mela and Ida rearranged the pillows, doffed their new clothing, and soon settled down. But Okra remained in a morass of emotions. She had had a chance to be a major character—and someone else had horned in! That elf had gotten it. She could smell the traces of Jenny Elf, who had been here. She smelled like no ordinary elf, because there was no particular elf scent associated with her. That was odd. But it made her easy to identify. Okra would not forget that scent.

Slowly a thought percolated through her ogre brain. Her Question for the Good Magician had already been half answered. Jenny Elf had gotten the status that might have been Okra's. But if something happened to that elf, then there would be only one person to have that status: Okra herself.

How could she get rid of Jenny Elf? That was now her Question.

In the morning they got up, dressed, and joined Sofia for a breakfast of pease porridge. Some of the peas were hot and some were cold and some looked as if they had been in the pot for some time. "This is just right for eating, now," Sofia said, confirming Okra's impression. "It is exactly nine days old."

Mela picked out some hot peas, and Ida selected cold ones. But Okra liked those that were nine days old.

At last it was time to see the Good Magician Humfrey. Sofia ushered them into the smallest, dingiest, most crowded chamber of the castle. There, almost lost amidst the piled tomes, was an old gnarled gnome of a man. This was Himself.

He looked up. "What do you want?" he demanded grumpily.

They hesitated. Then Mela spoke. "We—we have Questions, sir."

"Don't call me sir!" he snapped.

"No, your majesty."

"Don't call me that either. In fact don't call me anything. It only wastes time."

"Uh, yes," Mela agreed, out of sorts.

"Well, get on with it," he grumped.

Mela took a breath, which was impressive even in her clothing. "How can I find a suitable husband?" she asked.

He squinted at her appraisingly. "By that you mean a

nice, handsome, manly, and intelligent prince who is partial to sea creatures, of course.''

''Of course,'' she echoed.

He looked at Ida. ''And you?''

Ida was startled by the abruptness of his attention. ''I
seek my destiny. I—''

''Yes, yes, everybody does,'' he said. His gaze oriented
on Okra. ''You, ogress?''

''How can I get rid of Jenny Elf?'' Okra asked boldly.

Mela and Ida were appalled. ''You can't do that,'' Mela
said. ''She's a major character.''

''If there's a way, he should know it,'' Okra said.

''There is a way,'' Humfrey agreed. ''There's always a
way. There are Answers for all three of you. But I have
decided not to give them, on the grounds that it would be
counterproductive. Now go away and let me get my work
done.''

''But—'' the three said together.

''The Good Magician has Spoken,'' Sofia said gently.
''There's no arguing with him when he's like that. You
will have to go.''

''Now wait a minute,'' Mela said indignantly. ''We had
to go through the challenges, and we got thoroughly
gunked up in your smelly freshwater moat. At least tell us
a better why.''

The Magician ignored her. ''Please, don't aggravate
him,'' Sofia urged. ''He's difficult enough already.''

''At least a hint,'' Ida said. ''I'm sure he could spare
that much.''

''Yes,'' Okra agreed.

The Magician looked up, but did not speak.

''Yes, a hint,'' Mela said. ''Or else.''

Humfrey scowled. ''Or else what?''

''Or else I'll show you my panty,'' Mela said. She
turned around and put one hand on her skirt. ''And freak
you out.''

''Oh!'' Sofia exclaimed, appalled.

The Good Magician seemed almost to smile. "Then go see Nada Naga." He returned to his musty tome.

Sofia bustled them out. "What a disaster," she muttered.

"Well, at least we did get a hint," Ida said.

"But he'll be insufferably grumpy for a week!" Sofia said. "Oh, why did this have to happen on my watch?"

"I'm sorry," Mela said. "I suppose I shouldn't have threatened him. But he wasn't being nice."

"He's never nice. And he always has reason. There must be some calamity that will happen if you three get your Answers."

"What's wrong with my getting a prince to marry?" Mela asked.

"And my finding my destiny?" Ida asked.

"And my getting rid of Jenny Elf?" Okra asked.

Sofia looked at her. "That last I can answer, I think. Jenny is a nice girl. She doesn't deserve bad treatment."

"I don't want to treat her bad," Okra said. "I just want to be rid of her, so I can be a Major Character. Maybe she could go back to where she came from."

"I don't know," Sofia said. Then she bustled them on out of the castle. They had definitely overstayed their welcome.

Chapter 10. Gobble

Godiva led the way into Goblin Mountain. Che had visited here with Gwenny several times in the past two years, but this was different, because he was aware of a muted hostility in the other goblins which hadn't been there before. They knew that he was Gwenny's companion, and that she was first in line to be the new chief, and the goblin men feared and loathed that notion. The goblin women might feel otherwise, but they would not dare evince even half a scintilla of support for fear of retribution if Gwenny didn't achieve the office. Gwenny was essentially alone, for now, except for her mother and Che and Jenny Elf.

In Godiva's pleasant suite they had a proper meal (no tsoda popka) while she acquainted them with the situation. "It seems that when my husband died, in the general confusion Gobble was able to sneak into his father's chambers. He went there to steal anything of value he might find, of course, trusting that no one would notice. But he got something far more treacherous than mere objects. Gouty had a dragon's ear."

"A dragon's ear!" Che exclaimed.

She glanced at him. "I see you understand. A dragon's ear can be used to hear things magically, when properly

182

applied. Exactly what is heard varies with the species, and
sometimes with the dragon. Little is known about this, of
course, because dragons' ears are hard to come by. But
some ears will hear anything spoken about the one who is
listening with the ear. Some will tune in to any spoken
dialogue within a certain range. Some will attune to one
particular person, and overhear what he says and nothing
else; others will hear only what is said to him. Gouty's ear
was of the limited-subject type: it could overhear whatever
was spoken in Goblin Mountain on a particular subject.''

''What subject?'' Gwenny asked.

''Whatever subject the listener wished. I believe Gouty
used it to tune in on conspiracies against him. Only now
do I comprehend how he had such uncanny ability to discover such plots, as he had never seemed unduly intelligent. I despised him, of course, but I always supported
him because it was the proper thing to do. Obviously he
knew that, because of the ear; he allowed me more power
than is normally given a woman, and supported my effort
to obtain a companion for my daughter, because he knew
that I intended him no harm. Also because it gave him
more time to play with other women during my absence.''
She glanced at Che. ''But the companion was what was
essential, whatever the cost. You of course know how that
particular endeavor worked out.''

''I know,'' Che agreed.

Godiva paused as if gathering herself for something unpleasant. Then she continued. ''Gobble found that ear. He
had it for only an hour before he was discovered and relieved of it. But in that time the damage was done, for he
has always had an unerring nose for the worst possible
mischief. I think you can surmise to what subject he tuned
it.''

''The Adult Conspiracy!'' Jenny exclaimed.

''Exactly. You might suppose that a single hour would
not be enough, but it is with a dragon's ear. Gobble evidently did not learn the nuances or the rationale, but he

did learn the forbidden words." She glanced at Gwenny.
"I understand that you have now joined the Conspiracy."

"The Good Magician required it," Gwenny said. "All
three of us learned it. Actually we didn't learn the forbidden words, just the—the essential nature of it."

"You will recognize the words the moment you hear
them. They are superficial, but to those of a certain, shall
we say, mind-set, they are overwhelmingly important.
Certainly they have power, and this power should never
be abused. Naturally our menfolk do frequently abuse it."

"Naturally," Gwenny agreed without irony.

"Gobble learned the words, and now threatens to shout
them at the children of Goblin Mountain, as I mentioned.
That would of course do them incalculable harm, and perhaps destroy the integrity of the Adult Conspiracy itself.
This cannot be allowed."

"It cannot," Gwenny echoed, her dark face pale.

"But how can he be stopped?" Jenny asked.

"I have a plan," Godiva said. "But I think only you,
Gwenny, can put it into action, because you are the only
one who has any vestige of nominal authority over Gobble. You are technically his elder sibling. He does not see
it that way, but the men of Goblin Mountain dare not gain-
say it. I dread giving you this terrible duty, but I see no
other way."

Che saw Gwenny swallow, and knew she dreaded it
also. "I will try, Mother. What is your plan?"

"You must take the magic wand that only I and your
grandmother Goldy know how to use. I will show you its
secret. With it you will be able to hoist any person or thing
into the air and move it where you wish. That should suf-
fice to control Gobble physically, for a while."

"But he will still be able to speak the words," Gwenny
said. "I won't be able to keep him from the children very
long. And when it is time for the new chief to be selected
all the goblins of the mountain will be present, including
the children, and he will be able to freak out everyone
who isn't in the Conspiracy."

"I know that, dear. But that is only the first step. You must travel through the deepest caves to where there is an offshoot of the darkest river of all, called Lethe."

"Lethe!" Che exclaimed. "The river of forgetfulness!"

Godiva glanced at him appreciatively. "I see you are developing centaur knowledge. Yes, it is that river. It is dangerous, for a person who finds it and drinks can forget his way home. In fact he can forget his whole life, if he overdoses. But properly used, this enchanted water can cause selective forgetting, and that is what we want in this case."

"To make Gobble forget the words he learned!" Gwenny said.

"Even so. You must take him there, sprinkle him with just a few drops of Lethe water, and say the words you wish him to forget. Then he will be harmless."

"Why not just dunk him in the river so that he forgets everything, and can't even be chief?" Jenny asked.

Godiva shook her head. "That is not allowed. Gobble is illicit in birth and manner, but he is Gouty's child and must be protected by all goblins of the mountain. Gwendolyn must not begin her chiefship with a crime against the succession. The same law that gives her authority over her half brother requires her to protect him from harm. This treatment with Lethe water is part of that; his mind has been warped and must be restored."

"But how do I find that river?" Gwenny asked, evidently daunted by the prospect.

"Sammy can find it!" Jenny said. "Only—"

"Only he can't find home again," Che finished. "But I have a good memory. Once there, I will know the way back."

"But I wasn't asking the two of you to take this horrible risk!" Gwenny said. "This is something I must do myself."

"I am your companion," Che said firmly. "I shall not desert you in your hour of need."

"And I am Che's companion," Jenny said. "And

Sammy is mine. We are all with you, Gwenny, until you are chief. After that you will be able to dismiss us if you wish to. I will be going to the Good Magician's castle anyway."

"In my place," Gwenny said. "I already owe you so much! I just can't ask you to risk your life this way!"

"And you *didn't* ask us to," Che said. "We decided." Jenny nodded agreement.

Godiva looked at him. "You are the truest of companions, Che. Because of you my daughter has had two years of life on the surface which has surely been a delight for her, and has received an excellent education." She glanced at the elf. "And because of you, Jenny, she now has her magic lenses and a way to find the River Lethe. I have not yet properly demonstrated my appreciation, but I shall do so in due course."

"And so will I, somehow," Gwenny said, her eyes glistening. The lenses she wore were invisible; her eyes seemed entirely natural and beautiful. In fact the whole of her was the same. He remembered how nice it had been to kiss her, even in play. With his new understanding of the Adult Conspiracy, he realized why that was. Of course theirs would always be what the elder centaurs called a platonic friendship, because they were of different species, and crossbreeding was frowned on. His granddam Chem had scandalized the centaur community when she bred with Xap the hippogryph to produce the winged centaur filly Chex. The goblins had been similarly scandalized when Glory Goblin had married Hardy Harpy and the stork had brought them Gloha, the winged goblin girl. But there was more reason than scandal: he had a duty to preserve and extend the species that had come into being. But where would he ever find a winged centaur filly?

Che hauled himself back from the nebulous clouds of speculation to reality and turned to Godiva. "I assume that Gobble will be helpless as long as the wand keeps him floating, away from any handholds. But I suspect this trip to the River Lethe will be arduous. What happens when the tunnels become too narrow to keep him away from the walls? What happens when we have to sleep? How do we feed him without having him grab on to us?''

"I do not know the full route, but I know how it begins," Godiva replied. "There is a great vent in the stone, a veritable nether chasm. Only with the help of the wand will you be able to cross that. Once you are across, Gobble will not be able to return alone, and he will know it. Then you will be able to give him some freedom, because he will depend on you. He will of course try to steal the wand when you sleep, but he will not be able to use it. So that aspect should be satisfactory. No, what concerns me more is the danger of the Lethe itself, and of those dread deep caverns. You will have to start by traversing callicantzari caves.''

"The callicantzari!" Gwenny cried, horrified. Che knew why: those creatures were like huge, stretched-out goblins with their muscles tied on backwards, and they cooked and ate any creature they caught. They were so bad that even the goblins loathed and feared them.

"And perhaps worse beyond,' Godiva said. "I shall not minimize the risk, my daughter, because you must understand it before you undertake it. I fear you may never return. But if you do, you will be fit to lead this tribe. Of that, no one but Gobble will doubt. You must consider whether you would prefer to give up this ambition and go into exile, allowing Gobble to become chief. I am sure the centaur family will accept you.''

"It will," Che said. He could not say more; this was Gwenny's decision.

"Oh, I wish my father had waited a few more years to die!" Gwenny cried with no pretense of affection for the departed. "I am not ready for this!" Then her pretty jaw firmed. "But I will do it. I must save our tribe's children from violation of the Adult Conspiracy, and I must save Goblin Mountain from the horror of Gobble's chiefship. But most of all, I must fulfill the destiny for which I came to be: to lead the goblins into decency. If I possibly can.''

"I had almost hoped you would choose otherwise," Godiva said. "Come, then; I will take you aside and attune the wand to you." She glanced at Che and Jenny. "No offense; if Gwendolyn then chooses to inform you of its secret, that will be her privilege. But I must keep the covenant I made with my own mother."

"Naturally," Che said. The only way to keep a secret was to keep it, and much of the wand's power lay in the fact that no illicit party could use it. Smash Ogre had discovered the key to the wand and given it to Goldy Goblin, long ago, and it had served her and her daughter well ever since.

There was food and beverage on the table. While Gwenny and her mother were away, Che and Jenny sampled them. "Hey—this is tsoda popka!" Jenny exclaimed, tasting from a bottle. "Do you think we should—?"

"We're not children anymore, technically," he reminded her regretfully. "We have to set a good example. No more food fights."

"Too bad," she agreed.

Gwenny returned, holding the wand. "Now I must test this," she said wickedly. She pointed the wand at Jenny, and Jenny rose into the air. Then Jenny descended and the wand pointed at Che. He rose up, made a little circle, and dropped back to his hooves. The wand evidently worked.

"Now to use it on Gobble," Gwenny said. "This is going to be unpleasant, but I have to do it now, before he realizes. Mother will see to it that the children are confined so he can't corrupt them. We shall have to depart immediately. Mother is fixing us packs with food and tools."

"Grab a bite to eat," Che recommended. "It may be long before you have another chance."

Gwenny smiled and did so. Then she led the way through the labyrinth of the mountain toward Gobble's chamber. "He is gorging himself on cookies while waiting for everyone to agree that he must be chief tomorrow," she said. "I don't think he even realizes that I'm back, and if he does, he doesn't care. He thinks he has the ultimate weapon.''

''He did,'' Che said. ''Until you decided to nullify it.''

Jenny picked up Sammy and carried him on her shoulder. Che trotted along behind. He knew this was not going to be pleasant business.

They came to a tunnel where goblins were carrying baskets of cookies. There was no need to ask for whom those were. They followed a cookie toter into a chamber.

There was the twelve-year-old goblin boy, sitting in the middle of a pile of cookies, tossing them into the air and watching them crumble as they struck the floor. He must have eaten all he could hold, but couldn't give up the notion, so was wasting the rest. Only a real brat would do such a thing, but he was of course the realest brat available.

Gwenny went to stand before him. ''Gobble, I have come to put a stop to this,'' she said.

''Oh, hi, sis,'' he said. ''Wanna know what I think of you?''

''No. Come with me, please.''

''I think you're a crummy %%%%.''

There was a horrified intake of breath from a gobliness who happened to be passing by. Several cookies spoiled around the edges. The jaw of a male goblin dropped. Jenny Elf, who derived from a foreign culture, looked sickened.

It was to Gwenny's credit that she managed not to blush. Che realized that she was probably so concerned about the threat to the children of the mountain that she wasn't really absorbing the disgusting nature of the word. He had never heard it before, but its degrading essence struck right through to his mind and lodged there forever. Only his recent entry into the Adult Conspiracy enabled him to hear it without freaking out, and he knew that the tender minds of young children would be hideously warped, and that they would grow up to be the worst goblins yet, if such an utterance came their way. There was no doubt about it: Gobble had learned the forbidden words.

"I ask you again," Gwenny said evenly. "Come with me, and do not utter any more such filth."

"Yeah? Make me!" Gobble took a breath. Then he yelled "****!"

Now the cookies around him sent up wisps of filthy smoke. The gobliness, who had just been recovering from the last word, reeled anew. The male goblin began to smile. He of course lacked the gumption to perform such a violation himself, but he was typical of his ilk in his vicarious appreciation of it. Che felt sick, and Jenny was turning a faint mottled green.

"That does it," Gwenny said. Che saw that her jaw was clenching involuntarily. Only raw nerve kept her stable. She brought the wand around and pointed it at the brat. He rose into the air, spilling crumbs.

"Hey!" he yelled, startled. "Where'd you get that?"

"From my mother, not yours," Gwenny said. She moved the wand carefully, and Gobble moved along just above the floor.

"You can't do this!" the boy screamed. "I'm going to be chief! You're just a dumb girl!"

"I'm the daughter of Chief Gouty and his wife, Godiva," Gwenny replied. "As such I am the leading candidate to be the next chief, and I rank you by half your parentage. No one else can stop you, and no one at all can stop me. Now you are coming with me, regardless."

"No I'm not! No I'm not!" he screamed. "Guards! Arrest this impostor! Lock her in a cell!"

But the goblins in the vicinity did not move. They knew that Gwenny was Gouty's legitimate child, and that they could not interfere with her. Not openly. They liked the words, but at the same time knew that no child should be uttering them, so they didn't know quite what to do.

"####!" Gobble yelled. "++++!" But though those nearby blanched, they were all adults, so couldn't be freaked out, quite. The remaining cookies turned into steamy sludge, but the brat remained captive to the wand. So he took a breath and spewed out his ultimate: "$$$$!"

Che's young mind reeled with the onslaught of those abominable words. He felt nauseated, but managed to keep his stomach down and his face straight. He saw Jenny doing likewise, though she was turning a deeper green around the gills. That was a good trick for someone who had no gills.

Gwenny concentrated on her wand, causing the brat to float through the chamber door. He quivered a little, because her control was not yet quite assured, but got through.

"Help me, somebody!" Gobble shouted. "She's kidnapping me! I'm your future chief! Stop her!"

"Stand clear," Gwenny said, and the goblins reluctantly did so. She lofted Gobble on down the tunnel. Che and Jenny followed.

As they passed the nursery where the children were normally kept, Gobble managed to rip out one more word. "< < < <!" he bawled.

But there were no screams of freaked-out children. It seemed that Godiva had had them removed from the vicinity of the exit route. Gobble's awful ploy had failed.

Godiva met them farther along. "Here are your packs. They have food and water for a two-day trip; I hope you can complete it within that time. If not, I hope you can forage." She gave them each one, and tossed one to Gobble where he hung in the air.

"I don't want this junk!" the brat complained.

"Go hungry, then," Godiva said. "It isn't as if anyone would miss you if you starved."

Gobble reconsidered, and put on the pack.

Gwenny and her party moved on out of Goblin Mountain and around to the side where there was a crevice between it and the next mountain. At the end of the crevice was a boulder wedged in a hole.

"Now you will have to hold Gobble for a moment," Gwenny said. She lofted the brat over to Che.

Che grabbed one arm, and Jenny grabbed the other. Neither of them was a goblin, so Gobble had no authority over them. "****!" Gobble cried, struggling, but the word had less force because he had used it before. It seemed that he had learned only six of the seven forbidden words. Certainly they would not tell him the seventh!

Gwenny oriented her wand on the boulder. It looked as if it had been in place about four hundred years, but now it floated out and came to rest a short distance away. Behind it was revealed a dark and dreadful cave.

"Hey, that's where the callicantzari hang out!" Gobble cried, fear tinging his voice. "You can't dump me in there!"

"We are all going in there," Gwenny said.

"Help! Kidnapping!" he screamed in desperation. "We're all going to die in that hole!"

But the goblins on the mountain just stood there helplessly. Gwenny Goblin was the only one they could not interfere with, even if she had a suicidal nature.

Gwenny aimed the wand at Gobble again, and he floated up, his arms and legs waving wildly. He tried to hold on to Che and Jenny, but they stepped out of the way the moment they released him. "Aaaargh!" he wailed as he was lofted into the cave, just as if the others weren't going in with him.

"We need a torch," Che said.

"Yes, it is very dark and dank in here," Jenny agreed, shuddering.

"That, and the fact that the callicantzari are afraid of fire, though I understand they use it to cook their meat. That's part of their fouled-up-ness."

"No," Gwenny said. "A torch would advertise our presence. We must try to get through without alerting them. Mother said there is supposed to be fungus light when it gets deep enough."

"Ha!" Gobble said. "Hey, callicantzari! Come and get them!"

"You will be the first one they eat," Gwenny told him.

That set him back. Then he tried to bluff it out. "How

come? Everybody knows that girls taste better than boys. They'll eat you first, and I'll escape.''

"No. They will do something else to us first," Gwenny said evenly. Che was impressed by the way she was able to speak of that Adult Conspiracy secret without blanching. "And they don't like horsemeat as well as goblin meat, so they'll leave Che too. But you will be just right for them to start with, because you're small and loud and dusted with cookie crumbs. Also, you smell bad, and they have terrible taste. They prefer tainted meat.'' She was showing qualities of leadership, goblin style.

Gobble decided to shut up. He evidently realized that she was probably right, even if he didn't know exactly what the monsters would do to the girls first. It would hardly make a difference to him, if he got eaten first.

They moved on down below the mountain, Gobble not evincing so much as a peep. After a while the fading light from the cave mouth was replaced by yellow, green, and blue glows. The fungus light was showing, in many colors. The farther they went, the more colors showed, until there was a full rainbow spectrum. It was eerily pretty. It showed the outline of the tunnel, because the fungus lined every surface. It wasn't very bright, but would do.

They came to a larger cavern, and then to branching passages. Now it was time for the cat. "Sammy, find the River Lethe," Jenny said, setting him on the floor. "But don't run."

Naturally the cat bounded off at full velocity. That was because he was an animal who didn't truly understand human or centaur imperatives. Jenny started to run after him, but Che held her back. "You'll crash into a stalagmite," he warned.

"But I'll lose Sammy!"

"No you won't. See, there are dark spots where his paws crushed the fungus. We can follow his trail."

He was right, of course. Centaurs always were. The cat's trail was reasonably clear. They could follow it at leisure.

They did so, leaving their own trail behind. But Che knew better than to trust to that for their return; the fungus might regrow and reglow before they came back, erasing their trail. Or other creatures might pass this way, obscuring it. So he made sure to fix the exact route in his memory, so that he could find their way without reference to the fungus.

Then they heard something. A sort of ugly shuffling and scuffling, as if something awful was doing something worse. That must be one of the callicantzari!

"Can we hurry?" Jenny whispered.

They hurried. But when they did, they made more noise—and so did the unseen thing. Now there was more than one ugly noise, as if several things, each more grotesque than the others, were closing clumsily in on them.

Then one of them showed up ahead. It was even worse than Che had feared. It seemed to have started on the frame of a man, but gone astray. It had a grotesque furry face with a bulbous nose and two dirty eye slits and a mouth obscured by twisted fangs. The body seemed to have bones in the wrong places, and the muscles attached backwards, exactly as represented in the centaur classes. It it tried to jump forward, it might lurch backward, though probably it had learned to try to jump backward when it wanted to go forward.

But that was not the worst of it. Its breath was such a foul stench that the fungus around it was turning bilious green. Che knew that they would all choke if they got too close to the monster. "We had better run," he suggested.

"But it's right where we have to go," Gwenny said. "And we don't dare leave the trail; we might not find it again."

She had a point or two. But Jenny came to the rescue: "Use the wand on it!"

"But then Gobble will run away," Gwenny said.

"I don't think so, because there's another monster behind us. Gobble's safer with us."

Gwenny set Gobble down, and sure enough, the brat

did not run. She aimed the wand at the monster, and the callicantzari made a noisome moan, or maybe a moaning noise, and sailed away backwards.

Then the four of them charged forward down the tunnel. The monster behind pursued, but it was so disjointed that it couldn't keep the pace. The one ahead kept floating backward, because of the magic of the wand.

The tunnel widened into a passage, and the passage into a hall, and the hall into a gallery. They had to dodge around the many supporting columns. Fortunately the glow fungus made each one stand out, so they could see it coming.

Suddenly they came to a great dark cleft in the floor. There at the brink of it was a small furry shape, while the monster was suspended over the chasm. Che realized that this could be an extension of the great Gap Chasm, gone underground. If so, there was no hope of getting around it; they had to go over it.

"Sammy!" Jenny cried, swooping down on the small shape. Che realized that the cat had been stopped by the chasm, so had simply waited for them to catch up. That was just as well, because if Sammy had tried to hurdle the cleft, and missed—but obviously he had more sense than that.

Gwenny dumped the callicantzari on the other side, then aimed the wand at Che. "If the monster tries to get you, I think there's a knife in the pack," she said.

"I'll just make him light and throw him away," Che said more confidently than he felt.

Then he floated across the gulf, and landed on the other side. The callicantzari did come at him; he spun aside and flicked it with his tail. The monster, abruptly lightened, leaped into the air—and plunged into the chasm. Che was chagrined; he hadn't intended that. He watched the thing float slowly down. At least it wouldn't land hard.

Meanwhile, Gwenny was lofting Gobble across. Then she started on Jenny. "But wait—how will you get across?" Jenny asked.

"Oops—I hadn't thought of that," the goblin girl said, chagrined.

"There should be a rope," Che called, rummaging desperately in his pack. In a moment he felt it. Godiva had indeed had the foresight to provide them with this most useful tool for cave delving. "Catch this, and I will haul you across." He knotted the end and hurled it across the chasm.

But Gwenny was now facing the other way. One of the callicantzari was lumbering at her. She lofted it up and back, so that it tumbled into the one behind, and they both became a writhing mass of limbs and torsos, each part worse than the rest.

Jenny caught the rope and tied it to a column. "But then the monsters may use it too," Che said. "And we won't be able to get it back."

"Yes, we will," Jenny said. "You don't want to try to hold her full weight; she might drag you both down. So tie your end to a column, too."

Che obeyed, anchoring his end firmly. "But—"

Jenny turned to Gwenny. "Now you climb across on that rope. Quickly!"

"But I haven't lofted you across yet!" Gwenny protested.

"Right. I'll go last. Move!"

Gwenny put away her wand and took hold of the rope. She had strong goblin hands, and was able to hand herself across in short order. As soon as Gwenny completed her crossing, Jenny untied the rope at her end. It slid into the chasm, but Che hauled it up on his side.

But another monster was coming at her. "Look out!" Che cried as the monster reached a twist-fingered hand for her.

Jenny scooted away, but the clumsy arm came down, brushing her head. A backward finger caught the bow of her spectacles, and they were ripped off her face.

"Oh!" Jenny cried, suddenly blinded. She staggered forward, trying to see where she was going.

The callicantzari clung to the spectacles. It brought them to its face. It was trying to eat them! Che and Gwenny watched in horror as it crunched them between its tusks.

Jenny staggered toward the chasm. "No!" Che and Gwenny cried together.

Then Jenny stepped over the brink. She screamed as she fell into the awful depth.

But in a moment her descent stopped. Jenny rose back to the top, and came toward them.

Che let out his breath. Gwenny had used her wand to catch Jenny. That had been Jenny's intent when she decided to be the last to cross, but Che had mislaid that notion when he saw the monster almost grab her.

Jenny landed safely before them. Che embraced her. She wasn't as pretty as Gwenny, but she was his best friend, and he was greatly relieved to have her safe.

"Ha-ha, four-eyes!" Gobble said. "They gotcha spectacles! Now you're bat blind!"

Che suffered a surge of fury. He released Jenny and took a step toward the goblin brat. But Gobble was already rising into the air and floating over the chasm. Gwenny was just as angry.

"Don't drop me! Don't drop me!" he screamed. "I didn't mean nothing!"

Now Jenny realized what was happening. "Don't hurt him," she said. "He's just acting the way he is. That's what brats do."

Gwenny hesitated. Gobble shook over the chasm, because her hand was shaking on the wand. Che put his hand on hers and guided it so that the brat floated back to the regular cave floor and landed. He knew Jenny was right; a brat couldn't be blamed for being brattish. Also, Gwenny was supposed to protect her little brother, even if he was a disgrace to Goblin Mountain.

But how was Jenny to fare, now, without her spectacles? The light was dim enough already, and this would probably indeed make her effectively blind.

Gwenny put her hands to her face. Che thought she was

crying. But then she poked her own eye, and something came away from it. It was one of her magic contact lenses!

"Jenny, take this," Gwenny said, pressing the tiny lens into Jenny's hand. "Put it in your eye, and you will be able to see with that eye."

Jenny realized what it was. "But that's yours! You need it!"

"I have the other. We can share. One eye is good enough, down here. When we get back to the surface, you can get another pair of spectacles, and it will be all right. But down here, we need you to see, so you don't step off any more ledges."

Jenny had to acknowledge the truth of that. She rubbed the lens on her shirt, then brought it to her right eye. It went into place, and she blinked. "Oh, I can see again, better than before! But what's that Gobble has?"

Che looked. The brat was just standing there.

Gwenny looked. Her left eye had her lens. "Oh, that's his daydream. The biggest, fattest bottle of tsoda popka ever filled. He lives for junk food." There was a trace of sadness in her voice, which Che understood: now that the three of them had joined the Adult Conspiracy, they were no longer supposed to be interested in junk food. It would take time to adjust to that privation.

Gobble looked at them. "Hey, are you %%%%'s talking about me?"

"Oh, it disappeared," Jenny said.

"Because you jogged him out of his daydream," Che said, though he had never seen the dream.

"Gobble, if you keep using that word, I just may change my mind about dropping you in the gulf," Gwenny said.

Che could see why. That particular term was the most derogatory reference to the female persuasion that existed, which was why it was forbidden by the Conspiracy.

They returned to business. "I don't trust letting Sammy

go ahead loose,'' Jenny said. ''He could have plunged into that chasm himself.''

''Maybe we could tie a tope to him,'' Gwenny suggested.

''No, he wouldn't like that. Besides, it might snag and choke him. But we do need to find the—'' she hesitated, not wanting the cat to take off ''—whatever.''

''Maybe you could hold him, and see which way he wants to go,'' Che said.

''Yes, let's try that,'' Jenny agreed, relieved. She held the cat in her arms. ''Now, Sammy, I want you to stay with me, because it's dangerous here. But I also want to find the River Lethe, and by a safe route. So you just look the way you want to go, and we'll go there. Okay?''

The cat seemed satisfied to be carried. He looked down the tunnel ahead—and both girls jumped. ''Look at that!'' Gwenny cried, delighted.

''Oh, wonderful!'' Jenny agreed.

''What do you see?'' Che asked, mystified.

''Sammy is dreaming the route to the river,'' Gwenny answered. ''It's like a map, with the path highlighted. Now we know exactly where to go.''

''But doesn't your mentioning it make him stop?''

''No, it's still there,'' Jenny said. ''Maybe because he's an animal, and he has a very fixed attention span. When he sets out to find something, he doesn't stop until he has either found it, or been stopped from finding it. I never knew exactly how that worked before.''

''Hey,'' Gobble said, ''you mean those lenses make you see things? Like dreams?''

''Oops,'' Gwenny said. ''We shouldn't have let him know that. He'll blab it all over the mountain.''

''No, he won't,'' Che replied. ''We're taking him to the Lethe, right? That will be just one more thing for him to forget.''

''Hey, I'm not forgetting anything!'' Gobble cried. ''I'm going to remember all the great words, and how my stupid **** of a sister has to use a lens to see, which means she's blind too, so can't be chief, and how she's snooping on dreams.''

"You may forget more than those things, if you don't shut your fowl mouth,'' Gwenny warned him tightly.

The brat shut up for a while, realizing that she was serious. He knew that a fowl mouth was the very foulest mouth, because it referred to the way a harpy talked.

They went on, more rapidly now, because the girls had the cat's mental map to follow. They wound down through what would have been truly awesome caverns if they had been in less of a serious hurry. But they couldn't complete the journey in one trek, so they made camp in a dead-end offshoot chamber and had a meal. They took turns visiting another region for private business, and Gobble had the wit not to call it $$$$ out loud.

Then they settled down to sleep. "I appoint you the watch,'' Gwenny told Gobble. "I'm sure you'll let us know if any monsters approach.''

"Hey!'' he protested. "Why me? I didn't ask to come here!''

"Because you're the cause of this trip, because of the way you corrupted yourself with part of the Adult Conspiracy.''

"Well, how do you know I won't tie you all up and steal that wand, so I can get out of here?''

Gwenny handed him the wand. "Try it,'' she said.

He waved the wand. Nothing happened. "Hey—it's broke!''

"No. It's just not attuned to you. You can't use it. And if you were to tie us up, you would have to make your way back alone. If you manage to get across the chasm, I'm sure the callicantzari will welcome you with open maws.''

Gobble shut up. Che knew he wouldn't keep very good watch, but it didn't matter, because they had assigned him the place at the chamber mouth. Any monster who came would eat him first. His screams would alert the rest of them. Then Gwenny would use the wand to float the monster elsewhere.

It worked perfectly. No monster came.

After a reasonable sleep, they ate again and resumed their journey. Sammy's mental map remained clear to the girls, who seemed to do about as well with one seeing eye apiece as with two. He suspected that was because two eyes were necessary for the magic of depth perception, but dreams lacked depth and the caves had nothing *but* depth, which a single eye already knew.

Finally they reached the River Lethe. It was just a ribbon of dark water, evidently no more than a lost tributary, coming from some forgotten source and going to a forgotten end. But it was one of the most treacherous rivers of Xanth. Water from this river had caused the Good Magician Humfrey to forget his wife Rose for eighty years. That had complicated his life somewhat, when he remembered.

Gwenny got out a small cup and dipped out a tiny driblet. She faced Gobble, who tried to cringe away. But there was nowhere he could go. "Forget these words," she said, and sprinkled him with six drops. Then she gritted her teeth and uttered the awful crudities. "%%%%, ****, ####, ++++, $$$$, <<<<," she said, and then fell back, looking as if she wanted to wash her mouth out. Che knew how she felt; he wanted to wash his ears out.

"It didn't work!" Gobble cried. "I still know them! I can say ____! See?" Then he reconsidered. "Aarrgh! It's gone!" He looked chagrined.

Gwenny dipped out another driblet. "Now you will forget that I have any problem with my vision, or that anyone uses contact lenses, or that anyone can see any dreams with them." She sprinkled him with three more drops.

"Ha!" the brat said. "When I get home, I'll tell all Xanth about—" He paused. "About—oh, mice! I know there's something!"

Gwenny nodded. "Mission accomplished, I think. I wish I could make him forget to be a brat, but without his brattiness he would disappear, because that's his essence."

"Now all we have to do is get safely back to the surface," Che said. Somehow he knew it wouldn't be easy.

Chapter 11. Nada

"**Y**ou really shouldn't have threatened him," Ida said.

Mela nodded, shamefaced. "I know. I was desperate, and it was all I could think of under pressure."

"It's funny," Okra said musingly. "He did not seem frightened or angry, just amused. I wonder why?"

"Oh, I know!" Ida said, realizing. "Because that was the big Question he couldn't answer. So of course he would have made sure to learn it the moment the color was fixed. Probably Sofia told him. He must have been prepared, and wouldn't have freaked out at all if he had seen them."

"Oh, I forgot!" Mela said, chagrined anew.

"But at least we got a hint," Ida said. "We have to go see Nada Naga. I wonder what she has to do with us?"

"I never heard of her before you told the story about Marrow Bones, Prince Dolph, and how he agreed to marry her," Okra said. "Is she acquainted with Jenny Elf?"

"I believe she is," Mela said. "But I don't think she would help you get rid of Jenny."

"Would she know anything about my destiny?" Ida asked, getting interested.

"I don't see why. But if our only hint for our Answers is to talk to her, then we'll talk to her. I understand she's a nice person, and when in her human form, one of Xanth's most beautiful women.''

Ida looked at Mela, surprised. ''You mean you're not?''

Mela seemed taken aback. ''Why, I never thought about it. These legs aren't my usual state. I'm just a merwoman in drag, as it were.''

''In what?''

''In a wrong body, inverted, reversed, seeming other than I am, stranded out of my element—''

''Footsore?''

''Whatever,'' Mela agreed, smiling.

Ida looked around. ''Where do we find Nada Naga?''

Mela pondered. ''I suppose we'll have to go to Castle Roogna and inquire. I understand she lived there while she was betrothed to Prince Dolph. They should know where she is now.''

So they followed the enchanted path toward Castle Roogna. It was easy going, being fairly level, with regular camping places along the way. Ida was rather intrigued by the prospect of meeting royalty.

There was a swirl of leaves before them. The swirl assumed the shape of a voluptuous nymph. ''Did I overhear talk about beautiful women?'' it inquired.

''You don't count, Metria,'' Ida replied. ''You can assume any shape you want.''

''And you don't tell the truth!'' Mela said angrily.

''I always tell the truth,'' the demoness said indignantly. ''Except about my age, which is none of your business.''

''Not the *whole* truth. You didn't tell me to put on more than a panty.''

The demoness shrugged that off as she stepped out from the settling leaves. ''Well, you didn't ask me. What's this about Nada Serpent?''

Ida played the game. ''Nada who?''

''Snake, reptile, python, half human, crossbreed—''

''Whatever?'' Ida suggested.

"Naga," Metria agreed crossly. Then she did a double take. "Hey—"

"Do you know where she is?" Ida asked.

"Of course I know where she is!" the demoness said. "She's with my kind."

All three of them were astonished. "She's among the demons?" Mela asked.

"Correct. There's some very important project in the making, and she's part of it."

"But she's not a demon!" Mela said. "She's a naga princess. What would she want with your kind?"

"Nothing," Metria said. "But she doesn't have a choice. She tasted some red whine in the realm of the gourd. A person can't leave the dream realm if she eats of its substance. She didn't eat, she drank, and she didn't really drink, she only tasted, but it compromised her. So she has a debt to work off before she can be free. She's serving her time."

Ida found this confusing. "But I thought the demon realm was different from the dream realm."

"It is. But a beautiful creature like her is no good for bad dreams, so she's TDY to the demons."

"She's what?" Ida asked.

"Ha!" the demoness said. "Caught you! That's the term I meant to use."

"But I still don't understand it."

"It stands for temporary duty. Tee-Dee-Why. The dream realm is lending her to the demons."

"But what's she doing there that the demons couldn't do for themselves?" Ida asked.

"That's what I'd like to know," Metria said crossly. "But they won't tell me. It's some fat juicy secret, and they're afraid I'll blab it across Xanth if I knew it."

"Wouldn't you?" Mela asked.

"Of course I would! That's my privilege. I'm a gossipy demoness. It really gripes me that they are preventing me from doing my thing."

Ida, however, could see the point of the other demons.

They could not very well keep a secret if one of them blabbed it everywhere.

But Mela had an idea. "We have to go talk to Nada. But we don't know how to get to the demon realm. You, on the other fluke, want to—"

"The other what?"

"Sorry. I'm from the sea. I meant to say hand. You want to know what's happening there. Maybe we can make a deal."

Metria considered. "I get you there, you tell me what's going on?"

"That's it."

"But if they know you'll tell me, they won't tell you. And if I get you there, they'll know."

"You can assume any form," Ida said. "Why don't you assume human form and join our party? Then you can learn it yourself."

The demoness wasn't sure. "Demons are pretty good at recognizing other demons, because we all change form constantly."

"Suppose they never thought to check you?" Mela asked. "If you were beneath suspicion. Some harmless innocent waif, maybe."

"That should work," Ida said. "They *could* recognize you, but maybe *won't.* Because it never occurs to them."

Metria began to be convinced. "But I don't know any harmless innocent waifs."

"We'll invent one," Ida said. "Cerebral, my centaur tutor, told a story of a little human match girl. She was so poor she wore rags. She sold matches. They are magic splinters of wood that make fires when rubbed against things. But no one wanted them, so she froze to death."

"Why didn't she use her magic sticks to make a fire to keep warm?" Okra asked.

Ida shrugged. "I don't know. Maybe she didn't think of it. I think she wasn't a very smart little girl."

"Then that's perfect for Metria," Mela said. "No one will suspect her, because she's really smart."

The demoness seemed tempted. "But what would she be called?"

"Smart Aleck," Okra suggested.

"Perfect!" Metria said. Then she reconsidered. "Now just a minute! That won't do, because I'm not a boy."

"You need a name that is pitifully plain," Mela said. "Because woe betide us all if you get caught."

"That's it!" Ida exclaimed.

"What?" the other three asked in an imperfect but serviceable chorus.

"The name! Woe Betide."

The demoness fogged, then reformed as the smallest, cutest, most innocent ragged little girl imaginable. She carried a box of tiny wooden splinters with red tips. "Please buy my matches," she begged in the most waifish of voices.

"Oops," Mela said. "This is Xanth. We don't have money. So how can she be selling anything?"

"No problem," the waif said. "Demons do anything they want to. Since we can make coins from air, we use them to trade for things." She lifted one hand, and a bright golden disk appeared in it.

"But won't the coins turn back to air again soon?" Mela asked.

"Of course. As soon as we forget to concentrate. So what?"

"But then the sale isn't real!"

"Neither are the matches." The waif held up one, and it puffed into smoke and drifted away.

"But that will give you away," Ida pointed out. "A real waif would have real matches."

Metria sighed. The entire box of matches vanished. "We'll have to make real ones."

They found a Handy firewood tree and peeled off a number of splinters. These worked; when vigorously rubbed against a stone, they burst into fire. Then the demoness made a new box, and put the real matches in it. "That should surfeit them."

"Should what them?" Ida asked.

"Induce, inveigle, assuage, complete, qualify—"

"Satisfy?"

"Whatever," the waif said crossly.

Mela pursed her lips. "I don't think that will do. We shall have to keep the dialogue simple. You're supposed to be unsmart, anyway."

"Maybe just 'Match? Match?' " Okra suggested.

"That's fine," Mela agreed. "Waif, just say that, so you can't mix up the word."

The waif turned wonderful big brown eyes on her. "Match?" she begged pitifully.

"That's it!" Ida said. "That would melt a heart of stone."

"Oh, let's see!" the waif said. She approached a stone that was roughly heart shaped. "Match?" she begged so soulfully that it seemed impossible that she should be a soulless creature.

The stone began to melt around the edges.

"I think we're ready," Mela said. "How do we get there?"

"I can carry you there in a basket," the demoness said. A huge basket appeared.

Ida didn't like the look of that. She remembered how it had been told that Princess Rose had been taken to Hell in a hand basket. So she fashioned an objection. "If we enter the demon realm magically, they will know there's demon magic involved. So we'd better sneak in the way real folk would."

"That makes sense," Mela said. "There must be some secret access."

"There are several," the waif agreed. "But we're not supposed to tell mortals of them."

"And other demons aren't supposed to tell you what's going on there," Ida reminded her. "If we follow those rules—"

"There's one in the Gap Chasm," the demoness said quickly. "I can take you there."

"No, we had better walk there," Mela decided. "So we do it nonmagically all the way. And on the way we can get used to calling you Woe Betide, and you can get used to playing the part. That way we'll be less likely to make a stupid mistake."

To that the demoness agreed. They started walking north, along the first divergent enchanted path they came to.

By the time they reached the Gap, little Woe Betide seemed quite real to them all. She had trouble keeping the pace, and seemed to shiver in her rags though the day was warm, and she answered every question with the plea "Matches!" Ida hardly cared to admit it, but she was developing considerable sympathy for the waif despite knowing she wasn't what she seemed.

Ida was awed by the Gap Chasm. The centaur tutor had told her of it, but she had discounted it somewhat in her mind. Now she saw the vast expanse and depth of it, and knew that it had already been discounted by the centaur, whose memory of it might have fogged just a trifle. There were even small clouds hovering below her eye level, as if the atmosphere of the Gap were a world apart.

There was a bit of a rocky path down the sloping side of the chasm. Ida was nervous about falling off it and plunging down to the distant bottom, but she reminded herself that this couldn't happen if they were careful. The path led to a shallow hollow that didn't show from above, which fed into a cave, which debouched into a crevice, which finally gave up and let them into a tunnel down into the ground. There was a faint greenish glow which helped them see the walls; it was from mold coating them.

"This is an old vole hole," Woe murmured. "Demons don't need tunnels, of course, so they ignored this. But I found it one day while teasing a vole."

"Oh?" Mela said. "I thought the voles left Xanth a thousand years ago."

"Oh, was it that long? I must have been thinking of something else."

Ida wondered. Could the demoness be a thousand years old? It seemed possible.

"How far is it to where Nada is?" Mela asked.

"Oh, several days' walk through the labyrinth. No problem."

Ida exchanged a glance of dismay with Mela. It might be no problem for a demoness, who could jump there instantly, but it would not be any fun for them. For one thing, what would they eat on the way? She wasn't sure how much longer her magic sandwich would last. She also dreaded the notion of sleeping on cold stone in a perpetually dark tunnel. Who knew what monsters might lurk in this region?

"Are there rivers down here?" Okra asked.

A river! That notion was far less unappealing than dry tunnels. They might make a boat and float, saving their feet.

"Oh, yes, there are rivers galore throughout the caverns," the seeming match girl said. "Why?"

Ida and Mela explained why. Metria told them where some pieces of driftwood and flotsam were, and they made their way to these and dragged them to the water. The water had a faint blue glow of its own, contrasting with the green of the walls. It was rather pretty in its sinister way.

Okra used her ogre strength to bend the wood into new shapes and weave it together, forming the raft. She turned out to be good at it, and in due course they had not merely a raft, but a crude houseboat, with a woven shelter above.

"Now if only we had some food," Ida said.

"Oh, that's right; mortals like to eat."

"And match girls like to eat too," Mela reminded her firmly.

"Well, there are blind fish in the river, and water chestnuts and water biscuits and water taffy," the waif said.

"Oh, goody!" Mela said. She lay down on the raft and

put her face over the edge, into the water. In a moment her hand swept down, and came up with a fish. "It didn't see me," she said. "I'll ignite my waterlog, and cook it."

Ida and Okra managed to pick some of the chestnuts, biscuits, and taffy from the shallow edge of the river. In due course they had enough to fill out the meal.

It turned out to be nice enough, in the shelter. The burning waterlog warmed it as it baked the fish and toasted the chestnuts and biscuits.

There was a roar. The three travelers sat up, alarmed. "What's that—a waterfall?" Mela asked.

"No, only a water dragon," the demoness replied.

"Is it dangerous?"

"Only to mortals."

"We're mortals!"

"Oh, that's right; I forgot. In that case you're in trouble."

They peered out the door of the shelter. There was the glowing outline of the toothy head of a dragon. It was about to chomp the raft.

Okra grabbed the burning waterlog by its unburning end and hurled it into the dragon's maw.

The dragon swallowed the log. It looked faintly surprised. It burped. It was not a fire breather, of course; few of that kind liked the water. It gulped water from the river. Steam began to hiss from its ears. Then it submerged.

"Doesn't it know you can't put out a waterlog with water?" Mela asked. "Water is its fuel."

"I don't think it does know," Ida said, not feeling unduly sorry for the dragon.

"That one won't be back," the waif said. "It will take it days to digest that fire, and then it won't feel excruciatingly excellent."

"Feel what?" Okra asked.

"Never mind!" Mela said. "Just so long as it's gone."

"I'm sorry I used up your waterlog," Okra said contritely.

"Under the circumstances, I'll forgive you," Mela said with two thirds of a smile. "I do have another at home."

"Are there any more water dragons?" Ida asked.

"Not on this river," the waif said. "I'm afraid this will be a dull float."

"How unfortunate," Mela said dryly, which was a rare mode for her.

So for the next day or so—it was hard to be sure, since the light never changed—they ate and talked and slept, floating down the dark river. The word must have spread among the local water dragons, because there were no other attacks.

Finally they came to the appropriate region. They drew the house raft onto a dark beachlet and walked toward the increasing light of the demons' mysterious project. "Remember," the waif whispered, "the demons will try to fool you, without actually lying. Every time they do, I will try to sell a match. Then you will know."

Soon they encountered an office cave with a demon at a desk. "Who in heaven are you?" the demon swore.

Mela took the initiative. "We are merely three women and a waif, come to see Nada Naga."

"Who says?"

"The Good Magician Humfrey says. He told us to talk with Nada."

The demon looked at a book which appeared in his hand. "There is no demoness by that name here."

"Match?" the waif begged, proffering her box.

The demon scowled across the desk at her. "Who the delight are you?"

"I am just poor sweet little Woe Betide, eking out her paltry living selling accords."

Oops! Metria had tried to say too much, and had miscued a word.

"Selling what?" the demon demanded, a wisp of smoke curling up from one tusk.

"A cord of matches," Mela said quickly. "Or only one.

Whatever you care to buy, to help the poor innocent defenseless big-eyed cute little waif."

The demon frowned. The wisp of smoke formed a floating question mark. Possibly he was suspicious. A golden coin appeared in his hand. "I will buy a match," he said.

"O thank you ever so much, Sir Demon!" Woe cried ecstatically. She gave him a match.

He took the match and flipped it into the air. It did not puff into smoke and dissipate. He caught it and scratched it briskly across the suddenly marbled surface of the desk. It burst into flame. It really was a match.

Meanwhile Woe had given them the hint: the demon was trying to temporize. What? Ida asked herself. Deceive, cheat, dupe, mislead, delude, she answered herself. Fool? Whatever. So they had to find out what he was hiding. He had said that there was no demoness by the name of Nada Naga here.

Mela seemed to have pursued a similar chain of thought. "We did not say that Nada was a demoness. She is a mortal of the naga persuasion."

"Oh, *that* Nada. She is too busy for visitors at the moment."

"Match?" Woe inquired.

"I already bought one!" the demon snapped.

"No one can be too busy for the Good Magician's business," Mela said. "We must talk with her."

The demon sighed. The wind of his sigh was tinged with frustrated-looking smoke. "Very well. I will have a demon take you to her."

"Match?"

"If you bug me again, Ms. Betide, I will turn you into a silly piece of putty!" the demon snapped.

Woe puffed up. "I'd like to see you try, basilisk-breath!"

All three others closed in on her. "Oh, were you frightened by a basilisk?" Ida asked solicitously.

"Poor little thing!" Mela said.

"I will go stomp on it," Okra said.

Mela turned to the demon. "The poor waif isn't quite right in her mind. I think a basilisk thought about breathing on her mother. I think a regular demon would frighten her. Could you have a demoness show us the way instead?"

The demon blew a double smoke ring tinged with fire. "Anything to get rid of you. Which one do you want?"

"Magpie," Okra said.

Suddenly the demon's suspicion doubled. "How do you know of the one nice demoness?"

"I'm an ogre girl," Okra said. "Magpie came to help at our banquets. She told me how she helped similarly when Rose of Roogna married the Good Magician."

The demon turned pages in his ledger. "I see that Magpie did serve at the Good Magician's wedding to Rose of Roogna. That was a demon extravaganza."

"A what?" Woe asked.

"A bash, event, shindig, fancy occasion, celebration—"

"Blowout?" Woe offered.

"Whatever," he said crossly. Then he stared at her suspiciously. "There's only one creature I know who—"

"Please summon Magpie to guide us," Mela said urgently. "I'm sure she'll be just fine."

"Anything to get rid of you." He snapped his fingers, making sparks fly out, and a grandmotherly figure appeared.

"Magpie!" Okra exclaimed, hugging her.

"My dear, how you've changed!" the demoness exclaimed. "You look almost human!"

"It's this clothing I have to wear among the human folk," Okra said, embarrassed.

"But you look almost nice!"

"I know," Okra agreed, more embarrassed.

"And who are these folk with you? I see that one's human, one's from the sea, and one's—"

"A poor innocent match girl waif!" Mela cried.

Magpie gazed at Woe, evidently not for an instant deceived. "Yes, of course," she said. "Well, where is it you need to go?"

"To see Nada Naga," Mela said. "The Good Magician sent us."

"Very well. Right this way." Magpie walked briskly down a new tunnel that appeared in the rock.

They followed. First Mela, then Okra, then Ida, then Woe. Woe moved up to pace Ida. "She knows, but she's despicably nice," she murmured. "She wouldn't hurt anyone for anything, even another demon. So she's letting me pass."

"Maybe you can follow her example," Ida murmured back.

"Why?"

Ida realized that it was useless to suggest ethics or niceness to a demon. Demons had no souls. They merely did what pleased them, in their various ways. It pleased Magpie to be a nice emulation of a human being; it pleased Metria to be mischievous and curious. They could be trusted to be those things, and no more. Since there were times when it was necessary to work with demons—such as right now—it was best to have a realistic understanding of their natures.

So she revised her answer. "It might be entertaining."

"I doubt it."

So much for that notion.

They came to a cavernous chamber, or perhaps a chamberous cavern. A lot seemed to be going on at once. Demons were everywhere, doing mysterious things. There was a flying dragon in one corner, using a dummy model of a human being for target practice. The curious thing was that the dragon kept missing. Ida realized that it was trying to come as close as it could without actually scoring. Demons were measuring paths, apparently making them as narrow as possible without preventing human passage. Others were digging holes in the ground, and fashioning cunning covers for them, to make them look like safe paths that would actually give way under the weight of unwary travelers and dump them down.

"This looks like a bad dream factory!" Woe murmured. "I wonder whether they're setting up in competition to the gourd realm."

"Why?" Ida asked.

The demoness seemed taken aback. "It might be entertaining," she said after a pause.

"I doubt it," Ida said.

"So much for that notion," Woe said.

Ida had a feeling of déjà vu, but couldn't think of the term and wouldn't have known its meaning anyway, so had to let it go.

Magpie led them to a lovely young woman wearing a serpentine gown. She was standing before a demon in mundane costume, reading a script. "No, I will not do that," she said, facing a blue line which was painted on the ground before her.

"But how else will we get across the river?" the demon asked, reading from his own script. He sounded unconvincing.

"We shall have to find some other way. A princess does not disrobe before a stranger."

"No, no!" an imposing figure of a demon objected. He had gnarled horns and swishing tail, and fangs that shaped his mouth into a set snarl. "Do not volunteer the information! Make him ask for it."

"But it says here—" the woman protested.

"Not anymore, Nada," the old demon said.

Nada glanced at her script. It seemed that it had changed.

They tried it again. "We shall have to find some other way," Nada said.

"But why?" the mundane demon asked, managing to be just as unconvincing as before.

"Because a princess does not disrobe before a stranger," Nada read.

"But I'm not a stranger!" the mundane demon read. "We've been together for hours now."

"Oh. Well, in that case—"

"Cut!" roared the fanged old demon. "Never ad-lib! Is your brain full of mush? Follow the script!"

"But, professor, the script doesn't cover everything. Suppose he tries to kiss me?"

The mundane demon stepped forward and put his arms around her, happy to play the scene.

"Then you change into a serpent and slither away," the professor responded.

The mundane demon tried to kiss her. She became a serpent and started to slither. "No, you don't!" he said, grabbing her by the neck. She opened her jaws, about to bite him.

"Cut!" the professor cried. "You must not bite the Mundane. You are not allowed to hurt him. You are supposed to be helping him."

The serpent became the woman again. "But Mundanes are unpredictable," Nada pointed out. "How can I predict what he might do if I don't teach him some manners?"

"That's what we're doing now: working out all the variations, so that there can be no surprises. Now take it from the top. You come around the bend and spy the river, which bars the way to your destination."

"Oh, this is all so complicated!" Nada exclaimed, throwing up her hands.

The mundane demon reached out and started pulling up her dress. "Eeeeek!" she shrieked.

"Well, he might try that," the mundane demon said.

"Then let's add a motion to the script," she said furiously. "A punch in the snoot."

"A snake can't punch," the mundane demon pointed out smugly. "She has no fists."

"Then suppose I bite his face off?" she demanded, forming the head of a snake with a huge mouth.

"Take a break!" the professor snapped, evidently fed up.

Relieved, Nada walked away from the river. Magpie chose this moment to approach her. "Nada, you have visitors."

"Just so long as they're not from Mundania," Nada said wearily.

"Oh, no, we're from Xanth," Mela said. "The Good Magician Humfrey sent us to talk with you."

"Why would he do that? I don't know you."

"We don't know. We came to ask our Questions, and he wouldn't answer. Instead he told us to—"

The professor interceded. "Get organized!" he said severely, cowing them all. "First establish identities. I am Professor Grossclout, inducted into the direction of this ludicrous charade. This is Princess Nada Naga, one of the leading players in the game and ordinarily a nice person. You four are?" His terrible gaze turned to each of them in turn.

"Mela Merwoman."

"Okra Ogress."

"Ida Human."

"Woe Betide."

"Metria, what are you doing here?" Grossclout demanded. "Weren't you banned from the premises?"

The waif turned the biggest, hugest, meltingest, most tearful doll-brown eyes on him. "Please, professor, I want so much to know what's going on."

"Very well," he said grimly. "You will not only learn, you will participate. As part of that participation, you will be unable to tell any outside party anything about this project."

"I'm not sure I want to participate," Metria demurred.

"I don't recall inquiring as to your wants." The professor gestured. The waif was engulfed in a puff of smoke. When it cleared, Metria was herself again. "You are enrolled," he said. "You will be one of the list of authorized companions. Let's hope no one chooses you."

"I'm getting out of here," Metria said, alarmed.

"You are reporting to your station for rehearsal," he said. "Magpie! Take her there."

The grandmotherly demoness approached the beautiful young one, who seemed unable to flee. "Come, dear. It is really an interesting project." The two vanished.

"But Metria may not like the role," Nada said.

"To be sure," the professor agreed. Then he fashioned his set grimace into something very like a smile.

Ida suspected that the Demoness Metria was receiving her just desserts. Unfortunately such desserts seldom tasted very good.

The professor returned his attention to the three of them. "Now I happen to know Humfrey," he said. "He is a good man, for a mortal, and he normally has sufficient reason for what he does. What were your Questions?"

"How can I get a good husband?" Mela asked.

"How can I get rid of Jenny Elf?" Okra asked.

"What is my destiny?" Ida asked.

"Well, no wonder!" the professor exclaimed. "His Answers would be counterproductive."

"That's what he said," Mela confessed. "But I threatened to show him my panty, and then he told us to talk with Nada Naga. So we made a deal with Metria to get here."

"Now it all comes clear. He acted appropriately. Nada, take five."

The beautiful princess looked around. "Take five what, professor?"

Grossclout's eyes rolled up until the smoldering pupils disappeared, then on around inside his head until they returned to the front. "Five moments. Talk to these querents."

"But I don't understand—" Nada said, bewildered.

"Exactly." The professor stalked away.

Nada looked at them, baffled. "We don't understand any better than you do," Mela said apologetically. "We thought you would know what it was all about."

"I hardly know what *this* is all about!" Nada said, gesturing in a full circle.

Ida, seeing Mela and Nada standing together, found it hard to judge which one was more beautiful. Mela's body was fuller, but Nada's face was prettier. Then again—

"Could it be related to our Questions?" Okra asked.

Nada frowned. "A husband? Jenny Elf's riddance? Destiny? I somehow don't think so."

"I really don't want much," Mela said. "Just the most handsome, virile, thoughtful, intelligent prince available."

Nada stared at her a moment. Then she shook herself, as if not quite believing her own conclusion, and turned to the next woman. "Okra, why do you want to be rid of Jenny Elf? She's a nice girl, and surely never did any harm to anyone, especially you."

"She was chosen to be a Main Character instead of me," Okra explained. "If she goes, then I can be it, and then nothing bad will happen to me, and maybe I'll live happily ever after."

"How long have you been traveling with Mela and Ida?"

"Oh, days! We helped get Mela panted, even."

"Panted! You mean the Good Magician's Question has been answered?"

"Yes. Her panty is—"

"Don't tell me. Such things are not good to bruit about. But I think I'm getting an inkling of the Good Magician's reasoning." Then she turned to Ida. And stared again. "Oh, my! I think I do know your destiny."

"You do?" Ida said, delighted. "What is it?"

"But I don't know exactly why the Good Magician didn't tell you. So I think I must not say what I think. The Good Magician always has reasons, and I am afraid to interfere."

"But surely it can't hurt to—"

Nada shook her head. "I don't mean to tease you, Ida, but I'm afraid I must, to this extent. But I believe that my brother, Naldo, may be able to help all three of you and that the reason Humfrey sent you to talk to me was so that I would refer you to him. Indeed, you would have more trouble finding him than you did me. Here, let me see if I can arrange it.'' She walked to rejoin Professor Gross-clout, who was just standing up, aware of the end of her dialogue by some inherent professorish mechanism. Evidently the five moments were up.

"Yes, I will arrange it," the professor said. "Promise them to secrecy, then tell them what you wish.'' He vanished.

"Secrecy?" Mela asked.

"About this project. Surely you are curious."

"Oh, yes!" Mela agreed, echoed by the other two. "This is the strangest business."

"Then the three of you must agree not to tell any other person about what you have seen here. If you do that, the professor will not use magic to bind you to secrecy, as he has Metria."

The three exchanged a generous four glances. "We agree," Mela said.

"We are preparing for a marvelous game," Nada said. "It will be open to Mundanes, who will get to tour Xanth through it. Each player will be helped by one of us, so that he doesn't get into trouble, such as being eaten by a dragon. If he plays well enough, he can win a magic talent. If he doesn't, he'll be out."

"But what was all that business about swimming or kissing?" Ida asked.

"If I work with a male Mundane, he might get notions about seeing me in panties," Nada explained. "Of course we can't have that. So if we have to cross a river, I won't swim it, unless I change to serpent form. We're practicing how I can dissuade him, if he gets insistent. Everything has to be prepared for, so we don't mess up in the game itself. That's why the dragons are working on their accuracy; they aren't supposed to fry any players, just warn them. But of course the Mundanes won't know that."

"I don't envy you this duty," Mela said. "All because you tasted a bit of red whine!"

"Actually it is interesting," Nada said. "I wasn't doing anything much, after I stopped being betrothed to Prince Dolph. And once it's done, I'll be free. I'm learning a lot, and Professor Grossclout isn't bad, once you get to know him."

"What?"

Nada jumped. There was the professor. "I was only saying how terrible you are," she said quickly. "A real brute of a monster, with no consideration for personal frailty."

"That's better. Arrangements have been made." He faced the three visitors. "Group yourselves together."

"It has been nice meeting you," Nada said. "Remember, tell my brother what you have told me, but say nothing about what we are doing here."

"We will," Mela agreed.

Mela, Okra, and Ida drew together. The professor gestured. Abruptly the scene changed.

Chapter 12. Challenge

Jenny hoped that the worst was over. Gobble was still a brat, and she still had to use mainly one eye, and they were deep under the callicantzari mountain, but they had cured Gobble of his adult vocabulary and Che knew the way back.

Gwenny dipped some more Lethe water and screwed the cap on the cup. That elixir could be useful later. Then, just to make sure Gobble didn't steal it and use it on them, she sprinkled one more drop on him. "Forget about the Lethe water we have with us," she said.

They moved on up the winding tunnels and caves and galleries until they reached the place they had nighted before. They ate the last of their food, because they knew that the following day would see them either out of the nether region or in the fouled-up stomachs of the callicantzari. They let Gobble keep the watch again, because it still would be no particular loss if he got eaten by a monster. He was less obnoxious, now that he had lost his bad words, but they had to be careful not to say anything about the way the lenses let them see dreams.

Jenny was tired, and so fell immediately to sleep, not watching anyone else's dream. She woke refreshed, and trusted that the others were too, except for Gobble, who didn't matter.

They trekked on until they reached the chasm. There, unfortunately, was a phalanx of callicantzari, each one looking worse than all the others, as was their nature. What were they going to do now? Gwenny's wand could move only one monster out of the way at a time. They had hoped that these denizens would have forgotten about the travelers in the course of the last two days.

Forgotten! Obviously these creatures had better memories than bodies or natures. But that gave Jenny an idea. She drew Gwenny aside. "We can use some of the water to make them forget us," she whispered. "Then they'll go away, and we'll have no trouble."

"I knew I saved it for something," Gwenny said, brightening.

But how could they do this without alerting Gobble? Of course they could sprinkle him with another drop and make him forget again, but they weren't sure the Lethe water would be effective against the same memory twice. It would be better to divert or deceive him in some way, so that he just didn't learn about the Lethe again.

"Why don't I take Gobble and look for another way around the monsters," Jenny said. "Meanwhile you two can check in the other direction. Then we can meet back here and see who has the best route."

"That's a wonderful idea, Jenny!" Gwenny agreed.

"So I gotta be with the four-eyed freak elf," Gobble grumbled. Then he did a double take, or at least a one-and-a-half take. "Say, point-ears, how come you can see without your specs? I remember you lost 'em, and you're bat-blind without 'em, but now you're seeing okay."

The brat was entirely too cunning! Jenny thought fast. "Maybe I'm not as blind as you think I am, bratwurst."

He shut up, which was his usual reaction when bested. They walked down the tunnel away from the chasm, then turned right at the first intersection. Jenny made careful note, because she knew how important it was not to get lost.

They proceeded through assorted chambers, but none seemed to lead near the chasm, let alone across it. "There doesn't seem to be much here," Jenny remarked. Of course she wasn't looking for much; the point was to give Che and Gwenny time to cross and sprinkle the callicantzari with Lethe water.

"Why don't you have your dumb cat look?" Gobble asked.

"Sammy isn't dumb; he can speak if he wants to." Because dumbness had nothing to do with intelligence, and everything to do with silence.

"Yeah? Then let's hear him say something."

Sammy growled at him.

"That's not talking!" the brat said.

"That's cat-talk. But I won't repeat what he called you, junk-brain." Still, it was a notion. "Sammy, find the safest way out." She held on to the cat, just in case.

The cat map appeared, as it had before. It led straight back the way they had come. That meant that the others had cleared the way.

"See, he doesn't know anything," Gobble said.

"He's looking back," Jenny said. "That means we're going the wrong way. Maybe the others have found something."

"Yeah, sure," he said derisively. "They're probably just smooching."

That was all he knew about what adults did. The Conspiracy was holding.

They made their way back. Sure enough, Che was across the chasm and Gwenny was waiting for them. "The monsters went away," she called. "They must have forgotten about us."

Just so. "How nice," Jenny said.

"I never heard of the callicantzari forgetting about their prey," Gobble said suspiciously.

"Why, my dear little brother," Gwenny said sweetly,

"could it possibly be that there is something about yucky monsters that you don't know?"

He shut up twice as solidly as before.

They tossed the rope, and Gwenny used it to cross. This time Che had flicked her with his tail before he was lofted to the other side, so that she was light, and it was easy for her to hand herself along the rope. Then from the other side she lofted Gobble and Jenny across.

They hurried on, because there could be other callicantzari who hadn't been sprinkled with Lethe water, or some who had but might hear them and come in again. But they got through without event, to Jenny's relief. It was wonderful to see the faint splotch of light at the end of the tunnel.

"Do you know, Jordan the Barbarian explored this very passage, centuries ago," Che remarked. "But he managed to find another way out."

"Yes, he was the one who left the boulder blocking the entrance," Gwenny said. "I mean, they rolled it to shut him in, but he did get out. But he wasn't looking for—" She stopped just in time, remembering not to speak of it.

They walked on out of the deep cave and into the afternoon sunlight. It was a glorious feeling.

The goblin men came out to see them. "Very well, Gobble," Gwenny said. "You may go now. Thank you for a wonderful time."

Gobble opened his mouth. "_____!" he yelled, frustrated.

They returned to Godiva's suite and made a full report while eating a full meal. Then they retired to Gwenny's suite for a full night's rest. This, too, was wonderful. There was much to be said for fullness.

But there was no spare pair of spectacles in Goblin Mountain. Jenny had had a pair in reserve, but probably Gobble had sought them out and destroyed them out of sheer brattishness. So Gwenny insisted that she keep the one lens, until she could get regular spectacles. But she would have to act as if she couldn't see as well as she could, so that the goblins did not catch on that there was other magic in operation. That could make mischief for Gwenny.

Next day they walked around the passages of Goblin Mountain, talking with goblins. That was interesting and disquieting. "How do you feel about my becoming chief?" Gwenny asked one.

"You can be chief if you want to," the man replied. But he seemed evasive, and Jenny saw a daydream of Gobble wearing the mantle of the chief. This goblin actually supported Gobble, but didn't dare say so, in case Gobble didn't make it.

"How do you feel about me?" Gwenny asked another male.

"You're okay, I guess," he responded. But his mental picture showed her in a big pot of boiling water.

Jenny realized that not only were the goblins against Gwenny, they were lying to her about it, or trying to. The night mare lenses were acting like lie detectors, because the spot daydreams showed the truth. That made them very useful indeed! Perhaps it had actually been a good break, having to fetch these special lenses instead of regular ones.

They talked to some goblin women, too. Some said they liked Gwenny and hoped she would be chief—and their dreams showed they were telling the truth. Others said they thought a male should be chief—but their daydreams showed that it was Gwenny they really wanted. The men were pretty solidly against her, and the women similarly solidly for her, whatever either said openly.

Then they passed a chamber where goblins normally caroused. They had never been there before, because Gwenny had normally remained confined in her chambers, so that no one would realize that she couldn't see well. She never wore her spectacles here, of course; only Jenny did that. Che had helped greatly with that, so that she had been able to go out when she'd needed to, but they had never pushed their luck. How well Jenny understood, with the way Gobble had always tormented her about her spectacles and supposed blindness. But a chief would have to go about, so now Gwenny was doing it, demonstrating her ability.

But this chamber was a terror. They didn't even try to enter it, because they could see the daydreams floating out from it. They were of nymphlike goblin girls running around without clothing and flinging themselves on the men to perform Conspiracy acts galore. Both they and the men seemed tireless. It just went on and on, the variations parading through, but the underlying nature unchanging. It was really true: all those crude men wanted was one thing, and that thing was dreadfully dull. What was the matter with them?

Jenny exchanged a glance with Gwenny, and because their lensed eyes were doing it, they saw each other's fancies too. Both their spot daydreams were of a monstrous pot of boiling water, cooking all those dreaming males into mush. Then they laughed, though somewhat hollowly. Poor Che was perplexed, because he couldn't see the daydreams.

The following day it was time for the Challenge. This was to determine a candidate's fitness to be chief. Two challenging tasks were written out on paper and sealed into capsules. They would each draw one, and have to perform the task written. If one succeeded within the time limit, and the other did not, then the failure would be disqualified. If both succeeded, they would in due course move on to the next challenge.

Gobble marched up to draw first, without asking. Jenny knew that Gwenny would have protested, but did not want to be impolite. Gobble felt around for what seemed like a long time, trying to pick between the two. Finally he pulled one out, opened it, and exclaimed with satisfaction. "I have to get an old wives' tail, in two days," he said. "I can do it in one." He ran off. "Come on," he called to two adult goblins. "We gotta head for the harpy for-

est." He was allowed to have two helpers, because
Gwenny had two.

One capsule remained. Gwenny took it and opened it. She
stood there, appalled.

Jenny came and took it from her hand. She read it.
FETCH WHAT IS BETWEEN THE ROC AND THE HARD PLACE.

"What is that?" Jenny asked.

"The most terrible challenge of all," Gwenny said. "I
don't think I can do it at all, let alone within two days."

Che took the paper. "We must consult," he said grimly.

They went to Gwenny's suite and consulted. Che explained the meaning of the paper to Jenny. "In the Nameless Castle there is a great stone nest, and on that nest sits
a roc bird. Between the two is the roc's egg. That is what
we must fetch."

"But the egg must be huge!" Jenny said.

"It is. But Gwenny's wand will lift it. That is not the
problem."

"The roc—it won't give up its egg without protest,"
Jenny said.

"True. That is a problem. But not *the* problem."

"Where is this Nameless Castle, anyway?"

"That is the problem," Che said soberly. "No one
knows where it is. In fact the only reference to it we know
of is in the Good Magician's notes; it seems the demons
spoke of it. Humfrey searched for it and ascertained that
it was nowhere on the peninsula of Xanth, so he went on
to other things."

"Then how do you know about the roc and the hard
place?"

"The Good Magician had a footnote about that. Perhaps the great demon Professor Grossclout mentioned it.
But that is all we know."

"How could Gobble get such a simple task, while
Gwenny gets an impossible one?" Jenny asked.

"I suspect that Gobble cheated," Che said soberly. "He
must have switched the real capsule with this one. Unfor-

tunately we cannot prove that. I am afraid that we are stuck with this task.''

"But we should go to the authorities and complain!'' Jenny said.

"The authorities are male goblins.''

Jenny sighed. She had learned enough of goblin ways to know that protest was useless. "So what do we do?''

Che made half a smile. Unfortunately, it wasn't the nice half. "We find the Nameless Castle.''

"When even the Good Magician couldn't find it?''

"He didn't find it. That is not to say he couldn't. He probably had other things to do.''

"So how do we find it, then?''

"We ask Sammy.''

Jenny smiled. "Maybe that will work!''

So they replenished their packs and went out of the mountain. When they were in an open region, Jenny addressed the cat. "Sammy, find the first short stretch of the way to the Nameless Castle.'' For she had no notion how far the cat might run, if not limited, and she was learning how to use his ability more effectively.

Sammy bounded to the east. That was all right, since there was a path in that direction, leading to the river. They had used it not long ago. But they had not seen any castle on or near the river—and anyway, the castle was supposed to be not on peninsular Xanth. That probably meant the sea, which was less all right.

They followed. After a bit Sammy stopped and waited. When they caught up, Jenny had him find the next segment of the route. This was certainly a good way to use his talent.

But what would they do when they came to the sea to the east, and had to go beyond? Build another raft? That had worked for the river, but she wasn't eager to risk it on the sea. If Fracto spied them—

They came to the river. Sammy's mental map proceeded straight across. So they pulled out their raft and found poles and shoved across.

But this was the haunting ground of dragons. In a moment one or more of them would sniff them. So Jenny started singing, making a dream, and any local dragons who weren't already paying attention joined the dream instead. Che, who was doing the poling, paid close attention, so that he did not get caught in the dream.

When they were safely across and had trees to conceal them, Gwenny touched Jenny's hand. "Do you know, I could see the dream without being in it. That was fun!"

Beyond the river the route continued. But it was too good. There was an old wide path that curved along the contour, fairly level. Sammy bounded along it so swiftly that they were soon worn out trying to keep up. But that wasn't all.

"Nice paths too often lead to tangle trees or ogres' dens," Che said. "Now I know he's supposed to be following a safe route, but he might not realize who made the path. Maybe it is safe only so far, then it becomes unsafe, and whoever is on it is trapped."

"Or maybe it is safe only by day, but it will take more than a day to traverse, and we won't like the night," Gwenny said.

"Or maybe it just goes so far that we'll be hopelessly footsore by the time we get to wherever it goes," Jenny said. It was evident that none of them were eager to spend much time on this particular path. "I really don't think Sammy would lead us down an unsafe route, but we only have two days, so we need to go fast."

Che studied the path. "I think this is a serpentine track," he said. "See, its surface is oily green and very hard. Probably a giant serpent slithered along here years ago and is long gone, leaving only its imprint in the land."

Gwenny peered at the green. "I would hate to meet a serpent that big!"

"But if it makes its own trail as it goes, and doesn't return to it," Jenny said, "then it's free for anyone to use. Still, if the Nameless Castle is far away—and it may be, if Gobble wants to be sure we won't be back in time—we still need something more than just to walk along it.''

"Maybe we should try a diversionary ploy," Che suggested.

"A what?" Jenny asked.

"Ask the feline to find us something that will in an indirect manner facilitate our journey with respect to both velocity and safety."

"You weren't any clearer the second time," Gwenny complained. "You're getting to be too much like a centaur."

Che was taken aback. "I didn't realize. All I meant was that maybe Sammy can find us something to help."

"Oh. Good idea." Jenny addressed the cat. "Sammy—"

Sammy took off into the underbrush. "Wait for me!" Jenny cried, running after him.

"Here we go again," Gwenny said, following.

They trailed after the cat, who bounded through thicket and field and finally came to a peasant hut. There was a boy of about eight playing among a collection of toys, blocks, and things. He had black hair, blue eyes, and looked smart for his size. Sammy came up to him and stopped.

"Hey! A friendly wild creature!" the boy said, delighted. He reached out to pet Sammy, and Sammy did not avoid his hand.

Jenny saw that as she ran up. That meant that not only was this boy what the cat was looking for, he was an okay person. Those were good signs.

The boy looked up as Jenny arrived. "Look what I found!" he said, indicating Sammy.

Ah, the naivete of youth! Now that Jenny was in the Adult Conspiracy, she felt nostalgia for the innocence of the childish state. "Yes, that is Sammy, my cat. You didn't find him; he found you. I think you have something we want."

"I do? You can have all these things. I just made them for fun."

Jenny looked at the objects in the yard as Che and Gwenny caught up. They were of every type, but she didn't see how any of them would help them travel. "You made these?"

"Yes. That's my talent. I make in—inan—"

"Inanimate," Che said.

"Whatever—things into other things," the boy finished.

"Now that has possibilities," Che said. "Let's introduce ourselves. I am Che Centaur, and I am seven years old. These are Jenny Elf and Gwenny Goblin. They are older, but they have a right to be—they're girls."

"Yeah," the boy said, seeing the logic of it. "I'm Darren. I'm eight. I'm older than you, Che!"

"So you are. But I have wings."

"Gee, I wish I had wings! But I can't change myself, just bits of wood and stone and stuff."

Jenny and Gwenny stayed back and let Che interview the boy; he was good at it.

"We are traveling, but we are in a hurry," Che said. "We saw a path that goes where we want to go, but we need to go along it very quickly. Can you make anything that would help us do that?"

"Sure," Darren said. "A land sailer. You can go very fast in that."

"A sailor on land?" Che asked, perplexed.

"No. A sailer. Like this." The boy went to a big block of wood and touched it. Immediately the block started changing its outline, until it became a wooden boat with a thin wooden sail. At its base were several wooden wheels. "See? When you get in it, it attracts the wind, which blows it along. But Mom won't let me go very far. She says that there are dragons out there."

"Your mom is smart. There *are* dragons. I think we can use this sailer. What can we trade for it?"

Darren looked around. "How about this cat?"

Jenny jumped, but Che took it in stride. "No, we need Sammy with us. But maybe he could find something for you. Something you want."

"Oh. I guess all I want is to forget how dull it is being a child."

Che glanced at Gwenny. "I believe we can arrange that."

Gwenny brought out her bottle of Lethe water. She sprinkled one drop on the boy. "Forget how dull childhood is," she said.

Darren looked up. "Hey, it's fun being a child! I like it! I don't ever want to get into any of the Adult Conspiracy stuff."

Jenny turned away. How little he knew—yet how familiar was the sentiment.

Che made the sailer light and hauled it away, leaving the happy boy in his yard. They brought it to the path. Then they all got on it.

Immediately a stiff wind came up to address the sail. The sailer began to move. Soon it was moving so rapidly they had to hang on. But it was taking them where they wanted to go much faster than they ever could have done it on foot, and this was more restful, too. The scenery whizzed by so swiftly it became a blur.

But how were they going to stop? Jenny wished they had thought of that before they boarded this craft.

The blurred scenery turned dark. They were passing through a mountain cleft or perhaps even a tunnel bored by the serpent. Or maybe it had gotten bored after the serpent left it, since nothing interesting was happening. Then there were more trees and glades. Finally it opened out, and they could see far to either side, across a level plain or marsh.

"Where are we?" Gwenny cried in the wind.

"The east shoreline, I fear," Che cried back.

"But then we must be sailing into the—" Jenny started.

SPLASH! The sailer threw up a great cloud of beach sand and plowed into the water. It bounced and flipped as its wheels touched the liquid, and the three of them landed in waist-deep brine.

"The sea," Jenny finished belatedly. Now she had her

answer about how they were going to stop. At least they weren't hurt.

They plowed back to the beach, dragging the sailer. They were soaking, but there wasn't time to worry about that. The day was latening, and they didn't know how far they still had to go.

However, the beach itself glowed brightly, so that it seemed that the day would never end here. "I wonder where this is?" Gwenny said.

Then Che spied a sign. "That explains it," he said, pointing. The sign said DAY tona BEACH. "Though whoever painted this sign was sloppy; I think it should be DAY on a BEACH."

"Literacy isn't what it used to be," Gwenny agreed.

But Jenny remembered their mission. "Sammy—" she began, fearing where he might go next.

The cat walked a few paces south and stopped.

They came and stood by him. "But there is nothing here!" Gwenny said.

Indeed, the sand was bright and bare. There was nothing even close. Yet Sammy sat licking a paw, unconcerned.

"Maybe it is below?" Gwenny offered. But the sane was undisturbed, and the cat wasn't digging.

"Sammy, think of the route," Jenny said.

The cat's mental map appeared. The line went straight up.

They looked up. There was nothing there but a white cloud floating serenely by itself.

Yet that was where the route line went.

"The Nameless Castle is nowhere on peninsular Xanth," Che said. "We assumed that meant it was off to the side, such as in the sea. But it just might be *above* Xanth instead."

"We have to reach that cloud," Gwenny said.

"But how can we do that?" Che asked. "I'm not sure it's within range of your wand, and we have no way to fly."

Jenny had a bright notion. "Maybe Che could fly—" she began.

"If he just forgot that he could not," Gwenny finished. She brought out her bottle.

"The logic is fallacious," Che said. "I am simply not grown enough to—"

Gwenny sprinkled a drop of Lethe water on him. "You can't fly," she said, identifying what he was to forget.

"This is ridiculous," the little centaur protested. "I simply cannot yet—because my wings have not yet—" He hesitated, surprised. "What can I not do?"

"I'm sure we don't know," Jenny said. "But we are in a hurry, so please make us very light, and then you can carry us up as you fly to that cloud overhead."

"Of course." He flicked the two of them, and the cat, and then himself. Each of them took one of his hands, with Jenny holding Sammy. Then he spread his wings, which had grown and feathered out nicely in the past two years, more than had been apparent before. So had his chest muscles, which helped anchor the wing muscles. He pumped them, and the flight feathers caught hold of the air.

They lifted from the sand. At first things were unsteady, because this was his first flight, and he was supporting the others. But in a moment he got the hang of it, and was able to make a controlled spiral, ascending toward the cloud.

Jenny looked down. Already the ground was distressingly far down. She felt alarmingly insecure. But she kept a stiff upper lip, and a stiff lower one too. After all, this had been her idea.

So she looked up, and saw the base of the cloud approaching. It was quite ordinary. But how could there be a castle up here? Castles didn't float in air!

But clouds did, and a castle might rest on a cloud, if the right magic were in operation.

Che achieved the edge of the cloud, breathing hard. "My wings are getting tired," he gasped. Then his wing beat faltered. They began to sink down.

Jenny reached out and grabbed the edge of the cloud. It felt like cotton stuffing. She hooked her three fingers and thumb into it and pulled the three of them and Sammy in. She knew that she wouldn't have been able to do it, if there had been one more of them, or one less finger. Then Gwenny caught hold also. They were all still very light, so they were able to haul themselves and Che in without falling. They climbed onto the cloud and set the little centaur on his feet there.

"Thank you," Che said. "My wings got so tired! You'd think I had never flown before!" He cocked his head. "Actually—"

"They'll recover," Jenny said quickly. "It was a difficult climb, holding the two of us. But now we're here, and we can look for the—" She broke off, amazed.

All three of them stood gaping. For there before them was the Nameless Castle. It was cloud-colored and seemed to be made of cloud stones, but overall was solid and tall, with turrets and buttresses and embrasures and pennants and all. There was even a moat. One thing a cloud could provide was water. Jags of lightning jumped from its highest pinnacles. That was another thing a cloud could provide.

Sammy jumped down and walked toward the drawbridge. They followed, still awed. This would be a perfectly ordinary castle, if it weren't up here on the cloud. As it was, it was extraordinary.

The drawbridge was down and the porcullis up. It was almost as if the castle expected them. Yet they were here only because of Gobble's attempt to cheat. Jenny was amazed that they had managed to get this far. Could they actually fetch back the roc's egg?

They set foot on the drawbridge. It was made of the same tough cloud stuff as the rest, and readily supported their weight. Of course they didn't weigh much at the moment, but if they had, it still would have been strong enough. Jenny bent to tap its substance with her fingers, and it was like spongy tree bark, soft on the surface but with very little give beneath.

They walked on into the main doorway. It was huge, as was the castle. A giant could have used this!

The great hall led to a mighty central chamber, but it was empty. So they tried a side hall, but that led endlessly away, with many blank doors at its sides. Where was the roc?

"Sammy, find the roc," Jenny said.

The cat bounded off. She had forgotten to hold on to him! All she saw was his mental map, which disappeared as he followed the highlighted route. So she just had to run after him, as usual, trying to keep his tail in sight.

It turned out to be no easy route. They wound through halls, chambers, and galleries as devious as those of the caves they had left, wending their way gradually upward. It seemed there was no grand central staircase, but rather many little hidden stairs scattered around the castle. The only thing that enabled Jenny to keep up with the cat was the number of closed doors that balked him; he had to wait for her to come open them. This castle was a veritable puzzle box!

"This portion is made for folk our size," Che remarked. "In contrast to the main gate and hall, which is made for a giant. I wonder why?"

"Maybe this is the servants' quarters," Gwenny said.

"Yet there are no occupants of this castle, large or small," he pointed out.

"Except maybe the roc," Jenny said. Then she had a nasty notion. "Just what do rocs eat?"

"Any creature they can catch," Che said. Then he realized the significance of that. "The roc could have eaten everyone in the castle!"

"But the roc would be too big to get in here," Gwenny said. "And there's no damage to show that it ripped any of this open to get at anyone."

"So there must be some other explanation," Jenny said, relieved. "They must have gone elsewhere. We don't know how old this castle is, after all. They could have left centuries ago. It could have gotten boring on this cloud.''

Finally they came to the top floor. Here, there was a lone passage leading to the center of the castle. It opened onto a balcony overlooking another awesome sight.

For there below them, in a vast central chamber, sat the huge roc bird. It was of course roc colored, with a metallic sheen to its feathers. It was sitting on a monstrous nest fashioned of marbled granite. In the nest, just barely visible, was the rounded curve of the phenomenal roc's egg. It sparkled like a gem, iridescently.

"If just that one little sliver of it is that lovely," Gwenny breathed, "what must the whole thing look like?"

"Mind-bendingly spectacular," Che said.

They stared down for a while, but the big bird did not move. "Is it asleep?" Jenny asked.

"Do you know, I think it is a statue," Che replied. "See, it is not breathing. This is a statue, an exhibit: bird, nest, and egg. So we should be able to borrow the egg without any trouble after all."

That was a great relief. They all found a ramp leading down to the base of the exhibit, just right for them. They trekked down it. Jenny watched the roc somewhat nervously, but it was true: it neither breathed nor moved an eyelid. It was indeed a statue, so realistic that it would have fooled anyone who did not watch it closely for a time.

They came to the base of the nest. They walked around it. One of the roc's enormous tail feathers projected out and down. Jenny reached up and touched it. It was longer than she was and as hard as stone.

"Isn't that egg too big to fit through the doors?" Gwenny asked.

"It certainly is!" Jenny agreed.

Che looked around. "From here I can see that there is an opening to the sky. That must be where the roc flew in, before it was petrified. Or where it could have flown in, to provide the statue verisimilitude."

"You're getting centaurish again," Gwenny informed him. "I can't even imagine that word you just used."

Che looked abashed. "I only meant that if they wanted to make the exhibit seem realistic, they had to have a way for the bird to reach the nest. Just as if it really could fly."

"Why didn't you say that, then?" she said severely. But she couldn't maintain her frown, and the smile started leaking through.

"So maybe we can use the wand to float the egg out the top," Jenny said. "And down to the ground below. And you can fly after it."

"It does seem feasible," he agreed. "Provided I have some rest stops along the way."

"So how do we get the egg out from under the roc?" Gwenny asked.

"You can use the wand to loft the roc out of the way. Then I can flick the egg and make it light enough to lift. When Jenny and I have it clear, you can lower the roc onto the empty nest, and then use the wand to loft the egg."

Gwenny brought out the wand and faced the bird. She pointed the wand, moved it—and the roc rose smoothly up. The complete egg was revealed, and its luster magnified. It was indeed the most beautiful object Jenny had seen. She had not realized that a mere egg could be so magnificent. But of course this was not a true egg, but a giant gem, part of the exhibit.

"Our turn," Che said. He stood beside the egg and flicked his tail, touching it lightly, making it light.

The egg flashed. Light radiated out from its crystalline center, bathing them all. It did not blind them, but it added an iridescent cast to their hair, skins, and clothing. They were abruptly marked folk.

"Uh-oh," Gwenny said.

The roc squawked. It spread its wings and extended its legs. It stood on the nest, glaring down at them.

Huge panels slid across the skylight, sealing it closed. There was the sound of doors slamming throughout the castle. There was also the crash of the portcullis slamming down across the front entrance, and the squeak of the hinges of the lifting drawbridge.

They had just been locked into the Nameless Castle with an angry monster predator bird. Suddenly Jenny knew what had happened to all the other folk of this castle. They had come from their safe chambers into the roc's domain and tried to steal the egg. Touching the egg was what made the roc come to angry life. That was the terrible trap of the Nameless Castle. No wonder little news of it got out!

Bratty Gobble Goblin must have known or suspected that it would be this way. So that Gwenny would not only be unable to fetch the egg, she would be dead. And they had fallen for the dastardly plot.

Chapter 13. Simurgh

They were in a dusky cave. Okra and Ida stood on rock, but Mela stood at the brink of water. Before she could catch her balance, she fell in with an ungainly splash.

"Oh!" she spluttered, her hair turning sickly green. "Fresh water! Ugh!"

Okra immediately reached in and hauled her out by an arm. Naturally Mela had not changed to her tail, because of the awful water. Now she was soaked through.

"This is a weird place," Ida said. "What's that?"

Mela Merwoman looked around. They were standing beside a collection of bones and skulls. Mean-looking little bats hovered near, watching them suspiciously. Above, on a broad ledge; was what appeared to be a huge dragon's nest filled with gems—and the dragon was there! It rose up, jaws gaping, peering down at them.

Then its eyes fixed on Mela's soaking bosom. It froze.

Mela glanced down. It surely wasn't her sex appeal that mesmerized the monster. There on her bosom were the two firewater opals, gleaming brilliantly. So that was it! Naturally the dragon wanted those precious gems for its collection.

"Hold, friend," a voice said. "I recognize one of those damsels. She's my sister's friend."

Mela looked, and saw that beyond the dragon was a large serpent with the head of a man. One of the naga folk. "You must be Naldo Naga, Nada's brother!" she said, relieved.

He looked at her. "That I am. But who are you, and what are you doing here in Draco's lair?"

"Draco?" Mela said, appalled. "Draco Dragon?"

"To be sure," Naldo said. "You expected some other dragon?"

"He killed my husband!" Mela cried. "And stole our firewater opal!"

The dragon looked abashed. Naldo looked at him, evidently understanding him, then spoke again. "But he returned it, and its mate, so that you now have a matchless set. It was his way of apologizing for the incident. He recognized the set instantly, but has not before met you."

Mela's feelings were mixed. "It is true that Draco returned double, but I would never have been in difficulty if that same dragon hadn't rudely toasted my husband. I would not at this moment be in search of a new husband, having to go on land and wear these tiresome legs." She lifted her plastered skirt to show her legs, being careful not to raise it quite far enough to show her wet panty. There was no need to be an even worse sight than she already was.

"You came to a dragon's lair looking for a husband?" Naldo inquired with a droll lift of a brow.

"No. Not exactly. The three of us had Questions for the Good Magician, and he wouldn't answer, and he sent us to see your sister, Nada, instead, and she sent us to you. A demon conjured us here. I assure you, Draco Dragon was the last creature I ever wanted to see, and being dunked in his foul freshwater puddle was the last thing I wanted to do."

"My sister sent you to me? Then I must try to be a better host." Naldo's head turned to the dragon. "Draco, do you have any human-style clothing in your collection? Maybe left over from a meal? In her size?''

The dragon squinted, studying Mela's soaked torso. He disappeared, then reappeared with several items dangling from his toothy mouth. Naldo took them. ''Yes, here is some underclothing. Not ideal, but it will do until your regular clothing can be cleaned and dried. Here, I will toss it down, and you can retreat to a private crevice to change. Then we can talk, for it may be that we do have a dialogue coming.''

Okra extended a hand and caught the items as he dropped them. She brought them to Mela. They were a furry green brassiere, a silky white slip, and a pair of light slippers.

Mela took them to a private spot, got out of her clothing, dried, delved in her purse for a spare plaid panty, and donned the new clothing. The bra was odd but sufficient, even for her structure. The slip was so slick it seemed to want to slide right off her body, but it stayed once she was all the way in it. The slippers were similarly slippery. ''Just what kind of articles are these?'' she called.

Naldo consulted with the dragon. ''An algae bra, a Freudian slip, and Freudian slippers. Draco says they came from an unusual but sexy woman with erotic taste.''

Mela had never heard of such clothing. But it was the best that offered at the moment, so she didn't complain. It would do for the nonce. Certainly it was better than having the dragon discover what *her* taste was.

Then the dragon let down his tail, and one by one they got on it and were hauled up to the nest. It was beautiful; it scintillated with all manner of known and unknown gemstones. Mela had to admit that the dragon had taste.

''I see that you like Draco's display,'' Naldo said.

''It's the loveliest thing I've seen in my life, next to the deep sea itself,'' she breathed.

The dragon snorted. ''Draco says that *you* are the loveliest thing he has seen, next to the boiling lava of a fresh volcano.''

"Oh, really?" Mela said, flattered. "Oh, he means as a morsel for eating."

"That, too," the naga agreed. He looped his serpentine body into a pyramidal coil, with his head at the apex. "As I explained, it was a misunderstanding that caused Draco to toast your husband, and he much prefers not to quarrel with you. We were playing dominoes and discussing our mutual problem with goblin encroachment of our demesnes, never expecting company. Draco has had interesting news from other winged monsters, and suddenly I think I see a larger purpose in this encounter."

"A larger purpose?" Mela echoed.

"Because the Good Magician never does anything purposelessly. He surely had good reason to send you to my sister, and she had similar reason to forward you to me. Let's have formal introductions, and then perhaps I can clarify things somewhat. I am Naldo Naga, and this is Draco Dragon."

"I am Mela Merwoman, and this is Okra Ogress, and this is Ida Human. Okra wishes to become a major character, so needs to get rid of Jenny Elf. Ida needs to achieve her destiny."

The various named parties nodded at each other. But when Mela turned in the course of introducing the others, Ida's eyes looked troubled. "Naldo's staring at your backside," Ida whispered to Mela.

Mela put a hand back, and discovered that her slip had somehow slipped aside, and was revealing some of the color of her panty. Naldo had seen! She felt herself turning a rosy-cheeked apple red crosslined with other colors as she hastily pulled the slip back across her bottom. This could never have happened if she had been in her normal tail.

But the slip started to slip aside again, so she sat down on the raised edge of the nest. Unfortunately the slip rode up across her knees, and the slippers managed to make her feet slip apart, giving Naldo too much of a glimpse up her legs. What perverse items of clothing these were! She

had to concentrate on keeping them from embarrassing her
further, leaving the dialogue to the others. There had been
a time when she had not been concerned with appearance,
but that had been before she learned that males were not
supposed to see panties. She was now doing her best to
abide by the customs of landbound folk. So she firmly
crossed her legs and hoped for the best.

"What is this interesting news Draco Dragon has?"
Okra asked.

"And why do you think Nada sent us on to you?" Ida
added.

"I will answer you both," Naldo said, removing his
eyes from what Mela hoped he hadn't quite seen. "But
first let me learn just a little more about you. Okra, why
should getting rid of a harmless elf facilitate your situation?"

"Because there was an opening for one major character,
and the choice was between an ogress and an elf, and the
elf got it. Since Jenny was the elf, if I can get rid of her,
then there will be only one candidate, me."

"You don't actually wish her any harm?"

"No. I just want her out of Xanth, one way or another."

"So if there were some other way for you to gain the
status you desire, you would be content to let Jenny Elf
be?"

"Well, I suppose. But since there was only one character to be chosen, I think it has to be her or me."

Naldo nodded. "And, Ida, how do you propose to
achieve your destiny?"

"Well, I was going to ask the Good Magician, but he
didn't answer. So I thought I'd ask Nada Naga, but she
sent us on to you. So maybe you know how. I'm sure I
don't."

"You are sure you don't, but that I do?"

"Well, yes, really," Ida said. "Because we have been
sent to you. So you must know the Answer, or know how
to get it. Professor Grossclout seemed to know the An-

swers, but he's just like the Good Magician Humfrey: neither one will second-guess the other. They say our Answers would be counterproductive, whatever that means.
So you're our last hope. You must be able to help us.''

Naldo's human head nodded on his serpent neck. ''I
believe you are correct. Very well, now I will answer. The
news is this: Che Centaur is in trouble. The winged monsters have been keeping an eye on him, but aren't supposed to interfere. But they fear that if something is not
done soon, Che will not survive his difficulty. Neither will
his companions, Gwendolyn Goblin and Jenny Elf.''

''Jenny Elf!'' Okra exclaimed. ''I don't want her to survive!''

''And why should we care about Che or the goblin
girl?'' Ida asked.

Naldo smiled a trifle grimly. His face was rather handsome, and so were his coils, in a different way, Mela
thought. ''I asked myself a similar question, when I
learned that a goblin was a member of the party to be
saved; the naga folk do not get along well with the goblin
folk. But this particular goblin has a chance to become the
first female chief of goblins, and that would transform their
nature and make them halfway decent neighbors. And because Che Centaur is very important to the Simurgh, and
she will be most annoyed if he is harmed. We don't want
to experience her annoyance. She might let the universe
expire, so that another can start instantly in its place, one
without the annoyance.''

Mela thought about that, and realized that they did have
a certain peripheral interest in the matter, since they were
part of the universe. ''But we have concerns of our own,''
she said. ''Why would Nada send us here, when we can't
do anything about your other concern?''

''Ah, but perhaps you can,'' he said. ''But rather than
attempt to persuade you by logic, which is an imperfect
mechanism, let me be more direct. I believe I can solve
all your problems, or at least arrange for the satisfaction

of all three of your quests, if you will do something to help me handle my concern.''

''You can satisfy our quests?'' Ida asked excitedly.

''Yes. But I shall not do so unless you do something for me. I want you to help save Che Centaur. I suspect that this is what the Good Magician had in mind when he sent you to me via Nada.''

''But why not send us directly to you?'' Ida asked.

''Perhaps because Mela would not have come, had she known I was with Draco.'' He glanced at Okra. ''And you would not have come had you realized that I would require you to help save Jenny Elf.''

''Save her!'' Okra exclaimed. ''I don't want to do that!''

''But you do want to be a major character,'' he reminded her. ''Just as Ida wants to achieve her destiny, and Mela wants a husband. I do happen to be in a position to enable the three of you to fulfill these quests. But I do also have my price, which I think is not as great as the one the Good Magician exacts. The three of you must do what you can to save the three others from their predicament, regardless of your personal wishes. Only if you do that will I oblige your own wishes.''

Mela exchanged a good three and a half glances with Okra and Ida. She did not like this, but if he really could deliver, it might be worth it. She saw that the other two felt much the same. ''Then we'll do it,'' she said. ''Though we consider this to be unfair.''

Naldo shrugged, which was impressive with his serpent body. ''The price does not seem excessive considering that you are in no position to bargain.''

They could not argue with that. ''So what is it we have to do?'' Mela asked.

''You have to go to the Simurgh and tell her that Roxanne is about to eat Che.''

''The Simurgh!'' Mela exclaimed, horrified. ''No one dares go there!''

''Correction: no flying monster dares fly there,'' Naldo said. ''And other creatures had best practice extreme caution, because of the Maenads and Python. But I think three damsels in evident distress might manage to get through. So that is your task: to go to Mount Parnassus and tell the Simurgh. Then return here and I will make good on my promise.''

Mela knew that the naga folk always kept their promises. But she had another objection. ''We are north of the Gap Chasm, and Mount Parnassus is south of it. It will take us a long time to get there, and if the problem is urgent we may be too late.''

Naldo glanced at Draco, who slithered out of the nest, spread his wings, and flew down to the water. He dived in.

''I will show you out of this den,'' Naldo said. ''By the time we emerge, Draco will have some winged monsters ready to transport you.''

''Just so long as we don't have to go through that awful fresh water,'' Mela said.

''Unfortunately you do. But I trust all three of you can swim.''

Mela exchanged a few more glances with her companions. ''Yes. But we don't want to get our clothing wet.''

''Then take it off, by all means! I certainly don't object!''

''But if we do, you will see our—our unmentionables,'' Mela said, not wanting to say the *P* word to a male.

''I will transform to my complete serpent form,'' he said. ''The proscription does not apply to animals, of course, as they have no appreciation of the significance of such apparel.''

Mela wasn't quite certain of the logic, but couldn't refute it. So Naldo assumed his fully serpent form, and the three of them removed their clothing and then their panties, and stood in their altogether like three nymphs. They sealed their things in their purses, then looked at the snake.

The snake slithered to one side of the nest, and nudged something with his snout. It was a rope ladder. Mela went and tossed it over the side, and saw that it reached to the floor of the cave, and was firmly anchored above. That must have been how other visitors came up, when the dragon had company. She had never thought of dragons as sociable creatures, but it seemed that it was possible. After all, Draco had been playing a game of fire, water, sand with Merwin Merman when they had the altercation that led to the loss of the firewater opal. It seemed that though every mercreature knew that water doused fire, sand displaced water, and fire melted sand, the dragon had somehow thought that it was backwards, with fire evaporating water, water covering sand, and sand smothering fire. So each thought he had won, and that the other was cheating, and they had fought. What mischief had come of the confusions and aggressions of males! Still, males did make life more interesting. Perhaps not as interesting as females made life for males, but then the realms of life and love never had been quite fair.

They used the ladder in turn and stood by the dark water. The bats hovered again, watching. They were evidently guardians of the den. The snake slithered down the ladder and into the water. So they followed, distressing as it was for Mela. Once she landed her husband and returned to the sea, she would never touch fresh water again.

They swam in single file. The snake took a breath and dived under the surface, and Mela followed. She saw vicious little piranha fish, and was suddenly nervous, because without her tail (which she would not trust to this water) she could not swim fast enough to avoid them. But they did not attack; they merely watched. Draco must have given them the word. The dragon had guardians in both the air and the water, making his precious nest secure. Yet obviously the demons could reach it, since they had conjured the three damsels there, and the goblins had raided it. So nothing was perfect.

There was an underwater passage leading out. They used it, and soon came to an end of the water in a dry cave. Someone going the other way would never know that the dark pool led to a dragon's lair! Mela had been surprised to see the dragon swim away, but she really had never known a lot about dragons. It was evident that some flying dragons could indeed swim, and that some firedrakes could handle water. Just as some merfolk could handle land, when they had to.

They saw daylight beyond, so paused to put their clothing back on. Since Mela's original clothing remained wet, she had to use the Freudian slip and slippers again, and her algae bra. The bra was all right; in fact she hoped to continue using it after this was over, because it derived from the sea and was comfortable. But the slip was treacherous, and she didn't trust it at all. It seemed to be out to embarrass her by "accidentally" showing things she very much did not want to show. The slippers were almost as bad; they tended to slip on the ground when someone was watching. They caused her legs to slip out of their covering at odd moments, so that more of them showed than intended. This could have been very embarrassing, if she hadn't taken the trouble to form good legs.

They came to the cave opening. It turned out to be in the slope of a mountain, with a sheer drop to the level ground. What now?

A four-legged griffin approached, its fierce eagle's head orienting on them as the paws of its lion's body reached for them. It hovered as close as it could to the cave, but it was shaped the wrong way to land there.

Naldo resumed his naga form. "One of you catch onto the griffin's legs," he said. The downdraft from the wings was blowing his hair straight back.

"But—" Mela said, with a qualm that was more than mere doubt.

"Draco has enlisted them to carry you to Mount Parnassus," Naldo explained. "But one griffin can carry only one person. Gregor Griffin will set you on his back once you catch on. Trust him; he is sworn to protect Che Centaur."

Mela's faith was distinctly weak. Griffins had been known to slaughter and eat luscious merwomen such as herself. But she realized that she had to set an appropriate example. Besides, her slip was trying to slip to the side again, and her slippers were trying to make her feet slip out from under her so that she would sit down suddenly with her slip flying over her head. She had to get into a better situation. So she stomped on the nearest qualm, shored up her faint faith, and reached out to take hold of the monster's front legs.

The griffin flew up, and Mela was dragged off the mountain. She dangled in the air, under the griffin, feeling like the clapper of a bell. She tried to scream, but before she got enough breath for a respectable effort, the griffin hoisted his front legs and sent her looping up over his head. She did an appalled flip in the air and landed—*plop*—on his back, right between his beating wings.

She finally got her breath in order, and made ready to scream. But by then she realized that she no longer had cause. She was riding the griffin, and no one could see her panty even if the slip tried to show it, because she was too far from the ground.

She hung on to the griffin's feathery mane and glanced back. There was another griffin behind, with Okra on it. Farther back was a third, with Ida. They were all safely riding. What a relief!

Now the three griffins winged swiftly south. Surprisingly soon they were crossing the Gap Chasm. Mela peered down, trying to see whether the cave they had taken to the demons' realm was there, but they were flying so high that the details were only a blur. It was amazing the way Professor Grossclout had conjured them so far to the dragon's cave, just like that. She would never want to run afoul of the professor, for sure!

The griffins accelerated. Now the scenery fairly whizzed by. Xanth was like a huge carpet, with forests, rivers, lakes, and fields painted on. Most lakes were small, like puddles, but there was one larger one which looked like pursed lips. "Lake Kiss-Mee!" she exclaimed, thrilled by the identification. She had been there, not all that long ago. A line extended south of it which had to be the Kiss-Mee River, up which Okra had paddled.

They followed that line down until it touched a much larger lake. That would be Ogre-Chobee, where the curse fiends resided. Plus a few stray ogres, as Okra had shown. Then they angled southwest, crossing dense jungle. Finally the very tip of a mountain showed ahead—and the griffins swooped down to the land. That would be because they were not allowed to fly too close to Mount Parnassus. But it would still be a long walk for Mela and her companions.

But the griffins did not stop. They touched land, folded their wings, and ran on four feet on toward the mountain. So that was why Draco had enlisted the four-legged variety! They could take the travelers a good deal closer to the mountain without getting into trouble.

In due course the griffins halted. They were now quite near the base of Mount Parnassus, but not touching it. The winged monsters had gone as far as they dared go.

Mela dismounted. "Thank you, Gregor," she said with genuine gratitude. "You have saved me a long, hard trek." Then she kissed the griffin on the beak.

Gregor's face feathers changed from golden to beet. Mela was sympathetic, having experienced something similar when the Freudian slip misbehaved. Probably the creature was frustrated at not being able to consume her tender flesh.

Soon the griffins were running away. All the three of them had to do now was find a way to the top of the mountain without getting eaten by the wild Maenads or the monstrous Python. Mela hoped they were up to it.

Mela verified her memory of the hazards in her manual, then explained the problem. "We can't just climb up. The Maenads are wild women who chase down and eat any intruders, and those they don't catch the terrible Python does. There are Muses on the mountain, but they don't interfere, and anyway, it's the Simurgh at the top who we have to see.''

''Maybe I could bash a Maenad,'' Okra said.

''But they travel in wild screaming packs,'' Mela said. ''While you were bashing one, the others would get us. No, we want to avoid them entirely, if we can.''

''Maybe there's a path they aren't on,'' Okra said.

''Yes, maybe there is,'' Ida agreed. ''We have only to find it, and then we can go straight up and not have any trouble. No Maenads, no Python.''

Mela started to object, but realized that it was pointless. They had to go up the mountain, and hope that they did not encounter its menaces. Why make the others afraid? Even if they were doomed to be caught and eaten, there was no point in proceeding with fear. Okra believed that major characters never had anything really bad happen to them; that would be nice, if Mela cold be sure that she herself was a major character. Considering the death of her husband, Merwin, way back when, she doubted that she could be major. So she had no security, and neither did Ida. The only way to avoid the dangers was not to go up the mountain, and then they wouldn't complete their quests.

But she did think it was cruel of Naldo Naga to send them on this dangerous mission. He should have gone himself, but instead was saving his hide by making them do it. Maybe he really had no solutions for them, but figured he would not have to provide any, because they would not survive this mission.

No, that was unfair. The naga folk were honorable, and he was a prince, therefore responsible. So he would honor the deal. But he had certainly driven a cruelly hard bargain!

Okra and Ida were searching for a good path. Mela joined them, with less enthusiasm. She was older than they were, and versed in the horrors life could bring, such as the death of one's spouse. But it was better to leave them their relative innocence as long as possible.

"I found it!" Okra cried. "It's an invisible path!"

"Wonderful!" Ida exclaimed.

"Then how did you find it?" Mela asked more critically.

"I sniffed it out. See, here it is." Okra gestured to an impenetrable thicket of brambles.

Mela was trying not to be unduly negative, but was having a problem. "That doesn't look like a very good path."

"That's because you can't see it. Watch me." Okra stepped forward and disappeared in the brambles.

"Wait, you'll get all scratched!" Mela protested.

"No I won't," the ogress replied. "The brambles are illusion. The real brambles don't grow here because they think this space is already filled. That's what makes this such a good path: no one uses it, because no one can see it. The Maenads probably don't want to get scratched either. It probably goes right to the top of the mountain."

Mela poked a cautious finger at the mass of brambles. It encountered nothing. She put a foot in. Nothing. It really was illusion—which meant it was also a serviceable path. If it continued far enough.

Meanwhile Okra was forging ahead, ogre fashion. So Mela nerved herself and followed. Ida came last, smiling. She had been so sure there would be a path, and lo, there was. Mela feared that Ida's optimism would inevitably be disabused, but she didn't want to be the one to do it. Folk tended not to be as nice, after disabusement.

Okra followed her nose, and found the curves and twists of the path. Anyone without such a keen sense of smell would surely quickly go astray and wind up amidst real brambles. But the invisible path was kempt, not unkempt, with no blockages or gaps. Who had made it, and who used it?

When they were perhaps a third of the way up the

mountain, they heard a scream. There was one of the
fierce wild women! The Maenad stood on an intersecting path, and had spied them. She was as naked as a
nymph, and proportioned like a nymph, but her pretty
face was distorted into a grimace of hate. Her hair extended in a stormy cloud around her head. Her scream
was not because of any horror, but was to alert her
companions. In a moment the whole motley crew would
be in pursuit.

"Run!" Mela cried. She hoped the Maenads would not
discover the invisible path.

Okra ran, and the other two followed as closely as
they could. The Maenads charged for them, but did not
take the invisible path; instead they cut straight across,
through the brambles. In a moment they were howling
with pain as well as rage, for they were getting sorely
scratched. It seemed that, much as they delighted in
scratching others, they did not like being on the receiving end. Mela realized that if she thought about it, she
might remember others with similar attitudes. So she
didn't think about it.

It was working! The wild women did not know of the
path, and it seemed that their sense of smell was not as
acute as that of the ogress, so they couldn't sniff it out. So
they thought that brambles were the only way. They were
fighting through them, but losing ground.

Soon the Maenads were out of sight behind. But the
three moved on quickly, despite panting with the effort, to
be sure that they were truly clear of the threat.

Mela seemed to remember that snakes had acute senses
of smell. If the Python happened by . . .

But their luck held, and no monster snake appeared.
They slowed to a walk, and continued up the slope of the
mountain. They seemed to have had a bit of the luck normally reserved for major characters, as if the script had
slipped.

Finally they came to what seemed to be the end of the
path. It ended in a blank stone cliff. The cliff seemed to

extend indefinitely to either side; probably it circled the mountain, so that they could not go around it. They had to find a way up it.

"Maybe Okra could bash some steps out of the stone," Ida suggested.

Mela started to protest that that was impossible, but remembered that male ogres could bash stone. Okra was a far cry from a male ogre, but she had been able to nullify the dragon's breath on the Iron Mountain, so maybe it was possible. "Maybe she can," she agreed.

Okra made a fist and pounded the stone, tentatively. A chip of stone flaked out. She hit the stone again, harder, and a larger flake was loosened. "I can do it!" she said, surprised.

"Maybe you just never tried it before," Ida said.

"Maybe. I thought stone would hurt my hands. I'm really not much, as ogres go."

"You're enough for us," Ida said warmly. "Maybe you just never knew your own strength."

"Maybe that's right," Okra agreed, staring at the damage she had done to the face of the cliff.

Then she got serious. She used both fists, and bashed them alternately at the rock, and fragments fairly flew out. She was doing it!

In due course Okra had made a crude stone stairway, set in the rock like a relief carving. She even made stone handholds so they could climb the stairs without the danger of falling off. Mela had never really appreciated ogres before, but she was acquiring a taste for this one.

They wended their way up the stairs, and reached the upper level of the mountain. This was a slope leading directly to the gigantic tree at the top. They were in sight of the Tree of Seeds!

They approached it cautiously. They saw the tremendous bird sitting on a branch. The rays of the late afternoon sun refracted from her feathers iridescently. Then the bird turned, spying them. Mela was suddenly in a state midway between overwhelming nervousness and moderate terror.

AND WHO ARE YOU, WHO CLIMB MY MOUNTAIN UNINVITED? the Simurgh's powerful thought came.

"We—we are three maidens in distress," Mela said.

The great head turned, and a piercing eye fixed on them. YOU ARE NO MAIDEN, MELA MERWOMAN. YOU HAVE BEEN MARRIED AND WIDOWED.

"I—I meant two maidens and a woman," Mela said falteringly. "We have come to tell you something important."

I HAVE SEEN THE UNIVERSE DIE AND BE REBORN THREE TIMES, the Simurgh thought. WHAT DO YOU THINK COULD BE IMPORTANT ENOUGH TO WARRANT MY ATTENTION?

"Maybe nothing," Mela confessed. "But Naldo Naga sent us to you, to tell you—" She hesitated, fearing another overwhelming thought, but the Simurgh waited. "To tell you that Roxanne is about to—to eat Che Centaur." There: she had gotten it out, somehow.

WHAT? The thought was so strong it almost blew the three of them off the mountain. But Mela tried again.

"Roxanne is—"

I HEARD YOU, BRAVE CREATURE. I MUST CERTAINLY SET THIS RIGHT. BUT FIRST LET ME LEARN MORE ABOUT YOU. HOW CAME YOU TO BRING THIS MESSAGE TO ME?

"The three of us went to the Good Magician Humfrey with our Questions, but instead of giving us Answers he sent us to Nada Naga, who sent us to her brother, Naldo Naga, who told us he would grant us our desires if we took this message to you. So—"

HOW DID NALDO NAGA KNOW ABOUT ROXANNE?

"His friend Draco Dragon had it from the winged monsters. But they aren't allowed to fly here, or to interfere with your designs, so—"

JUST SO. WHAT WAS YOUR QUESTION FOR THE GOOD MAGICIAN?

"How can I get a good husband? All I want is the handsomest, nicest, smartest prince—"

TO BE SURE. THE ONE YOU MARRY WILL ALSO HAVE A CERTAIN SENSE OF HUMOR.

Mela frowned. "I suppose I can live with that, if he has the other qualifications." Mela was developing a slow thrill, realizing that there really was a husband for her. She had begun to doubt.

HE DOES. NOW LET ME ACQUAINT MYSELF WITH YOUR COMPANIONS, WHO ARE NEW TO ME. The huge bird aimed her eye at Ida. Mela saw the Simurgh blink, almost as if startled. What could account for that? Ida was a nice but ordinary young woman, pleasant company but without any evident magic. What could there possibly be about her to surprise the wisest creature of Xanth? WHO DO YOU THINK YOU ARE, AND WHAT DO YOU THINK YOUR QUEST IS?

Ida made the effort to speak. "I—I—I think I am Ida. I was raised among the otterbees. I came to seek my destiny. I don't know what that is, but I hope it's nice."

IT IS AS NICE AS ANY DESTINY POSSIBLE IN XANTH. BUT IT MUST WAIT ITS TURN, FOR YOU HAVE THINGS TO ACCOMPLISH FIRST.

"I do? What are they?"

IT WOULD BE COUNTERPRODUCTIVE TO TELL YOU AT THIS POINT, INNOCENT DAMSEL.

"That's what the Good Magician said!" Ida said, sounding frustrated. "And Grossclout Demon. Naldo Naga claims to know something, but wouldn't tell us right away. Isn't this sexist or something?"

OR SOMETHING, the Simurgh agreed with a wry curve of her beak. BUT NECESSARY. Her eye moved to fix on the ogress. AND YOU?

Okra looked up at the bird. "I am Okra Ogress. My quest is to get rid of Jenny Elf, so I can become a main character."

AND INSTEAD YOU MUST SAVE HER. THAT MAY
SEEM LIKE IRONY.

"That seems like nonsense," Okra said. Mela was
alarmed, fearing that the ogre girl would bring destruction
on her head, but the Simurgh seemed not to take offense.

NEVERTHELESS, THIS IS YOUR COURSE, UN-
LESS YOU DEFAULT. NOW I SHALL SEED YOU.
STEP CLOSE, OKRA.

The ogress stepped closer to the Simurgh. "I don't understand."

NATURALLY NOT. MUCH OF WHAT I DO, I DO
THROUGH SEEDS. FIRST I SEED YOU. The Simurgh
turned to pull a scintillating feather from her wing. She
held this in her beak and brought it down to tap Okra's
head. Mela could not see anything happen, and could not
fathom the significance of this action.

NOW I GIVE YOU TWO SEEDS. ONE IS TO GIVE
TO ROXANNE. HOLD OUT YOUR HAND. The bird
jumped slightly, causing the tree to shake, and a single
round seed fell down to land in the ogress's outstretched
hand. THIS IS A SEED OF THYME. ROXANNE WILL
UNDERSTAND ITS USE. NOW HOLD OUT YOUR
OTHER HAND.

Okra obediently held out her other hand. The Simurgh
shook the tree again, and a cylindrical seed fell into it.
THIS IS A ROC-KET SEED, WHICH WILL ENABLE
YOU TO TRAVEL THERE WITH YOUR FRIENDS.
STEP INTO IT AND GO THERE NOW.

"But—" Okra started, confused.

Then Mela saw that the second seed was growing. It
expanded until it was too large for the ogress's hand. She
had to set its flattened end on the ground, but its pointed
end kept growing. It was assuming the form of a cylinder,
with a sturdy central section. It was translucent, so that
they could see that it was hollow: a cylindrical chamber.
Soon it was large enough to hold all three of them, and it
had a panel/door in the side.

So the three of them slid open the panel and got into

the seed. It was crowded, but they did fit. The panel slid closed behind them. The seed had become a prison!

But before Mela could work up a decent fright, the thing exploded.

Chapter 14. Roxanne

Gwendolyn Goblin stared up at the giant bird. They had walked right into a trap and were locked into the Nameless Castle with a righteously angry roc. Whatever were they to do now?

"Scatter!" Che cried. "It can't catch us all!"

Good strategy! Gwenny ran in one direction, and Jenny Elf in another. Che himself leaped straight up, flicked himself with his tail, and flew farther up. But Gwenny saw that all three of them still sparkled slightly with the radiance of the egg; they could not hide from the roc, because that sparkle called attention to them. Even if they had been able to flee into a crowd, the bird would have been able to pick them out.

The roc oriented on Che first. Gwenny stood by the ramp and watched, helpless and horrified, and the terrible bird stalked him. The roc was so big that it did not need to fly; indeed, there was little room here in the castle chamber for that. It merely walked, stalking the tiny figure.

It? This was surely a female bird, because she was egg-sitting. They had thought her to be a statue; now they knew that she had merely seemed that way, and that their touch of the egg had instantly awakened her. This was an enraged mother bird.

Che couldn't fly out of the castle, because it was now sealed. He couldn't hide in the small halls and chambers, because these were now shut off. All he could do was try to dodge and elude the huge awful beak of the roc.

"But you're a winged monster!" Jenny cried from the other side of the chamber. "All the winged monsters are sworn to protect Che from harm!"

She was right. But Gwenny saw with dismay that the roc was taking no notice. Evidently she had not gotten the word. Maybe that made sense. She could have been sitting here for years, out of touch with recent events, so simply didn't know about the Simurgh's requirement. And if she did not understand human speech, they would be unable to make her realize that she wasn't supposed to eat the winged centaur. Maybe some other year she would learn, but that would be way too late.

Then Gwenny had a desperate notion. Maybe she could distract the roc! She walked back toward the center of the chamber. She aimed her wand and concentrated on the lovely crystal egg. It rose and hovered above the stone nest. "Look, roc!" she cried. "I'm taking your egg!"

The bird's head snapped around. The huge eye fixed on the floating egg. *"Squawk!"*

So the monster did understand human speech well enough. "Don't move, or I'll drop it," Gwenny said.

The roc took a step toward her. Gwenny shook the wand, and the egg bobbled dangerously. "It will shatter on that stone," Gwenny warned. "If you take another step, I'll do it. After all, it's my friend's life I'm fighting for."

The bird considered. Rocs were not known for their imagination, as they were bigger than anyone's imagination, but now Gwenny saw a mental picture forming. It seemed that the bird was trying to get the picture straight so that she would know how to act, and at the moment the picture was somewhat tilted. In the center of that picture was the shining egg precariously balanced above the nest. To the side was Gwenny with her wand.

In the picture, the roc launched at Gwenny, snapping her up and swallowing her in a trice. But the egg dropped on the hard place in another trice, and shattered into one thousand and one glittering fragments. The picture tilted worse and dissolved; that was definitely no good.

The picture formed again, of floating egg and standing goblin girl. This time the roc launched at the egg, trying to catch it before it fell. That seemed more promising.

"Oh, no, you don't, Rocky!" Gwenny cried, moving the wand so that the egg sailed away from the bird.

The roc's picture tilted and dissolved. It was replaced by one of herself, somewhat fuzzy, as if something was interfering with her thought.

"Her name's probably not Rocky," Jenny called. She was able to see the mental pictures too, because she had the other lens.

"Rockhead?" Gwenny asked. The picture fuzzed worse. "Rockhound? Rock-a-bye-baby? Rockfall? Rocking chair? Rock-'n'-roll?" The picture blurred into obscurity.

"Try female names," Jenny suggested.

"Rochelle?" The picture brightened. "Roxanne?" Suddenly the focus was perfect: that was the name.

"You are able to communicate?" Che inquired. He had landed at a safe distance. "Then get her to talk about herself. Then maybe she'll forget about chasing us."

Good idea! "Well, Roxanne," Gwenny said, "we didn't know you were alive. We thought you were part of an exhibit. We have to get the egg if I am to become chief of my tribe. It's nothing personal. It doesn't look like a real egg. Are you sure you couldn't let us have it for a day or two? Then we could bring it back."

Roxanne's mental picture exploded into smithereens. One smither zoomed so close that Gwenny had to duck. It seemed that the egg was not available for a loan.

"But the egg won't be much good to anyone if it shatters," Gwenny said. "And I'll drop it or loft it against a wall if I have to."

The roc moved sideways, not approaching the egg, but also not retreating from it. Gwenny didn't drop it, because once it shattered, she would have no hostage against the rage of the bird. So they were at an impasse.

"How did you come by this egg, since I don't think you laid it?" Gwenny inquired conversationally.

That set off a new picture. Roxanne was flying across Xanth, covering an ordinary landbound creature's hour's travel with every wing beat. She was young and her feathers were bright. She saw a high mountain and flew to investigate it, having the curiosity of youth.

"What are you seeing?" Che called.

"A big, tall, two-peaked mountain," Gwenny called back. "With a temple at the base and a giant tree growing on the summit."

"But that's Mount Parnassus!" Che protested. "No one's allowed to fly there!"

"And on the tree sits a bird the size of a roc," Gwenny continued, "with iridescent feathers. Roxanne is flying right toward that bird, thinking maybe it's another roc."

"That's the Simurgh!" Che cried. "The oldest creature in Xanth! She has seen the world end and be recreated three times! She doesn't allow anything to fly in that vicinity!"

Roxanne heard him speaking. Her head cocked toward him. Then she leaped. Che tried to take off, but couldn't get his wings properly set. He tried to gallop away, but the great talons of the roc's foot closed about his body.

Gwenny and Jenny screamed together. Then Gwenny collected a few of her scattered wits. "Let him go!" she cried. "Or I'll drop the egg!" She wiggled the egg with the wand.

Roxanne refused to be bluffed. Her mental picture showed the egg dropping—and right after that, the little winged centaur being squished into purple pulp.

Gwenny didn't dare drop the egg while Che was all right. But she certainly would if the roc hurt him. So it was another impasse, but now Roxanne was in a better bargaining position than before.

The big bird carried Che to a cage set high against a wall. She popped him in and slammed the door closed with her beak. Gwenny saw Che try the door, but it was securely locked; he could not get out. He was all right, but captive.

Gwenny knew that if she shattered the egg, the roc would simply go back and squish Che, so the impasse remained. How was she going to get him free?

She decided to try the dialogue again. Maybe she would learn something that the roc wanted more than the three of them to eat. "Roxanne, what happened after you encountered the Simurgh?" she asked.

The roc came to stand at the same distance from the egg as before. However, Gwenny took the precaution of lofting it so that it hovered above the rim of the stone nest. If it dropped there it would certainly shatter, with half of it falling outside the nest. She wouldn't have to guide it at all; if she simply dropped the wand, the egg was doomed. It was evident that Roxanne understood. It was dangerous to go after Gwenny herself.

However, Jenny Elf was not necessarily safe. "Jenny, don't let the roc get near you!" Gwenny called.

"I won't," Jenny agreed. She was hiding under the ramp, where it would be difficult for the big bird to grab her.

The picture formed again. Young Roxanne in her innocence was flying directly toward the Simurgh. The sitting bird glanced at her. The picture filled out with increasing detail, becoming a full-fledged dream, so that Gwenny found it easy to follow. In fact it was as if she were experiencing it herself. That was part of the nature of dreams: they were magically easy to believe, even when they made little or no sense. So she seemed to be flying over Mount Parnassus.

She looked around and saw that the mountain was actually made of huge scrolls and books. Many were weathered, with bushes and even trees overgrowing them, so that on the surface they might not be evident, but from this vantage they were. Well, Parnassus was known as the residence of the Muses, who were reputed to be literary folk; maybe these were books they had written. Roxanne had no interest in the Muses and less in books, but was slightly intrigued by the fact that the tomes had accumulated into a mountain. What a lot of waste effort!

The sitting bird twitched one feather.

Suddenly Roxanne's wings lost purchase. She flapped them wildly, but they had little effect. It was as if the air had stopped having substance, so that she could not fly. She barely made it to the ground without crashing. After that she could not take off again no matter how hard she tried. She was mysteriously grounded.

She was on the side of the mountain. She had to move by walking, which was embarrassing; trees kept obstructing her, and she had to knock them down. What had happened to her?

She found a pool and waded in it to cool her feet. Then she dipped her beak and took a swallow. The water was cool, but it warmed her throat. What kind of water was this?

Then she identified the taste. This was a wine spring!

Tiny folk of the human persuasion appeared around the edge of the pool. They seemed to be all female, and very active. They charged in and tried to attack Roxanne. Well, that made them that much easier to snap up; a good meal was here for the taking. She caught one in her beak and took a closer look. Didn't human folk normally wear clothes? She must have misremembered, because this one wore none. Maybe they had come to swim. Well, it hardly mattered. She dipped the one in the wine for better flavor, then gulped her down. She was as delicious as any giant worm. So there was no danger of going thirsty or hungry here.

The wild women kept coming, so Roxanne kept swallowing them. She had never had as good a meal this readily. Not since she had split a fat sphinx with her male friend Rocky. They had gorged until satiated. "I can't believe I ate the whole thing," he had squawked. That was an exaggeration; he had eaten only half. But she knew exactly how he felt. They had been too heavy to fly, and had had to sleep on the ground for several days before getting trim enough to resume normal elevation. But it had been worth it.

That reminded her. She spread her wings, pumped them, and leaped into the air. Only to flop back into the drink with a ferocious splash that nearly drowned several wild women who had been trying to hack off her feathers. She remained ground bound, and it wasn't from overeating. Something was seriously wrong.

She waded from the pool, seeking a suitable roost for the night. The wild women followed, still trying to stab her, so she made a sweep of one wing and dumped them in a pile back in the pool. Then she made her way to a niche in the mountain, found a suitable outcropping of rock, and settled down to rest. When the wild women came at her again, she spread her wings and flapped forward, and the wind blew them back into the pool. After a few times they realized that they weren't getting anywhere, and let her be.

Now she had time to think. How was it that her wings had the power to blow enough air to sweep the wild women into the drink, while they couldn't lift her into the air? They seemed to be functioning normally, except when she tried to fly. What could account for this?

Offhand, the most reasonable explanation seemed to be magic. Some kind of curse. But how had such a thing come about?

Then she remembered that the other big bird she had been about to visit, the one with the iridescent feathers, had glanced at her, then twitched one feather—just before

Roxanne fell to the ground. That twitch could have been an enchantment! That must be a bird with a magic talent.

But why? Roxanne had been innocently coming in for a visit. Why should another bird choose to mess her up like this? That was where her thinking faltered; it didn't seem to make sense.

She snoozed, and when she woke it was morning. She got up and went to the pool for a bath. The foolish wild women appeared again and tried to interfere, so she ate a few more and blew the rest away. She finished her bath, took another sip of the warm-tasting wine-water, and strode to the bank. She shook herself dry, then spread her wings and tried to take off.

Again, she could not. Her wings beat the air furiously, blowing up a great cloud of dust, but she didn't rise. It was as if she were tied to the ground. She could not fly.

A large snake slithered into view. A very large one. Rather than being a morsel for eating, this was a potential enemy. She set herself, making ready to fight.

"Hold," said the snake in bird talk. "I have not come to quarrel, but to advise."

Roxanne was astonished. "How is it you speak my language?" she squawked.

"I am the Python of Parnassus," he replied. "I speak all languages, for it is my duty to guard this mount from intrusion. The Maenads inform me that you are causing them difficulty."

"Oh, the wild women? They taste good when dunked in wine."

"I agree. However, they too guard the mount, and should not be preyed upon too savagely, lest the supply of them be exhausted. That would deprive me of my tastiest morsels. I must ask you to cease your depredations on them."

"I will gladly do so, the moment I can fly away from this place. I never wanted to stay here anyway, but something funny happened to me on the way to visiting the roc at the summit."

"That is no roc. That is the Simurgh, the senior creature of Xanth and the mortal realm. She is the Keeper of the Seeds, and she sits in the Tree of Seeds and protects the mountain from intrusion by air. She allows no flying monsters here. You intruded, so she grounded you."

"Grounded me! But I was only coming to say hello! I didn't know she was so fussy about visitors."

"Now you know," the Python said.

"Well, tell her to lift the spell, and I'll fly away. I certainly don't want to associate with anyone so unfriendly."

"The Simurgh is not unfriendly. She merely enforces the rule. She lacks the patience to educate those who somehow remain unfamiliar with her edict."

"You mean she won't let me fly again?" Roxanne asked, alarmed. "What a mean creature!"

"Not mean. Merely firm. Ignorance of the requirement is no excuse."

"But I can't endure forever on the ground!" Roxanne protested. "I'm a bird! I need to fly!"

"Then you will have to petition the Simurgh for a release from grounding. Perhaps she will be lenient, considering your innocence."

So it was that Roxanne made her way laboriously by foot up to the top of Mount Parnassus to petition the Simurgh.

YOU MUST PERFORM COMMUNITY SERVICE, the Simurgh's powerful thought came. WHEN YOU HAVE COMPLETED IT SATISFACTORILY, YOU WILL BE UNGROUNDED.

"What is this service?" Roxanne squawked.

YOU MUST GO TO THE NAMELESS CASTLE AND HATCH THE EGG THERE.

That seemed simple enough. "Where is the Nameless Castle?" she asked.

The Simurgh did not answer directly. Instead she twitched a feather. Suddenly Roxanne was there.

The egg was beautiful, but slow in hatching. Roxanne lost count of the centuries, but was sure she was making progress toward her ungrounding. She followed the rules of this service scrupulously: she could eat only those visitors who approached close to the egg. Sometimes they came in bunches, and sometimes singly. When there were several, she locked the extras in cages awaiting her appetite. The spaces between such visits could be brief or long. It didn't matter. She snoozed betweentimes. Somehow it seemed to work out; she was usually somewhat hungry, but never starving. It was not bad service, actually, but she would be glad when it was finally over.

Gwenny was amazed. "You have been here for centuries?"

Roxanne's thought reviewed the time scale. Yes, there did seem to have been several centuries. She slept so much and so deeply that it was hard to tell.

"But who built the Nameless Castle? Who laid the egg? What will hatch from it?"

Roxanne did not know. It was not hers to reason why, merely hers to do and fly. To egg-sit until it hatched. That she would faithfully do, because she did not want to annoy the Simurgh again.

"But Che Centaur is protected by all winged monsters, by order of the Simurgh," Gwenny said. "The same bird who sent you here for your community service. You will annoy her something awful if you eat him."

Roxanne knew nothing about that. She had never left the Nameless Castle, because she couldn't fly, and had not questioned any of the intruders before eating them. Why should she take the word of an attempted thief that the Simurgh had said not to eat him?

Gwenny shook her head, baffled. The roc's thought made sense, on her terms. How was she to be convinced that she was mistaken?

Then Gwenny heard something. It was a low humming, perhaps singing, the words not quite distinguishable. The roc, intent on Gwenny and the endangered egg, was not listening to it.

It was Jenny Elf—trying her magic. It worked only on

those who were within hearing range but not paying attention. So it wouldn't affect Gwenny this time, because her mind was right on things, but it just might work on the roc, if the roc's attention remained distracted from the elf.

Gwenny saw the dream forming, however, because of the lens in her eye. It was like a cloud over Jenny's head, where she hid under the ramp. Within that expanding cloud a scene appeared, at first vague, then clarifying. It was of a grassy glade, with flowers in the foreground and misty mountains in the background. In the middleground were glades and sparkling streams and all manner of handsome trees. It was completely lovely, as Jenny's scenes usually were.

Gwenny wished she could step into that dream, as she had so many times before, but she couldn't afford to. If she did, she would lose concentration on the wand, and the egg would drop and shatter, leaving the roc nothing to do but destroy all the intruders immediately. If she set the egg down first and stepped into the dream, the roc could recover the egg and then hunt them down. So she had to remain alert. But she could watch it from outside. This was a new experience, seeing reality and the dream at the same time.

Jenny appeared in the dream. She walked among the flowers, which was one of her favorite things to do, being careful not to step on any. She bent down to sniff a big purple passion flower, carefully, because girls were not supposed to get too much of that sort of thing. Not even those who had been inducted into the Adult Conspiracy.

Sammy Cat appeared in the dream. He was snoozing in life, near Jenny; he did the same in the dream. There was even a dreamlet cloud over his head within the dream, but its details were obscure. Probably he was dreaming of himself dreaming of himself dreaming, and so on, each dream cloud smaller until they became pinpoint small and vanished.

Roxanne Roc appeared in the dream. She looked surprised. She *was* surprised; her own thought cloud showed it, with a picture sliced diagonally. One part was where she had just been, in the Nameless Castle; the other was where she was now, in a lovely glade with an elf girl. Which one was she to believe?

"Why hello, Roxanne," Jenny said in the dream. Gwenny couldn't actually hear the words, but she saw Jenny talking and knew that was what she would be saying.

"What am I doing here?" Roxanne asked. She could talk directly to Jenny now, because that was the way of it in her dreams. All barriers between creatures were broken down, and everybody got along harmoniously.

"You are in my dream," Jenny said. "It is nicer than reality, because everything is perfect, here."

"Things won't be nice for me until I can fly again," Roxanne said.

"Why, you can fly, here," Jenny said.

Amazed, Roxanne tried it. She spread her wings and took off—and sailed into the deep blue sky. In a moment she was playing tag with a passing cloud. It was wonderful!

But Gwenny couldn't watch all of this. Jenny had given her a chance to get them free. So she moved her wand and set the egg carefully back down into the nest, then stashed the wand in her pack. She ran across the chamber to the row of cages against the wall. They were up above her head, because though Roxanne could not fly, she was such a big bird that she could reach far up. So Gwenny had to climb up the wall. That was no trouble, because the wall here was made of rough-hewn cloud stuff and was easy to grab on to. Also, she remained fairly light, because it had not been all that long since Che had lightened her so that he could carry her up to the Nameless Castle.

She climbed, glancing back to make sure that Jenny's dream remained effective. She saw Jenny by the ramp and Roxanne sitting beside the nest, and the dream cloud between them, filled with its pleasant wonders. The dream roc was looping and swooping in the air, absolutely delighted. For centuries she had been grounded, for all that she was in a castle on a cloud in the air, and she was reveling in her newfound flight. She would not be eager to leave that dream in any hurry.

Gwenny reached the bottom of the cages. She hooked her fingers into their cloud-strand wire and pulled herself up to the front of Che Centaur's cage. "Che!" she whispered. "How does this thing open?"

"It is tied by a fragment of a Gordian not," he said sadly.

"A what?"

"A Gordian not. It is a magical knot that cannot be untied by anyone except the one who tied it. The roc tied it, so she's the only one who can untie it."

"But then how can I rescue you?"

"You can't," he said sadly. "Nor can you rescue Jenny, I fear. See whether you can find some way to rescue yourself."

"I'll do nothing of the kind!" she said indignantly. "You're my companion and next-closest friend. I must rescue you both." She looked at the not. "Maybe I could cut it."

"I don't know whether that is wise."

Gwenny glanced over her shoulder at the continuing dream scene. "Jenny can't hold the roc forever. I've got to act now, if I'm ever going to."

"You may be correct," he agreed reluctantly.

Gwenny hung on with her left hand, and dug her knife out of her pack with her right hand. She set the blade at the top of the not and began sawing through it.

The not screamed and flashed. The light was almost blinding, and the sound was a shrill keening that made the very walls shudder.

The roc snapped out of the dream. She gazed wildly around, catching on to what was happening. Then she leaped at Jenny Elf, catching the girl in her huge talons before she could scramble around the ramp. She carried the girl across to the cages.

"Flee!" Che cried to Gwenny.

Gwenny let go of the cage and dropped to the floor. Her lightness made the landing tolerable. She scooted off to the side, avoiding the big bird. She found a rocky region and dived behind a boulder.

Meanwhile Roxanne had opened the cage, tossed Jenny in with Che, and retied the Gordian not. Now two of them were caged.

Gwenny realized that she should recover her control of the egg. It was the only way to restrain Roxanne, who really was trying to do her job, misguided as it was in this case.

She ran toward the egg, bringing out her wand. But Roxanne was already running toward it too, and her steps were a whole lot bigger. So Gwenny aimed the wand, but before she could loft the egg, the roc reached it and threw herself on it. She pulled cloud cord from somewhere and wrapped it around the egg and nest, tying it with another Gordian not. It was now impossible to loft the egg; it was anchored to the nest, and the nest was anchored to the floor. Gwenny had lost her chance at it.

She should have used her wand as soon as she landed on the floor, instead of mindlessly fleeing. She had panicked, and given up her last real chance to make an even fight of it. That was hardly a chiefly thing to do, not that she would ever get a chance to be chief. So maybe she really wasn't qualified to be chief. But she hated getting her friends into this disaster with her.

The roc finished binding the egg and turned her head to fix on Gwenny. Then she pounced.

Gwenny lofted the bird high into the air and over her own head. She hadn't even planned on that; it had just happened. The huge creature hurtled like a stone and crashed into the opposite wall, denting her tail. Her thought cloud showed a mass of squiggles and exclamation marks; she was really confused.

Well, now! Maybe Gwenny did have a chance! Because Roxanne couldn't fly, she was now helpless in the air. The wand could control her. Maybe if she got bashed around enough, she would give up the battle.

The roc righted herself and started for Gwenny again. This time she didn't leap, she walked. It didn't matter; Gwenny lofted her again and smacked her into another wall.

The third time the bird got smarter. She extended her talons and drove them into the cloud stones of the floor. When Gwenny tried to loft her, it didn't work, because she was locked onto the floor. She took one step, and then another, keeping one foot anchored.

Gwenny thought of something desperate. She ran toward the bird's anchored foot. Roxanne, surprised, yanked that foot out of the floor so as to grab her—and Gwenny struck with the wand in that moment and lofted her high.

But this time she did not smack the roc into the wall. It was her own turn to get smarter. She held the bird aloft. Now Roxanne was unable to move, because she had no purchase and could not fly. Gwenny had captured her, in a fashion.

But what was she to do with her captive? She couldn't hold the roc there forever, because she would have to sleep sometime. Apart from that, she had to take the egg back to Goblin Mountain within a day, and there was hardly enough time remaining for that even if she had her friends free and possession of the egg. Her situation remained desperate, no matter what happened to Roxanne.

A new cloud formed in the air between them. Whose dream was this? But it didn't form a picture; rather the entire cloud assumed a shape. The shape became that of a woman, a grown woman, with a voluptuous figure and clothing designed to advertise every curve and contour. Then the face formed, and it was familiar.

"Metria!" Gwenny exclaimed. "What are you doing here?"

The demoness drifted to the floor, peering at her. "The goblin girl," she said. "I might ask you much the duplicate."

"Much the what?"

"Alike, identical, double, reproduction, transcript, replica, remake—"

"Same?"

"Whatever," she said crossly. "I am here on business. I thought you were going home to be monarch."

Gwenny elected not to correct the misnomer. "I am trying to, but I had to meet my little brother in a challenge. He changed the paper, and I had to fetch what was between the roc and the hard place. So we came here to fetch the crystal egg, only we're in trouble."

"Now that's interesting. How soon do you think you'll be through here?"

"If I'm not back at Goblin Mountain within another day, nothing will matter. So I guess I'll be through in a day, one way or another."

The demoness produced a notepad and pen, and made a note. "I'm working for Professor Grossclout now, setting up the special bleep, and I have to survey exotic settings such as this one. So I'll report that it will be clear next year. Thank you."

"A special what?"

"That's not a confusion, it's a censorship. I'm not allowed to say anything about it. I tried to sneak into it to find out, because curiosity is my dominant emotion, and I did see Nada Naga rehearsing, but the professor caught me, and no one ever told the professor no on anything. So now I know all about it, but can't tell anyone else. It's a phenomenal frustration."

"Well, can you maybe help us while you're here? Che and Jenny are locked in a cage, and I'm lofting Roxanne Roc, but it's an impasse and I don't know what to do."

"Oh, hasn't the rescue party found you yet?"

"What rescue party?"

"The one the Simurgh's going to send, when she learns of this." Metria looked around. "It will be interesting to see whether she learns of it in time. Well, toodle-oo."

"The Simurgh doesn't yet know?" Gwenny cried despairingly. But the demoness was already fading out.

Gwenny was alone again. Her friends remained caged, and the egg was tied down. There just didn't seem to be any chance to save them and the egg and get back in time.

She pondered, and came to a conclusion. She did not have to be chief. She was not sure she was qualified for it anyway. But she just could not let her friends be eaten.

"Roxanne," she said. "I came here to steal your precious egg. I admit that. I would be willing to borrow it and return it, but I don't think you'll agree. So now I'm ready to compromise. Let my friends and me go, and we'll leave your egg alone."

The bird considered. But Roxanne had heard what the demoness said, and now knew that Gwenny was desperate. Her thought cloud showed Gwenny falling asleep, when the roc could then get back to the floor and grab her.

"But you also heard that the Simurgh does have an interest in us," Gwenny said.

It seemed that Roxanne dismissed that as irrelevant or as an attempt to fool her. She would wait.

"Then I'll bash you against the wall!" Gwenny cried, suddenly furious. She waved the wand, causing the bird to circle wildly in the air. But she did not follow through, because she feared that Roxanne would sink her talons into the wall and so regain her footing, which would give her the victory.

Gwenny cast about for something else. She saw the rocky region where she had hid for a moment. That was a rock garden! Now she remembered that rocs liked rocky things, such as rock candy, rock music, and rock gardens. That must be the bird's private garden.

"I'll mess up your rock garden!" Gwenny said.

Roxanne squawked. That had gotten to her.

"Let my friends and me go," Gwenny repeated.

But the roc wouldn't. So Gwenny walked back to the rock garden, which she saw was composed of rocks of several sizes ranging from large to huge. She pushed against one, but it was too heavy for her to budge. They all were.

Well, she could use the wand. She brought it around—and the bird gyrated. Oops! If she used it on a rock, she would have to let Roxanne go, and that would be disastrous. She couldn't make good on this threat either.

Gwenny sat on a rock, baffled. The guilty sparkle that stained them was finally fading, but that didn't make any difference now. Two of them were caged, and the third was mostly helpless.

She felt tears starting. What was she to do?

Chapter 15.   Rescue

Okra Ogress reached out and grabbed Mela on one side and Ida on the other, holding them steady as the roc-ket seed capsule exploded. Fire and smoke billowed out all around them, and the capsule shook as if grabbed by a giant. Then, slowly, it rose in the air. Mela and Ida were frozen with their eyes welded closed, but Okra of course lacked the wit to do that, so she was peering out through the transparent seed casing.

She saw the capsule rise up through its own smoke, which was coming from the bottom end of it and bouncing off the ground. It went up higher than the great Tree of Seeds, and headed for an innocent cloud floating above. The cloud, affrighted, tried to scud out of the way, but the roc-ket seed was too swift for it. The capsule caught the edge of the cloud, and knocked the cloud into a spin. Rain sprayed out as the cloud lost continence. It did not look pleased.

Now the capsule was headed up toward the sky, fire and smoke still thrusting from its base. OGRESS—GUIDE THE CRAFT, the Simurgh's thought came. POINT IT AT THE NAMELESS CASTLE.

"But where is the—?" Okra started. Then she saw a panel, and on the panel were several little pictures. Some were of mountains. One was of a mountain with a big tree at the top, like Mount Parnassus. Another had goblins swarming over it. That would be Goblin Mountain. Another was flat-topped mountain: Rushmost. Another showed creatures sleeping: Mount Ever-Rest. Several more pictures were of castles. One had a zombie by it: Castle Zombie. Another had a grumpy old gnome by its turret: the Good Magician's castle. Another was in a lovely orchard: Castle Roogna. And one was perched on a cloud.

Okra pondered a moment, and thought for another moment, and cogitated for a third moment, and considered for a fourth moment. At that point her head was beginning to overheat, so she knew she would have to stop. That meant that she would have to take the fourth choice: the castle in the air. That had to be the Nameless Castle.

CORRECT, OGRESS. NOW SET THE INDICATOR THERE.

There was a glowing dot. At the moment it was in the middle of the sky, but it was too small to be the sun. Okra's arms were both busy holding her companions in place, so she used her nose to nudge the dot across the panel to the Nameless Castle.

The capsule veered wildly as the dot changed position, but steadied on a new course when the dot was left on the Nameless Castle. Okra hoped that meant that the capsule was now headed for the right place.

CORRECT. PART OF YOUR TASK IS DONE.

Part of it? "What's the rest of it?" Okra asked. But the Simurgh did not answer. Probably she had more important business to attend to. Why should she care about a minor character ogress, except as a momentary tool to accomplish a purpose?

The craft, as the Simurgh had called it, was now flying horizontally across Xanth. Okra pondered that a moment, and managed to translate the key word into one she understood: level. The craft was flying level instead of up. The Land of Xanth was zooming along below.

They seemed to be flying northeast, back the way the

griffins had brought them, but faster. Soon Okra saw Lake Ogre-Chobee again. Her home region seemed so different from above! She had never dreamed that she would go so far or have such adventures when she set out to achieve Main Character status! There was the Kiss-Mee River she must have paddled up. But the craft did not follow the river north; it continued northeast across the jungle. Just as the great sea to the east came into sight, the capsule slowed. The fire stopped belching from its tail, and it coasted to a halt on a cloud. It bounced and lay still. It had arrived.

Okra removed her arms from her companions. "Relax, friends," she said. "We're there." She slid open the panel, and fresh air wafted in. "But don't stray far; we're on a cloud."

"A cloud!" Ida exclaimed as she drew herself out of the compartment. "How can that be?"

"The roc-ket flew to the Nameless Castle, which happens to be on a cloud," Okra explained. She poked a finger into the cloud stuff, testingly. "It seems strong enough to support us—and the castle."

Mela emerged, brushing back her hair with one hand. "I thought we were being incinerated," she confessed. "Other things being equal, I'd rather drown."

"But merfolk can't drown!" Okra protested.

"Precisely."

They stood and looked at the castle. It was as white as the cloud itself, with cloud gray shadows. It was large enough for a tribe of ogres. Okra wondered why it didn't weigh down the cloud and make it sink to the land below. But of course it was magic, and magic didn't have to account for itself to anything else.

"Roxanne must be inside," Mela said. "She must be a mean-spirited woman, if she is going to eat a centaur."

"Maybe she's a demoness," Ida suggested.

"Or an ogress," Okra said. "Most of them are more ferocious than I am."

Mela frowned. "That brings to mind a possible problem. If Roxanne likes to eat folk, what is to stop her from eating us?''

''But we are bringing her the seed of Thyme,'' Ida said. ''So she shouldn't eat us.'' But she seemed uncertain.

''Would the Simurgh have sent us here if we were only to be eaten?'' Okra asked.

Mela smiled, faintly reassured. ''No, I think she expects us to find a way around the problem.''

''Maybe we could use the seed of Thyme,'' Ida said, ''to protect us, until we can give it to her. Then maybe she won't want to hurt us.''

''But how do we use it?'' Mela asked.

''Well, Okra was seeded, which I suppose must mean that she was given the seeds until she could pass one on. Maybe she can use it, the way she used the roc-ket.''

Okra looked at the seed still in her hand. She had no idea how to use it.

''Maybe you can invoke it,'' Mela suggested. ''That's the way some magic objects are used.''

Okra held the little sphere up before her. ''I invoke you, seed of Thyme,'' she said.

Nothing happened.

''But of course you still have to make it do something,'' Mela said. ''Tell it to do something thymely.''

''Thyme, speed me up,'' Okra said.

Still nothing happened. ''Any more ideas?'' she inquired.

Neither of the other two answered. They stood as if frozen, not even blinking. What was the matter with them?

Okra walked to the edge of the cloud and looked down. Xanth lay below, with the edge of the sea in sight. Nothing seemed to move there either.

Then Okra realized that if she had speeded up, but the others hadn't, it might be this way. ''Slow me down, Thyme,'' she said.

Mela and Ida blurred into action. Their voices came like the quacking of frenzied ducks. One zipped out of sight, then back. What a change in them!

But there was a change in the rest of Xanth, too. In the distance the sun nudged on toward the horizon, as if impatient to be done with its day's work. The gray shadows of the castle grew longer. She could see it all happening.

Oh. Xanth hadn't really speeded up; she had slowed down too far. "Make me normal again, Thyme," she said.

". . . must tell it to speed you up again," Mela was saying. "Please, Okra, we don't have much time!"

"I'm back," Okra said.

"Oh, wonderful!" Mela said. "First you got blurry fast, then you were like a statue. It must be the magic of the seed of Thyme."

"Yes," Okra said. "So if Roxanne attacks us, we can just speed up and get away from her."

"I wonder whether it also affects others?" Ida asked. "It seems me that if it can affect one person, it might affect another."

Okra tested it. "Thyme, speed Ida up and slow Mela down."

Ida became a blur of motion. Mela became a statue. "Quick, Thyme, change them back!" Okra said.

Ida slowed to normal, and Mela quickened to normal. The three compared notes, and concluded that the seed of Thyme could indeed affect others.

"That means it can slow Roxanne down, without affecting us," Ida said. "That might be the best way."

Mela looked at the castle. "Maybe we should slow the whole castle down," she said. "So that if Roxanne is about to eat Che, she won't do it before we come in to rescue him."

Okra faced the castle. "Seed of Thyme, slow everyone in the Nameless Castle down," she said.

Nothing seemed to happen, but they realized that that was deceptive. They walked up to the castle.

The drawbridge was up and the portcullis down. The moat was full of water, and they did not quite trust what might be in it. But Okra solved that. "Water, slow down."

The water froze. They walked across the frozen surface.

But how were they to get into the closed castle? There were no low windows, and the door was firmly shut.

"Maybe you could bash a hole in the wall," Ida suggested. "The way you bashed steps into the cliff."

Okra made a fist and tried a tentative bash. She managed to chip off a flake of cloud stuff. "This stuff doesn't seem tough, but it is," she said. "It will take me some time to bash a hole in it."

"I don't think we have a lot of time," Mela said.

"Then speed us up," Ida added. "So that we can get into the castle quickly."

Okra speeded the three of them up. Then she started bashing. The work was slow, but they had plenty of time, because she was actually working quite swiftly. She bashed a dent in the cloud wall, and then a depression, and finally a hole. Then she put in her hand and yanked out more around the edge, widening it until it was big enough for them to crawl through.

They did so, and found themselves in an empty cloud chamber. The door was closed, but Okra pushed it open. When they passed through, it slammed closed again. Mela tried the handle, but the door was locked. It seemed that it would open only from the inside.

Now they were in a small hall. Its walls were made of cloudstuff, as was everything else here. They followed it until it debouched into a medium hall, and followed that until it emptied into a large hall. That hall proceeded on into the depths of the castle, making the acquaintance of other halls of its size and accepting the tribute of smaller halls. This was one huge castle!

They came to another closed door. This time they fetched a cloud couch and used it to wedge open the door, so that they could return this way without having to bash the door down. Then they moved on out into what appeared to be a huge dining hall, to which every other door was closed.

"It's a good thing we are speeded up," Mela remarked,

"because otherwise we would not be getting anywhere fast."

"Maybe the folk here are upstairs," Ida said. For they had seen no sign of any person other than themselves.

That seemed to make sense. They looked for stairs, but wherever they were was sealed behind another door. So Okra piled chairs on the dining table, and stood on them so that she could reach the ceiling. Then she bashed a hole in it. This, too, took time, but there was no other way.

When the hole was big enough, Okra drew herself up through it. She was on the floor of a monstrous chamber. There in the center of the chamber was a huge pedestal supporting what looked like a nest. Floating above the nest was a roc bird. What was going on?

Okra helped haul Mela and Ida up into the upper chamber. The three of them remained speeded up, while the creatures in the castle remained slowed down, so they did not have to hurry. They stood beside their bashed hole and surveyed the situation.

"Roxanne!" Ida exclaimed. "She's the bird! Rocs-Anne!"

On the floor below the bird was a rather pretty goblin girl holding a wand. The wand was pointed at the bird as if holding the roc at bay. To the side were several cages, and in one of the cages was a winged centaur and an elf girl.

The centaur would be Che, whom they were supposed to save from getting eaten. The elf would be Jenny.

Okra's eyes narrowed. That was the one who had taken her status as a main character! She certainly didn't look like much. She was big and ungainly for an elf, and her ears were pointed in a way Okra hadn't seen before. And her hands—she was missing one finger of each hand! What had happened to her? More important, what could there be about this odd creature to make her worthy of major character status?

"That must be Gwendolyn Goblin with the wand," Mela said. "I think I once heard something about a magic wand the goblins had that would move things around. So maybe she's been moving the roc away from her, so she won't get eaten.''

"And the roc caught the other two before," Ida agreed. "Maybe we should free them first. Then we can bring the goblin down through our hole, and take them all out before we give Roxanne the seed of Thyme.''

That made sense to Mela. Okra wasn't sure about releasing the elf, but decided not to argue. They had to complete their mission for the Simurgh, so that they could return to Naldo Naga and gain their quests.

They went to the cages. These were set above the floor, but it was easy to climb the rough wall to reach them. Okra went up, and found that the cages were tied shut. She tried to untie the knot, but it wouldn't budge. So she bit through it instead.

The knot screamed. But she didn't care how it felt; it should have let her untie it. In a moment she had it severed and the cage door open.

Then she took the loose cord left over from the knot and tied it around the body of the winged centaur in a crude harness. She carried him out and dropped him down, using the rope to prevent him from falling. Mela and Ida caught him below and guided him to a place on the floor. It was surprising how slowly he fell through the air—but of course he was falling at the normal rate, which seemed far slower than it was. They untied the rope so that Okra could pull it up.

Now for the elf. Okra was tempted just to toss her out without the rope. But she knew that Mela and Ida wouldn't appreciate that. Of course she might make a mistake and tie the harness just a little too tight; who would know it hadn't been an accident?

But she discovered that no matter how hard she tried, she couldn't make the harness too tight. Her hands insisted on doing it just right. What was the matter with her?

Then she realized that it was because of the same thing she resented about this elf: her status as a major character.

No major character could suffer anything truly bad. They could be frightened, and get into extremely awkward situations, but they always somehow got out of them. The irony was that it was Okra who was getting Jenny Elf out of this awkward situation. She had to help her enemy, because of the power of the magic that Jenny's illicit status had. How disgusting!

So she carried the elf to the edge and let her gently down, resenting it all the way. She would have to find some other way to be rid of her.

Okra jumped down, then carried the two creatures in turn to the hole in the floor. Again she let each down, while Ida went below to remove the harness.

Finally they took the goblin girl and lowered her down to join the others. All three were safe, because the roc bird was far too big to fit through the hole.

Now it was time to deal with the roc. Ida remained with the three below, while Mela and Okra made ready to brace the big bird. If Roxanne tried to attack, Okra would slow her down again. But they needed to be in the same time frame now.

Okra held the seed of Thyme. "Slow us down to regular speed," she told it.

That was the wrong directive. The huge bird, formerly hold aloft by the goblin girl's wand, and only now beginning its slow fall, dropped to the floor with a feather-denting plop. She blinked and looked around.

Okra realized that Roxanne had just been dealing with a goblin girl with a wand, and now faced an ogre girl instead. Well she might blink; she might think that the one had changed into the other. But in a moment she would realize that the wand was gone.

She did. She pounced on Okra.

"Slow her down!" Okra told the seed. Then the roc was frozen in the air just before her talons were able to close on Okra.

Okra walked around to the bird's rear. Mela had been standing to the side; now she went to hide under the ramp that led up to closed doors. "It's your show," Mela said. "Keep getting behind her, until she pauses long enough to listen."

"Suppose she doesn't understand me?" Okra asked.

"Then we're in trouble. We may just have to leave the seed of Thyme here, with the roc in slow motion, and hope the effect wears off after we are safely away from the castle."

Okra thought about that. "Let me test it," she said. She set the seed down.

Immediately the roc resumed motion. She bounced on the floor, her talons closing on air.

Okra hastily picked up the seed again, and the bird stopped moving. Now she knew: the seed obeyed only the one who was holding it. If they tried to leave it behind, Roxanne would get it and be able to slow the escaping party down, and they would all be in her power.

"We *are* in trouble," Mela said.

Okra had another notion. "Seed, speed the roc up to about three-quarter speed." Ogres couldn't do fractions, but she was distressingly lacking in stupidity and did understand them. It was one of her several secret shames.

The bird finished her bounce and skidded along the floor. Then, realizing that she had missed her prey, she got her balance and looked around. Her motions were moderately slow, as if she lacked urgency. At regular speed they would have been alarmingly fast.

"Roxanne!" Okra called. "We must talk!"

The bird turned, set herself, and leaped again at Okra. This time Okra walked away, and Roxanne missed. The slowdown was just about right; Okra now had better reflexes, and could avoid the pounces.

"We must talk," Okra repeated.

But the bird would not listen. She continued to go after Okra, thinking she was just about to catch her.

"Speed us up," Mela said. "We'll have to talk with the folk we just rescued, so that we can get them to use the wand for us. Then we'll be able to suspend the bird in the air again, and make her listen.''

Good notion! Okra speeded them up, and the big bird went still. They climbed down through the hole to where the other four waited. ''It's been such a long time, I was getting worried,'' Ida said.

''That's because you remained in fast speed,'' Mela said. ''We slowed down to normal speed to try to talk to the roc, but she won't listen. So now we need to consult with these three, to see what they know that might help us.''

Okra stood before the three. ''Speed them up,'' she told the seed of Thyme.

The three became animate. ''Oh, where are we?'' the elf girl said. Okra saw that the elf was holding a cat; somehow she hadn't noticed, before. Maybe she had more ogreish dullness than she thought.

''How did I get down here?'' the goblin girl said.

''Who are you?'' the winged centaur foal said. All three of them seemed somewhat confused. That might be because two of them had been in a cage a moment before, by their perception, and the third had been facing the roc.

''I am Okra Ogress,'' Okra replied. ''This is Mela Merwoman, and this is Ida Human.'' She indicated her companions. ''We have come to save you and to give the seed of Thyme to Roxanne Roc. But Roxanne won't listen to us.''

The centaur seemed to reorient most swiftly, as was to be expected. ''You used magic to conjure us out of the roc's chamber?''

''This seed of Thyme,'' Okra said, showing it. ''We made it speed up our time so we could rescue you without the roc stopping us. But now we need to talk to her.''

''Jenny can do that,'' Che said. ''But the castle remains sealed. So unless you can persuade her to let us go, it may be pointless.''

''Well, maybe she will let us go in exchange for the seed,'' Mela said. ''We brought it to her, but we don't have to give it to her until we're safe, I think. And the Simurgh did want her to understand that you are not to be hurt."

"Yes, the winged monsters are supposed to protect me," Che agreed. "Because I'm a winged monster too. But Roxanne has been egg-sitting here for centuries, so didn't get the word. I'm glad you came; we do need help."

"But we can't just go without the egg," Gwenny said.

"And we'll need to travel very swiftly," Jenny said. "Because Gwenny has to take the egg back to Goblin Mountain tomorrow." Then she looked uncertain. "Or maybe today; we can't be sure how much time has passed, now."

Okra frowned. She wasn't here to help the elf! "We're just here to save the centaur and give the roc the seed of Thyme."

"But I am Gwendolyn Goblin's companion, and I am here to help her get the roc's egg," Che said. "So if I am to be saved, Gwenny must be helped."

Mela frowned. "That doesn't sound quite like centaur logic."

"Well, I'm not a grown centaur. It is centaur foal logic."

"And Jenny is my friend, and she's giving a year of service to the Good Magician to help me in my quest, so she must be helped too," Gwenny said. "Otherwise she won't be able to meet her commitment."

"I'm sure that's not what the Simurgh said," Okra said.

"But as it happens, you need Jenny," Che said.

Okra almost choked. "I don't need the elf! I want to be rid of her!"

"She's right," Jenny said. "Because I got the character she wanted."

Okra stared at her. "You know?"

"I learned. And I didn't even seek it. I didn't know there was a choice being made. I just got lost following Sammy, and showed up here. Maybe I should go back, after I finish my service to the Good Magician."

Okra was getting to dislike her less. She turned to the centaur. "Why do you say I need the elf?"

"Because her cat can find almost anything, including what you might need, and Jenny can talk to Roxanne with her dreams."

Okra had to admit that those were adequate recommendations. "So we find out how to settle with Roxanne, and set you three free," she said grudgingly. "Then we go."

"We shall need your help also to get to Goblin Mountain in time," Che said. "The Simurgh surely sent you for this reason too."

"Yes, that makes sense," Ida said.

Okra, about to disagree, found herself agreeing. She was getting as confused as the rest of them! "Well, let's get this done," she said.

So Jenny Elf went up to the roc's chamber with them. There she did her thing, which turned out to be a sort of stupid humming or singing. Okra soon lost interest and looked around the chamber—and found herself abruptly in another world. This one was very pretty, even to an ogre's perception, with hard gray mountains on the horizon, turbulent storm clouds in part of the sky, and big gaunt ironwood trees in the foreground.

How had she come here? She was the one with the seed of Thyme, so she couldn't have been slowed way down and moved. She would have had to be moved a long way, because this scene was on the ground, while the Nameless Castle was on a cloud in the air. In fact, she saw the castle, on one of the clouds in the distance. Who had conjured her to the ground?

Jenny Elf and her cat were also there. "How did this happen?" Okra asked her.

"I did it," Jenny said. "It's my talent."

"You're a sorceress!" Okra exclaimed.

"No, only an elf girl. I can imagine a nice place, and anyone who hears me sing and isn't paying attention can join me in it."

"But what's the point?" Okra demanded. "We need to talk to the roc."

"That's right," Mela said, appearing. "Because now I'm in it too. But this isn't getting our business done."

"When Roxanne appears, we'll be able to talk to her—in this dream," Jenny explained.

"So where is she?" Okra asked, looking around.

"Well, her attention has to wander, before she can come in. But we talked to her before." Jenny looked around also. "Funny she isn't here yet, though."

"Oh, I just realized!" Mela exclaimed. "She's still in slow motion, or we're in fast motion. It will take ages for her to join us!"

Okra glanced at the seed. "Maybe I can speed her up. But if I do, could she eat us instead of joining this dream?"

"I'm not sure," Jenny said.

"Well, let's find out," Okra said, satisfied to make Jenny squirm. "Seed of Thyme, make Roxanne join our speed."

"But—" Mela and Jenny said together.

Then the roc appeared. "Hey, I'm here again!" she said. She spread her great wings and launched into the sky.

"Hey, Roxanne," Jenny called. "We have to talk to you."

The roc looped about. "Who has to talk to me?"

"Okra Ogress, there," Jenny said.

Okra realized that Jenny had done it back to her. This might be a dream world, but could the roc eat a person here?

"Well, then, I'll eat her first," Roxanne said. "I don't know how you got out of the cage, but this time I'll make sure of all of you. You won't escape after I've eaten you." She oriented on Okra and swooped down.

Okra lifted the seed. "Slow her to three quarters of our speed," she said.

The bird's wing beats slowed. She lost elevation faster than she wanted to. She had to pump harder to avoid crashing into the ground. Even in a dream, that might hurt. "What have you done to me?" she squawked. Even her words were slow.

"I used the seed of Thyme to slow you to three-quarter speed," Okra replied. "I can slow you further, if you don't behave."

The roc landed bumpily on the ground and hopped toward them. Her hops were slow, and she seemed to hang longer in the air than she should. It would be easy to avoid her. "What is this seed of Thyme?" she asked, still speaking in a somewhat measured manner.

"The Simurgh gave it to me, to give to you. But you must free your captives and not try to eat them."

"And you must give us the egg," Jenny called.

"Never!" Roxanne cried. "The Simurgh sent me to egg-sit, and I must protect that egg until it hatches."

"But we need it," Jenny said.

"You can't have it! I know the Simurgh would never have given it to you."

It did seem odd to Okra that the Simurgh would send a roc bird to protect the great crystal egg, then allow it to be taken to a mountain of goblins. "Why do you have to have it?" she asked the elf.

"Because Gwenny Goblin has to fetch what is between a roc and a hard place, or she won't get the chance to be the first female goblin chief. And the egg is what's between the roc and the hard stone nest."

"You can't have it!" Roxanne repeated.

Okra realized that there might be something else here. "Is the egg the only thing in the nest?"

"It must be," Jenny said. "We saw it."

"Yes, that's all I allow in the nest," Roxanne agreed.

"What about stray feathers?" Okra asked.

Jenny looked at her, astonished. "Why that would count, too! Maybe we don't need the egg!"

"Still, you tried to steal the egg," Roxanne said. "So I must eat you."

"But you can't eat Che Centaur," Okra said. "No winged monster can."

"Nobody ever told me that," Roxanne said. "As far as I'm concerned, he's a thief, too, and deserves to be eaten."

"But if we took only a feather, and promised never to return," Jenny said. "Then—"

"No. You tried to take the egg."

"But suppose we gave you the seed of Thyme?" Okra asked. "Would that make you change your mind?"

"I don't want to slow myself to three-quarter speed!" Roxanne said.

"But with it you could make yourself any speed—or anything else any speed," Okra said. "It is a very powerful thing. That is why I am able to stop you. I just change your speed to something that can't hurt me. If you had it, you—" She paused, realizing the roc-sized significance of it. "You could speed up the egg until it hatches, and you would be free!"

"Free!" Roxanne exclaimed, excited.

"And all you have to do is let them go, with a feather," Okra said. "Will you do that?"

It was evident that even a firmly mind-set roc had her price. "If that is all, yes."

"Then let's get out of this dream and fetch that feather," Jenny said.

But Okra was more cautious. "Truce?" she asked the roc.

"Truce," the bird agreed. "But if you try to steal the egg again, I'll eat you."

Jenny clapped her hands, creating her own distraction, and the dream vanished. They were all back in the roc's chamber. They could no longer talk with Roxanne, but the bird understood them well enough.

"I'll go get the feather," Mela said. "You don't want to get in range, Okra, just in case."

That made sense. Mela walked to the egg. Roxanne approached it also, but did not try to attack. Actually she was still at three-quarter speed, which helped.

Mela looked in the nest. "There's no feather here," she said.

"Oh, there must be!" Jenny cried in anguish.

"Maybe something else?" Okra asked.

"Nothing but an old shed claw," Mela said.

"A claw will do, if it's been between the roc and the hard place," Okra said.

Mela hauled out the claw. It was as long as she was, a talon like a long sword. "Come to think of it, this must always have been between the roc and hard places, because every time she lands on a mountain or the floor or the nest, or picks up a stone or a bone, this claw was between her and it. Once she lost it, it's been in the nest." She faced Roxanne. "Is it all right to take this?"

The bird nodded. It wasn't as if she didn't have plenty of other talons.

"Then will you let us go, if we give you the seed of Thyme?" Okra asked.

Reluctantly, the bird nodded again.

"And you know that if you break this agreement, you'll be in trouble with the Simurgh?" Okra asked. "Because she's the one who sent us here?"

Roxanne jumped. It was obvious that she didn't want that. The Simurgh had given her a way to get free whenever she chose; why should she throw it away by angering the Simurgh anew?

So Mela hauled the talon away, struggling with its weight, and Okra walked to the nest and put the seed of Thyme in it. Immediately the time became normal for all of them; her commands no longer applied. "All you have to do is hold it and tell it what to speed up or slow down," she said. "Maybe you had better test it before we go, to make sure it understands you."

Roxanne came to the nest, reached inside it with her beak, and brought up the seed. She tucked it under a wing feather, and squawked.

Suddenly she was a blur of motion. Light flooded into the chamber. The bird had activated the seed and speeded up, or made the rest of them slow. They were now at her mercy.

Then things returned to normal motion. Mela, Jenny, and Okra stood unharmed. The bird had not taken advantage of her power over the seed to eat them. She had only tested it. Fortunately.

"Then we'll go now," Okra said.

Roxanne nodded.

They climbed back down through the hole, and then walked out through the open castle. Okra carried the talon, which was too heavy for Mela to haul for long. Soon they came to the front gate and crossed the drawbridge, which was now down for them. Roxanne had opened everything during her trial with the seed.

Okra had wound up helping Jenny Elf, too. Okra hoped she would not regret this foolishness. It was unogreish, for one thing. And it still didn't help her achieve her desire to become a major character.

Chapter 16. Arrival

Che was amazed at recent developments. One moment he had been in the cage; the next he had been in the downstairs chamber with his friends, facing a buxom merwoman with legs, a surprisingly small and unugly ogress, and a young woman whose identity he had almost mistaken. But he had been able to reorient rapidly, as was proper for a centaur, because he had seen two of them in the tapestry. They were Mela Merwoman and Okra Ogress. Even as he placed them, they were introducing themselves and the third, who turned out to be Ida Human. They had been sent by the Simurgh to save Gwenny Goblin's party, for the Simurgh was the original winged monster who had declared that Che would someday change the history of Xanth and should be protected. To facilitate that, the ogress had brought Roxanne Roc a seed of Thyme.

That had proved to be a bit complicated, but now it was done, and all six of them were on their way back to Goblin Mountain. Because Che, realizing that they could get there in time only with the help of the other three, had used juvenile logic to persuade them. He would not be able to get away with that when he grew to be an adult, but he wasn't there yet. Except for the business about the Adult Conspiracy, which perhaps he could pretend to forget for a few more years. It really didn't apply when centaurs weren't with humans or crossbreed humans, so was of limited concern. Centaurs preferred to fetch their progeny directly, not trusting innocent babies to the carelessness of storks.

Now they stood at the edge of the cloud, the Nameless Castle behind them. The day was waning, and circumstantial evidence indicated that it was their second day of this quest; they had perhaps an hour to get back to Goblin Mountain. He hoped their new companions could enable them to do it.

"Will all of us fit in the roc-ket seed?" Mela asked. She wore what Che recognized as a Freudian slip, which tried to slide around to reveal a peek at a truly intriguing panty. She also wore Freudian slippers, which tended to set her feet down where her legs showed a bit too much. There was surely an interesting story behind her attire.

"Surely we will," Ida said optimistically. "It's such a big seed!"

Now Che saw the seed to which she referred. It was a big cylinder with translucent sides and a panel. It lay on the edge of the cloud. He doubted it would hold six folk. In any event, what was the point? They didn't need to cram into a seed, they needed to travel swiftly.

The ogress went to the seed and hauled it up so that it pointed toward the sky. "Pile in," she said gruffly. Che could see that she was not enormously pleased about this association, and she especially did not seem to like Jenny Elf. Well, she had reason. It was a real irony that the Simurgh should have required the ogress to help rescue the elf. Did the Simurgh have a mean streak?

They piled into the big seed, and lo, it turned out to be even larger inside than out, and they all did fit. Then the ogress slid the side panel shut. She did something—and fire and smoke billowed all around the seed and hurled it up off the cloud. Now the fire and smoke seemed to be coming from the base of the seed, blasting out and down as if eager to get away from it. Well, that was better than

having it try to burn up the seed! Maybe that was why the
seed was moving so swiftly: to escape the fire.

Jenny and Gwenny were hugging each other, terrified,
but Mela and Ida were taking it in stride. Che looked at
the ogress, and saw that she was looking at a panel on
which were several pictures. One picture was glowing: a
messy pocked rubble heap of a hill. That would be Goblin
Mountain!

He looked out through the transparent side. The seed
leveled off, then zoomed across Xanth, headed inland. Che
peered down, realizing that though he still seemed to be
standing upright with the others, all them were actually
lying flat with respect to Xanth. This was most interesting
magic!

The cloud bearing the Nameless Castle had evidently
traveled a fair distance during their stay on it, because they
were not traveling west, but northwest. He saw the Isle of
Illusion, and the Gap chasm, and dragon country. Ahead
was the smoke of the Element of Fire. But that was beyond
their destination; was the ogress overshooting the mark?

Then the roc-ket seed dropped down, already arriving
at Goblin Mountain. They were going to be there on time!
It came right at the mountain, frightening the goblins on
it; Che almost laughed as he saw them scatter into their
holes.

The seed came to rest in sight of the mountain. Okra
slid the panel open. They were there.

Gwenny got over her fright. "Oh, how wonderful!" she
exclaimed as they piled out and stood beside the seed.
"You have done me such a favor!"

"We did it because of the Good Magician," Mela said.
"And Nada Naga and her brother, Naldo, and the Simurgh. We are each supposed to have our Questions answered when we're done. So now we'll go back to find
Naldo, and hope that he makes good on his word."

"Oh, Naldo will," Gwenny said. "He came to help us
when the goblins fought the winged monsters, because of
the alliance. He doesn't like goblins at all, in fact his peo-

ple and ours have been at war for centuries, but he did it. He's the very best creature.''

Okra made a wheezing sound.

Che glanced at her. "What's the matter?''

"Just my asthma," Okra wheezed. "I must have changed altitude too swiftly. It will pass in a moment."

But Che was alarmed. "You mean you have an illness?"

Okra coughed weakly. "It comes and goes. It makes my breath clog up so I lose my strength. I've been lucky recently, and hardly felt it at all, but now it has caught up with me."

"We must get a cure for you," Che said.

"No, it will pass," she repeated. "I'm surprised it hasn't caught me more often since I left home. Maybe I've just been moving around so much that it hasn't been able to keep up. So maybe it just lay in wait for me here, and caught me." She coughed again, wheezingly. "You must get on to the mountain with your prize." She laid down the roc's talon, which now seemed to be too heavy for her to carry.

Che didn't like this, but knew she was right: Gwenny had to get promptly to Goblin Mountain. "I hope you get better soon," he said. "You have been a real help to us."

"I'm sure you'll think of a way to get rid of it," Ida said with her characteristic optimism.

"That would be nice," Okra agreed, making an effort to smile.

Mela and Ida and Okra climbed back into the seed and pulled the panel closed. Che and the girls quickly retreated, knowing that the fire and smoke would come again. Goblins were reappearing at their holes, and Gwenny waved them back.

But nothing happened. The seed capsule just lay there.

After a while the ogress slid open the panel. "It won't go," she reported gruffly. She still looked weak and worn, and her voice was faint.

"Maybe you are not yet done with us," Che suggested.

"Yes, that must be it," Ida agreed, climbing out.

It did seem to make sense. So they remained a party of six, for the nonce, and Gwenny led the way to the mountain.

They started toward the mountain. The sun was almost singeing the trees to the west. There was just time to make it before the day ended, so that Gwenny would not be disqualified.

Suddenly a monster loomed up on the path before them. It was massive, with the head of a stag but with a single black horn in its forehead. It had four elephant's feet, a boar's tail, and the body of a horse. It lowed challengingly.

Che happened to be in the lead. He stopped. This was certainly a monster, but not a winged one, so it could be a threat to him. "We're only passing by," he said.

"Halooo!" it bellowed in its low voice. "You must pay to use my path."

Gwenny stepped forward. "I know you, Hugh Mongous Monoceros! You're always lurking around, trying to take what isn't yours. This isn't your path! This is a goblin path."

"Who says?" the monoceros demanded.

"I say!" she said.

He thumped the ground with an elephantine toe. The ground shuddered. "Who are you?"

"I am Gwendolyn Goblin, soon to be chief of Goblin Mountain. Now get out of the way before I move you out."

"Ho, ho, ho. It is to laugh. You can't move me out, you skirted goblette. You must pay."

Gwenny brought out her magic wand. She aimed it at Hugh Mongous. One of his forefeet lifted. "Uh-oh," she said.

The monoceros laughed again. "Ho, ho, ho. Is that the best you can do, you cute morsel?"

"What's the matter?" Che asked.

"The wand's weakening," she said. "I've used it a lot today; on the roc and such, and after a while it loses power and has to recharge overnight. The monster is now too heavy for it.''

Che looked at the sun, which was hastening to end the day. They could not afford to be delayed long. ''Is there another path we can take?''

''Yes, but it will take too long. This is the only direct one from here.''

''So you're stuck, goblette,'' Hugh Mongous said. ''Pay.''

''This is outrageous!'' Gwenny said, stamping her little foot. ''We have to get through immediately!''

''We shall just have to make a deal,'' Che said, disgusted. He faced the monoceros. ''What is your demand?''

''I demand that you pay me something for using my path. Something interesting and different. Such as maybe that magic wand.''

''Never!'' Gwenny said.

Okra Ogress came forward. ''Maybe I can help,'' she gasped.

''No, you can't!'' Gwenny protested. ''You're not well!''

''Let me try. I've been trying to think, because that heats my head and sometimes helps clear my throat, and I may have found an idea.''

Ida clapped her hands, maiden style. ''Wonderful, Okra! I knew you could do it.''

Che kept silent. That foolish optimism could become wearing, in time.

Okra faced Hugh Mongous. ''I have something that you might consider to be interesting and different,'' she wheezed. ''Do you want it?''

''What is it?'' the monoceros asked.

''My asthma. It makes me wheeze.''

Che had to clap a hand to his jaw to prevent it from dropping. Could the ogress be serious?

''What a wonderful idea!'' Ida exclaimed brightly. There it was again; she was thrilled about anything at all.

"It does?" the monster asked, somewhat stupidly. "How loud can you wheeze?"

Okra took a labored breath, then forced it out. "WHEE-EE-EEZ!"

The creature would never fall for this! Meanwhile, they were wasting precious time. Che was disgusted.

"I'll take it!" Hugh Mongous said.

This time Che did not manage to catch his jaw in time. That creature was even more stupid than an ogre!

Then Okra straightened up, extending a hand. "Here it is," she said, no longer wheezing. She set an invisible something on the monster's nose.

"Wonderful!" the monoceros wheezed. Satisfied, it moved out of the path and let them pass. They could hear it happily wheezing as they left it behind.

"As a stupid person, you are a complete failure," Che murmured to the ogress.

"I know," Okra said sadly.

They moved rapidly to the mountain. The goblins stared at the three additional folk, but did not attack them because they were with Gwenny. All three were twice the height of any goblin, but Gwenny chose a tunnel that was large enough to accommodate them.

They trouped to the central chamber. There were Gobble and his henchmen. The brat was holding a soiled harpy feather. He had found the old wives' tail, and figured he had won. He was just waiting for the day to end without Gwenny's reappearance. It was a joy to see his crestfallen look as they entered the chamber.

Godiva entered. Her expression was the opposite of the brat's. "You have returned, my daughter!" she exclaimed, hurrying across to embrace Gwenny.

Behind her were the three male goblins who had served her loyally for years, Moron, Idiot, and Imbecile. Che had gotten to know them, and they really weren't bad sorts, for goblins. When the children had wanted to sneak in tsoda popka to substitute for ugh healthy drinks, these three had always been willing accomplices. Godiva had been aware of this, but elected not to make an issue, because she was unusually liberal, for an adult: she thought children should be allowed to have a little bit of fun, if it wasn't overdone. So while Godiva was hugging her daughter, the three halfway decent goblins came across to congratulate Che and Jenny, and to meet their new companions.

"These are Moron, Idiot, and Imbecile," Che said. "Those are their names, and there's nothing odd about them." That was so the women wouldn't laugh. Then, to the goblins: "And these are Mela Merwoman, Ida Human, and Okra Ogress, who are here temporarily until their roc-ket seed is ready to move again. See that no one messes with it."

"Right," Moron said, hurrying out. The other two remained, looking at Mela.

Che realized what was happening. "Mela," he murmured, "straighten out your slip."

The merwoman quickly adjusted the Freudian slip, which still conspired to give stray males flashing glimpses of her panty. Che would have to speak to Godiva, who was an excellent seamstress, to see about making Mela a regular dress. After all, suppose underage goblins saw? It wasn't as if it was a dull panty; its pattern was a most intriguing crisscross of colors that would surely madden the mind of an adult male.

"But where's what's between a roc and a hard place?" Gobble demanded, recovering some impudence.

"Right here," Gwenny said, gesturing to Okra, who still carried the roc's talon.

"But that's just an old claw! It's supposed to be the fancy egg."

"It was in the stone nest, under Roxanne Roc," Gwenny said evenly. "It was between the roc and a hard place. It qualifies."

"But that wasn't what I meant!" he protested. "I meant the egg!"

Gwenny stared at him. "How could you mean the egg,

if you didn't write it? And if you wrote it, you cheated, because you weren't supposed to know what the challenges were.''

Gobble was silent, realizing that he could only get himself into trouble. ''So okay, you got it. But you're not home free, sis. Tomorrow's the physical combat.''

''Physical combat!'' Che exclaimed, appalled. ''Girls don't do that!''

''Yeah. So she loses,'' Gobble said with satisfaction. He glanced darkly at the three male goblins with Gwenny's party. ''And after that I'll deal with you traitors.'' Then he slunk out of the chamber.

''I knew there were three challenges, like the ones for getting into the Good Magician's castle,'' Gwenny said. ''I know the first consisted of merely being qualified to assume the chiefship, which narrows it down to Gobble and me. The second was performance, which we have just finished. The third is physical, but I thought that just meant building something or showing I could hold a club. Combat—I fear that is beyond me.''

''But he's just a little brat,'' Okra Ogress said. ''You could club him with one fist.''

''No, I couldn't,'' Gwenny said. ''I'm a refined goblin girl, and we are never violent in that way. It simply is not our nature. If we could fight, we would not be nice, and there would be no point in having a female chief to make the goblins nice.''

Che saw the logic. ''But Gobble cannot be trusted,'' he said. ''We must check the original document. Where is it written how the chiefship is won?''

Gwenny took them to a small separate chamber. There in a chest to which she had the key was an old dirty scroll. She brought it out, and they read it.

It was indeed the list of rules for the succession. ''Ha!'' Che said as he read it. ''There is a combat, but it's a combat by selected champions.''

''Gobble and me,'' Gwenny agreed glumly.

''No. By champions you select. So you don't have to

fight yourself. You merely choose a tough goblin to fight for you, and if he wins, so do you. Gobble won't fight himself either; he'll have someone bigger and meaner.''

"But no male goblin will fight for me!" Gwenny said. "They don't want me to be chief."

Che pondered. "That does present a problem," he said, stumped for a solution.

"But I'm sure you can solve it," Ida Human said brightly. "Because centaurs can solve almost anything."

Then, oddly, Che did get a notion. "But maybe a female could fight for you," he said. "Goblin girls are all nice, but that's not necessarily the case for the females of other species."

"I'll fight for you!" Jenny Elf said.

"No, Jenny, no!" Gwenny said. "You would be no better than I, because you're not mean or tough."

"She's right," Che said. "I meant a female from somewhere else, tough enough to do the job."

"But who would that be?" Gwenny asked. "The females of other species really don't care much about goblin politics. In fact they don't care much about goblins, period."

"I don't know," Che admitted. "But I know how to find her."

"Well, tell us!" Jenny said. "Because there's less than a day to get her here."

"I can't say it directly, until certain arrangements are made," Che said. "Because a certain party has been known to take off without warning, seeking what has been mentioned."

"Oh," Jenny said, glancing at her little cat. "Sammy, come here." The cat did, and she picked him up and held him firmly. "But with a—a certain device I can see where he is going, and—"

"Suppose the one we want is far away?" Che asked. "You could not keep up. But I think I might." He looked at the goblin girl. "Gwenny, do you have any light cord? Something that might tie a very light person to another, so that he might be hauled along at whatever velocity is necessary?''

Gwenny nodded. She hurried away. ''Imbecile, help me fetch the cord,'' she said, and that goblin immediately followed her.

''But suppose he goes through some small hole?'' Jenny asked.

''We can frame the search to exclude that sort of thing.''

''What are you folk talking about?'' Mela asked.

''Jenny's cat can find anything except home,'' Che explained. ''So if we ask Sammy to find something, and I follow him, we'll find it. I will be away for a while on that search, but Gwenny will see that you three extra visitors have a room and food for the night. Perhaps tomorrow your roc-ket will be recharged, and you can be on your way. We do appreciate the way you have helped us, and regret that it has diverted you from your quests.''

''That's very nice of you,'' Ida said. ''But it seems that our quests are linked to yours, and that when you have yours fulfilled, then ours will be too. I still don't know my destiny.''

He shrugged. ''Perhaps. Maybe you are a lost princess, and your kingdom will find you after this is over.''

''Or maybe she's someone's twin sister,'' Mela said. ''And her twin will find her, and they'll live happily ever after.''

''Or maybe she'll turn out to have a Sorceress-caliber magic talent,'' Okra suggested. ''Just waiting to be discovered.''

''Oh, if only any of it could be true!'' Ida said, clasping her hands with longing. ''But first we must help Gwenny, if we can. And I'm sure you can do it, Che, because you are so smart and talented.''

Che tried to resist the obvious flattery, but it did buoy his confidence. Maybe this desperate ploy wasn't as farfetched as he feared.

Gwenny returned with some twine. ''This is spider cable,'' she said. ''It is very light but very strong.''

They wove the threadlike twine into a harness that fit about Che's body. Then they made a smaller harness at the other end of the silken line for the cat. Now the two were firmly linked. Che flicked himself several times with his tail, making himself so light he almost floated, but he did not try to fly. "I am ready," he announced.

Jenny put the cat down on the floor. "Sammy, where is there a female creature who can and will be Gwenny's champion?" she asked. "Who can be safely reached by one of us?" It was a good thing she had remembered to add that last.

The cat took off. Che found himself being hauled along, bumping the floor and walls. But he was so light that the bumps were not uncomfortable. They were zooming through the goblin tunnels, then out of the mountain and away to the south. Where were they going? Not the way they had before, when they sought the Nameless Castle.

Then he remembered something he had forgotten: to ask Godiva Goblin to make a better skirt for Mela Mer-woman. Oh, well; maybe he would be back at Goblin Mountain soon, and could do it then.

Soon they were passing the elf territory. A startled band of Flower Elves stared as they whizzed by the Elf Elm. That reminded Che of the strangeness of Jenny Elf, with her pointed ears, four-fingered hands, and huge size. For the normal Xanth elf was a quarter the height of a human being, while Jenny was more than half human height, matching or slightly exceeding goblin stature. She had come from a world unlike Xanth, and might someday return to it. After she completed her service to the Good Magician.

That reminded him of something else. He had been the closest of friends with Jenny for two years, ever since she had accidentally crossed into Xanth while following Sammy. She had been a great comfort to him in his time of need, and a great companion since then, along with Gwenny Goblin. He privately hoped that she would never return to her World of Two Moons. But even if she did not, there was something that was bound to separate them. For the three of them were growing up. Already they had been inducted into the Adult Conspiracy, and had acted to enforce it on the obnoxious Gobble Goblin. As adults, they would have to start going their own separate ways, for that was the way of adults.

So Jenny's year of service would be only the start of the separation. Their idyllic juvenile association was doomed by one thing or another. That was the tragedy of becoming adult. Perhaps someday he would understand where it was written that compatible childhood associations should be sundered in favor of new associations with adult strangers.

Darkness was closing. It had been late when they returned to Goblin Mountain, and it was later now. Che would rather have retired for the night. But he had to do what he could to help Gwenny. Because if she did not win that final challenge, she would be dead, and the hope for a kinder, gentler goblin tribe would be gone. It was his destiny to change the course of the history of Xanth, and this seemed like the way to do it. For this would eliminate the scourge of the goblins in one region of Xanth, and perhaps sow the seed of a change in other goblin tribes. Goblins were, taken as a whole, one of Xanth's worst scourges, along with dragons, tangle trees, and individual menaces such as Fracto the cloud and Com-Pewter and the Demoness Metria. So it would be well worthwhile to change the nature of the goblins.

They passed through the land of the dragons. Actually, all Xanth was the land of dragons, but they were especially thick here. Che couldn't see them, because it was dark, but he could see their plumes of fire. It seemed that several dragons were toasting a cloud that had tried to sneak in under cover of night. Clouds could be very foolish.

He was bumping worse, and realized that some of his weight had seeped back, as it did with time. He flicked himself again, lightening up.

Then Sammy leaped into a void. It was the Gap Chasm! What was the fool cat up to?

But Che's lightened body now served as a brake, so that the cat did not fall at full speed. They descended to the depth of the chasm, Sammy landing neatly on his four paws and Che hardly touching. Then they were off across the floor of the chasm. It was a good thing that the Gap Dragon didn't hunt at night. Che was probably safe, but Sammy Cat might have been chomped.

The cat found some sort of path and bounded up the other side. Che kept himself light so that he wouldn't pull Sammy off the steep slope. Near the top, Che judged, they plunged into a deep cave. This was amazing! He was sure that Gwenny didn't have any friends under the ground.

On and on they went, through caves and passages and caverns. At one point they even hurdled a subterranean river. Sammy couldn't be looking for one of the callicantzari, could he? Or a demon? Neither of those types would care to support anything like decency in the goblin succession.

At last they came to much larger caverns, illuminated by glowing fungi. Sammy bounded to a chamber set in the wall of this region, and came to a sleeping serpent. He stopped.

"This is it?" Che asked. "This big snake?"

The snake woke. It looked at them. Then it formed a lovely human female head, without changing the rest of its body. "Why Che and Sammy!" the head said. "Whatever brings you here?"

"Nada Naga!" Che exclaimed. Suddenly it made sense. This was one formidable female creature who had an interest in better goblin relations. The naga folk had even made an alliance with the human folk to help contain the goblin menace to their own tunnels. That was how Nada had once gotten herself betrothed to Prince Dolph. "We need your help."

Quickly he explained. Nada's human head nodded. "I see your need, Che, and I would really like to help, but I have another commitment. I must devote my full energy to rehearsing for the Xanth Game that the Muse of History is about to write about. If I took time away from that, I might not do as good a job, and if something should happen to me they would have to train a whole new companion, and that would be awkward.''

''Companion?'' he asked, a bit blankly. ''I am Gwenny Goblin's companion.''

''Yes, that's the same type of thing. As you know, it is not necessarily an easy thing to be. You wouldn't take a day off from being Gwenny's companion, would you?''

''No!'' For he had agreed, and a centaur never went back on his word. ''But it is to save Gwenny that I am here. We need a female to fight for her, so that she can be chief, and Sammy led me here to you. If you can't do it, she won't be chief, and the goblins will kill her, and Gobble will be chief, and they'll be worse than ever.''

''Oh, we can't have that,'' she said. ''Believe me, Che, I do want to help, and ordinarily I would, because the goblins are a worse bane to my kind than to your kind. But I am under contract to the demons, and I must fulfill it. However, Sammy did not lead you falsely. I can refer you to one who should be able to help you more effectively than I could, if you can answer one question.''

''What question is that?''

''Why do you seek a female to help Gwenny?''

''Because no goblin male will help her, so it has to be—'' He paused, realizing his error. ''Oh, this is horribly embarrassing! I made an uncentaurly assumption! It doesn't have to be female. We're not looking for a goblin, but any creature who is capable and willing to support Gwenny's cause.''

Nada smiled. She was lovely when she did that, even with her serpentine torso. In fact, she was lovely when she did anything. Gwenny Goblin was quite pretty, and Mela Merwoman was physically luscious, for all that he was too young to notice, but Nada was beautiful. It was easy to appreciate why Prince Dolph had loved her, even at a young age. ''So my brother, Naldo, should serve your need.''

"Naldo!" Che said, seeing it. Naldo Naga was trained in combat, and had even directed the defense of Goblin Mountain when it had been under siege by the winged monsters. He was no friend of the goblins, but there was an ancient convention that united the ground monsters against the winged monsters, and he had honored it. He knew Gwenny and her mother, Godiva, personally, and he certainly wanted the goblins to reform themselves. "Where is he?"

Sammy bounded off. But Che stretched out his hands and caught the sides of the chamber door. The spider cable went taut, holding the cat back. "I didn't say to find him, Sammy!" he said. "I was asking Nada." Then, to her: "You see, we used up much of the night getting here, and our champion has to be there at noon tomorrow. If we go searching all over Xanth for him, we may be too late for Gwenny."

"Perhaps I can arrange help," she said. Then, to the air: "Professor Grossclout, may I disturb you a moment?"

A horrendous demon appeared. "What mush-head dares disturb my repose!" he thundered. Then he looked into Nada's beautiful face. "Oh, it's you, my dear." Che realized that Nada's perfect features had the power to soothe even the worst of demons. That was fortunate.

"Professor," Nada said winsomely, "my friends Che Centaur and Sammy Cat need to be transported quickly to my brother, Naldo, because—"

Grossclout gestured negligently. Suddenly Che and Sammy were in a dragon's nest. A dragon and a naga were rolling bones in some kind of game. Such games were notorious; they could last for days and nights, and this one seemed to be no exception.

The dragon's near eye widened as he spied Che. "I'm a winged monster, and so are you!" Che said quickly.

"Why, hello, Che," the naga said. He was Naldo, of course. "Draco won't eat you. After all, he knows you and is sworn to protect you. It is obvious that you are here on some sort of business. Or did you come to join the game?''

That was right! It had been several years since Draco had visited the winged centaur family, and dragons tended to look somewhat alike to Che, but now he recognized the firedrake. He quickly explained, again.

''Yes, certainly, I will be Gwendolyn's champion,'' Naldo said. ''I shall be glad to facilitate the succession of the first female goblin chief.'' He glanced at the bones. ''But first I must finish my game here.''

''But the champion must be there by noon!''

''Never fear, I'll be there. Goblin Mountain is not all that far from here, and I can travel rapidly in my large serpent form. Just put out a direction sign indicating exactly where the match is to occur, and I will appear promptly at noon.''

''Thank you,'' Che said. ''I will return now with the good news. How do I get out of this cave?'' For he could see that the nest was in a closed cave, with a lake at its base.

''I will take you out and to the ground,'' Naldo said. ''Hang on.''

Che got on the serpentine back and hung on as well as he could. Naldo slithered out of the nest, down the vertical side of the cave, and into the lake. Che held his breath, and hoped Sammy was also holding his breath as he was dragged along at the end of his tether. In a moment they were out of the water, and in another moment out of the cave, and, then Naldo was slithering down the clifflike mountain slope to the ground. He really knew how to travel, in this body!

''Tell them I am coming by invitation, not invasion,'' Naldo said as they stood on the ground. ''So we don't start another war.''

''I'll do that,'' Che agreed.

Then Naldo slithered back up the mountain, and Che set Sammy on his back and set off at a light-footed gallop to the north. The cat could not lead the way, for they were in effect going home now: from the place they had started. Anyway, Sammy was surely very tired after his wild run past the Gap Chasm.

For that matter, Che himself was tired. He had gotten no sleep, and he was still young enough to need it. But he had a job to do, and he would do it. He moved as fast as he could, never pausing, knowing the way to go. He could rest after he got there with his message of hope. Gwenny would be so pleased!

As dawn came, Che reached Goblin Mountain. The sentry recognized him and let him pass. "But after noon, you'll be horsemeat, you little winged freak," the goblin said pleasantly.

Che went to Gwenny's suite, where Idiot stood guard. The goblin seemed glad to see him. "I hope you got someone good," Idiot said. " 'Cause it won't be nice if Gwenny loses." That was surely the understatement of the day.

"I did," Che said, and knocked on the door. Gwenny opened it, garbed in her nightie. "Oh, Che, you're back!" she cried, hugging him.

"Naldo Naga's coming at noon," he gasped. "To be your champion. Put out a sign saying where the contest is to be." Then he found a pile of pillows waiting for him and collapsed into them. He was asleep almost before he landed, but knew that the girls would take care of things.

Chapter 17. Chief

Ida was worried. It was almost noon, and Naldo Naga had not yet shown up. It wasn't that she didn't believe him, but that she feared that something could happen to delay him, and that would be disastrous.

The contest was to be held in the main chamber of the mountain, where there was plenty of room for both the combatants and the bloodthirsty spectators. It was even possible for some of the lady goblins to peek in from the doorways. Gobble's champion was already there: a horrendous male ogre, who was gnawing on a pile of bones while he waited for the fun to begin. Gobble had promised him a year's supply of bones if he won, and of course he expected to win.

Moron, Idiot, and Imbecile formed a tight group near Gwenny. They were armed, now, with goblin-sized clubs, and looked ugly. Ida knew this was because they were afraid they were going to have to use them. But they were a pitifully small group compared to the hundreds of goblins who surrounded Gobble.

"Do you know him?" Ida asked Okra.

"No. He is from the Ogre-Fen-Ogre Fen," Okra replied. "My tribe hasn't had much contact with them in the past few centuries. I understand that they are fierce, uncivilized, and crude. In short, the very ideal of ogre-dom.''

"I realize that ogres are justifiably proud of their strength, stupidity, and ugliness," Ida said. "It must be a horror, being of their number." Then she paused, suffering a new idea. "Or is it possible that your tastes could run to what is typical for your ogre kind? Suddenly I can see the sense that would make."

"Yes, that's the kind of male I like," Okra said. There had been a time when her taste was different, but she had evidently matured during her travels, and now the notion of a brute male appealed. "But of course one like that would never notice me, because I'm not strong, stupid, or ugly."

"Well, I must admit that you're not stupid or ugly. But you were strong enough to bash a hole in the wall of the Nameless Castle," Ida reminded her.

"That was because of the seed of Thyme, which gave me time to bash as long as I needed. I couldn't do it otherwise."

"And you breathed so hard that it stopped that dragon on the Iron Mountain," Ida said.

"Well, then I had the madcap on. That entirely changed my nature. I couldn't have done it in my normal state."

Ida nodded. "I suppose you're right. You don't have the qualities a regular ogre would like. But I have to say that those same deficiencies appeal to me."

"Too bad you're not an ogre," Okra said, gazing longingly at the male ogre.

Noon neared and still Naldo did not appear. Gwenny looked nervous. "Are you sure you told him here, at noon?" she asked Che, who had dragged himself up from his slumber for this occasion.

"Yes. You did have a sign put out for him?"

"Yes. Moron made it. It said CHIEF CHALLENGE—GOBLIN MOUNTAIN."

"Let me go check that," Mela said.

She walked away, to the crude whistles of the goblins,

and some cries of "Get out of here, fish-tail!" Then her Freudian slip slipped around to flash a naughty glimpse of her panty, and the goblins went silent, freaked out. It served them right. Moron went with her, to show her where the sign was. His eyes had been where they belonged, straight ahead.

"I must ask Godiva to make her a new skirt to cover both her Freudian slip and plaid panty," Che murmured beside Ida. She could only agree.

Gobble marched into the chamber, surrounded by his henchmen. "Well, sis, where's your champion?" he demanded obnoxiously.

"He's on his way," Gwenny replied.

"Well, he'd better be here at noon, or you forfeit. Won't that be awful, ha-ha." And the henchmen joined him, laughing coarsely.

Mela returned. "Someone's changed the sign!" she said indignantly. "Now it says CHIEF CHALLENGE—MOUNT EVER-REST."

"Mount Ever-Rest!" Gwenny exclaimed. "But that's far away from here!"

"He must have seen the sign and slithered off to the other mountain," Ida said, realizing what a dastardly deed had been done. "He can't possibly get back here in time!"

"It's another one of my brother's horrible tricks!" Gwenny said, devastated.

"But then we don't have a champion," Jenny said.

"Noon!" Gobble cried exultantly. "Come on, Smithereen! Time for the bashing!"

Okra, standing beside Ida, jumped. The jump wasn't noticed by anyone else in the general hubbub, but Ida wondered what had caused it. So she inquired. "Why did you jump?"

"Smithereen—that's the ogre I was to marry! He was on his way south when I fled home."

"Oh, then you have met him halfway. That's nice."

"But I ran out on him," Okra said. "He won't like that."

"Maybe he doesn't know, since he hasn't yet reached Lake Ogre-Chobee." That seemed reasonable.

The ogre crunched the last of his bone and tramped to the center of the chamber. "Me bash, make hash!" he grunted, pounding his hairy chest with his ham fists. Then he lifted his club from the harness on his back and waved it in the air.

Ida was disgusted. But she noted that Okra was licking her lips. Tastes certainly did vary!

"So where's your champion?" Gobble demanded. "If he's not here, Smithereen gets to crunch your bones first, sis!"

The horror of it was that he wasn't joking, because it was the nature of goblin males to be awful and the nature of ogre males to eat folk. Gwenny's life really was on the line.

"You changed the sign!" Gwenny accused him.

"So what? So show your champion or forfeit," Gobble said exultantly. It was obvious that he had planned exactly what had happened. The girls had been trusting, while the brat had cheated without hesitation. Ida could see that it really would be better for the goblins to be ruled by a female chief.

"I'll have to do it myself," Gwenny said bravely. "I've got the wand, at least."

"Hey, no wand!" Gobble cried. "That's magic at a distance! That's outlawed!"

"Oh, no, he's right," Gwenny said, looking ill.

"You mean he can cheat and you can't?" Mela asked.

"I didn't catch him cheating in time," Gwenny said. She handed the wand to Godiva.

"No, you can't!" Jenny Elf said. "I'll do it instead!" She stepped out into the center.

"Hey, four-eyes is coming in!" Gobble cried. "Only now she's bat blind instead! What a show!"

"She can't see?" Okra asked.

"Her spectacles were lost, and she didn't have time to

get new ones,'' Che said. "She can see in a special way,
but that won't help her against the ogre.''

Mela glanced at Okra, sadly. "It seems that your desire
is about to be granted. You'll be rid of Jenny Elf.''

Suddenly Okra strode forward. She caught the elf by
the collar and hauled her away from the arena. "Get out
of here, girl. I'll do it.''

Astonished, Ida tried to protest. "But this isn't your
quarrel, Okra! You don't care about the goblin succession,
and you have good reason not to help Jenny Elf! And you
can't fight Smithereen either! None of us can!'' Yet even
as she spoke, the idea was growing that maybe it was
possible.

Okra bent to pick up the roc talon they had brought.
"It's a dirty job, but somebody's got to do it.'' She walked
out to meet Smithereen.

The male ogre stared. "Who you?'' he demanded.

"I am Okra Ogress, whom you were supposed to marry.
Instead, I am going to bash you into oblivion,'' Okra said.
She poked at him with the point of the talon.

It was evident that Smithereen didn't recognize the
name. He might never have been told, or he might have
forgotten, since bad memory was part of ogre stupidity.
"Ho-ho! You no O,'' he said, grabbing the talon in a ham
hand. Okra was jerked off balance. She was only half his
size, and lacked muscle. She was obviously no match for
him.

Gobble and the henchmen were doubling over with
laughter. "What a silly filly!'' Gobble exclaimed.

"She's no filly, she's an ogress,'' Che muttered. "And
a brave and selfless one.''

Then Ida got another idea. "The madcap, Okra!'' she
called. "That's what you need!''

Okra heard. She reached into her pack and pulled out
the cap. She jammed it on her head.

"Ho ho!'' Smithereen roared. "Fat hat!''

But Okra was changing. Her body seemed to be growing larger and hairier, and her face uglier. She was en-

raged. "Sneer he at she?" She jerked on the talon, pulling him forward, then pounded a fist into his belly. "Smelly belly!" she screamed.

"OOOF! POOOF!" Smithereen gasped, surprised. The blow had evidently had a good deal of force.

"Never underestimate the ire of an ogress scorned," Che murmured, intrigued.

Ida's belief increased. After all, Okra had fought the dragon. The madcap made all the difference. Perhaps even more so than usual, for Okra had seemed to like the ogre, and it might be reversing the power of her liking, turning it into hating. As Che observed, women did not like to be scorned.

Now Smithereen was catching on that there was after all some opposition. He straightened up, forming a ham fist. He lifted his massive club, whose mass seemed to be almost as much as Okra's whole body. He swung it viciously at her head.

But Okra stepped back and swung the talon. It met the club and stopped it. Ida realized that the talon itself must have magic, to enable the roc to land on the toughest surface with all her weight and not break a nail, and to hold on to whatever it touched. It made a good weapon.

Then Okra took the offense. She swung the talon, bashing his arm out of the way, then stabbed him in the chest with the point. The thrust wasn't strong enough to impale him, but it did make him stagger back. She followed up with another stab, this time at the head.

But Smithereen did know how to fight. He swung his club around again, and when Okra countered with the talon, he reached down with his free hand and grabbed her by the hair. He lifted her into the air. Her cap tilted crazily, but remained in place.

"Hey, that's a foul!" Jenny Elf cried.

"There are no fouls in this type of combat," Gwenny said morosely. She seemed not to have phenomenal confidence in the outcome.

Okra heard that. "No fouls?" she asked. "I can do anything I want?"

"That's right, hair-face!" Gobble answered. "Whatcha going to do, kiss him?" And he rolled over again with laughter, and his henchmen with him. To a brat his age, kissing was contemptible.

Okra hauled up both knees and bashed the ogre in the chin. He fell back, dropping her. She landed neatly, then used the talon to stab between his legs. She wedged it around so that it made him stumble and fall. Then she leaned over him, taking the talon in both hands. She was using her hidden advantage, and fighting intelligently.

Suddenly Gobble got nervous. She was actually making a fight of it!

"Ha-ha!" Jenny Elf cried, getting into it. "Your ogre can't match that madcap!"

"Madcap!" Gobble exclaimed. "That's magic!" He ran into the arena behind Okra, made a terrific leap, and grabbed the cap from her head.

"Hey!" Ida cried, outraged. "That's cheating! You can't interfere!"

"So whatcha going to do about it, girl-face?" the goblin brat demanded, tossing the cap to a henchman.

Without the madcap, Okra lost her furious power and initiative. She stood there over the fallen ogre as if not knowing what to do next. In a moment he would jump back up and pulverize her. She couldn't even give him her asthma, because she had already given it to Hugh Mongous the monoceros.

"You can do it, Okra!" Ida cried, desperately believing.

Che could only shake his head. Optimism was about to collide with reality.

Then Okra threw herself down on Smithereen's body. Her face landed on his face. She put her mouth to his mouth.

"She's doing it!" Mela cried, astonished. "She's kissing him!"

For a moment Smithereen lay still. Then he threw Okra off, clambered to his feet, and opened his huge ugly mouth. "Ugh! Ugh!" he cried. And charged out of the chamber.

The goblins gaped. "Huh?" Gobble asked intelligently.

Then Ida caught on. "She did what you said!" she called. "She kissed him! And he couldn't stand it! He fled! And Okra's the winner! She beat your champion!" Yet Ida realized that this had been a sacrifice for Okra, because she would rather have made Smithereen like her instead of being revolted by her. She had thrown away whatever chance she might have had to get together with him.

Gobble's mouth dropped open. "No fair!" he cried.

But Gwenny seized the moment. "It's fair! There are no fouls. She beat him by disgusting him so much he fled. He lost and she won. And you have lost and I have won! Now I am chief."

"No!" he cried despairingly.

Gwenny whirled on the henchmen. "Now you will obey me, or be banished. Arrest Gobble!"

Stunned, the henchmen stood still. But Moron, Idiot, and Imbecile strode eagerly forward, ready to do their duty.

"No, she's just a stupid girl!" Gobble cried, as his henchmen blocked off Gwenny's three goblins. "You can't obey her! Kill her!"

"Now that makes me mad," Okra said. She lifted the talon and strode toward Gobble. The henchmen scattered at her approach.

"You can't be mad!" Gobble said. "You lost the madcap."

"I don't need the madcap to be mad at a sniveling brat like you," Okra said. She caught him by the collar and lifted him into the air, much as Smithereen had lifted her. She brought the talon around.

"No! No!" he screamed, waving his stubby arms and legs helplessly. "Don't kill me! Don't kill me!"

"Why not?" Okra demanded. "You were going to kill Gwenny."

"But she's just a stupid *girl!*"

"Well, so am I. And you're just a bratty boy," Okra retorted. She aimed the point of the talon at his face.

Gobble burst into tears.

"This is what you want to be chief?" Okra asked the henchmen. She let Gobble drop and turned away.

She had made her point. One by one the henchmen turned to Gwenny. "You are chief," one said. "We don't like it, but we must obey you."

"Thank you," Gwenny said, as if the issue had never been in doubt. She faced Gobble. "Get out of here, brat. I hereby banish you from Goblin Mountain. If you ever return, the first goblin who sees you will kill you, or suffer the consequence himself."

Gobble got up and attempted some bravado. "You can't do this! I'll get you!"

"If you don't leave immediately, I might change my mind about letting you live," Gwenny said evenly.

The brat hesitated. Then Okra took a step toward him.

Gobble quickly fled.

Gwenny acted as if the brat had never existed. "Moron!" she snapped.

Moron came forward, somewhat apprehensively. "Yes, chief."

"I appoint you Head Honcho," Gwenny said. "All these henchmen will answer to you. You will keep order in Goblin Mountain, and report to me alone."

"Gee," Moron said, abashed.

"We have to report to that slug?" a henchman demanded incredulously.

Then he sailed into the air. Ida saw that Godiva was using her wand.

"You have a problem with that?" Gwenny inquired.

The henchman sailed over a stalagmite near the edge of the main chamber, and hovered over the sharp stone point. "N-no problem," the goblin said quickly.

"Are you sure?" Gwenny asked sweetly.

The henchman descended toward the stalagmite, butt first. "Quite sure, %%%%!" he muttered.

"I don't think I heard that," Gwenny said.

The goblin landed on the tip. "I HAVE NO PROBLEM!" he bellowed.

"I am so glad you got the point," Gwenny said.

Only then did he nudge off the stone column and come to rest gently on the floor, rubbing his posterior.

For some reason none of the other henchmen expressed any problems either.

"Idiot," Gwenny said, and that goblin came forward. "I am placing you in charge of Intelligence."

"Uh—what's that word?" Idiot asked blankly.

"Spying," she said. "You will make sure that there are no spies in Goblin Mountain. You will give any you find a bath."

"A bath?"

"You will keep a big pot of water here, which you will heat to boiling," she explained. "For the bath."

He began to get a glimmer. He glanced at the henchmen. "But how will I know who's a spy?"

"That's easy. It is anyone who says a word against the new chief, or any friends of the chief. Or who does anything that might reflect adversely on Goblin Mountain."

"Might what?"

"Look bad," she clarified. "Dirty deeds. Dirty words."

"Actually, those henchmen already look sort of dirty to me," he said. "And I think I heard a dirty word in the mouth of one of them." He glanced meaningfully at the one who had said "%%%%."

"Then set up the pot and give them a cold bath," she said. "That should clean them off. Use soap to wash out their mouths. If that doesn't do it, heat the water. I'm sure they will improve as it warms."

Ida saw that Gwenny had a fair notion of how to enforce her leadership. Probably her mother had instructed her.

Idiot set about the job with gusto. A huge kettle floated in, no doubt assisted by Godiva's wand. Goblins started carrying buckets of water to dump into it, and bars of soapstone. There would not be much spying in Goblin Mountain after this day.

"Imbecile," Gwenny said, and the third goblin approached. "I am appointing you the Foreign Relations Officer. You will make arrangements to meet with representatives of the other folk of the neighborhood, such as the Flower Elves, the griffins, and especially the naga. We are henceforth going to live in peace with them all."

"In peace?" he asked, amazed.

"And cooperation. We may even trade goods with them. If any doubt, I will go personally to clarify the new order."

A new figure appeared. It was a huge snake. It formed a handsome human head. "Hear, hear!" it exclaimed.

"Naldo Naga!" Che exclaimed. "You found us!"

"A bit late, I am afraid," Naldo agreed. "There was some difficulty with a sign. I turned around as soon as I realized. Where is the opposing champion?"

"He departed," Gwenny said. "That was Smithereen Ogre."

"Oh, that must have been the one I saw crashing through trees and mountains. I asked him where he was going, and he said he didn't remember. So I asked him where he was coming from, and he said he was fleeing a cute ogress."

"That was me," Okra said. "I beat him by kissing him." Yet she looked sad rather than happy.

Naldo glanced at her. "He said that ogress wasn't very ugly or stupid, but she had a secret weapon that destroyed his will to fight. I think you impressed him."

"Oh!" Okra said, thrilled.

Naldo turned back to Gwenny. "So it is done? You are now chief of Goblin Mountain?"

"Yes, thanks to you," Gwenny said. "You sent Mela,

Ida, and Okra to rescue us, and then Okra won the final challenge for me. I owe them all so much, and you too!''

"I don't think so," Naldo said. "I believe the scales are even, now."

"But without their help, I would never have made it!''

"Bear with me," Naldo said. "If you will allow me to explain, I think I can satisfy everyone." He glanced around. "And if you will post a lookout, I am expecting another person shortly. She should be treated with respect."

"By all means." Gwenny sent a goblin off to keep an eye out for the person. Then they gathered in a corner of the chamber, so as to be away from the clamor of the ongoing goblin bath.

Naldo coiled his serpentine body and addressed those around him. "These three," he said, indicating Mela, Okra, and Ida herself, "came to the Good Magician Humfrey to ask their Questions. Instead of answering, he sent them to my sister, the Princess Nada Naga, who sent them on to me. When I talked with them, I realized why the Good Magician acted as he did, and I did what I had to do."

"You sent us to the Simurgh!" Ida said. "And she sent us to rescue Che Centaur. You said you would grant all our wishes, if we did."

"Precisely. Now I shall do that." Naldo looked at Okra. "It is your desire to become a major character."

"Yes," Okra said. "And you did give me the chance; I see that now. But I threw it away, because I didn't get rid of Jenny Elf."

"You saved me!" Jenny said. "I would have been destroyed, but you stepped in and beat the ogre!''

"You sacrificed what you perceived to be your own welfare, for the sake of one you didn't want to help," Naldo said to Okra. "Why did you do that?"

"Well, it just wasn't right to have a blind person fight an ogre," Okra said. "And I saw that Gwenny did need to be chief. So I just had to do it. I know I messed up, but I guess I just didn't want to get what I wanted that way. But maybe it's not so bad being a minor character. Maybe I can work something out with Smithereen.''

"Maybe you can," Naldo said. "But that will be another story. In *this* story you do achieve your desire, Okra.''

Okra shook her head, confused. Ida was confused too. "I told you, I gave it up," Okra said.

"And I told you that you didn't," Naldo said. "It may have been true that there was an opening for a particular major character, and that Jenny Elf got it. But new openings occur all the time. The thing is, they are not just given out to those who want them. If that were true, every Mundane would be overrunning Xanth; we'd have Mundanes clogging the drains. So few have the chance, and fewer are called. I saw that you had a chance, but only if you qualified, and the only way you could qualify was by doing something noble, so that others would want to see you as a major character. That is why the Good Magician did not answer you; he knew that you did not want the thing you asked for, and that you could achieve your true desire only if you acted appropriately without knowing its significance. You could not act unselfishly if you knew the reward for it. You had to remain ignorant until your chance came. I gave you that chance, and it seems you came through. You earned your status.''

"I did?" Okra asked, bemused.

"You acted selflessly, and did a truly good deed at great risk to yourself. You saved Jenny Elf, and won the chiefship for Gwendolyn Goblin. In those actions you became a major character." He bowed his head, briefly. "I salute you, Okra Ogress, and congratulate you on the charmed life which will now be yours.''

"Can this be true?" Okra asked dazedly.

Jenny Elf went to her. "Oh, yes, that's the way it works." She kissed Okra on the cheek.

"Jenny knows," Naldo said. "She routinely does similar things. She is about to go to give a year's service to the Good Magician, which she undertook on behalf of her friend Gwenny. Decency and generosity are the hallmarks of major characterdom. Perhaps the two of you can be friends, now.''

''Oh, I'm sure they can!'' Ida said enthusiastically as the two looked at each other.

''And you, Ida Human,'' Naldo said, turning to her. ''You may be the most remarkable case I've seen. You sought your destiny—but your destiny was beyond your dreams. You, too, had to remain ignorant, if you were to achieve it, so the Good Magician also declined to answer you. Instead he gave you the same chance he gave Okra.''

''But what *is* my destiny?'' Ida asked, as bemused as Okra had been.

Naldo turned to Che Centaur. ''What do you think it is?'' he asked.

''Why, I don't know,'' Che said, surprised.

''But you have an idea. Come on—I know you do, because I see it reflected in Ida. You have conjectured.''

''Well, we only made idle guesses,'' Che said, ''when I was about to set off to find a champion. We speculated how she might be a princess, or somebody's twin, or have a Sorceress-caliber magic talent. But it didn't mean anything.''

''It means everything,'' Naldo said firmly. ''I suspected it the moment I saw her, but I couldn't figure why the Good Magician had declined to tell her. So I assumed that the two aspects of three were fixed, but that the third required special handling, just as was the case with Okra's major character status. That premature telling would spoil it. So I postponed answering until I could verify it—and now I have. Ida is all those things.''

''What?'' Ida squeaked, thrilled and appalled. ''A princess? A twin? With a strong talent? I've never shown any sign of—''

''I asked a friend to come here,'' Naldo said. ''After she made sure it was safe, of course. She should be arriving just about now.''

Indeed, the posted goblin appeared. Behind him was a cloaked figure. It seemed to be a woman. Her face could not be seen behind the thick veil, yet she looked oddly familiar. She came to stand before Naldo, remaining anonymous.

"Ida," Naldo said, "your destiny was to be all the things you ever dreamed of being. It was your talent which confused me, but now it can be revealed. First, the other two." He nodded at the anonymous woman. "Meet your twin sister, who was as surprised by the news as you are."

Ida opened her mouth, but could not speak. She actually was a twin?

"But who is she?" Che asked.

The woman lifted her veil. The others stared. "They look almost alike!" Okra said.

"So they do," Naldo said. "But there are those here who know our visitor."

"The Princess Ivy of Human Xanth," Godiva exclaimed.

Now Ida stared. "The Princess Ivy?"

Ivy took her hand, then embraced her. "I did not believe it at first, but now I do," she said. "We finally verified it on the Tapestry. The stork tried to bring two, but lost one, and I was the only one who reached Castle Roogna. I never knew!"

"So you are Princess Ida," Naldo said. "And now your talent, and the reason the Good Magician declined to identify it. It complements Ivy's talent of Enhancement, but is even more subtle. Your magic is that of the Idea, as your name suggests. When you get an idea, it comes true."

"Every time Ida said she was sure something would work, it did!" Mela exclaimed. "She even suggested that Okra don the madcap, so she could beat the ogre."

Ida realized that it was true. She had come to believe that Okra had a chance, and then Okra had won, even without the madcap. She had believed that Che would find a champion, and he had, even if Gobble had managed to mess that up. Everything she truly believed in had happened.

"But that must be Xanth's most powerful talent," Godiva said. "She could make anything happen, just by deciding that it should!"

"No," Naldo said. "It is obvious that it has never been that easy for Ida. Because her talent has a crucial liability. The idea has to come from someone who doesn't know her talent."

"But *she* didn't know her talent," Mela said.

"Correct. That was vital, because it meant that she could get ideas on her own, and make them come true. Now that she knows her talent, she can no longer do that. And none of us, here, can do it either, because now we know her talent. So it will continue to be just as tricky to invoke it as it has been before. But when it *is* invoked, it is certainly of Sorceress caliber, as befits a princess."

"But the Good Magician," Che said. "Surely he knew!"

"Surely he did," Naldo agreed. "As did the demon Professor Grossclout, and the Simurgh. But they also knew that Ida would not achieve her destiny unless someone who did *not* know suggested it. They also knew that her talent was needed to help rescue you, Che, and to enable Gwenny to become chief. Because Ida is a nice, optimistic person, inclined to believe the best of people and situations. Without that special type of support, your prospects would have been bleak indeed. But now the important things have been accomplished, and it is only fair that Ida know her own nature." He turned to her. "You will be going home to Castle Roogna with your sister, now."

"You—you recognized me," Ida said. "When the demon professor conjured us to Draco's nest."

"I thought I did," he agreed. "I thought you were Ivy. Then I realized that you weren't, but that you were so very like her that something special was going on. So I started investigating, and gradually it came to make sense. But you could not be allowed to know until you had seen

Gwenny through to victory. The matter was too important to be risked. Every person who recognized your nature had to conceal that knowledge, until the time was right.''

''Yes,'' Ida agreed faintly. She turned to Ivy. ''But was I really your twin sister, before someone thought of it? I mean, if it is my talent that makes things come true—''

''It's true now,'' Ivy said. ''We no longer need to worry about what might have been, or what might not have been, or how any premature revelation of your talent might have changed things.''

''That's beautiful,'' Mela said. ''I'm so glad for you, Ida. I hope we can still be friends, even if you are now a princess, and Okra and I are just people.''

''Of course we can!'' Ida exclaimed, going to hug her and the ogress. ''I'm sure it makes no difference.'' Then she had a painful second thought. ''Except that if my own ideas don't work, now—''

''Friendship is not an idea, it's a personal choice,'' Godiva said. ''You will remain friends if you want to be.''

''Oh, I want to be!'' Ida said. Then a third thought came. ''But you, Mela—what of your quest? You haven't found a husband, and now I can't get the idea that you will.''

''Yes, it is time to address that matter,'' Naldo said. ''I promised all of you fulfillment, and now it is Mela Merwoman's turn. Mela, for the record, exactly what kind of husband do you seek?''

''Oh, nothing much,'' she said, abashed. ''Just the smartest, handsomest, nicest, most manly prince available who won't mind my swimming in the sea often, and who likes raw fish, and who will help me brush out my hair. Some folk seem to think there is something wrong with a tail or with greenish tresses. But—''

''Which is why the Good Magician sent you to my sister,'' Naldo said. ''And she sent you to me. And why you wore that Freudian slip, and slowed me the color of your panties. I must admit, that very nearly freaked me out.

But I knew I had to wait until the rest of your quest was done and your friends had achieved their desires.''

Mela blushed a solid plaid. ''You saw my panty?'' But there was more to her blush than that; she was evidently foolishly smitten with Naldo, just as Okra was with Smithereen.

''Just a wee glimpse,'' he said. ''But that was sufficient. I know that you are the sexiest crossbreed human in Xanth, which defines my own simple desire in a wife.'' He changed to his human form, and stood there as an extraordinarily handsome man. ''I am the one you seek: Prince Naldo Naga, until this moment Xanth's most eligible bachelor. I will marry you, Mela, and fulfill your dreams, even as you fulfill mine. I have no objection to a pretty tail, having one myself.'' He changed briefly back to his naga form. ''And I do like to swim on occasion, and eat raw fish, especially with compatible company. I shall be happy to help brush out your greenish hair, if you will wear that slip and those panties and sit in my lap while I'm doing it.'' He shot her a glance that nearly violated the Adult Conspiracy.

''Oh, yes!'' Mela exclaimed swooningly.

''My sister has been trying to marry me off for years,'' the prince confided. ''And she has at last succeeded. Come, I shall kiss you now, and seal the betrothal.''

Ida could not even marvel at his assurance, because he was a prince, and he had been instrumental in helping them all complete their quests. He was horribly smart, yet as it turned out, he had had a nice reason for making them work for their answers. Mela could not have found a better match. She too would become a princess, because she would marry a prince. All because of that Freudian slip and her fancy panty. Who would have thought that the color of her panties would be so important!

Mela seemed ready to faint, but she managed to stave it off, because there was just too much to appreciate in the conscious state. Ida saw that Prince Naldo was indeed the most intelligent, handsome, nicest unmarried prince in

Xanth. It hadn't been clear before, because he had never shown them his human form, but now it was impossible to doubt. Mela's dream had been realized.

The prince took Mela in his arms and kissed her. They made Xanth's loveliest couple, even if they were both in human form at the moment. Only the goblins seemed bored.

Then the Freudian slip flashed a glimpse that nudged the male goblins across the line into freakdom.

Naldo drew back half a smidgen and gazed into Mela's oceanic eyes. "How do I love sea?" he asked rhetorically. "Let me count the waves." The merwoman seemed about to dissolve. She had been warned about his humor.

A hand touched Ida's arm. She turned to find Princess Ivy there. "Come, sister: we must take you to Castle Roogna to meet your family."

Ida realized that she had indeed achieved her destiny. They all had.

Author's Note

Jenny Elf reported to the Good Magician's castle. "I am here to do my year's service," she said.

Magician Grey Murphy was there. "But you're in the wrong place," he said. "This is the Author's Note."

"The what?"

"Never mind. You're supposed to be in your own chapter, in the main body of the narrative."

"No, the story is done. Gwenny Goblin is chief of Goblin Mountain, and Che Centaur is helping her. Okra is a major character, Ida is a twin princess, and Mela is showing Naldo Naga her two very fine—"

"Beware of the Adult Conspiracy!" he said, worried.

"Her two very fine firewater opals," Jenny continued. "And maybe something else, but that's their business. So everything has been wrapped up, and I'm here for my year."

"I see you don't understand," he said. "It has to do with the way the Muse of History organizes these narratives. This one has two groups of three characters each, and they take turns with the viewpoint. So a cycle was Mela, Ida, Okra, Che, Gwenny, and you, Jenny. Three such cycles complete the narrative. Eighteen chapters in all. It's done to confound the cri-tics, I think, who don't know anything about literature. You're supposed to be viewing Chapter Eighteen.''

"What Chapter Eighteen?'' Jenny demanded. ''I gave Gwenny back her contact lens when I got a new pair of spectacles, so I can't see dreams anymore. Is it a dream chapter?''

Grey looked flustrated. ''It's the final chapter! Where everything gets wrapped up with a happy ending, according to the formula.''

''But everything's already wrapped up. So there's nothing left for me to view. So here I am, ready to get this yearlong chore out of the way, though I'd rather be with Gwenny and Che.''

''Maybe Humfrey can explain it to you,'' he said.

They went up to the tiny study with its piles of everything. The old gnome looked up. ''About time you got here, Jenny,'' he grumped. ''What kept you?''

''But she's supposed to be running Chapter Eighteen,'' Grey protested.

Humfrey scowled. ''Clio glitched,'' he said. ''A chapter got mislaid. Probably because Jenny came from a foreign world, and so doesn't mesh perfectly with Xanth. There is no Chapter Eighteen.''

''But that means Jenny doesn't get her allotted viewpoint,'' Grey said. ''That isn't right.''

''So let her handle the credits,'' Humfrey said.

Grey threw up his hands. ''All right. Jenny, you will begin your service by handling a mundane chore. It's highly irregular, but we just have to make do. Here is the list of credits; just describe them in your own words. I'll show you to your room, so you won't disturb Humfrey.''

Jenny took the list. It was a strange thing, but then everything about the Good Magician's enterprise was strange. Hers, she realized, was not to reason why, hers was just to wash and dry. Or whatever.

She took a breath and started reading: ''The hit men and the mitten bush were sent by Tim Hittle. The piggy bank was from Guy McCutchan. The road hog is Robert

Turbyfill. The lemon tree is Kanayo Agbodike. Electra's daughters, Dawn and Eve, and their talents are from Abbey Wray. Esk Ogre and Bria Brassie's son, Brusque, is from C. M. Keller, and his talent of making things hard and heavy or light and soft is from Jason Menefree. Calling a goblin child a goblet is from Ronald Foster.''

Then she came to a paragraph. This was a big one. It was also a surprise, because it related to a character she had just come to know. ''Okra Ogress and the related detail is from Barbara Hay Hummel, she of the pain medicine who brought us Rose of Roogna in *Question Quest.* Barb is also responsible for the fanciest of the panties Mela modeled but did not choose, and for Canis the dog and the seed of Thyme.'' Jenny shook her head. Okra had not only been a minor character, she had been fashioned by a Mundane? No wonder she had been eager to changer her status! And what was this about pain medicine? Someone in pain would really have the desire to escape to fantasy! This whole thing was weird.

She took another breath and resumed. ''The asthma is from Carson Fredericks. The idea of the healing water for Gwenny Goblin's eyes is from Deborah Jones. The reason healing elixir did not cure Gwenny's or Jenny's vision is from Woodrow W. Windischaman III. The contact lenses for Gwenny are from Kit Arnold, Rene Alexander, Lisa Campbell, and Ann Franklin. The multiplication table is from John C. Wear.'' Jenny looked up, unable to restrain herself. ''Thank you, John Wear!'' she said with the heaviest irony she could muster. What a mess that had been!

She took another breath and went on. ''The pulpit and the putrifly are from Patrick Brown. Attila the Hunny Bee is from John Brummel. The leaves of absence are from Eric Meyersfield. The gunman is from Mark Richman. The winged fauns are from Brent Kauffman.'' She looked up again. She hoped those folks would just keep their future suggestions to themselves! Did they have any idea how they had complicated her life and the lives of her friends?

But then the endless credits took another tack. "The otterbees are from Virginia A. Johnson. The hoof-in-mouth disease is from Christopher Onstad. The tickle- and gooseberry bushes are from W. G. Bliss. The madcap is from Zoe Selengut." She looked up again. That had turned out to be really useful in the end. So maybe these credits weren't all mere mischief.

"Alister and his dog, Marbles, are from Jody Lynn Nye, the nymph who authored *The Encyclopedia of Xanth*. The Propeller Plains are from Mayfair Games. The doldrums are from Carol Jacob. The Dragon Dola is from Russell Duffer. Joy'nt the little skeleton is from David Edison. Thomas Hardy provided the inspiration for the pun on *Far from the Madding Crowd*. Nada Naga's debt to the gourd was pointed out by Patrick Ware. The problem of children exposed to what the Adult Conspiracy conceals was suggested by N. N. Reits, though that treatment may not be precisely what was envisioned. This is, after all, Xanth." Jenny looked up again. "But it was bad enough," she said to no one in particular.

She resumed her reading. "The old wives' tail and air brush were by Tamara Bailey. Darren, the boy with the ability to make things into other things, was suggested by Melinda Gordon, who was age eight when she wrote. Isn't it odd that she was just his age? The roc and the hard place was the genius of Jason Rodrigues; there will be more about that concept in Novel nineteen. The algae bra was from Robert A. Hubby, relayed from his math teacher, Dick Greseth. Who says math can't be fun? The Freudian slip was by Cynthia Bellah, and Mount Ever-Rest was by Charles E. Brown. Ivy's having a twin sister was the idea of Joanna van Oorschot, who used her magic to make it come true. It came true for Ivy's mundane identity, too: the author's daughter Penny found a friend, Joana Jansen, exactly her age to the day. Obviously that's no coincidence; Joana with the one *N* must have come into being when Joanna with the two *N*'s thought up the notion."

Jenny looked up again, startled. "So that's how it happened! It came from Mundania!'' She was amazed at these revealed interactions between Xanth and Mundania. She returned to the list. '' 'How do I love sea,' etc. was spoken by Suzan Malles.'' Jenny sighed. When would it ever end?

It got worse. ''The derivation of the title was devious. In the dawn of history there was the promise or threat of the sound of his horn, or the playing of the Angel Gabriel's trumpet, signaling the end of the world. Then Stephen Donaldson used a similar patterning for his novel *The Mirror of Her Dreams*. Then came Powers's *The Stress of Her Regard*. Xanth of course is lower brow—in fact about halfway from the brow to the ground—and distressingly naughty. Thus *The Color of Her Panties.* '' This time Jenny merely shook her head, realizing that Xanth was incorrigible. Anyway, they were nice panties, and they had helped Mela Merwoman to nab her husband, which was the point of the whole adventure. If Jenny ever decided to look for a husband herself, she would remember how it was done.

She resumed reading. ''But why that particular color? Indeed, who says it *is* a color? Well, the official colors of the author's 1952 class at Westtown Friends School in Pennsylvania were plaid and white, partly in honor of their chosen female faculty member, Teacher Rachel Letchworth, who had Scottish blood. But the printer was unable to reproduce plaid for the yearbook, so brown had to be substituted. (There was a male faculty member, Master Charlie Brown, but it is unknown whether he had anything to do with this.) Ever since, the class colors have been erroneously listed as brown and white. Those are actually the *school* colors. Perhaps this helps correct the record; it has been a forty-year indignity. This, at any rate, is the precedent for using plaid as a color. You have a problem with that?''

Jenny shook her head, listening to what she had read. ''I never questioned plaid as a color,'' she said quickly. She looked at the list again. ''There were several more suggestions, but they didn't manage to squeeze into this volume. Probably they will be used in the next."

Then it got really odd, because she found herself reading about herself—only not exactly. "Jenny of Mundania, the model for Jenny Elf, who was paralyzed by a drunken driver, continues to improve." She paused. She herself derived from a Mundane? Just as Okra did? And this Mundane had chosen her instead of Okra, to represent her in Xanth? The concept was so strange she set it aside and resumed reading. "This report will be over a year out of date by the time you read it, but here it is:

"Jenny is now able to use a cup and drink by herself. She can sit in a chair in the shower, washing herself. She is in the hospital, being trained to use her computer, and is getting more facile with it. She can use it to call home, and her mother has made a game of it by installing a security code, so that Jenny has to figure out how to break it in order to gain entry to the home computer. The first code was simple, but each subsequent one is harder, so that Jenny really has to use her mind. Since she has much more use of her mind than her body, this is good. Her speech is improving too, but she needs surgery on her jaw—I would mention the temporomandibular joint, but only a nerd would understand the term—so that her mouth will be able to move for better enunciation. Remember, Jenny was really bashed up, and some things that don't show cause her endless complications. Her mother estimates that Jenny has now received over two thousand nice letters, and they are still coming in at the rate of three or four a day from all over the world. They would really like to answer them, but are presently unable. It's pretty much a full-time job just surviving. However, one letter writer happened to be in the area, and recognized Jenny at a store—oh, yes, it is possible to shop in a wheelchair—and exclaimed 'I wrote to you!' Just so."

There was a knock on the door. Jenny opened it. Grey Murphy was there. "There's been another mistake," he said, embarrassed. "Good Magician Humfrey forgot. You

are supposed to report to the demon's game, to work with
Nada Naga. That will complete your service.''

Jenny was pleased. ''Nada's nice!'' She handed him the
sheaf of credits. ''These are weird.''

''They always are,'' he agreed. ''Yet also true. I once
lived in Mundania, and saw how Xanth looks from there.''

''If I could believe more than just a little of this, I would
be extremely mixed up,'' she said.

He nodded. ''It is probably best just to forget it. The
Good Magician will conjure you to the demons' studio.''

Jenny followed him down the hall. She knew she would
have an interesting experience in the game. But she wasn't
sure she would forget what she had just read.

And so we finally get it straightened out, and I, the
author, will finish this Author's Note myself. I have just
one thing to add. It is of a personal nature, but important
to me. While working on this novel in Mayhem 1991 I
attended a memorial service, and I spoke there. The person being honored was extremely popular in her community, and there were many there to speak well of her. I
think my own words are self-explanatory. Actually I did
not speak as well as this rendition makes it seem; my
thoughts got tangled by emotion, and some were left out.
So this is the full text, including what I meant to say as
well as what I did.

''My mother said 'Oh, I'm going!' and she died. I was
not ready. I did not want her to start that journey so soon.
I cannot change it, but perhaps I can conjecture where it
was that she was going. Call this a fantasy, if you will.
My mother was in her way a creature of trains; when she
traveled she did not like to fly, though she would do so
when she had to, and I don't think she really liked long
car drives either. I share these sentiments. So I'm sure it
was a train she chose when it came time to make this final
journey. There is just something about a train, in its beauty
and power and reliability. A train is like portable civilization. Everything you need or want is there. Edna St.

Vincent Millay put it nicely: 'There isn't a train I wouldn't take, no matter where it's going.' You can trust a train. Now we are here at the station to see my mother off. This is a special train; it comes from eternity, and it is making a round trip. When she boards it, she finds that many of her friends are on it, having boarded at prior stations, and more will join them down the line. She has a window seat, and beyond that window is all the universe, past, present, and future. There is land and sea and sky, cities and forests, houses and people. There is the joy of day and the mystery of night. Everything is out there, and none of it is ever lost; one has only to look. But there is no need, for there is also much within the train. There are sleeping compartments, and a dining car, and a pleasant hall for games and conversation. She has the companionship of compatible people, including many she never met in life but who are well worth knowing now. It is a nice place, and she is happy there, as she was here; and though I am so sad to see her go, I hope she rides that train forever.''

And the usual note: readers who want a source for all of my news and available titles can call 1-800 HI PIERS.